PRAISE FOR EMBOOZLEMENT

I loved this book. Rich Leder's newest installment of the Kate McCall Crime Caper comedy/mystery series is a tour de farce and probably his best work yet. Leder's writing is fast and smart, opinionated and adult, and unashamedly funny. The story follows Kate McCall, private investigator, and an astoundingly varied cast of New York characters through a tightly wound maze of plot lines...dishing out plenty of crime and mystery, suspense and murders, romance and eccentricity but best all, lots of laughs! Leder's expert storytelling is so rich and layered, using city attitude, off-beat character perspectives, and inside language, and always with his distinct comedic point of view, that the reader is anxious to turn the page, always wanting more. Such a joy, so much fun to read. Five (5) Stars! Highly recommended!

— OLSADEYES REVIEWS

Kate McCall strikes again! Wacky, offbeat, hilarious! Emboozlement will make you laugh out loud! Leder's suspenseful and entertaining new installment will have you waiting for the next one!

— THE COMFORT LOVER REVIEW

PRAISE FOR EMBOOZLEMENT

So funny! One of the best books I've read in a while. Murder, mystery, drama and humor intertwine to create a fun, funny and interesting read. I will definitely be reading the first two books of the series and waiting on the next book to arrive!

—5-STAR AMAZON REVIEW

I just put down my Kindle, and I have a big smile across my face! Emboozlement was so much fun! So many great moments and images from this story have burned into my brain. I'm going to spend a lot of time laughing to myself thinking about all the crazy situations! This is the first book in the Kate McCall Crime Caper series that I've read, and I didn't miss a beat. You don't need to read the first two to enjoy this one. But after reading Emboozlement, I'm going back to the beginning and read the first and second books too!

—5-STAR AMAZON REVIEW

A fast-paced, funny detective story with a feisty, gutsy main character, Kate McCall!

—5-STAR AMAZON REVIEW

EMBOOZLEMENT

THE THIRD KATE MCCALL CRIME CAPER

RICH LEDER

LAUGH
RIOT
PRESS

1

THE PROBLEM IS THAT'S A PROBLEM

"Your bird has a big mouth," Blue said.

"The biggest," I said. "But he's not my bird. His name's Jerusalem Joe. He's an Amazon parrot from Jerusalem, the Finger Lakes town, not the center of world religion. I bought him for my maintenance man, Fu, because he saved my life four or five times. Fu, not Joe. Joe never saved my life. Joe's a jerk. Actually, so is Fu."

"Fu's the bulldozer cooking the ribs?"

"Fu Chen. My maintenance man, yes, that's him."

We were eating barbecued Chinese ribs and drinking beer at the kitchen table in my apartment, looking out through the bars that covered my plate glass window to the backyard, where the tenants of the House of Emotional Tics were gathered around the grill to celebrate the arrival of Fu's parrot, *who was also eating ribs* in the custom cage Fu had built. The cage was constructed of wood beams and steel bars and was the size of a phone booth—when there used to be phone booths.

"I didn't realize it was so dangerous to manage a brownstone," Blue said.

He'd smiled when he said it, letting me know *he* knew there was no such thing as a lethal brownstone management job— that he was in on the joke somehow.

Ha-ha.

It wasn't managing the House of Emotional Tics that had Fu rushing to my rescue four times, maybe five. It was working Jimmy's murder. I'd been after my father's killer since, more or less, the last weekend in July, much to the exasperation, frustration, and consternation of my son, Matthew, an assistant district attorney in the borough of Manhattan, and to the acrimony, animosity, and hostility of Homicide Detective Lew Logan of the Thirteenth Precinct, who was also investigating my father's death. Logan had arrested me three times in the last ten weeks.

I hadn't caught the killer, but my investigation had struck a nerve because he, the killer, had tried to murder me twice. Now, I was texting him, he was texting me back, and I had a bad feeling about where that was going.

"Fu helps me with my cases," I said.

"And he saved your life five times?" Blue said.

Again, I could tell he didn't think Fu had *literally* saved my life. He probably thought Fu had saved my ass somehow. I mean, who saves somebody's life that many times anyway? Whose life needs saving so often?

"Four. Or five," I said. "One of those is in dispute."

Blue's real name was Steve Stark. His nickname was Blue because his eyes were the color of a Carolina sky. He owned Blue Bar, one of the biggest and best sports bars in New York, and someone had their hands in his cash register. Mel Shavelson, Jimmy's lawyer, had sent him to me, saying it was my kind of case.

Blue had been a Major League Baseball player, a relief pitcher who, over the course of his career, had bolstered the bullpens of the Dodgers, Braves, Reds, Giants, and Mets. After a few seasons mopping up the middle innings at Citi Field, he'd retired and become a sportscaster for PIX. After that, he'd opened Blue Bar in an Upper West Side, doublewide brownstone—three floors of flat-screen televisions, sliced steak sandwiches on homemade sourdough, dozens of craft beers on tap, and a hundred years of sports memorabilia covering every inch of every wall.

He was cocky and, in the same breath, humble the way many professional athletes seem to be, like, on the one hand, they know they're physically superior, rich as Robert Redford, and living the life of royalty and rock stars and there's nothing anyone can do except stand in awe and ask for an autograph. And on the other hand, they're the same gosh-darn Little League kid they were way back when, grateful to Mom and Jesus for the gifts they've been given.

One of Blue's gifts was that he looked like the Marlboro man, if the Marlboro man were Ralph Lauren: gorgeous, prematurely gray hair; bright, beautiful smile; and strong hands—the hands of a professional athlete. Maybe he was six two or a tad taller, and my age, forty-five, or a bit older. He was unshaven the way rodeo cowboys are unshaven, which is to say handsome as hell. He wore a gray work shirt, a black bomber jacket, and jet-black jeans.

"Maintenance man, bodyguard, grill master, movie star," Blue said. "Not your everyday resume."

Ten minutes ago, at the backyard barbecue, Blue had heard me commit to playing the role of renegade cop Cassie Barnett in *Kung Fu Fu*, the less-than-zero-budget martial arts masterpiece LaTanya (House of Emotional Tics resident/filmmaker/cab driver/badass/friend) was writing, directing, and shooting guerrilla-style—meaning without permits—on the streets of New York. Fu was the Fu in the film. As Blue and I left the party to talk business, Fu had announced he was a movie star.

"Fu's full of surprises," I said, thinking, *Understatement of the decade.*

"So are you," Blue said. "Shavelson didn't mention anything about you being a PI *and* an actor. That's a crazy combo."

Yes and no, I thought. I had been an actor since I was cast as Kim MacAfee in our seventh-grade production of *Bye Bye Birdie*, and I had never stopped being one since that moment, cobbling together a career that included local late-night television commercials, no-budget independent films, not-ready-for-prime-time cable pilots, and off-off-off-off-Broadway musicals. I had used my acting expertise, my theatrical flair, and my dramatic savvy to solve my cases.

And that had been for about all of ten weeks, since Jimmy was found murdered at the Monument Life Insurance Company, tied to a chair in an empty elevator, eyes blown out of his head. He was killed by a corporate hit man, a high-society assassin who was still on the loose. I'd inherited Jimmy's business, McCall & Company: Private Investigations, at the reading of his will at Shavelson's office, where I had also inherited Shavelson. I didn't want either one. But Shavelson had sent me cases, and I had taken them, and then I was chasing my father's killer, and here I was with Steve Stark.

"Crazy as Nick Nolte," I said.

"My bar's as crazy as Nick Nolte too," Blue said. "Check that. Crazier. If we're talking about crazy, Blue Bar is in Gary Busey territory."

"In what way?"

"Start with the premise there's nothing nuttier than a Major League Baseball team. And trust me, nothing is more out of bounds than a Major League Baseball team. Dozens of grown men crisscrossing the country on chartered jets, all of them making stupid money to play a sandlot game—baby-faced rookies who've never been off the farm, grizzled veterans drinking bourbon for breakfast, all-stars taking buck-naked selfies with supermodels...I'm talking Charlie Sheen crazy. Wesley Snipes. Lindsay Lohan."

"Crispin Glover, Joaquin Phoenix. Got it."

"Blue Bar's like that but worse. Think Randy Quaid. We've got owners, managers, coaches, superstars, switch-hitters, Hall of Famers, wannabes, bums, has-beens, and hangers-on, and every day's a sold-out doubleheader, meaning lunch and dinner. There's no looking back. Yesterday's games are gone, and more money's missing, and I've got two more games today and two more tomorrow and two more the day after that, and I have to try to keep *that* cash in my pocket."

"I'll need unrestricted access to every bar, office, and employee on every floor."

He shook his head and said, "That's a problem."

I shook my head and said, "The problem is that's a problem."

"The problem is no one, not even my managing partner, can know I hired a private investigator to catch the asshole who's stealing my money."

"Why not your managing partner?"

"Because I think it's him, and I don't want to scare him off. I want to catch him in the act."

Perfect, I thought. *Three floors of certifiable Randy Quaid, sports bar insanity and both hands tied behind my back before the first pitch is thrown.*

"So no one knows *you* know someone's stealing from you?" I said.

"Whoever it is, they think they're getting away with it," he said.

"They *are* getting away with it," I said.

"That's why I'm hiring you," he said.

And then he smiled, and his eyes caught the light and twinkled. I mean, holy shit, they actually twinkled, and I thought, *Jesus Christ, he's not playing fair with those eyes and that smile and those pro-athlete hands. If I were a woman on the fence about being his baseball groupie, and, repeat after me, I am definitely not a woman on that fence, but if I were, just saying, one look in Steve Stark's eyes and I'd jump into his arms.*

2

THE PROMISED LAND OF PECULIAR THEATER

"Welcome to Wonderland, Professor," I said, stepping out of Peter Paul Rubens's *Venus and Adonis* in the hallowed halls of the Metropolitan Museum of Art one fine hippy-dippy day in 1968. I was playing the role of Venus—*from the painting!*—Roman goddess of love, sex, beauty, fertility, victory, and even prostitution, part of poor Professor Johnny Jedry's impromptu acid trip. The heartbroken Columbia University art instructor had impulsively downed a dose of LSD in a cab on her way to the Met, where she'd hoped to rediscover her lost passion for art and life and love and had instead discovered Venus and Adonis, who'd popped out of the painting in three-dimensional flesh and blood. It was Jedry's first time tripping. "The love you seek is but a song and dance if you rock with the gods of Rome," I said.

And then the music was supposed to swell, and we were supposed to launch into a ZZ Top-type toe tapper titled, as you might have already guessed, "Rock with the Gods of Rome."

But Dennis stopped the rehearsal right there. "I'm not feeling a rock star-goddess commitment from you, Kate," he said.

"You're still struggling with Venus?" Posey said from behind her piano.

"I'm still struggling with what I'm struggling with," I said, actors all around me nodding in agreement. "When I figure *that* out, then I'll struggle with the goddess."

"Ten minutes, people," Dennis said.

We'd been rehearsing *Psychedelic Sunday* since early September, and the show was in the tall grass. Granted, we'd been rehearsing this nonsensical musical while we were performing another nonsensical musical, *Blood Song and Dance*, so some amount of chaos and confusion was to be expected, but *Psychedelic Sunday* was opening after Halloween weekend —in four more weeks—and no one, cast or crew, had any idea why any of the characters would do or say the things they did and said.

For instance, why an esteemed Ivy League art professor, heartbroken or not, would accept and drop a tab of LSD from a cab-driving stranger when she had never-not-once done an impetuous thing in her entire fictional backstory was a motivational question that would go unanswered for the entirety of the run, as most story and character questions did at the D-Cup.

I had acted in more than a dozen D-Cup musicals since joining the Schmidt and Parker Players, and each production had been progressively more preposterous. When the curtain rose five weeks ago on *Blood Song and Dance*, Dennis and Posey's ridiculous, outrageous, and incongruous blood-spewing show about a wannabe nightclub-singing vampire (me), who sells train tickets in Grand Central Station as her day job (a singing-and-dancing vampire with a *day* job was the *least* ludicrous plot point of the play), it broke all theatrical barriers in terms of indecipherable absurdity.

Nothing, we thought as an acting troupe, *can surpass* Blood Song and Dance *as an illogical, irrational, and unreasonable musi-*

cal. Blood is the mountaintop, the Promised Land of Peculiar Theater.

And then Posey wrote *Psychedelic Sunday*, a musical so inane, arcane, and insane that we could all see *Blood Song and Dance* in its rearview mirror. Which is not to say D-Cup productions weren't fabulously entertaining for their season subscribers, who came to every show for a happy assault on their theatrical senses, because they were.

D-Cup cofounder and co-creative director Posey Schmidt composed and orchestrated terrific songs; her husband and theatrical partner in crime, Dennis Parker, was a fantastical, frenetic, and commercially crazy director and choreographer; and their all-original musicals were uproarious romps, spectacular celebrations of singing and dancing, enormous fun for actors to perform, and great good times for the audience, though no one in the theater had a clue what the shows were about.

"I'm torn between two camps," I said, grabbing my phone to check voicemails and messages (like all the other actors) as Dennis crossed the stage, Posey beside him.

"What are you thinking?" Posey said.

"Is Venus the Venus in Johnny's LSD brain, meaning does the goddess behave as the professor envisions her, meaning is she the goddess Johnny thinks she is while she's tripping, meaning is she the goddess Chloe thinks Johnny thinks she is while she's tripping? Or is Venus the Venus of Roman mythology? Am I creating the character from myth, or am I Chloe's creation of Jedry's acid queen? Which Venus is this Venus?"

"A character conundrum," Dennis said.

"A Rubik's Cube of character," Posey said.

"Does anyone think it's a good idea to chart a course through the maze of Chloe's mind?" Dennis said.

Without glancing at each other, Posey and I responded

instantly, at the same second, and with equal amounts of dread. "No."

"Then it's settled," Dennis said. "Venus is the Venus of Roman mythology."

"Of course, she does pop out of a painting," Posey said, "and she is bisexual, so I imagine she's trippier than Virgil thought she was."

"But not as cracked as Chloe," Dennis said.

"Agreed," Posey said, and we all looked at the other end of the stage where Chloe was either practicing dance moves or trying to break her own bones—it was hard to tell.

"Body of a centerfold, face of a cover girl, talent of a starfish," Dennis said.

"Work in progress," Posey said.

Chloe Burns, from Akron, Ohio, had left the Midwest for the Big Apple to become an actress though she had never acted before, as in *never*, meaning not one time ever. Posey and Dennis had cast her in *Blood Song and Dance* as a lesbian lover of vampire women thinking they could mitigate Chloe's singing, acting, and dancing deficits and accentuate her appearance, making the play *look* much better.

It might even have worked except Chloe lost her mind, her sense of self, and her innocence during rehearsal and every performance had become an adventure in existential theater of the absurd: Who would Chloe be in this scene and the next scene—herself, her character, a character from some other play?

"She should never have dropped the LSD," Dennis said.

"She was trying to find the professor," Posey said.

"Her first trip," Dennis said.

"And she never quite came back," Posey said.

"Now Jedry is as cuckoo as Chloe," Dennis said.

Making matters more mental, Dennis and Posey had instituted a new rehearsal/performance schematic for the D-Cup season. Normally, the Schmidt and Parker Players performed the play they were performing for eight weekends, Friday and Saturday night shows only. When the curtain closed on that particular show, rehearsal started on the next production the next day and would last four intense weeks, then would run for eight weeks, and so on throughout the year.

The "improved" plan had us rehearsing *Psychedelic Sunday* while we were performing *Blood Song and Dance* so that the new play would open the very next weekend after the old play closed. It had been five weeks of double duty, and there had been a kind of full-cast derailing of which Chloe was the poster child. It was a scheduling experiment to see if the D-Cup could mount a few more plays during the season. But the result was a troupe of chickens without their heads, cast and crew exhaustion, and musical schizophrenia.

Dennis and Posey, their own heads hurting, had announced the experiment would end when *Blood* closed in four weeks. There would then be one week to dress-rehearse *Psychedelic*, and then that play would open the first weekend of November, and then we would be back to the old schematic: eight weeks of performance followed by four weeks of rehearsal followed by eight weeks of performance followed by four weeks of rehearsal followed by, followed by, and followed by.

In other words, normal D-Cup delirium would resume.

"So...any page one PI headlines?" Dennis said, changing the subject.

"Hot pursuits off the presses?" Posey said.

"Convoluted cases coming around the corner?" Dennis said.

I could hear it in their voices and see it in their eyes. Like Peter Graves in *Mission Impossible*, I had used them and Chloe and Roger Platt, my cocky D-Cup costar, as well as the rest of the Schmidt and Parker Players, to help me solve both my stolen identity debacle, which ended this past Friday, and the workman's compensation case before that, and they could still taste the adrenaline of those real-life, real-time performances and were hungry for more.

"Around the corner, up the stairs, and in my office," I said. "Signed and sealed today before rehearsal."

"A new case?" Posey said.

"What's our role?" Dennis said.

"When do we start?" Posey said.

But before I could tell them about Steve Stark and Blue Bar and Stark's partner embezzling money, I got a text from the corporate killer who murdered my father, and my head went haywire, and I couldn't recall the color of Blue's eyes.

3

——————

JUST ENOUGH CLUE TO GET MY EYES SHOT OUT

I DIDN'T WANT DENNIS AND POSEY TO KNOW MY HEART WAS pounding and my head was spinning because then they would have asked me why and that would have led to an additional conversation about Jimmy's murder and how I came to be texting with the corporate killer who shot my father in the eyes at the end of July. And *that* discussion would have taken a heck of a lot longer than the ten-minute rehearsal break Dennis had announced two minutes ago. I needed to excuse myself with low-key comportment, words and emotion that wouldn't give me away.

"I have to pee like a racehorse and talk to my father's murderer," I said like a racehorse that had to pee and talk to her father's murderer, and then I stepped off the stage (with velvet curtain and proscenium), and hurried across the loft before Dennis and Posey could pick their jaws up off the floor.

The Schmidt and Parker Players were spread around the third-floor theater, listening to voicemails, making phone calls, and reading and replying to text messages before the break was up. I went around and through them toward the bar and the bathrooms at the other end of the loft, past the large, faded pictures of women's torsos wearing huge, half-century-old brassieres that were painted on the exposed brick walls in the 1940s when the D-Cup was a three-story bra factory. I weaved my way between the two rows of steel support beams that lined the length of the space, ensuring partially obstructed views for the seats situated behind them. I rushed past the old-world industrial elevator, dead center in the middle of the long wall opposite the ten-foot, floor-to-ceiling windows. The elevator bell rang as I went by (meaning the car was on its way up or down) just like it did all hours of the day and night, including during rehearsals and performances, signaling a parade of people coming and going and going and coming, usually ringing at the most imperfect moment possible.

I arrived at the bathrooms—both facilities were unisex— and chose the former men's room because it had urinals tall enough to stand in, and Jimmy had liked them—*"In case you were taking a leak and wanted to move in,"* he'd said when I showed them to him.

I crossed to the sink—there were two of them and two toilets and two move-in-ready urinals—looked at myself in the mirror, and told myself to get a grip.

But thinking about my father—unexpectedly and out of context, Jimmy talking about a urinal, for God's sake—momentarily blew me apart.

Right after his murder, I was inconsolable, sobbing my guts out, snot flowing, shoulders heaving, pressure and pain where my heart used to be, eyes unfocused, drowning in grief. It had happened like that several times a day for three or four weeks —I would think of my father tied to a chair, seated in an insurance company high-rise elevator with his eyes shot out, and lose my shit on the spot: eating Chinese food at Wo Hop with Harriman, riding in a cab, cleaning my living room and finding an old picture of Jimmy and Matthew between the sofa cushions.

I loved my mother, Christine, with all my soul. She died of cancer when I was ten, and I took it as hard as any ten-year-old girl could take it. But my father was my hero, my idol, my mentor and protector and teacher. He was everything to me. I had all of his DNA in my blood, all of it, and remembering my life with him—as a little girl in Queens when we were a family, as a pregnant sixteen-year-old, as a young mother, as a struggling actress and occasional PI—would make me realize again that he was gone for the rest of time and tear me to pieces.

I knew most everyone on the planet since the beginning of everyone being on the planet felt that way about their father when their father died. And I knew everyone's father died. It didn't help knowing this. The loss was too deep, too vast, too final.

The explosions of debilitating grief faded to frozen moments of paralysis—minutes, hours, entire days when I couldn't get the chill out of my bones, out of my blood, when I couldn't do anything except sit on my sofa and stare into the empty space where Jimmy used to be.

And then I was moving again, back in my life, though there remained holes in my heart I knew would never be filled. But I *was* back in my life—the opening of *Blood Song and Dance*, the workman's compensation case, *Psychedelic Sunday* rehearsals, the stolen identity case—and the most powerful part of the grief, I thought, was past me.

And then I stood at the D-Cup sink and thought about Jimmy joking about the urinals and bawled my eyes out.

After a few minutes, I looked at my phone, Jimmy's phone, actually—mine went into the Hudson River when Jimmy's killer tried to kill me too (the *second* time he'd tried to murder me)—and I saw the text-only number of the assassin who'd murdered my father. Ironically, the Industrial Douchebag who'd ordered my execution only four days ago had whispered *The Number* in my ear with his last breath, a final mea culpa that probably did nothing to save his soul. I will never repeat it out loud. It will forever and a day be known as *The Number.* The killer's text read: *Conducting business with Lowry Lowe partner by end of week. See you there.*

Our total conversation so far had been short and sweet.

Me on Thursday: *0 for two. I'm coming and will never stop.*

Him on Sunday afternoon: *Never say never. Third time's a charm. Clue coming soon.*

Him on Sunday night: *Conducting business with Lowry Lowe partner by end of week. See you there.*

0 for two let him know it was me texting him—he had twice tried and failed to kill me. *I'm coming and will never stop* meant "Fuck you for killing my father, you piece of shit. I will get you if it's the last thing I do."

Never say never meant one day I would stop coming for him because I would be dead because he would kill me like he'd killed my father and leave his calling card by shooting my eyes out. *Third time's a charm* meant next time was when he would kill me. *Clue coming soon* meant he would text me again, which he had just done.

A partner at Lowry Lowe, whatever and wherever that was, was going to be murdered by the end of this week. Just enough clue to get my eyes shot out.

The door to the bathroom opened at that moment, and Chloe came in. She walked to the sink beside me, looked at her reflection, reached into her purse for lipstick, started to put some on, and then saw me in the mirror and stopped short, lipstick suspended in front of her lips. Seeing her stop in mid-motion made me look at myself. I was a drowned rat. She was Marilyn Monroe.

"I know it's hard, Kate," she said, continuing on with her lipstick, a pale translucent pink, "and I'm sorry about that."

How does she know I was crying about my father? I thought.

"But that's what we do as actors," she said. "We suffer in

silence as we search for the souls of our characters. Trust me, you'll wake up one morning and Venus will be there with bells on, and all of this will be a bad dream."

Acting, I thought. *Not Jimmy. She's giving me philosophical advice about acting.*

When Chloe Burns is giving you philosophical advice about acting, it's time to wake up and smell the crazy.

She put her lipstick away, turned to me, smiled an understanding smile, and said, "Venus with bells on. That's the answer. Think about it."

"Maybe later," I said.

As the door shut behind her, I typed a reply and hit Send: *Not if I see you first.*

4

LOWRY LOWE ARE YOUR LAWYERS

AFTER I HIT SEND AND BEFORE REHEARSAL STARTED AGAIN, I called Al Cutter. He picked up on the fifth ring, so I suspected he was busy.

"You better be offering me money, McCall," he said, "because I'm in the middle of a monster trade."

"I have a job for you," I said. "How long will it take to finish the trade?"

"Counting this conversation or if I hang up now?"

"Counting this conversation."

"Too long. Got a call from a keeper in the Keystone State, so I'm trucking twenty hives of honeybees from Hartford to Harrisburg."

"Pennsylvania?"

"No. Harrisburg, Norway. Yes, McCall, Pennsylvania. It's a million bees making a thousand pounds of honey, and that means money."

During the day, Al was a hellacious eBay trader. And if I'd learned anything about his trades, it was that they were biblical in nature, meaning one thing begat another.

"What do the bees turn into?" I said.

"Twenty-five boxes of bottle rockets on a bus bound for Baltimore, where they become a couple hundred crab cakes on a train to Trenton that get traded for a dozen trumpets that travel back to Bethlehem, where it all started in the first place."

"Israel?"

"Pennsylvania, McCall. It's an eBay deal, not the book of Genesis. Pay attention."

"What happens to the horns?"

"The trumpets join a juco marching band that plays a song that sounds like, wait a minute, listen to it, six grand. Figure twenty-seven hundred for the bees, and Big Al clears three large and change. So are we done? After this, I got to deal with the cars until dawn and Warren gets back. Plus, I'm fucking with Elliot's power bill, which will be more than the gross national product of Botswana when it arrives at his Brooklyn abode."

Sleep was not part of Al's calculus. He was a thirty-four-year-old insomniac who had not slept more than one or two hours a night since his freshman year at Fordham, when he was eighteen and his roommate, a psycho rich kid named Elliot Morgan, woke Al up from a deep sleep, put the barrel of a loaded .357 Magnum in Al's mouth, and held him hostage for ten hours, SWAT team in the dorm hallway, while Elliot negotiated an F to an A with his biology professor. *"A for Al,"* Elliot had said ad nauseam, finger on the trigger.

After a slap on the wrist and a few years of counseling, Elliot's wealthy parents set their sick son up as a commodities broker. He lived in a Brooklyn townhouse, where Al tortured him by manipulating his utilities.

The cars Al was talking about were three stripped-down Toyota Corollas owned by Warren White that made up the uninsured, unlicensed, and illegal Warren Rental Car fleet.

Since sleep was not in the cards, Warren had hired Al as his night manager. Al lived in 5A. Warren lived in 4B. They were each other's only friends, and they couldn't stand each other.

When he wasn't trading or working, Al's special talent was hacking. He was a first-team, all-world hacker. *"When it's four fifteen in the morning and you haven't slept in seventy-two straight hours,"* Al once told me, *"recalibrating the orbit of an old Soviet satellite seems like a swell way to kill some time."* Other overnight Al Cutter projects were, for instance, having a look at Walmart's interoffice executive memos, checking US corporate accounts in questionable Cayman Island banks, and playing with Pakistani Parliament personnel files.

Like I had done with the Schmidt and Parker Players, I had used Al and Warren and Fu and the other House of Emotional Tics tenants to help me with my cases. Actually, one case in particular: catching my father's killer.

"It's a research project," I said.

"Cut to the chase."

"I want to know everything there is to know about Lowry Lowe."

"Cut to the chase means 'How much are you paying me?' Jesus, McCall, get with the program. What the hell is Lowry Lowe?"

"That's the first thing I want you to find out."

"You hear me groaning? I'm groaning because you don't pay me enough."

"How much is enough?"

"More than you pay me."

"Lowry Lowe. I'll knock on your door at ten."

"Bring cash."

"Ten o'clock."

"Cash on the barrelhead."

I knocked on his door at ten. He opened it, shook his head

with disgust, and walked away from me. I followed him into his apartment and shut the door behind me.

There were two units per floor in the House of Emotional Tics, and all the apartments were railroad flats, meaning the rooms were set in a straight line, like the cars of a train, one leading into the next and then into the next. Each living room was at the front of the building, looking out on East 83rd Street, with the last room, the kitchen, at the rear of the building, looking out over the brownstone's backyard.

Al's living room was the darkened bridge of a Klingon Bird of Prey. There were glowing multiple monitors, images and text flying across the half dozen screens at warp speed. Each monitor had its own tower and was accompanied by all kinds of keyboards on disparate desks, connected to speakers and printers and scanners and other equipment that baffled me, all of it scavenged and jury-rigged and communicating in codes that mere mortals couldn't comprehend. The whole system fed into two six-foot-tall mainframes that seemed like cybernetic soldiers, mechanized and mighty, blinking in the background, probably once the property of NASA or NORAD or NSA or NOAA, surfing and sailing over, under, around, and through top-secret digital security gates, keeping Al occupied through his endless days and nights.

"You're interrupting my beauty sleep," he said.

It was too late for Al as far as beauty sleep was concerned, meaning no amount of sleep could beautify him. He was very tall and very skinny—crack cocaine skinny. His hair was long and stringy. He had thin lips and a long, thin nose. His skin was pasty white, as if he'd lived his life in the dark shade of night. But it was his eyes that made him appear undead. They were set deep in his skull, skeleton deep, and they were terminally bloodshot, devil red. It was his eyes that made mothers hold their children close when he passed by in, say, a Korean market or when waiting at the corner for a light to change. He was a strung-out addict zombie on the streets of Manhattan, minus the drugs. Al did not do drugs. He didn't need them to achieve the look of a strung-out addict zombie on the streets of Manhattan.

"That's ironic," I said.

"You have no idea," he said.

For months, Al's plumbing had been badly misbehaving, working intermittently or not at all—mostly not at all—acting impulsively with a vindictive mind of its own, sending Al a not-so-subtle message: *Fuck you and forget flushing as a modern convenience.*

An apartment without a consistently working toilet would be enough to send most New Yorkers running for new digs, but Al lived life below the legal radar and had secrets to keep and didn't want anyone to know where he was at any given time. And he wanted the folks from the IRS and other federal and state agencies to forget they ever knew where he was in the first place. Not to mention, Al's apartment was rent controlled, and in New York City, no one moves out of a rent-controlled apartment for any reason, including ghosts, poisoned paint, or a defective flusher.

Fu had been in Al's pipes a dozen times to no avail. Finally, Zombie Al had taken to buying cases and cases of yellow Gatorade, drinking the liquid, then refilling the empty bottles with his own urine. The bottles were lined up everywhere around the apartment. Telling piss from Gatorade and vice versa could not have been a picnic.

"Lowry Lowe," I said. "What did you find out?"

He lifted a stack of papers off the desk, held them up, and fanned them with his thumb. "How much money did you bring?"

I held up five twenty-dollar bills and waved them back and forth.

"You going to slap me in the face with them?" he said. "Because that's what a hundred bucks is, a slap in the face."

"Fine," I said, turning to let myself out, "I'll do it myself."

"Keep your shirt on. I'll take your money."

"Lowry Lowe first."

"Cash first."

"Both at the same time."

He nodded, and I held up the money. He crossed to me and held up the research.

"On three," I said. "One, two..."

He took my cash, and I took his paperwork. We never got to three.

As I skimmed through the pages, he moved away, pocketed the bills, and checked columns of code racing up and down one of the monitors—like in *The Matrix*—maybe the flight plans of the French Air Force, maybe the emails of a Philippine minister to his mistress, maybe Exxon's undisclosed political contributions, maybe the secret recipe to Kentucky Fried Chicken batter, maybe Elliot Morgan's Con Ed bill.

"If you're a senator or the CEO of a big-bucks bank and you're reaming your soon-to-be ex while she's reaming you and it's the Battle of Bull Run," Al said, "Lowry Lowe are your lawyers. Penthouse ass-wipe attorneys for corporate carnivores fighting for custody of kids, control of accounts, and keeping the canine."

"High-society midtown law firm," I said, ticking off basic facts.

"Soul-sucking lawyers for hedge fund heroes clawing each other's eyes out over monthly alimony that could feed half of Africa."

"Specializing in divorce mediation and settlement."

"Cold-blooded, 30 Rock counselors for real estate royalty ripping each other new assholes over who gets the family jet."

"With offices in Rockefeller Center."

"The top one percent of the top one percent of dickwad wives and fuckhead husbands fighting it out to the death with lawyers from hell who make fifteen hundred bucks an hour."

I looked at Al and his computers and his Gatorade bottles of piss and thought, *And one of the partners gets their eyes shot out by the end of the week.*

5

———

LET ME PAINT YOU A THEATRICAL PICTURE

IN THE BOX I'D INHERITED AT THE READING OF JIMMY'S WILL WAS a bottle of Wild Turkey, a satellite cell phone, a digital camera the size of a credit card, a miniature photo printer, a six-inch restorer's pry bar, my father's open case files, his recently closed case files, his Colt .45 pistol, an old-fashioned brass nameplate that read *McCall & Company, Private Investigations* (which Fu had attached to my front door without my permission), a beer stein urn holding my father's ashes, and a sealed manila envelope with my name written on the front.

Inside the envelope were incorporation transfer documents, other official papers, Jimmy's business and individual PI licenses, and a handwritten letter titled *Jimmy's Rules of Private Investigation for Kate*. Rule number three was *never kiss a cop on the first date*.

I could hear Jimmy's voice in my head: *"Don't cozy up to the cops, Kate, because even though you might be investigating the same case, you don't have the same feelings about it, you don't have the same facts at hand, you don't want to solve it the same way, and you don't have the same rulebook, the same motivation, or the same endgame."*

Since inheriting Jimmy's business and tracking his killer, I had learned firsthand that first dates with most cops last forever—but not with Homicide Detective Lew Logan.

Logan and I were three dates (arrests) into our relationship, meaning me wearing Logan's handcuffs because we'd both been investigating Jimmy's murder at the same time: him on his side of the law, me on my side, which is why I'd been in handcuffs.

Although we'd been seeing each other regularly, Logan did not like me. He had told me this to my face on several occasions —each time he'd arrested me, for instance, and a few other times on top of that. There had been moments of begrudging respect, but they were fleeting, replaced with frustration, incredulity, anger, and dismay because I wouldn't stop my investigation even though he'd told me to in no uncertain terms.

The point is I had promised him—and Matthew, I might add—in exchange for not putting me in jail, that I would tell the police what I knew about the corporate killer the next time I knew something before I did something about what I knew. And now I knew one of the Lowry and Lowe partners would be dead by the end of the week.

It was late Monday morning. Logan was seated behind his desk. I was seated at the unoccupied desk across from and abutted to his desk—Harriman's old desk. My relationship with Logan's ex-partner—*The Harriman Affair*—had done nothing to change my luck with men, which had been rotten since I was sixteen years old and the boy who got me pregnant left the East Coast for the West Coast while simultaneously leaving being straight for being gay. Matthew's father had happened twenty-nine years ago, *The Harriman Affair* was six weeks ago, and pretty much every relationship I'd had between and including those two had been either misguided, unwarranted, unwise, shortsighted, untimely, naïve, unfortunate, inadvisable, foolhardy, or demonstrating some kind of questionable judgment on my part.

Believe me, I wanted to have a serious, loving, monogamous relationship with the man of my dreams; I was just no good at finding him so far, or recognizing him, or roping him in, or settling down when I did find, recognize, or rope him in, or whatever.

Okay, I was bad at it.

But *The Harriman Affair* was history, and a person's romantic luck can change any time, like the weather, rain to sun. Anyway, that's what an optimistic, independent, strong-willed, singing-and-dancing, single, mid-forties woman with a wicked right cross has to believe.

"Let me paint you a theatrical picture, McCall," Logan said, "so your half-baked, off-off-off-off-Broadway brain can somehow wrap itself around these particular, fucked-up fences that you yourself have no doubt constructed."

If you turned to *crusty, son-of-a-bitch cop* in the dictionary, Logan's mug would be looking back at you. He was in his late fifties and had been a homicide detective for three decades. He was five foot ten and fit for a man his age or ten years younger. My acting career annoyed him almost as much as my PI career, though plenty of other things annoyed him too, so in some ways I was just another name on his shit list. I'd been on that list since the first day we'd met. I'd slipped off it a couple of times, but had always found my way back. Now that I had committed to being a PI, I was on the list for good.

My permanent position was secured by the fact I had promised him I was "all done investigating any damn thing in New York" and then kept right on investigating damn things in New York. I'd meant the promise when I'd made it, but as Jimmy had said to me more than once, *"Some promises you can't keep until later."*

This was one of those promises.

"The curtain opens as I arrive at Lowry Lowe," Logan said, "and tell the partners someone in their dipshit divorce factory is going to get murdered at the end of the week by a serial corporate killer for hire whose calling card is he shoots your goddamn eyes out after he murders you. How am I doing so far?"

"Born playwright."

"The partners ask me how in the hell I know this information, as in what gives me the right to scare the crap out of everyone in sight, meaning right at the top of the first act is where the play runs off the rails. See where I'm going?"

"Page one rewrite."

"I tell the partners I heard it from an actor who thinks she's a private investigator because she inherited her father's PI business after he was murdered and shot in the eyes ten whole fucking weeks ago. Half the time, I tell the partners, the actor can't tell her ass from her elbow, and the other half I'm arresting her for idiocy beyond the pale."

"I can tell my ass from my elbow two-thirds of the time at least."

He'd reminded me of my father more than once, Logan had, including right then. Jimmy had spent a good deal of his life frustrated by my life. Frustration that sounded like, *"Jesus Christ, Katie, does your brain not work at all?"* which is a question he'd asked me daily since I was sixteen. Truth be told, I'd asked myself the same question a ton of times too.

But Jimmy had never given up on me, even when he probably should have, and he'd listened to me more than he'd ever admit, even when he probably shouldn't have.

The same was true of Logan.

"'How does the actor know this?', the partners ask me," Logan said. "And I reply, 'Voodoo, the eclipse of the moon, and the wind in the willows.'"

"Yes, the last one, tell them that, the wind in the willows."

He sat back, shook his head in disbelief like Jimmy used to do, gestured at his desk, and said, "Can you see my mountain of paperwork?"

"They can see your mountain from the Mount Airy Lodge."

Logan's desk would one day be in the Smithsonian or maybe Ripley's. Every kind of paper possible was scribbled with names and addresses and phone numbers and chicken-scratch notes and was haphazardly piled higher and higher until it looked like the Poconos, with valleys that exposed a corner of his phone here, the edge of his old-school Royal typewriter there. He had multiple Rolodexes so jam-packed the cards randomly popped off the rolls in futile attempts to escape suffocation. Logan would grab the offenders and shove them back in place without a second thought.

I was like one of those cards.

"These are homicides ranging in temperature from hot to cold, ranging in age from four o'fucking clock this morning to a lifetime ago," Logan said. "The reason they remain on my desk instead of in some faraway file cabinet is that they—each and every one—have a source, a justification for me to insert myself in the downward-spiraling circumstances. Without a source, I cannot walk into a law firm that chews married people to pieces and spits out divorcees and announce that murder is on their menu."

"I'm your source."

"You are not my source. You are my painful reminder that morons make law enforcement harder than it has to be. The laws of logic prohibit me from opening an investigation based on the premonition of a reckless actor who I have arrested on multiple occasions. 'The sky is falling' is not how NYPD Homicide conducts business. How do you know Lowry Lowe is the next name on the list?"

This is where the private investigator thing got tricky for

me. *How much of the truth is too much?* I thought. *And how soon do you put it in play?*

"Someone told me," I said, deciding that amount of truth at that moment was plenty for now.

"Who?"

"I don't know him." It was mostly true. I knew it was the killer, but I had no idea who the killer was. "An anonymous source."

"So an anonymous source you don't know called you out of thin air and said, 'I was going through my address book and came across your name and thought you might like to know the next pair of eyes going to be shot to shit.'"

"Text."

"What?"

"He texted me."

Logan narrowed his eyes. Three decades of investigating murders in Manhattan had imbued him with radar that could read the dimmest light of truth in a pitch-black tunnel of bull-shit and vice versa. I had not lied to him about Harriman, I had not lied to him about the Industrial Douchebag, and I was not lying now. I wasn't telling him the whole truth, but we were only dating. We weren't married or anything.

"Did you text the anonymous source back?" Logan said.

"Yes, I did."

"What did you say?"

"I told him I was going to the police." Total lie, I admit. But I had kept part of my word, which was better than keeping none of it. The point is the ball was in Logan's court now.

"You're not going to tell me his number, are you?" Logan said.

"He's my source, Logan, and he's kind of jumpy. If *you* start messaging him, he'll stop talking to *me*. I'm your best bet here," I said, and I pushed back from Harriman's desk and stood up.

"I don't want you anywhere near Lowry Lowe. Do you understand what I'm saying?"

"You don't want me anywhere near Lowry Lowe."

"And I want every text he sends you and every reply you send him. Every one."

"Anything else?"

He opened a desk drawer and removed my father's Colt—my Colt.

"I retrieved your gun from the Weehawken Police Department, and I am returning it to you," Logan said, placing it on top of the chaos that covered his desk. "I am not doing this because we are friends."

"We're not friends?" I said. I didn't reach for the gun because his hand was still on it, meaning he was giving it to me, yes, but not quite yet.

"Not even during my nightmares, in which you are often the star. I'm doing this because you will not listen to a word I've said. You will instead continue to investigate your father's murder, putting your life at grave risk. If something were to happen to you—dismemberment, for instance, or death, more likely—and it was intimated that having your gun might have somehow saved your sorry ass, then I would be plagued by your absence, though your absence is what I hope for on a daily basis."

He handed me the Colt, and I could hear, not see, the smallest smile in his voice, and I thought, *Just like Jimmy.*

6

THREE TO ONE SHE'D BE DEAD BY THE END OF THE WEEK

Every year for my birthday—three days before Christmas—until I turned ten and my mother died of cancer, Jimmy took Christine, Marilyn, and me skating at the rink in Rockefeller Center.

Those were some of the happiest, most loving memories of my life. Christine was beautiful on the ice, a swan on a lake—face flush with winter chill, eyes bright and alive with life and love. She would skate backward, looking at me and my father as he held my hand, and sing us Christmas carols as we went round and round the rink. Even Marilyn, six years older than me and too cool for family events, would skate beside us for a minute or two before zipping off on her own. (She zipped off to Cleveland, of course, when I was twelve, and she never came back.)

We would rest along the rail and drink hot chocolate and look at the twinkling colored lights on the tall tree, and then we would skate again and again; maybe not the perfect family but damn close. Jimmy and Christine were fantastically in love, and my sister and I would let bygones be bygones for just this one night—I can remember skating while holding Marilyn's hand, if you can believe it.

Thinking of my life at that time, of my mother and father, brought tears to my eyes, a bittersweet sadness born from the idea that the memory of them skating at Rockefeller Center was all I'd ever have. I would never actually skate with them again. The moments themselves, the people themselves, were gone forever.

Anyway, the point is my family did not skate at some midtown rink on the island of Manhattan; we skated at the Rink at the Rock, as Jimmy used to call it—the Rockefeller Center skating rink. When a National Historic Landmark has a landmark of its own more iconic than the National Historic Landmark itself, you're into something much more than a landmark; you're into something *sovereign*. The overwhelming breadth and elegance and history of Rockefeller Center makes it an island unto itself, dazzling and incomprehensible in size and scope and cultural significance that cannot be understated even in New York...which is an understatement.

It's a huge chunk of change: twenty-two acres in the dead center of some of the world's most expensive commercial real estate. *Twenty-two acres*—the mind boggles—encompassing nineteen commercial buildings, including the internationally recognized art deco dozen, constructed by the Rockefeller family in the early 1930s with renowned architectural features, steel frames, and limestone facades. Taken in total, Rockefeller Center covers six square blocks, from 48th to 51st Streets between Fifth Avenue and Avenue of the Americas, and offers more than *nine million total square feet* of rental space.

The legendary Radio City Music Hall is also part of Rockefeller Center, which means there's a designated New York City Landmark, one of the most famous theaters on Earth, *inside* a National Historic Landmark. (As an aside, I'd never performed there, but Jimmy took me to see The Rockettes when I was eight, and for the rest of his life, he blamed that show for me becoming an actor. He wasn't wrong.)

The tenant roster is ridiculous. There's the Bank of America Building, the Simon & Schuster Building, the GE Building, the McGraw-Hill Building, the Time-Life Building, and the Comcast Building—30 Rockefeller Center.

30 Rock, seventy stories and nearly three million square feet, is so famous for being home to the NBC family of networks, including the offices and studios of the *Today* show, *The Tonight Show Starring Jimmy Fallon*, and *Saturday Night Live*, that the great and funny Tina Fey named her hit TV show after it. (Another aside: I auditioned for that show, absolutely killed it, and didn't get a call back. Ms. Fey was in the room. I was pissed, but I was over it now—mostly over it, not really over it, probably never would get over it.) But NBC is not 30 Rock's only claim to fame. The building is also home to the Rainbow Room, the Observation Deck, the Lower Plaza, Deloitte & Touche...and Lowry Lowe.

"The girl on the phone said you're licensed to practice law in California, Florida, New Jersey, and New York," I said with a Texas twang to the Scandinavian supermodel sitting across the conference table.

"That's true," the Scandinavian supermodel said.

"Good," I said. "Tommy and I have houses in all those places. And Austin, of course."

First thing this morning, before I saw Logan at the Thirteenth, I'd gone online and surfed around and discovered the story of a reclusive, super-geek software genius who'd gone so far off the grid that probably even he had no idea where he was. He was rich as a king and so skilled at all things Internet that he'd virtually erased himself from the real world. He'd been in and out of trouble with the law, the story said, for being dangerously eccentric, and now he was gone. No one knew anything about him or his life beyond the fact that he was a real software guy, he was from Texas, he was loaded, he was crazy, and he was MIA. His name was Tommy Baynes.

Second thing this morning, I'd called Lowry Lowe and told them I was Tommy's wife, Emily Baynes, I'd just flown in from Austin, I was shopping for a divorce attorney, and I was going to hire one today. Then I asked to meet with a partner who could make me stinking rich by the end of the week. *"Oh, yes, we can do that for you,"* the receptionist had said.

Then I'd gone to the Thirteenth. I'd left Logan—with implicit orders to stay away from Lowry Lowe—went to the ladies' room on the first floor of the police station, and changed my clothes and my shoes. And my hair. And my eyes. And my accent. And my name. I'd arrived as Kate McCall, actor-PI, carrying a large tote. I'd exited as the maritally misfortunate Mrs. Emily Baynes.

I had chosen the shoulder-length red wig with bangs, the green contact lenses, and the gray business suit I'd worn in a woebegone TV pilot called *When We Were Dead*. I'd played the role of Wanda Ward, wife of Wally the Wastewater Worker and mother of twins Wesley and Wayne. We'd all died when Wally drove into a wall in Wisconsin, and the sitcom was about us living life in Milwaukee as a deceased family. It had no hope from inception and died ten minutes after it wrapped. But the clothes I bought from the bankrupt production company at bargain basement prices were wonderful. In the show, Wanda was a worldwide weatherwoman with taste and style, and death didn't slow her down one whit. She'd remained a shopaholic even after her life ended. That was the only part of the program I found believable.

I'd grabbed a cab, sat by the Rink at the Rock, and thought about my parents before taking the elevator to the sixty-second floor for my eleven o'clock meet and greet. As the elevator went up and up, I'd remembered *Jimmy's Rules of Private Investigation for Kate, Rule Number Two: don't trust anybody who lives or works above the twenty-fifth floor.* Lowry Lowe had missed the mark by a long shot.

"What does your husband do for a living, Mrs. Baynes?" the Scandinavian supermodel said. "And what do you imagine your estate is worth?"

The Scandinavian supermodel was Michelle Lowry, one of the four Lowry Lowe partners, younger than me, maybe thirty-seven or so, and as beautiful as a Swedish queen, white-blonde hair in a French braid to the middle of her back, icy-blue eyes, full lips, majestic cheekbones, tall and curvy and ready for the cover of *Cosmo*. Did I mention sharp as a shark? She was a great white in Armani. And the odds were three to one she'd be dead by Friday.

"I had this conversation with the girl on the phone," I said with impatience, as if I was accustomed to getting everything I wanted as soon as I wanted it and this whole annoying divorce thing was already taking too long.

"I want to make sure she heard you correctly," Michelle Lowry said.

"Fine," I said. "Tommy writes software. He's the geek who created the essential piece of code for the first voice-chat program—as in *first ever*. He wrote it for a Chinese company in China—I hated China, they all speak Chinese—and took a contractual piece of the pie everywhere they licensed it, and they licensed it everywhere—Apple, IBM, Microsoft, Skype— so we're worth two hundred forty million, not including the real estate, the cars, the artwork, the future income, whatever. The point is he's a mess, socially, sexually, culturally...he's an irreconcilable fucking mess, excuse my language, and he'd be worth nothing without me, that's the point. Am I right, Ms. Lowry?"

"Call me Michelle," she said. "And you're right. That is precisely the point."

"Good," I said. "Call me Emily."

"Emily."

The conference room door opened and two of the best-looking men in Manhattan walked into the room. *Since when did male models go to law school anywhere other than on TV? I thought. Jesus Christ, this is like an episode of* Suits *or* The Good Wife *or* LA Law. They were both in their mid-forties, like me, and had movie star hair, rock star confidence, and political *savoir-faire*. I expected them to pose for paparazzi and kiss babies any minute.

"These are two of my partners," Michelle said. "Emily Baynes, Jack Lowe. Jack, Emily. And this is my husband, Christopher Lowry. Jack's wife, Lisa, is the fourth partner, but she's out of the office; otherwise, she'd have dropped in too. You'll meet her next time, assuming you decide to move forward with us."

In the packet of papers Zombie Al had downloaded for me, I'd already learned that Lowry Lowe was composed of two married couples. There were photographs of them as well, but nothing had prepared me for how goddamn good-looking they all were.

I'd also learned the Lowry Lowe partners shared clients, meaning two or three or all four of them got involved in every case so each client could feel connected and cared for at all times, so there would always be a partner to talk to, a legal shoulder to cry on. It was a business model that had worked wonders. They'd made a fortune in money, they were famous in certain circles, and they were respected, renowned, and feared for collecting armored truckloads of cash for their clients.

"A friend of mine in Dallas told me you occasionally work for a percentage of what you collect, if the settlement is potentially big enough," I said—I'd read that in the Zombie Al literature, so I already knew it was true. "Is that true?"

"If circumstances warrant," Jack said.

"Do they?" Christopher said.

"You tell me," I said. "Tommy's attorney has offered me twenty million, and he wants to settle before Friday. I could pay your retainer—what is it, thirty-five thousand?—and you could fetch it for me tomorrow, but I'm thinking the number is one hundred twenty million, and I'll pay you twelve percent if you get it, twelve percent of anything more than thirty million. Less than that, I'll pay your retainer at settlement."

"Divorce is sometimes about needing things besides money, Emily," Jack said. "Closure. Revenge. What else do you need?"

"There are certain aspects of my husband's private life, let's call them strings, that he can't allow to go public," I said. "What do I need? I need to spend time with each of you this week so I know which strings to pull with which partner," I said. "I need lawyers who know how to play hardball."

The three Lowry Lowe partners, two of them married to each other, had an entire conversation with their eyes, and then turned back to me.

"Batter up," Michelle said.

7

NEUTRALIZE THE NEGATIVE

I stood across the street from Blue Bar and took the place in. I'd been here with Jimmy to watch ball games, drink beers, and eat steak sandwiches but not for years. So it was a bittersweet feeling to be back—fond memories mixed with deep loss and sadness.

The bar was in the middle of the block on the north side of the street. An extra-wide flight of stairs on the east side of the building led up to the main entrance on the first floor. Exterior lights on either side of the double front doors were fitted with blue bulbs. There was no exterior signage, just the blue lights. A discreet, street-level door on the west side of the building had a single blue light and brass plaque that read *Office*.

With the money he'd made throwing breaking balls out of the bullpen, Blue had bought a condemned, doublewide brownstone on West 83rd Street, between Amsterdam and Columbus, saved as much of the four-story structure as he could, gutted the rest, and turned the place into sports bar heaven.

That it was directly across the park from the House of Emotional Tics—same street, other side of the city, straight line between the two—was coincidental. *I hope the rest of this case is as straight a line*, I thought.

I crossed West 83rd, climbed the steps, and went through the front doors. It was just past noon, and the bar was already alive with lunch hour. I remembered the energy, the pulse of the place, immediately—the all-encompassing sounds of sports and music and chatter and buzz, the smell of grilled steak and beer and bourbon, the overwhelming collection of memorabilia, the sense that no matter where you thought you were going, you had arrived at the place you needed to be.

The entrance area held a hostess stand, several plush blue velvet sofas, and a huge wall with rows of framed jerseys, including those of Jeter, Pettitte, Rivera, and Posada—the Core Four, the most famous Yankees since Guidry, Jackson, Piniella, and Munson, whose jerseys were also framed and were hanging right below the Core Four. As if this wasn't enough of a championship statement, these eight World Series winners hung shoulder to shoulder with the framed jerseys of Seaver, Koosman, Ryan, and Gentry, the starting staff of the 1969 "Amazin' Mets," *and* the framed jerseys of Frazier, Reed, Bradley, DeBusschere, and Barnett, the starting five of the 1969 champion New York Knicks, *and* the jerseys of the 1987 Super Bowl champion New York Giants legendary linebackers Banks, Carson, Taylor, and Johnson, *and* the framed jerseys of Namath, Sauer, Maynard, and Snell, the New York Jets who won Super Bowl III—after Broadway Joe predicted they would.

These twenty-five iconic New York City jerseys covered the entire east wall of the lobby like some kind of super-duper wallpaper that, if you were a sports fan, would drop your jaw. If you were a New York sports fan, the sofas were there so you would have something soft to catch you when your knees buckled in awe.

Jimmy had said, *"That's a real Wall of Champions,"* every time we'd come here.

Straight ahead were the stairs up to the second and third floors and down to the office. To my left, was the hostess stand. Three attractive young women—all actors, no doubt—took names, organized menus, escorted folks to tables, pointed them toward the bar or the stairs, and smiled as if Blue Bar were a play and they were the chorus.

The staff wore blue work shirts, blue jeans, and blue high-top Chuck Taylors. Waiters also wore a blue apron tied around the waist that dropped down to their Converse sneakers.

I walked to the hostess stand and smiled at the girls. There were two blondes and a brunette looking at a computer screen. "Hi. I'm meeting Blue and Dave for lunch at one o'clock," I said like I'd lived in New Jersey all my life.

I'd left Lowry Lowe as Emily Baynes, a married and miserable Texan, and arrived at Blue Bar as Danielle Sullivan, Big Apple-by-way-of-Bayonne management consultant specializing in bars and restaurants. I was still wearing the shoulder-length red wig with bangs, the green contact lenses, and the gray business suit.

"Danielle Sullivan?" one of the blondes said, checking the computer.

"Dani," I said.

"Follow me," the dark-haired hostess said.

I walked past and around the blondes and followed the brunette out of the lobby and into the first-floor bar. The floor was dark-stained oak; the walls—where you could see them through the memorabilia—were exposed brick. Overhead Tiffany-style lights gave the room a soft, warm glow. The handsome mahogany bar ran the entire length of the west wall, long enough to accommodate forty leather barstools and keep four bartenders hopping. There were several dozen craft beers on tap and dozens more in bottles. Huge chalkboards stated both the beverage and kitchen specials. Mirrored walls behind the bar reflected top-shelf bottles of booze and also made the room feel much larger than it was, and it was a good-sized space to begin with—occupancy on this floor, and every floor, was two hundred people, so on game days, six hundred-plus fans packed the place. Between the bar and the opposite side of the room, tables and chairs and sofas created intimate dining and drinking areas that felt like your living room at home, except a thousand times better.

But like the lobby, it was the massive volume of *sports stuff* that took your breath away. It was as if a volcano holding every famous American sports memory since the early 1900s had erupted in this very spot. All collegiate and professional sports were represented: baseball, basketball, football, soccer, hockey, golf, tennis, car racing, rodeo, cycling, MMA, fishing, fencing, the Olympics, and every other game under the sun. Paintings and photographs and trophies and autographed baseballs and footballs and basketballs and soccer balls and hockey sticks and tennis rackets and golf clubs and many hundreds of pennants and plaques and flags and helmets and hats covered the walls from top to bottom and side to side. It was exciting to be in the middle of something so hip and happening, something so perfectly plugged into its universe.

Flat-screen televisions were everywhere—twenty at least—tuned to live games and replays of games and drafts and combines and preseasons and every color of ESPN and every flavor of Fox. If it was sports and it was happening—or had ever happened—it was on TV in Blue Bar. Throw in a cold craft beer (or five) and a sliced steak sandwich on homemade sourdough and, holy shit, what a place!

"I'm Dave Griffin," Blue's managing partner said, standing as the hostess and I arrived at a comfortable table for two in the middle of the room. "Blue couldn't make it." He nodded at the brunette, and she went back to her post.

"I'm Danielle Sullivan. Dani," I said, and we shook hands.

"Griff," he said, and he gestured for me to take a seat.

We sat at the table, across from each other, bustling bar business all around us. Like Blue, he was around my age or a little older, and he was taller than me but not by much, possibly five ten. He was handsome in an athletic way, as if Blue had rubbed off on him, except with dark hair, stylishly long, and dark eyes that gave away nothing. *It's intentional with the eyes*, I thought. *He's consciously giving nothing away. Either he doesn't trust anyone or he can't be trusted. I bet both.*

"I'll go first," he said. "Blue called me this morning and told me he'd hired a management consultant to help us be more efficient."

I knew Blue had called him, of course, since I'd called Blue before that to tell him to arrange a lunch meeting and tour that Blue himself would then conveniently miss so I could spend quality time with his managing partner.

"He didn't ask me what I thought about it," Griff said. "He just told me he'd done it, and I was to help you any way I can, total access to everyone and everything everywhere. So right off the bat, that sounds inefficient. I'm the managing partner, and Blue didn't discuss you with me. Does that sound efficient to you, Dani?"

He was one part asshole and two parts prick, which was what I'd expected. Blue had told me about him at the House of Emotional Tics during Fu's parrot party, less than twenty-four hours ago. *"The truth is hard to track with Griff,"* Blue had said. *"He tells you one story, but he's on the move, so you don't get it all, so you follow him down the street and around the corner to get the rest, but when you catch up, it's not the same story. The truth has changed along the way. That's how it's been since we were kids."*

"It sounds like we need to neutralize the negative, Griff." I had once upon a time been a receptionist at a management consulting firm in Tribeca and knew the lingo.

"What does that mean?"

"You assume there's something wrong with you—so you go

negative—because Blue acted in the best interests of the business without your input when in reality he was being efficient, streamlining time and effort while keeping management—you—focused on the immediate. Blue wants to do better than he's doing in terms of processes and profitability. I'm here to help you both make more money. Negativity is a drag on productivity. That's a long-winded way of saying there's nothing wrong with you, Griff."

Another man joined us—an All-American kid in his mid-twenties with close-cut curly hair the color of coal, black eyes, and a cocky vibe I didn't like.

"This is Adam Stoker," Griff said. "He's my bar manager. He's going to give you a tour. Show her everything, Adam, but be efficient, or she'll pink-slip you."

"Will we be having lunch after the tour?" I said to Griff as I stood.

"You and me," Griff said, "do not have lunch in our future."

8

WHAT BRINGS YOU TO THE DUNGEON?

THE SECOND-FLOOR FOOTPRINT MATCHED THE FIRST FLOOR, except an open, gleaming, commercial kitchen dominated the length of the west wall instead of a bar. Stainless-steel refrigerators and freezers and dishwashers and sinks of all sizes, butcher block and marble countertops, a huge industrial hood covering two wide grills and two big, badass fryers (aside from the salads, almost everything on the menu was either grilled or deep-fried), and a cook staff of ten wearing blue-and-white-checkered, custom kitchen clothing, including Blue Bar baseball hats and navy-blue kitchen clogs, filled the tiled space and pumped out pub food from noon to two in the morning every day except Christmas.

The third floor was identical to the first floor, but instead of sofas and dining room tables and chairs, the back of the big, open room featured two pool tables, two foosball tables, an eighteen-foot Grand Champion shuffleboard table, a tournament dart board, and tall bistro tables with matching barstools. Flat-screen televisions and sports memorabilia were, again, the overpowering decor.

As we walked from the third floor down to the office, I

asked Adam to describe how Blue Bar worked, the ebb and flow of the various processes and systems, the checks and balances, the chains of command. He answered my question with a question.

"Exactly what are you looking for?" he said.

"Inefficiencies," I said, thinking he intended to tailor his description to some specific, management consulting goal I had in mind. "Weak links in the Blue Bar business model chain."

"You mean theft."

"Why would you say that?" I said, thrown off balance. Either he was lucky to have landed on the truth, or I had underestimated him. *He couldn't be that smart*, I thought. *Could he?* On top of that, he again answered my question with a question.

"Where did you go to grad school?" he said.

"Excuse me?" I said, thinking, *Breathe, Kate. You couldn't have given yourself away already. No way. You know the lingo, and you've got the wig and the eyes and Wanda Ward's worldwide weatherwoman wardrobe.*

"You're a management consultant. I'm assuming you have an MBA. Where did you get it?" he said.

I didn't like the way he was glancing at me as we passed the second floor and continued down to the first floor, I didn't like the way he answered my questions with questions, and I especially didn't like the questions he was answering my questions with.

"Rutgers," I said, trying to stay in control of the conversation.

"Chicago," he said.

"Chicago what?" I said.

"My MBA. University of Chicago."

He was my height, five seven, and thin and wiry like a long-distance runner. He had small teeth, two neat rows of Chiclets that popped bright white against the blackness of his eyes and hair. The subtext was *I am way smarter than you, and I know you're full of shit.* If I wasn't lying about having an MBA from Rutgers and about being a management consultant and about being a green-eyed, redheaded Jersey girl named Dani, if it weren't my first day on the Blue Bar case, I would have punched him in the nose.

In fact, I could feel my hand forming a fist when we passed the main-floor bar and started down to the street-level office and caught Griff coming up the stairs.

"She make us any money yet?" Griff said to Adam.

"Cost us," Adam said. "The monetary value of my time added to the profit I would have made us during the tour."

"How much?" Griff said.

"Thousand bucks so far, but she's just getting going," Adam said.

"Put it on Blue's tab," Griff said.

"Already did," Adam said.

And then Griff was gone, and we were in the office, which had the same footprint as the other floors, except along the west wall, where the bars and the kitchen were situated upstairs, was a row of three offices. Opposite the offices were a walk-in fridge, a walk-in freezer, a dry storage room, a liquor-beer-wine storage room, various housekeeping closets, and one room that held building systems: security, gas, power, computer, HVAC, and so on. Like the upper floors, the bathrooms were at the far end.

"First office is Griff's," Adam said, gesturing at the room closest to the front of the building, "then Blue, then Mary."

"Who's Mary?" I said.

"I am," came a voice at the end of Office Row. "Office manager, bookkeeper, den mother, jailer, judge, and jury."

She stepped out of her office and walked down the hallway toward us. She looked about sixty-five years old, maybe closer to seventy, and like everyone else in the city of Manhattan, she resembled somebody famous: Doris Roberts.

Jesus, I thought, *it's Ray Romano's sitcom mother.*

"Mary Capp," she said, and we shook hands.

"Danielle Sullivan," I said.

"What brings you to the dungeon?" Mary said to me while looking at Adam for the answer.

"Blue hired a management consultant to make us more efficient," Adam said, and he actually put the words *management consultant* in air quotes, which pissed me off and shocked me at the same time. "Open access to books, printouts, everything."

"Did you give her the ten-cent tour?" Mary said.

"Yes, except the true cost was a quarter," Adam said, and then he looked at me. "I can explain that to you if they didn't teach it at Rutgers."

The blood must have drained from my face because Mary took one look at me and said, "I'll take it from here, Adam."

"That's a relief," he said, and he turned to head upstairs but then turned back to me as if he'd forgotten something. "Can I have your card?"

"What?" I said.

"Your business card," he said. "I'd like to have it in case I need a management consultant when I open my own place."

He locked his eyes on my eyes, and his look said, *Gotcha.*

"I left them in my car," I said. "I'll get you one as soon as I'm done with Mary."

"Sure you will," he said, and he went up the stairs.

In my mind, I said, *What just happened?* But I must have said it out loud too because Mary said, "Adam and Griff think you're a PI. I *know* you are."

I felt a billion brain cells explode in my skull, and I turned to her and moved my mouth, not expecting words to actually come out, though one did. "What?"

She took my arm and led me down the hall to her office at

the end of the row. It was a good thing she did because my legs would not have moved without her assistance.

"I know who you are and why you're here," she said.

"You do?"

"You're a private investigator pretending to be a management consultant. Blue hired you yesterday, and you told him your plan this morning."

"How do you know that?"

"He told me after you told him."

When I'd called Blue this morning to tell him my plan, a part of my plan—a big damn part of my plan, in fact—was that he was supposed to *not tell anyone at all* about my plan, meaning not even Doris Roberts. "He told you?"

She shut her office door and said, "I'm the office manager. He came to me as soon as he realized someone was stealing from us."

"He did?"

"I told him we needed to hire a PI so we could catch Griff in the act."

"You think it's Griff?"

"Oh my, yes."

Her office was good-sized and homey, with exposed brick walls and stained oak floors, a colorful Asian rug, a wrap-around maple desk with a matching credenza and two leather guest chairs, a wall of file cabinets, a bookshelf, pictures of grandchildren, and a round conference table with four chairs. We sat at the conference table.

I wasn't the fastest horse on the track, but I wasn't the slowest either. Most of the time, I was fast enough to know when I was a rail off the pace. But now I felt like I'd missed the gun and was already five lengths behind the pack.

"Blue didn't tell me he told you," I said.

"I didn't think he would. He told me you told him not to tell anyone, and then he told me not to tell you he told me. Does that make sense?"

"If Blue told you not to tell me he told you, then why did you tell me? That's the part that doesn't make sense."

"Because Griff is shrewd and connected and dangerous, and he thinks Blue is on to him, and Griff told Adam that, and Adam's with Griff, so it's two against one, and that's not fair, so I wanted to be your inside man."

"Inside man?"

"You're going to need me," she said, putting her hand on my arm. "I know where the bodies are buried."

It was like someone had hit the Blue Bar jigsaw puzzle table and a thousand pieces were flying through the air and falling willy-nilly to the floor. I had not expected a minute of what had happened, and it was hard for me to think my way through it. But there was one puzzle piece I knew I had to catch.

"Blue told you my name?" I said, thinking, *If he's given me all the way away, I'll have to drop the case, and I don't want to drop the case because I want to nail Dave Griffin to the wall and punch Adam Stoker in the nose before everything is said and done.*

"No. You did. Danielle Sullivan, right?"

"Dani, please. Nice to meet you, Mary," I said.

9

OH MY GOD, IT'S STANLEY STEIN

Two years after my sister left for Cleveland, when I was fourteen, Jimmy and I were eating Chinese takeout on a bench overlooking the lake in Kissena Park in Flushing. Jimmy was on surveillance, watching a woman who was cheating on her husband, a heavyweight who trained at Raul's, a hole-in-the-wall, second-floor boxing gym in Hell's Kitchen near the Port Authority. Jimmy boxed at Raul's too, and the heavyweight found out Jimmy was a private investigator and hired my father to catch his wife and the guy she was cheating with in the act and bring the son of a bitch to the back alley behind Raul's so he, the heavyweight, could beat the guy to a bloody pulp.

It was a Saturday afternoon, and Jimmy had taken me with him because he'd needed cover in Kissena while he watched the heavyweight's wife, who, it turned out, was cheating with another woman, meaning there was no back-alley beating at the end of that unhappy rainbow.

Anyway, while we ate Chinese takeout, Jimmy said it was time for me to learn how to defend myself. He took me to Hell's Kitchen the next day, and presented me to Raul, who took one look at me and told Jimmy I was a soft taco. "*Taco suave*," he'd called me.

I'd been training with Raul ever since. Four days a week for three decades, I'd jumped rope, pounded out push-ups and pull-ups and sit-ups, shadowboxed, and hit the pads and the speed bag and the heavy bag for more rounds than I could count. I'd done roadwork—running around the reservoir in Central Park—between training sessions for just as many years, so fast-forward three decades, and I was in excellent physical condition, which is another way of saying I looked great.

I mean, I was forty-five, not twenty-five (for Pete's sake, I don't *want* to be twenty-five again), but I was tight and strong and lean—not that I wasn't feminine and sexy and curvy, I had curves in all the right places (and in some places I *didn't* want them), and I was plenty sexy when I wanted to be. But sexy aside, I was a woman who could handle herself with a heavyweight husband in a back alley, meaning I could hit like a man who's been trained in the ring, which was why Jimmy took me to Raul's in the first place.

But the truth is I boxed to clear my head, not to beat up heavyweight husbands in back alleys, and my head needed clearing big-time when I left Blue Bar. It was Monday, and I was already up to my neck at Lowry Lowe *and* at Blue Bar—maybe over my neck. *Jesus*, I thought as Raul ran me ragged, *it's only the first day*.

When my tank was empty and I couldn't throw one more punch, I took a taxi back to the House of Emotional Tics, where I found the call sheet for *Kung Fu Fu* taped to my door.

In the wonderful world of film production, the call sheet is the logistic summary of the next day's shooting schedule, including cast and crew involvement, locations, times, scenes to be shot with page counts, special notes, and so on. It's usually distributed at the end of the shooting day so everyone is ready for tomorrow and tomorrow and tomorrow and tomorrow.

That LaTanya's no-budget guerilla film had a call sheet in the first place was both cool and crazy. Cool because when you get one, it means you're in a movie, and before the thing becomes a cyclonic disaster, it's cool to be in it. Crazy because the cast was Fu, Al, Warren, Charlie, LaTanya, and me. And the crew was Fu, Al, Warren, Charlie, LaTanya, and me. We could have used the lobby intercom to work out the details. But LaTanya had told me she was going for the Academy Award for Karate (even though there was no such thing) and wanted *Kung Fu Fu* to be professional from the get-go, so a call sheet was called for. Anyway, it said we were meeting Wednesday at six o'clock in the backyard for a table read of the script.

I took a shower, put on blue jeans and a gray silk blouse, drank a glass of white wine at my kitchen table while I wrote case notes, then grabbed a cab on First Avenue and went through the park back to Blue Bar—as myself this time, no wig, no colored contacts, no voice adjustment.

Just so you know, plenty of people had told me I looked like Sandra Bullock from *The Blind Side*, the Sandra Bullock from *Crash*. Sometimes I could see the resemblance, and sometimes I couldn't. Either way, I didn't mind the comparison. We were both actors, we were the same height, around the same age (she was older—sorry, Ms. Bullock), and we both had some smartass in us. Plus, who wouldn't want to look like Sandra Bullock from *The Blind Side*? I mean, come on.

I met Matthew and Vainglorious Nina, my son's significant other, in the Blue Bar lobby beneath the Wall of Champions. They had both come straight from work, so he wore Brooks Brothers and wingtips, and she wore tailored Ann Taylor from head to toe.

The first and second floors were full houses, meaning not one empty table, so one of the blonde hostesses from lunch, doing a Monday double, led us to a table near the long bar on the third floor, which was packed to near capacity. There had to be six hundred people in the doublewide brownstone, all of them pounding beers and chasing them with shots and then chasing their drinks with sliced steak sandwiches on home-made sourdough. *Holy shit*, I thought. *Blue Bar is raking it in.*

Matthew and I ordered Allagash White on draft. Nitwit Nina ordered an Absolut martini. We all ordered the steak sandwiches and then talked about work and the weather and my new show. Numbskull Nina, who despised the D-Cup with every molecule in her highbrow, snot-faced, know-it-all soul, lectured me on the negative impact the show's LSD-positive message would have on American youth.

"It's the irresponsibility of the cultural underpinnings that will ultimately undo your absurdist musical," Parasitic Nina said. "Greek Gods popping out of paintings and having acid-induced orgies in the Met as a way to teach ill-conceived lessons of love? Seriously? You can't disregard, dislocate, and disrespect accepted mores in the face of our next impression-able, wide-eyed generation and expect to create something of societal significance for entertainment-seeking adults. The audience is not smart, but it's conditioned to sense and ignore artistic irrelevance. Your musical is destined for theatrical insignificance. I'm sorry to be the one to have to tell you, Kate. I really am. *Psychedelic Sunday*? Even the title is inconsequential."

Egomaniacal Nina had lived with my son for several years. We could barely breathe each other's air for five minutes. For her, everything about me was tied too loose. For me, everything about her was wound too tight. Was she beautiful? Sure. But if you're full of shit and a total snot-bag about it, you wear your welcome out fast no matter how beautiful you are, no matter how much my son loves you. And when you're an overbearing, NYU art appreciation assistant professor who thinks she knows more about film and theater and art and literature and televi-sion and food and culture and style than the rest of the world *and* you make a habit of telling the rest of the world how they should feel about those things no matter how they actually feel about them *and* you're full of shit and a total snot-bag about it, then I want to hunt you down and run you over with a crosstown bus.

"I'm sorry, Nina," I said. "I dozed off as soon as I heard your assistant professor voice. Were you saying something societally significant? Or was it destined for inconsequentiality? Want to try again? I'm listening now. I really am."

We smiled, coexisting with snide reluctance because I loved my son and he loved her. Nonetheless, she got an adjective at all times because she deserved one.

"Changing the subject," Matthew said, "Detective Logan called today and said he returned your gun."

"Why did he do that?" I said, knowing exactly why Logan did it: the more people trying to keep me off the case, the better, especially if one of them was my son.

"Professional courtesy," Matthew said, "and beside the point, which is that you went to the Thirteenth to tell him you had a secret, anonymous source that told you, texted you, one of the Lowry Lowe partners would have their eyes shot out by Friday. I think that's the point, don't you, Mom? That you're still investigating Jimmy's murder even though you promised not to?"

My son was born on my seventeenth birthday. I can remember that day and most every other day of his life just by closing my eyes—birthdays, graduations, Little League games, Christmas dinners, days at the beach, camping with Jimmy, first words, first steps, first dates. He was a beautiful boy then, and he still was now. Except now he was a twenty-eight-year-old assistant district attorney for the city of New York. Jimmy helped me put him through NYU undergrad, but Matthew had paid his own way through law school, graduated with honors, clerked for a superior court judge for a few years, and then joined the DA's office, where he was a rising star. He was smart, handsome, talented, funny, honest, sincere, and genuine.

Proud mama bear? Oh yeah, that was me.

Perfect mother and son relationship? Uh, not so much.

To be blunt, Matthew thought I was wasting my life aspiring to be an actor. He thought I was stubborn and irresponsible and immature. I had all those traits, it was true, but for a single teenage mom in New York, I had done all right by him, and I'd done all right for myself too—not great, but good enough. I loved to act. I loved to box. I had a job and a place to live and a few nice friends. I had a life. Matthew disagreed. But if I'd been "a flailing and failing aspiring actor for thirty years" (his words), at least I was always "a good mom, a good person" (also his words), right up until, that is, I'd inherited Jimmy's PI business and my ride went off the rails.

Matthew has always parented me, which was cute when he was eight but was aggravating at twenty-eight, though now he was worried about my safety—not just living a good life but staying out of jail in the process...and staying alive. Anyway, since I'd become a PI, Matthew had put his parenting engine in high gear: scolding me, warning me, bossing me, bribing me, begging me, and lawyering me because he loved me. I knew he loved me. And I loved him so much I could feel it in every heartbeat.

"You should be proud of me, Matthew," I said. "I promised I would tell Logan when I knew something as soon as I knew something, and that's what I did."

"Anonymous source? You haven't been doing this long enough to have an anonymous source. Who is he?"

"I don't know his name. That's what *anonymous* means."

"What's his text number?"

"I can't tell you. Private investigators protect their sources. So do reporters, by the way. It's not like this is unheard of."

"Nobody in their right mind, and that's what this conversation is actually about, nobody in their right mind, no matter what they do for a living, protects a source that's trying to kill them."

I knew he would suspect I was texting Jimmy's killer. He couldn't outright accuse me because he was a prosecutor and needed evidence to make an accusation, but he could float the idea he was onto me so I would know he was onto me. Now I knew.

"Logan told you to stay away from Lowry Lowe, did he not?" Matthew said. He was upset with me, but I had actually gone to the police, and he'd recognized that as a gold star instead of a demerit, so the evening was not yet lost.

"He did."

"Good. I'm telling you too. Do not under any circumstances stick your nose into...oh my God, it's Stanley Stein."

He was looking past me, straight at the bar. Deplorable Nina and I followed his eyes to a white-haired, seventy-something-year-old man in a suit who took a seat at the bar and nodded at the bartender, who put a drink down in front of the man without having to be told what kind of drink. The man opened the sports section of his newspaper.

"Who's Stanley Stein?" I said.

"One of the biggest bookies in New York," Matthew said. "Top three."

"What's he doing here?" Despicable Nina said.

"Taking bets," Matthew said. "Blue Bar is one of his watering holes."

10

LOOKS LIKE IT MIGHT BE THREE ON ONE

It was a cloudless October, Tuesday morning. The view from the Lowry Lowe conference room on the sixty-second floor of 30 Rockefeller Center was spectacular. A wall of windows on the north side presented a panoramic view of the island of Manhattan in all its magnificent, mind-blowing splendor. The East River, the Hudson River, the iconic bridges, the awesome and eclectic skyscrapers, the glorious green parks and gardens set between the great grid of avenues, the endless electric ballet of city buses and checker cabs and nearly nine million people living life in the fast lane.

The view inside the law offices of Lowry Lowe was pretty swell too. The partners had spent a not-so-small fortune to have the place professionally designed and decorated with upscale elegance and style that could only be called super-ultra-high-tech modern. The floors were natural maple, polished to a perfect sheen. The walls and ceilings and doors were African ebony, gorgeous beyond gorgeous. Stainless-steel lighting fixtures were artistically placed to accentuate the original, avant-garde paintings and sculpture that could fill a fabulous wing at the Museum of Modern Art. The lobby, conference rooms, and offices were tastefully set with coal-black leather chairs and sofas that had gleaming stainless frames, walnut desks and credenzas and conference tables, and wireless, cutting-edge, state-of-the-art media and office electronics. There were wide hallways, tall ceilings, and exotic plants and flowers.

Everything dripped money, including the staff. Finely styled attorneys, paralegals, assistants, secretaries, and receptionists went about their business, charging fifteen hundred dollars an hour to empty the bank accounts of unhappy couples.

It was sleek. It was slick. It was superfly.

"The partners apologize for making you wait, Mrs. Baynes," Michelle Lowry's assistant had said when she deposited me in the north conference room thirty minutes ago. "But they're meeting with a detective behind closed doors, and it's taking longer than expected. Can I get you a bottle of chilled water? I have Veen."

I'd accepted the Veen (*twenty-three dollars a bottle!*), thinking, *Divorce attorneys definitely dance with detectives to dig up dirt, so it's probably got nothing to do with anyone getting their eyes shot out.* But thirty minutes later, I had to take a twenty-three-dollar pee and decided to find out what kind of dirt took a half hour to dig.

I opened the north conference room door and poked my head out. "Ladies' room?" I said with a Texas twang to a passing paralegal. I was wearing the Wanda Ward red wig, the green contacts, tight jeans, Tony Lama cowboy boots that would make El Paso proud, a white silk blouse, and a blue blazer.

The paralegal pointed me down the hall. I smiled because the bathroom was the same direction as the south conference room—just beyond it, in fact. I nodded thanks, and started that way.

When I got to the south conference room door, I looked

around, took a breath, grabbed the handle, and went in as if I knew where I was going.

"Oh dang," I said, acting thoroughly surprised. "I thought this was the ladies' room. I'm sorry."

I wasn't sorry. Lew Logan sat at the table with Michelle and Christopher Lowry and Lisa and Jack Lowe. Lisa was the only one I hadn't yet met. She was every bit as impressive, imposing, and beautiful as Michelle, the Swedish Queen, except her exquisite gene pool had originated 1,665 miles due south of Sweden, meaning she was an Italian bombshell, as in Sophia Loren, as in Monica Bellucci, as in shimmering black hair and deep, dark eyes and picture-perfect olive skin and full lips and a killer body, as in Lisa Lowe rules the world if she wants to.

"It's the next door down the hall, Emily," Michelle said. "So sorry. We're almost done. Two minutes."

"That's fine," I said, smiling as I backed out of the room. "I've waited twenty years for Tommy's money. I can wait two more minutes."

It turned out two minutes was the precise amount of time I needed to recalibrate my Lowry Lowe equation. Until now, I had no way of knowing whether the partners knew about the sword of Damocles hanging over their heads. I'd planned this first meeting to be a fishing expedition: Did they know anything? If so, how much? But I had thought I'd be fishing without a pole.

Now, thanks to Logan, I had a pole and a hook and a hunk of bait.

Speaking of Logan, the homicide detective hadn't given any indication he knew Emily Baynes was really me. There was no narrowing of his eyes, no tightening of his jaw, no cocking his head in that special way that said, *You've got to be kidding me with this shit. Does your brain not work at all?*

That didn't mean he didn't know it was me. Logan could

hold his cards so close to his vest you couldn't tell if he had cards to begin with. If he did know, he didn't give me away because he was hoping I'd learn something and tell him what it was before the contract killer did some contract killing. And if Logan didn't know, then I was as good an actor as I'd hoped I was.

The north conference room door opened, and Michelle and Christopher Lowry came in and sat down across the table from me. Michelle opened a MacBook Air. Her husband had a legal pad and a fancy pen, which made me think of Jimmy, who always used the cheapest Bic he could buy. *"It's lose-lose, Katie,"* he'd told me. *"Either you're an asshole because you think you can impress someone with an expensive pen, or you're an asshole because an expensive pen impresses you."*

"Lisa and Jack had a midtown mediation and asked if they could meet with you later today or tomorrow," Michelle said.

I knew I was meeting Blue later today, and tomorrow afternoon I'd be at Blue Bar, and then six o'clock was the table read for *Kung Fu Fu.* "How about tomorrow morning?" I said. "I can be here at ten thirty."

"Done," Christopher said, making a note with his fancy pen.

"Naturally, we have a list of questions for you," Michelle said. "And I'm sure you have a list of questions for us as well."

"Client comfort comes first," Christopher said. "After you, please."

He and his partner, Jack Lowe, had reminded me of two specific actors since I'd met them yesterday: Patrick Dempsey and Eric Dane—McDreamy and McSteamy from *Grey's Anatomy.* Jack was McSteamy. Christopher was McDreamy.

I smiled and said, "How come there's a homicide cop in your conference room? If your husband's dead, there's no point divorcing him. Bank account belongs to you. Same thing the other way around. If the wife's murdered, what's the husband need you for? He's got the money. He needs a criminal attorney."

Michelle and Christopher looked at each other. The question surprised them, but they were a cool couple.

"How do you know he's a police officer?" Michelle said.

"Your assistant told me you were meeting with a detective when she apologized for you making me wait thirty minutes," I said with just the right amount of snark. The Swedish Queen would eat me for breakfast if I let her. I had to be as tough and cocky and confident as she was to get anywhere worth going.

"How do you know he's homicide?" Christopher said, and I felt like I was in a *Grey's Anatomy* episode, the one where the redheaded Texan firecracker lights up Seattle Grace Hospital. I shook it off and thought, *A pole and a hook and a hunk of bait.*

"Because Tommy killed a man in Austin, and we met with homicide cops every day for ten months," I said. "They've got a life-and-death look I know by heart. It's like a neon sign comes with their badge."

There was a moment, maybe just the tip of a moment, where Christopher looked at Michelle in a way that registered as deeper than professional, that registered as personal, as husband to wife. It was a glance that said they somehow knew something about killing a man, about homicide cops, about life-and-death looks.

He was looking for his wife's support, not his business partner's support, and she totally rejected him in an equally personal way. There was something cold about Michelle Lowry —cold-blooded.

She smiled ever so slightly, as if something had clicked for her below the surface, as if the game had changed for her in the same way it had changed for me when I'd seen Logan in her conference room.

"There's been a death threat made against the partners," Michelle said. "It's not unusual in high-dollar divorce settlements for someone to threaten us. Generally speaking, there's a very angry spouse on the other side of the table."

"Good to know," I said, nodding my approval of both her answer and attitude.

"Your husband killed a man in Austin?" Christopher said. He'd recovered from his wife's subtle rejection and was back in lawyer mode.

"One I know of," I said. "Couple others I suspect."

"Why didn't he go to jail?" Michelle said.

"Tommy's a twisted pervert geek—wait until I tell you about the underage girls—but he's also a goddamn genius," I said. "If he sets his mind to getting away with murder, you have to wake up early in the morning to catch him. That's why I hired Lowry Lowe. I figured four on one, I might have a chance at the big money."

I loved playing the role of Emily Baynes. I'd thought she'd be arrogant and spoiled, but I'd never expected her to be so feisty. She was a hot handful, which is why Tommy had married her, I realized. She wasn't as smart as he was by a long shot, but she was a challenge and a half, and that was enough...until it wasn't. And by then, Emily was sick to death of his special brand of bullshit.

"Except now," I said, "it looks like it might be three on one."

"Excuse me," Michelle said, drilling me with her icy-blue eyes.

She was good. I knew she knew what I'd said *and* what I'd meant, but she wanted me to say it again—to see if there were cracks in my confidence. Of course, there were cracks up and down my confidence, but I was a trained and skilled actor, and I wasn't going to let her see them. Which seemed only fair because she was a trained and skilled attorney, which is a lot like being an actor, so she didn't let me see her cracks either. Although it crossed my mind she might not have any.

"The detective delivering a death notice, did he say which partner was being threatened?" I said.

"No," Michelle said.

"He didn't know," Christopher said.

"That's a whole other rodeo," I said. "If you had to pick one, who do you think it would be?"

They shouldn't have answered the question. They should have let it go. Given me lip service. Changed the subject.

But the question itself was thought provoking enough to throw them both off balance. They didn't look at each other. They just opened their mouths at the same time.

"Jack," Christopher said.

"Lisa," Michelle said.

11

———————

SOMETHING PRIVATE BETWEEN YOU AND ME

IT HAD STARTED YESTERDAY MORNING WHEN I'D CALLED TO TELL
him my plan.

"You pick the place," he'd said, "and I'll buy you lunch tomorrow, and you can tell me what happened."

"Or I could call you tonight when I get back from the bar," I'd said.

"You could, but then I wouldn't get to see you," he'd said.

Right there, that was it. I could hear it in his voice. I could see his smile in my mind, his twinkling eyes. Blue was flirting with me. Was it because he liked me, because he was attracted to me? Or was it just how he was wired after so many years of beautiful baseball groupies in hotel bars? It didn't matter. He was my client. I wasn't getting involved with him under any circumstances.

"I pick Calexico," I'd said.

"Which one?"

"Flatiron."

"I'll be there."

On Broadway, near the Flatiron Building, between 24th and 25th Streets, rules the mother of all food carts. It was called

Calexico, after the Imperial Valley border town that separates Mexico from California. Half the town is south of the border. The other half belongs to Uncle Sam.

Once upon a time, three brothers who called that part of the world home moved to Manhattan and, homesick for hybrid Calexico cuisine, set out to bring a taste of the border to the City That Never Sleeps.

They didn't have the money to open a restaurant, so they bought a food cart instead. These were the dark days of New York, before fabulous food trucks ruled the roads, when rolling carts served hot dogs and pretzels and not much more.

As fast as they could fill a taco, the brothers won a Vendy— the Oscar for street food—built a fleet of carts, and opened a couple of brick-and-mortar joints for folks who like to sit inside.

If you don't get there by eleven forty-five, the line wraps around the block, and you take agonizing baby steps toward the grill while the heavenly aroma of roasted tomatillos and ancho chiles and sizzling steak, pork, and chicken fills your head with anticipation and makes your mouth water. As you might imagine, when your mind is full of tacos and burritos and rolled quesadillas and your mouth is watering, it's hard to have a serious conversation, if you're having a serious conversation, which I was with Blue.

We'd both arrived at twelve thirty. The line was already long, so we had time to talk.

"Did you catch him?" Blue said, mostly kidding.

"Not yet," I said.

"Did he tell you anything important?"

"He told me lunch was not in our future."

"He thinks you're a PI."

"I am a PI."

"That's what he thinks. Adam too."

"I know. Mary told me."

"I know. She told me too."

After I'd left Michelle and Christopher Lowry, I'd used the ladies' room near the Rink at the Rock, lost the red Wanda Ward wig and green contacts, and brushed my hair and freshened my makeup.

While I looked at myself in the mirror, I'd had a feeling in the pit of my stomach. I tried to ignore it, but it moved to my head and turned into a thought that became a voice in my mind that said, *You're getting involved with Steve Stark. You're attracted to him.*

I couldn't let that go, so we had a little discussion, the voice and me.

I'm not getting involved with him. I admit he's handsome and successful and single. But I'm forty-five years old, for God's sake. I'm a grown-up. I can be attracted to handsome, successful, single men without turning into a hot-to-trot, grade-school girl. I can compartmentalize these things. It's a business lunch. I'm a professional PI. He's my client. I'm not getting involved with him under any circumstances.

The lady doth protest too much, methinks, the voice said.

And then we'd met on Broadway, Flatiron Building in the background, and his eyes were somehow bluer than they'd been on Sunday at Fu's parrot party, and his smile was more gorgeous than I'd remembered, and I could feel a microscopic twinge of heat on the back of my neck. Nothing I couldn't control, but there it was.

"Right, about that, about you telling Mary my plan after I told you not to tell anyone my plan," I said.

"I know," he said.

"If you know," I said, "then why would you do that? The whole *private* thing about a private investigation is that it's *private*. If I tell you not to tell anyone, you can't tell anyone. That's what makes it private. It's between you and me."

"I like the sound of that."

"The sound of what?"

"Something private between you and me."

He held my eyes with his eyes, and he smiled, and the microscopic hot spot on the back of my neck grew to the size of a dime.

"Then let's keep it that way," I said, smiling back at him. *Oh crap*, I thought. *That was very close to me getting involved right there. He started it, and now I'm doing it too. Right here in the middle of the day on Broadway.*

"Bad habit," he said. "I knew you'd need Mary's help. I'm always two pitches ahead in the count, if you know what that means."

"My father was a pitcher," I said. "He was good too, but he blew out his shoulder and became a private investigator instead. He took me to tons of games. I can score nine innings like a beat reporter."

"So you know what it means."

"If you're always two pitches ahead, don't think of me as the batter. I'm your catcher. You can't be ahead of your catcher, Blue. And you can't shake me off. I'm calling the game."

"I never had a catcher who looked like you," he said, and the dime of heat grew to the size of a quarter.

The line inched forward, and a wave of pollo tocino—chicken and bacon simmered in roasted tomatillo salsa—filled the air and made my knees shake.

"Mary said Griff was shrewd and connected and dangerous," I said.

"He is."

"So why is he your friend? And if he's your friend, why is he stealing your money?"

"He's my friend because we grew up on the same street in Montclair. Played ball together. Little League, Babe Ruth, American Legion. Joined at the hip."

"What position did he play?"

"Second. We were high school state champs four years in a row. And then the Dodgers drafted us. Different rounds. Total fluke they took us both. We'd dreamed about playing in the bigs together, telling our story to *Sports Illustrated*—Little League to Major League, Montclair to LA, side by side the whole way, and now it was happening. I did three years in the minors and moved up to the show. He did three years in the minors and was released—not big enough, not fast enough, not good enough."

"You stayed friends?"

"You share your whole life with somebody, you stay friends even if you're not friends, even if some things change."

"Sounds like everything changed."

"Pretty much. He moved back to New Jersey, got out of baseball, and sold cars. But there were allegations he was stealing from the dealership, so he left that job and became a bartender, hooked up with a rough crowd in Trenton, and bought a bar. And then he lost that bar and bought another one in Paterson and lost that one and bought another one, and, meanwhile, I played pro ball and made a lot of money and got on TV and lived the life we'd dreamed of. The life we were supposed to live together."

He smiled, ever so slightly wistful. I noticed he had one wave of unruly hair, like Superman. I wanted to gently brush it away with my hand, but I didn't.

"And then you retired from the Mets, and there he was again," I said.

"There he was. I worked at PIX for a few years, and that was good, but I knew I wanted to own a sports bar in New York. It was a vision I'd had for years, and then I got a shot at the building on 83rd, and Griff wanted in."

"Was he still running with the Trenton crowd?"

"Up to his ass."

"And you let him buy in as your managing partner?"

"Not exactly. I lent him two hundred fifty thousand dollars. I paid his share."

"Not your smartest move."

"Not my smartest move. But he was Griff, and he'd owned bars before, and, well, he was Griff."

"Did he pay it back over time?"

"It was a five-year balloon due July first, three months ago, and as of the last week of June, he didn't have the money. I know because he told me."

"Pretty sure I don't like where this is going."

"He borrowed it from Trenton. Now he owes them a quarter mil, and it's not a balloon. The way guys like that work, your payments never go down—three grand one week, thirty-two fifty the next. You can never get even. And if you don't make good, they bury you in pieces up and down the turnpike. Anyway, that's why he's stealing my money."

"But you can't prove it's him."

"There was cash missing July second. I caught it the end of that week. I knew it was Griff. It had to be. Maybe it would just be one time, I thought. But then it kept happening. At first, he's giving it to Trenton, making payments, that's what I'm thinking. Then one month goes by and then another, and I can't catch him, and Mary can't catch him, and now he's not just taking money to make payments, he's taking money to make payments *and* he's taking money to bet at the bar, swinging for the fences so he can pay the whole thing off. But you're right. I can't prove it. That's your job. And, I have to say, I'm liking that more every day, the idea of working with you."

He moved a little closer to me when he said it so I would know he meant he was liking *me* too, not just the *idea* of me. Apparently, he was also a professional at body language. The heat moved down my neck and across my shoulders.

Stop it with the heat down your neck and across your shoulders, said the voice in my mind. *You have to control it right now. If you can't take the heat...*

Get out of the kitchen, I said to the voice. *I know.*

"Which leads us to Stanley Stein," I said.

He smiled, and the line moved, and he took my elbow with his hand and guided me forward, and the heat shot through my whole body at his touch.

"If you wait long enough," he said, "everything leads to Stanley."

12

CRAZY THE SIZE OF THE SUN

Blue had the pollo asado, grilled marinated chicken with pico de gallo and an avocado sauce that made you think you died and went to Heaven. I had the pollo tocino because I'd caught the aroma in line and the chicken and bacon simmered in roasted tomatillo sauce hooked me hard and reeled me in.

Stanley Stein, Blue told me over lunch, seemed like a nice guy, unassuming, soft-spoken, somebody's grandfather, somebody else's uncle—everybody's bookie. He came into Blue Bar several times a week, but there was no pattern to his arrival. Stanley could show up any day or night of the week at any time. He always went to a different floor and ate at the bar. He *never* had to order his food or drinks. Every bartender knew what Stanley wanted and made sure he got it pronto.

None of that was unusual, Blue told me. Stanley was a Blue Bar regular, spent good money, left big tips. What *was* unusual was there were *always* two empty stools waiting for him—no matter what day of the week, what time of the day or night, or which bar on whatever floor he landed. Two stools. Every time.

Stanley would sit at the bar and read every New York newspaper. Throughout the night (or day or sometimes both), people would sit beside him, talk to him for a minute or two, shake his hand, pat his back, practically kiss his ring, and then vacate the stool. And then someone else would join Stanley at the bar and do the same thing, and so on and so on until Stanley folded his papers and left.

There was no doubt, and also no proof, Stanley was taking bets: no cash changed hands, and the bookie never wrote anything down. Not a word or a number. Nothing.

"Does Griff sit at the bar with Stanley Stein?" I said to Blue.

"Since August," Blue said, "all the time."

After lunch, I caught a cab to the D-Cup for an afternoon *Psychedelic Sunday* rehearsal. Dennis devoted the entire session to the crescendo of the show, the grand finale, the curtain closer at the end of act 2: a full-cast striptease in the American Wing of the Met that led to the second orgy of the play. Yes, the play had *two* orgies.

An orgy ended the first act too, so there was a kind of symmetrical madness to the musical. The first-act orgy was set in the Greek gallery, where, in Johnny Jedry's LSD-soaked brain, the mostly naked statuary came to life as the cast performed a Posey rocker called "Lusty Ladies of Greece" after the professor and Venus shared the Kiss of All Kisses—meaning Chloe and me locked lips like there was no tomorrow—while the jealous Adonis watched from the wings.

And while we all thought nothing could top an onstage orgy like that in terms of basic insanity—an orgy of naked Greek statues—we soon learned that an orgy including George Washington, the signers of the Declaration of Independence, and the women of the colonies, all of whom pop out of Early American paintings and strip to the Freddie Mercury/Queen-like anthem "Love and Death and Sex and Me" after Adonis shoots Jedry in a duel to the death so he can reclaim Venus as his lover, we soon learned an orgy like *that* was crazy the size of the sun.

The only thing weirder than watching Americans of the Revolutionary War pop out of paintings, strip down to their powdered wigs, and get it on while singing and dancing across the D-Cup stage was *being* Americans of the Revolutionary War stripping down to powdered wigs and getting it on while singing and dancing across the stage.

You might think a rehearsal like that would have held my attention, but it was hard for me to concentrate on Venus and Adonis and Professor Jedry and the orgiastic colonists because I couldn't stop thinking about Dave Griffin and how his life mirrored my life but for how the wind blew him one way and me the other.

All *my* life, since Jimmy took me to see the Rockettes, since my seventh-grade star turn in *Bye Bye Birde*, I had been an actor. I had not *aspired* to be one, like my son said; I had *been* one, with every heartbeat, every breath, every thought, every line, every note, every dance, every drop of my blood, every minute of my days and nights.

I had not envisioned myself consigned to a way-off-Broadway life of nonsensical nightclub-singing vampires and psychedelic orgies. I'd seen my future unfolding in front of the bright lights on Broadway. That it hadn't happened that way for me had not stopped me from being who I was: an actor. In other words, I'd never confused what I wanted to do with who I was. And so my life, while challenging in many ways, had always featured me living as an actor. No matter what, I was *me* because I was living my acting life. Granted, I'd taken a recent left turn after Jimmy willed me his PI business, but I was still acting—Emily Baynes, Danielle Sullivan, and Venus, for instance, were current roles—I was still an actor in my guts. That's how the wind blew me.

All *his* life, since he and Blue had played Little League in Montclair, New Jersey, Griff had been a baseball player. On they went to high school and four straight state championships, and life was sweet for Dave Griffin. Life was perfect. He was drafted by the Dodgers and was living right smack-dab in middle of the life he knew he wanted to live, was supposed to live. He was a baseball player. And then he wasn't big enough or fast enough or good enough to play in the majors, and that was when he confused what he wanted to do with who he was, when the wind blew him sideways, when he made a choice that redefined his sun and moon and stars: he stopped living his baseball life.

Maybe if he'd gone into scouting or coaching or managing or announcing or something that kept him in the game, living his baseball life even if he wasn't playing at the highest level, maybe then he would still have been who he was, maybe then he wouldn't have hooked up with Trenton and dug himself a quarter-million-dollar ditch. That was how the wind blew him.

Or maybe the wind wasn't even blowing. Maybe Griff was born a con man, always a dishonest prick who would steal from his childhood friend. How would I know? I popped out of paintings in wackadoodle D-Cup musicals with *two* orgies and loved every minute of it.

13

CAN'T DO WITHOUT FU

WHEN I GOT BACK TO THE HOUSE OF EMOTIONAL TICS, I FOUND Fu on a ladder, fixing a light in the Lobby That Never Cheers Up. With its dim-grim amber glow and its sad and sagging 1940s feel, it was always the most depressing day of the year in the House of Emotional Tics lobby—even the brightest midsummer morning came off as a dreary winter afternoon. The staircase was on the right side, the west side of the long lobby, and the mailboxes, the intercom, and my apartment, 1A, were on the left side.

Fu had built a portable perch out of wood and metal so Jerusalem Joe wouldn't be stuck in his telephone booth-sized cage all day. The bird had belonged to a bitter, Brooklyn middle school gym teacher named Gianassio, who'd retired upstate near the Finger Lakes and had taught the parrot to be a smart-mouthed son of a bitch. I'd owed Fu an Amazon parrot for saving my life four times, maybe five, but how Fu found Joe in the Finger Lakes was a mystery. Anyway, the Chinese mainte-nance man and the colorful bird were fast friends—maybe because they were both wise guys.

"Who invited you, sad sack?" Joe said as I crossed the lobby.

"I don't need an invitation," I said to Joe. "I'm the manager."

"Good luck with that," Joe said.

"You're a douchebag, Joe," I said.

"Kiss my ass, girlfriend," Joe said.

Jesus Christ, I was having a conversation with a parrot that was spitting out mindless invectives he'd been taught by Gianassio. He was a parrot, for Pete's sake. We couldn't *really* have a conversation. But somehow we were. And I was losing.

I took out my keys, and Fu said from the ladder, "When tell Fu Lowry Lowe?"

There were no secrets in the House of Emotional Tics. If it was my business, it was everybody's business. Especially Fu, who seemed to know my business before *I* knew my business.

"Why do I have to tell you? You already know," I said.

"Already know more than you," Fu said in a smirky voice.

No one beside my sister knew how to get under my skin the way Fu did. It was instant and effortless, like a summer splinter. I walked to the ladder and looked up.

"Even if you know *something* about Lowry Lowe," I said, "you don't know more than me. I've been there twice. I've met the partners. You've never been there. You've never met the partners. How do you even know about Lowry Lowe?"

He kept working on the light. "Fu fix Zombie toilet. See Lowry Lowe papers on desk. Ask Zombie why papers on desk. Zombie say papers for you. Fu say no kill Zombie if Zombie tell Fu everything you tell Zombie. Zombie tell Fu everything so Fu no kill. That how Fu know." Then he looked down into my eyes. "How *you* know?"

We'd arrived at the House of Emotional Tics around the same time, a little more than two years ago, and for those two years he'd said exactly six words: *yes, no, Fu, say, you, too.* Then one day, in the middle of my first case, with our lives on the line, he let on he knew all the damn words in the dictionary, and there had been no shutting him up since then—and no winning an argument either.

"Because the killer told me," I said, understanding there was no point keeping it secret since it would probably be common knowledge anyway by tomorrow's table read. "He texted me."

Fu smiled a snarky smile that pissed me off and turned back to work on the light. "Fu figure."

"Fu figure? You just figured the killer was texting me? Really?"

"How else you know? No have crystal ball. No have swami in back pocket. Have Fu."

"Way to go, meathead," Joe said to me.

"Shut up, Joe," I said to the bird, and then I looked up the ladder. "Okay, so you know about Lowry Lowe. What do you know that I don't know?"

"Lowry Lowe lawyer dead Friday," Fu said, climbing down the ladder and turning so we were face-to-face. "Fu know why."

He was forty-two years old and my height, but three of me could hide behind him. He was two hundred fifty pounds of pure muscle, solid as a block of granite, wide as a VW bus. He had short, spiky black hair, smooth skin, and hands that could crush concrete—I had seen him do it. He had the power of a bulldozer, the grace of a ballerina, the speed of a sprinter, the agility of a gymnast, and the wiseguy grin of a mafia assassin, which is what he'd been in China before the Chinese mob sent him here for whatever nasty reason they'd had to get him out of China in the first place. He was the most singular human being in the city of New York, the quirkiest of the quirky, the oddest of the odd, the deadliest of the deadly.

He never knew his mother, and his father had abandoned him at a Shaolin temple when Fu was a young boy. He'd been raised by a mysterious shifu who had trained him to be a tenth-degree, black belt/red belt, martial arts killing machine in a dozen different disciplines, taught him to love Italian opera, and showed him how to bake tea cakes like a Chinese Betty Crocker. Somehow that path had led Fu to the Chinese mafia, where he'd killed more mob enemies than he cared to recall. "No more kill. Kill too many. Kill enough," he'd once said to me. Along the way, he'd developed a special bond with birds of all feathers—except pigeons, he hated pigeons—and made bird movies in China, which only proved Fu was the rarest bird of all.

"No way," I said.

"Way," he said.

"*I* don't know why. How do *you* know why?"

"Fu read Lowry Lowe paper. Read between lines. Fu better than swami."

Freaking Fu, I thought. *He is better than a swami.* It took all my acting prowess to keep that thought off my face.

"Fine, Fu. Why?" I said.

"Affair."

"Affair?"

"Lowry Lowe partners divorce many time. Many affair."

It was true. I'd read that in the Lowry Lowe papers Al printed for me. "So?"

"Fu say two Lowry Lowe partners have affair. Fu say Lowry Lowe affair go too far. Fu say one Lowry Lowe partner want revenge. Hire killer."

Was it possible? It was. Was it probable? I didn't know. I couldn't think it through because I was too pissed off that Fu had read between the lines and I hadn't.

"Okay," I said. "Let's say you're right. Let's say two of the Lowry Lowe partners had an affair and one of the other husbands or wives found out about it. And then let's say whoever found out was so bent out of shape they hired the corporate killer who murdered my father to kill one of the partners in the affair. Let's just say that's what happened."

"Fu say that what happen."

"Then who is he going to kill?"

And then came the Fu Chen smirk. Oh yes, the smirk that pushed my buttons. "How Fu know? You go twice. You meet partners. Fu no go. Fu no meet partners. Fu ask you. Who kill first?"

He climbed back up the ladder, and I could hear him smiling and smirking and smirking and smiling. I turned away and walked across the lobby to my door.

He was right. I had been there twice as Emily Baynes. I had met the partners. I had asked Christopher and Michelle that same question this very morning. "That's a whole other rodeo," I'd said with a Texas twang. "If you had to pick one, who do you think it would be?" I'd been there twice, and I had no idea who it would be.

Christopher had said Jack. Michelle had said Lisa.

I would ask Lisa and Jack the same question tomorrow morning.

I put my key in the door, and Fu called across the lobby, still pretending to work on the lobby light. "Fu not know more than you after all."

I turned to him. "Good," I said, knowing he didn't mean it as an apology but futilely accepting it as one anyway.

"Fu know *much more* than you."

Jesus, I thought. *Just like my sister.*

"You know why I didn't tell you yet, Fu?" I said. "Because I don't need you yet. When I need you, then I'll tell you. You don't decide when I need you. I decide."

Ha, I thought as I opened my door. *I finally get the last word with Fu.*

"May not need now," Fu said, stopping me before I went

inside with the sheer power of his snarky smirk. "But need soon. Can't do without Fu."

"Heck of a job, Brownie," Joe said to me.

"Shove it up your beak, bird," I said. "And Fu you, Fu."

"Fu you too," Fu said.

14

WONKY WEATHER IN MY MIND

It was nine thirty, Wednesday morning, one hour until my meeting with Jack and Lisa Lowe, and the weather report in my brain was dense fog.

I'd woken up early and gone for a run, something I often do to clear my head. If my head needs deeper clearing, I run west on 83rd Street to Fifth Avenue, cruise into Central Park, and follow the footpaths to the JKO Reservoir, one of the best places to clear your head in New York. Between Blue Bar, Lowry Lowe, *Psychedelic Sunday*, Al Cutter, and Fu, my head needed industrial-strength clearing.

I ran west on 83rd to the park.

The one-hundred-six-acre, decommissioned reservoir was named in honor of Jacqueline Kennedy Onassis in 1994. One of the city's most famous and beloved daughters, Jackie O, being the true New Yorker she was, liked to run around the reservoir too. I can only imagine the kind of clearing her head needed.

The reservoir is as popular with tourists as it is with New Yorkers. Side by side, they run laps around the one-and-a-half-mile track, taking in the serenity of the water and the surrounding city skyline, hoping the grandeur of it all works its magic and opens their minds. Or maybe they ride horses on the bridal path, which also encircles the JKO, wondering, like the runners, how the heck they got into whatever mess they got into and how the double heck they get out of it. Or maybe that's just me.

Fu liked the reservoir because it's an ecological sanctuary unlike any other in the city: home to more than twenty species of waterbirds. He went there from time to time to commune with the mallards and geese, the coots and loons, the gulls and grebes and gadwalls, the herons and egrets, the mergansers and shovelers and the buffleheads.

I did two laps around the reservoir and then ran back to the House of Emotional Tics, a five-mile workout that cleared my head just enough for me to know what I wanted for breakfast. I showered, ate a bowl of Greek yogurt with berries from the Korean market near the corner of 83rd and First, and went into my walk-through closet to become Emily Baynes.

Like all the apartments in the brownstone, 1A was a two-bedroom/one-bathroom railroad flat. The front door opened into the living room, which opened into the bedroom, which opened into the second bedroom—that I'd turned into a walk-in/walk-through closet—which opened into the dining room, which opened into the kitchen, all the rooms in a row. The bathroom was a separate room off the kitchen.

I had lived in the House of Emotional Tics and been the building manager for more than two years, but I'd collected plenty of thrift store and yard sale shabby chic furniture, rugs, eclectic lamps, and decorations before I'd arrived on East 83rd Street, and so my place had a French countryside flea market feel to it the day I moved in. *Mucho* memorabilia from my acting career—playbills and posters and props and scripts from several decades of irreverent musical theater, faded cable commercials, failed TV pilots, and forgotten indie films—was everywhere, as were framed photographs of Matthew and me and Jimmy and Christine and even Marilyn.

It was clean but cluttered. I liked my things around me. I liked to see them all the time. I liked to pick them up and feel again the feelings I'd felt when I'd first felt them, when I was living that moment in time. I wasn't good at putting things away is what I'm saying. I didn't keep everything. I got rid of boxes and boxes of junk all the time. But I held onto things that held onto me, if that makes sense. In other words, my walls and shelves and tables were full of my life, the events and feelings and moments that had made me, me.

And the room most full of my life was my closet. Two built-in units, a large armoire, an art deco makeup vanity, a full-length mirror, two dressers, and shelves upon shelves upon shelves upon shelves of the clothes and shoes and jackets and sweaters and accoutrements I'd accumulated over the course of living a working life in Manhattan that included dozens of different jobs in dozens of different businesses—receptionist to waitress to dog walker to florist to messenger to secretary to retail to wholesale to everything beyond, betwixt, and between. I wasn't especially a clothes hound—except when I was, which is probably more than you might think what with living and working in Manhattan but is still not too much. I was a casual New Yorker who enjoyed getting dressed to the nines now and then but owned lots of blue jeans and flats and T-shirts and silk blouses and sweatshirts.

Thanks to Raul and the JKO Reservoir, I was in good shape, so my real-life clothes from jobs gone by, the classics that stayed in style, still fit me fine—better than fine.

My real-life clothes shared the space—were overwhelmed, actually—by the decades of costumes and props I'd worn and collected from defunct wardrobe and prop departments throughout my roller-coaster career. Wigs and gowns and suits and shirts and skirts and pants and dresses and bags and glasses and hats and belts and faux watches and rings and jewelry from a wide variety of roles in an even wider variety of productions that had an even wider variety of implosions, explosions, and unfortunate endings were all in the mix. Including the red Wanda Ward wig and the green contact lenses.

Anyway, when the reservoir run wasn't enough to clear my head, when there was still wonky weather in my mind, then getting into character, putting on the clothes and the wig and the makeup and the contact lenses, adjusting my accent and the register of my voice, changing my posture, my handshake, my stride, my laugh, and my attitude often burned away the last of the fog so there were clear skies as far as thinking through whatever I was thinking through.

But becoming Emily Baynes, Texas twang and all, wasn't helping. As I got dressed, I couldn't see five feet in front of my face as far as Lowry Lowe was concerned, and my meeting was in one hour.

I felt like Fu had read it right—there'd been some not-so-funny funny business between the husband and wife partners. I'd had a momentary sense of bad marital juju when I'd met with McDreamy and the cold-blooded Swedish Queen. But I had no idea what the moment meant or how to relate it to my morning meeting with McSteamy and the Italian Bombshell.

It occurred to me as I pulled clothes from dressers and drawers that to clear my head and wrap my mind around Lowry Lowe I would have to run around Lake Michigan.

I'd better start now, I said to myself with a voice straight out of Abilene, *because someone will be dead by Friday.*

15

———

TWO PARTS TRUTH AND ONE PART PASSION

AND THEN SOMETIMES, WHEN YOU'RE SITTING IN A CONFERENCE room with Jack and Lisa Lowe, for instance, dressed up as Emily Baynes from Austin-by-way-of-Abilene, for instance, and you can't drive the conversation where you want it to go because the fog is so thick, for instance, even then, sometimes the wind blows, the clouds clear, and the road ahead runs plain as day.

"Michelle mentioned in her notes that your husband murdered a man," Lisa said, sitting across from me at the conference table, taking notes and reading from her iPad. "Maybe more than one man, you told her, but one you know of." She looked up from the iPad and met my eyes. "We have to be sure of ourselves when we negotiate with Tommy and his attorney Friday afternoon. Divorce mediation is two parts truth and one part passion. If we're going to tap an emotional vein in order to move the settlement in our direction, we have to know the facts are true and the passion is real. Is that true, Emily? You know for a fact Tommy killed a man?"

Yesterday, when I'd met with Christopher and Michelle, I'd said Tommy wanted to settle by the end of the week, and today, when Jack had pressed me about the settlement time, I'd told him and Lisa a meeting had been arranged with Tommy and his attorney for four o'clock Friday.

Hearing Lisa confirm that meeting produced two internal reactions at the same time.

The first was, *Holy shit, now I have to arrange a meeting.*

The second was, *Holy shit, Lisa Lowe really does rule the world.*

The Italian Bombshell was the polar opposite of her partner, the Swedish Queen. Whereas Michelle was cool and calculating, dispassionate, icy, and aloof, Lisa was impassioned and vibrant, spirited, fiery, and intense.

She wore a tailored coal-black Armani suit. Her stylish, shoulder-length black hair framed her face, which became more beautiful the longer I looked at it. Her nails and lipstick were blood-red. She wore little makeup because she didn't need any. Her Mediterranean, movie star skin, naturally kissed by the sun, was unblemished but for a supermodel mole, perfectly placed near her upper lip.

"Let's say it's something I know firsthand," I said.

"He was acquitted?" Jack said.

"Never arrested," I said.

Jack stood at the windows, looking out over the city, taking no notes of any kind. He was from the town of New Canaan in Fairfield County, the Gold Coast, horse country—a zip code that meant big money and, apparently, also meant other people take notes for you, even your own wife/partner. He was an only child. His mother and father were divorced divorce attorneys, something Jack's parents had in common with their son and with the other Lowry Lowe partners, all of whom had been divorced multiple irreconcilable times, meaning the extramarital affairs for Michelle and Christopher and Lisa and Jack had been salacious and mainstream—and searchable on the web, where Al Cutter's supercomputers had found all the scandalous details.

Jack had graduated from Fordham University for both undergrad and law school. He was smart, handsome, confident, and handsome. Did I mention he was handsome? He was freaking McSteamy, for God's sake.

"If it was something you knew firsthand," Lisa said, "why wasn't your testimony enough to file charges?"

"Stalemate by necessity," I said.

"I don't know what that means," Jack said. "But I do know what *firsthand* means. Are you saying you were there when Tommy killed him?"

Before Jack pushed me about the settlement meeting and I'd created one out of thin air, there had been ten minutes of small talk when we'd all first entered the conference room—the pretty October morning, the New York network news anchor who'd been caught with his pants down, literally, in a public restroom with his weatherman, of all people. And in that time, McSteamy and the Italian Bombshell had never made eye contact. Not once. And it was deliberate. They were professional and pleasant to me, but they were avoiding each other in the sense there was something unmistakable between them—something personal and unpleasant.

And they still hadn't looked at each other.

And that's when the clouds cleared and the road ahead ran plain as day.

"I had an affair," I said, "with Tommy's chef. And Tommy found out about it by walking into the kitchen when we were doing it on the marble island."

Chatting about cheating on my husband while adopting a Texas twang made the story sound like an episode of *Dallas*.

"Tommy took a butcher knife and buried it in the cook's back," I said. "While we were doing it. Yes, I'd say I was there."

The word *affair* and the fact (lie) I was having one and the further fact (lie) it had led to murder went off in the room like a grenade. Jack and Lisa Lowe stared at me in silence, shell-shocked in a way that made me feel the meeting had become as much about them as about me. But they still didn't look at each other.

"Tommy pulled the knife out of the chef," I said, "and the guy fell dead to the floor, and Tommy said he wasn't going to kill me because he wasn't done making me miserable. Death by a thousand cuts instead of one badass butcher blade. That's what he had in mind for me. And that's how it's been ever since."

"You said stalemate by necessity," Lisa said, finding her professional voice.

"Tommy couldn't claim the affair because then the question of motivation would have been answered," I said. "And I couldn't claim it because then it would have been part of the public record and held against me when I went for the big money. So Tommy got away with murder, and I'm going to get a hundred twenty million dollars, and the chef took a ten-inch knife for the team. His name was Arty Seabury. I barely knew him."

There was a reason I'd christened the dead chef.

And that reason was no one expects a person to tell a spectacular, cohesive, and convincing lie and claim it's the truth. Even high-society divorce lawyers—*especially* high-society divorce lawyers—don't think Mrs. Tommy Baynes from Austin-by-way-of-Abilene is going to arrive in their office on the sixty-second floor of 30 Rockefeller Center and tell a tale like the one I'd just told them. It couldn't be a lie. It just couldn't.

Jimmy had said no one wants to believe they're being lied to. People want to believe they're hearing the truth. And the bigger and better and bolder the lie, the more that's at stake in the story, the more they want to believe it's true. *"If there's enough on the line,"* Jimmy had said, *"then they have to believe it's true."*

So if Emily Baynes says her Silicon Valley husband, the actual, real-life Tommy Baynes, is worth two hundred forty million dollars and he murdered a chef in cold blood while she was screwing the chef's lights out in the kitchen, you don't assume that's a lie. You believe it because it *sounds* true because there's a fourteen-million-dollar legal fee on Friday hanging in the balance.

Arty Seabury was a grace note in a true-sounding lie.

"I guess the lesson here is an affair can make one man kill another man," I said. "Or one woman kill another woman. Or one partner kill another partner."

I could see it in their faces. It was a lesson they had already learned.

"I read about you," I said. "It's why I chose this law firm, because you two and both your partners had butcher-blade affairs of your own. You know what I'm talking about. You want truth and passion? Tommy and me got that in spades—just like each one of you. I'm not saying that's why there's a death threat hanging over Lowry Lowe—only you know what kind of truth and passion are in play with your partners. I'm saying that's what we're going to use to motivate my husband to give me a hundred twenty million dollars."

Yes, their eyes said, *that's what we'll use to motivate your husband.*

And *yes, yes, yes,* their eyes also said, *one partner is getting into all kinds of kinky truth and passion with another partner—and those two partners aren't married to each other.*

"So now that we're talking about it, the death threat, if you had to pick a partner, who do you think it would be?" I said.

They looked at each other for the first time since the

meeting started. It was not a pleasant moment. *Lots of bad water under that bridge*, I thought.

"Michelle," Lisa said.

"Christopher," Jack said.

16

STANLEY STEIN IS UNHITTABLE

I grabbed a cab to the Upper West Side and met Blue for lunch at Blue Bar. The place was packed. We sat at a table on the second floor, midway between the kitchen and the bar, and for the life of me, I couldn't make up my mind what to order. The waitress arrived, and I looked at her like she was speaking Swahili.

There were three reasons I couldn't concentrate on the menu, three separate irons in the fire pulling my mind in three different directions.

Blue was distraction number one. I had seen him yesterday, and I'd already forgotten how gorgeous he was, how polished professional athlete, how rugged rodeo rider, how *Top Gun* fighter pilot, how Wild West gunslinger. He got a kick out of my Wanda Ward wig and told me I was as good-looking a redhead as I was a brunette. He was charming and fully present, which is a big turn-on for me after being on dozens of dates with men who were somewhere else instead of with me. Blue held my eyes with his eyes, listened to, and actually heard what I said. The older I got, the more certain I was that nothing was more important in a relationship than listening to your partner and hearing what they said. It didn't hurt when you looked like Blue and you played Major League Baseball and you owned one of the most successful sports bars in New York, but throw in paying attention to the conversation and was it any wonder I could feel the heat on the back of my neck? Did I mention I could feel the heat on the back of my neck?

But we weren't on a date. And our relationship was strictly client-private investigator. It was a business lunch. I reminded him my name was Danielle Sullivan and not Kate McCall, and he winked at me like he was in on the ruse, and I told him to stop winking at me like he was in on the ruse and to call me Dani. I told him we had business to discuss. I told him I wanted to talk about Griff and Adam and Mary, about the cash registers, the bartenders, and everyone who handled the money.

But first I had to order lunch, and I couldn't put two words together, and the waitress was, well, waiting. So Blue ordered for both of us: Ommegang Scythe & Sickle, a harvest beer from a brewery in Cooperstown, home of the Baseball Hall of Fame, one of Jimmy's favorite places on Earth; Steamroller Chicken, half a chicken pounded flat and grilled with rosemary and olive oil; and smoked, house-made brats with mustard hot enough to start a wildfire. It was the first time I'd ever eaten at Blue Bar and not ordered the sliced steak sandwich on homemade sourdough.

Jack and Lisa and Christopher and Michelle were distraction number two. I felt sure someone was screwing someone at Lowry Lowe—there was bad juju between the husbands and wives, but there was also no way to know which husband was sleeping with which wife. In two days, one of them would be as dead as James Dean, and I wanted to stop that murder and catch the prick who killed Jimmy. Oh, and I'd scheduled a meeting for Friday with my fictional freak husband, Tommy Baynes, and Tommy's attorney. There was that too.

Stanley Stein was distraction number three. He was seated

at the bar, an empty stool to his left, eating his lunch, reading the papers, and drinking a beer. People kept coming up to him, sitting beside him, chatting for a moment or two, and then shaking his hand and going back to wherever they came from, all of them happy as hippies to talk to Stanley and place a bet with the big-time bookie.

Except no one could prove he was taking bets.

"Why do you let him do it?" I said, pointing my eyes toward the bookie at the bar. "Why don't you bounce him?"

"Because fifty people follow him everywhere he goes, including to my bar. All those people buy a beer and watch the game and eat something and buy another beer. Adam ran the numbers one time. It came close to a grand a day, three, four days a week, one hundred fifty thousand a year, give or take, because Stanley Stein likes to read the paper at Blue Bar."

Stanley wore a gray suit with a matching fedora. He was a retired mortician, or a haberdasher hanging on to his trade, or a middle manager for some copier company.

"It's against the law," I said. "Why don't the cops arrest him?"

"He has friends."

"I have friends, and the cops arrest me." Detective Lew Logan had arrested me three times, in fact. Although in all honesty, we weren't actually friends.

"Not like Stanley Stein. Stanley has friends in positions of power, top of the ladder—police department, government, courthouse, mafia. He has friends everywhere he goes because everywhere he goes his friends and their friends and their friends bet on games."

"If everybody's betting," I said as another man sat beside the bookie, "somebody should be able to catch him in the act."

"You can't catch Stanley. He doesn't take money, and he doesn't write anything down. What are you arresting him for? Talking about a box score?"

I watched Stanley Stein chat with four people. *How many more are waiting?* I thought. *How do they know he's here? What the hell are they betting on?*

"What the hell are they betting on?" I accidentally said the last one out loud.

Blue didn't answer right away because he was signing a menu for a strawberry-blonde beauty who couldn't have been more than thirty years old. In his bar, on his home turf, signing autographs for fans was part of the job for Blue.

He had done more than a decade in the majors, played for a handful of big-market teams, and been to the playoffs five times. Throughout his career, he threw junk, meaning he didn't have an overpowering fastball, so he had to rely on sinkers and sliders, changeups and curveballs, spit, wit, and guile. He'd been a middle-innings specialist. If the starting pitcher got hurt or tired or pounded, the manager would signal for Blue.

His claim to fame, and the reason he'd made millions, was that he had never given up a run in a playoff game. He'd pitched in the postseason fourteen times and his ERA was nothing. Nada. Zippo. Not one run. For teams hoping to make it to the World Series, Blue was worth three mil a year. If you're smart about it, it doesn't take too many years of making three mil before you're rich enough to lend Dave Griffin two hundred fifty grand.

It wasn't just women who wanted Blue's signature, although there was a long line of them. It was also Mets fans and stat geeks and New York sports junkies and out-of-towners who knew their baseball. Blue had been on TV too, so there was a crowd that recognized his face from the evening news sports report and wanted his name on a menu or cocktail napkin or credit card receipt just so they could say they saw him up close and in person.

"American League Division Series," Blue said as our beers arrived. "National League Division Series. Under/over. Runs per game. Hits per game. Highest average. Most walks. Most strikeouts and steals and errors. Number of pitches thrown in the top of the third inning. How many balls. How many strikes. You can play the odds and place a bet on anything that happens in a baseball game every minute it's happening—or in any other game. Look at the TVs, Kate."

"Dani."

"Look at the TVs, Dani. Auto racing. Mixed martial arts. Rugby. WTA tennis. Volleyball. Soccer. Horse racing. PGA golf. Field hockey. Cycling. Cricket. Boxing. Billiards. You can bet on any of them. You can bet on all of them."

Another man took the stool to Stanley's left, and our food arrived. We shared everything, and it was delicious.

I wanted to talk about the case, about Griff and Adam and Mary and the missing money, but the conversation didn't flow that way. Instead, we talked about our lives, how we grew up, how we turned out to be who we turned out to be.

It was somewhat surreal to talk about Jimmy and Christine and Matthew and myself while wearing the Wanda Ward wig and pretending to be someone named Danielle Sullivan, but Blue didn't mind. He understood what it was like to have a public persona. "I know the difference between the me people think they know and the me I know," he said.

He knew what I meant. I knew what he meant. It had been that way since we'd first met. We liked each other then, and we liked each other even more now. And we both knew that too.

And throughout lunch, there was Stanley Stein, shaking hands and taking bets.

The waitress took our plates. Blue said he had a meeting with his attorney, signed the check, and stood, leaning back over the table in such a way that made me think he was going to kiss me. I even got ready for a kiss. But he didn't kiss me. He just didn't want anyone to hear what he had to say.

"Want to know what I'm thinking?" he said.

"Yes," I said.

"If you're going to catch Griff stealing Blue Bar money, you're going to have to catch him betting with Stanley first and work backward. And that's a tough at bat."

"Tough at bat?"

"Half a dozen undercover cops have cozied up to the bar beside Stanley since the day I opened the doors, and every one of them struck out. Stanley Stein is unhittable. And if you get too close to the plate, he'll throw one at your head."

And then he smiled and said he'd see me tomorrow and walked across the room, signing two menus and a cocktail napkin before he disappeared down the stairs.

I watched him go and then looked at Stanley and thought of my father, a former pitcher himself, a lifelong baseball fan before someone blew his eyes out. We were at Yankee Stadium, upper deck behind home plate, drinking beers and eating peanuts. Matthew was with us. He was seven. The Yanks were getting shut out, and I'd said the pitcher, a Baltimore heat thrower whose name I forget, was unhittable.

"Nobody's unhittable," Jimmy said.

Next guy up doubled to left center.

Guy after that took a fastball in the middle of his back.

17

HOW THE MONEY MOVED

I GOT BACK TO THE HOUSE OF EMOTIONAL TICS AT FIVE THIRTY. According to LaTanya's call sheet, the *Kung Fu Fu* table read was scheduled for six o'clock. I had thirty minutes to reconcile my Wednesday afternoon at Blue Bar, which had been irritating, frustrating, aggravating, and illuminating.

Throughout my many years as a struggling actor, I had worked as a hostess, waitress, and bartender, so I knew there was a money trail, meaning once it left the customer's hand, restaurant revenue followed a path through the business back channels all the way to the bank, where it then paid bills and taxes and wages and more bills.

So I'd decided to work backward through the back channels, starting at the end of the money trail—my logic being if I started at the beginning, I'd have no way of knowing where I was supposed to go and what it was supposed to look like when I got there. If I started at the end and landed at the beginning, I could put the path together in a somewhat more cohesive way.

Granted, Griff and Adam and Mary all either strongly believed or knew for a fact I was a PI and not an actual management consultant, but still, I had to play the part to understand how the money moved.

After lunch with Blue, I'd sat next to Mary in her cozy basement office, going backward, step-by-step, through the Blue Bar books. We'd started with the bank deposits—direct deposits from the credit card companies and cash deposits made at the bank by Blue, Griff, or Adam. The deposits squared, meaning the amounts deposited, as recorded by the bank, matched the amounts written on the deposit slips—so Griff wasn't stealing money on the way to the bank, not that I thought he was. I felt sure Blue's managing partner had his hand in a register—or two or three.

Then we'd run through the register printouts and cross-checked them with the kitchen and bar orders. The Blue Bar operating platform was fully digital. There were four registers at each bar and four wait-station computers on each floor—a total of twelve itemized bar printouts and four times three servers per computer on each floor, so thirty-six or so itemized food printouts times two—lunch and dinner. Again, the bottom lines across the board were square.

For internal security, Mary had told me, Blue Bar had implemented a check and balance recommended by the restaurant software company that sold Blue the system and also installed it: only Blue, Griff, and Adam had access to program administration, which did not include generating checks. Only those three guys could *sign* checks, not Mary. But Mary kept the checkbook, meaning checks had to be requested through her, meaning she cut the checks and no one else. And anyway, the checks squared too. Griff wasn't forging checks. He was taking cash, though the money trail didn't show where his fingers got sticky.

In other words, all the numbers added up except for the ones Blue knew by heart: the cash that should have been in the account at the end of each day, week, and month. Blue's cash.

There was history for those numbers, and those numbers were short by sixty-eight thousand dollars and change since July.

During our stroll through the Blue Bar books, Mary had told me all about her family in Pennsylvania—her children and her grandchildren. Her husband, an electrical contractor, had died of cancer ten years ago, and after three years of sadness and sorrow, she'd decided she was ready for an adventure. She sold everything and moved to New York. She'd been an office manager and bookkeeper at a sports bar in Allentown for many years, so when friends of friends of friends told her former pro pitcher Steve Stark was opening Blue Bar on the Upper West Side of Manhattan and was looking for an experienced book-keeper and office manager, she got herself an interview and then got herself the job. She'd been with Blue since day one.

She was as proud of her children, two daughters still living in the Lehigh Valley, as I was of Matthew. And her grandkids? Forget it. There was no way to measure that level of delight. That amount of pride and joy could power the five boroughs.

One day, God willing, I'll feel the same way about my grandchil-dren, I'd thought, watching her beam at the framed photos around her office. *And even their mother, Highfalutin Nina, won't be able to rain on that parade.*

I sat at the makeup table in my walk-through closet, took off the Wanda Ward wig, popped out the green contacts, and considered a future that included Matthew having kids of his own. It was a warm feeling that didn't last long because Griff popped into my mind. After I'd met with Mary, I'd walked up the stairs and met the managing partner by the first-floor bar.

He'd been all business. No handshake. No hello. Straight into the demo, which was showing me how the registers worked, how the bartenders rang up drinks and made change, how the waitstaff input orders, how he or Adam closed out registers as shifts ended, how he made sure the tapes balanced with the money in the drawer, how he reset the registers for the next day, how he counted and banded the extracted cash for deposit, and how he locked it in the safe in Blue's office. Blue Bar took in around eighteen thousand dollars on an average day, close to thirty grand on a big game day, so if the money didn't get to the bank for a few days, there could be fifty or sixty or seventy thousand bucks in cold cash sitting in that safe. Only Blue and Griff had the combination.

Throughout the demo, it was as if Griff couldn't deal with me on any level—management consultant or private investigator—because some deeper, darker thought pattern required all his contemplative power. It didn't matter who I was or what I wanted; there was someone or something else he had to deal with first. It was the unpleasant look on his face, the distant, preoccupied glaze of his eyes that gave him away. There was trouble brewing on Griff's horizon.

We'd walked to the second floor and watched digital orders from the waitstaff arrive in the kitchen, where they were automatically printed and expedited. Then we'd gone back to the basement office suite, where he'd showed me the computer room, which held the mainframe and ancillary machinery.

"Mary told me only you and Blue and Adam are system administrators," I'd said. "I'm assuming you have access from your office computer?"

He'd looked at me like he would kill me if he didn't have this other thing blocking the sun. "You have no idea what you're into here. No clue whatsoever. You want to fuck with me? Get in line and wait your turn, whoever the fuck you are," he'd said, and he'd walked down the hall and into his office, shutting the door hard behind him.

I took off the Danielle Sullivan business suit I'd worn to Blue Bar, put on an old pair of blue jeans and a soft sweater, went into the kitchen, and grabbed a beer from the fridge. I thought the trouble on Griff's horizon might have something to do with Trenton, but Adam Stoker quickly replaced that thought.

As soon as Griff had gone, Adam had appeared and said, "Oh good, my turn." I'd asked to meet everyone who handled the money, but to shove it in my face in the most annoying way possible, Adam had introduced me to every bartender, every server, every hostess, everyone in the kitchen, and everyone on the janitorial staff. To one Hispanic dishwasher who didn't speak a word of English, Adam introduced me as a private investigator doing a bad rendition of a management consultant. Okay, maybe it wasn't my best performance, maybe I was distracted by Adam's asshole behavior, but it definitely wasn't a bad performance. I was an actor. I knew the difference.

When we were done, Adam had walked me to the front door and said, "You never gave me your card."

"It's in my car," I'd said, without turning around. "I'll get it for you."

In the cab back to East 83rd Street, it had occurred to me that Griff had figured out how to beat the system, and there was no catching him. Blue Bar money was spot-on when it went into the safe, meaning there was no proof Griff was stealing anything out of the registers, and likewise, from the safe to the bank the numbers all added up. If Blue and Mary couldn't catch Griff after watching him for three months, it wasn't likely I could nail him before Blue Bar was out another sixty-eight grand. Blue was right. I was going to have to start with Stanley Stein. And maybe take a fastball in the back.

Imagining the pain of a Stanley Stein heater, I walked to my kitchen window, looked through the bars to the backyard garden, and saw Al and Warren rehearsing for the table read. A new thought took the place of the bookie throwing a hard one at my head. It was a thought about Al and Warren. A thought so outrageous I dismissed it in a blink. But when my eyes opened again, it was still there.

18

FRATERNAL TWIN SONS FROM
DIFFERENT WORLDS

AT THE FAR END OF THE BACKYARD, BEYOND THE BRICK PATIO, PAST
the ancient, wrought-iron furniture and rusted Weber grill Fu
had turned into a brownstone birdbath, near the scrubby
bushes where Charlie had planted his marijuana farm, beneath
the shade of the elm tree, beside which I'd buried my father's
ashes, was a beat-up picnic table.

Near the table, Zombie Al and Warren White were
rehearsing a scene from *Kung Fu Fu*. They were standing—well,
no, actually they were moving around as if the cameras were
rolling on an actual Hollywood set—holding their scripts and
spouting dialogue that sounded suspiciously extemporized.

I crossed the yard and found four more scripts on the table.
Each one had a character name written in bold black marker
across the top of the title page. The scripts looked very thin, as
if pages were missing. I grabbed the script labeled *Detective
Cassie Barnett*—my role—took a seat, and scanned the screen-
play. The script was thin because there was no dialogue. That's
what was missing. What we were supposed to say.

Like the great and grumpy Larry David, the wizard behind
the curtain of *Curb Your Enthusiasm* (and *Seinfeld* before that),

LaTanya had written a movie meant to be improvised by the actors. She'd spelled out the big picture of each scene—where it was, who was in it, what was meant to happen, and the kinds of things the characters were thinking and so might say while the action was happening. But scripted words? Dialogue to remember, internalize, and deliver in character? Nope.

Kung Fu Fu was the story of Fu Steinberg, a Jewish, Chinese homicide detective, played by Fu, and his partner, Cassie Barnett. We were, the script said, renegade cops framed by renegade drug dealers, played by Charlie (of course) and Al, fighting to clear our names and stop a mad scientist (also a renegade), played by Warren, who had hidden a bomb on a bus. Throughout the five boroughs, at any given time, there are five thousand buses on hundreds of highways and byways, so finding the bomb before it blew up was of paramount importance. At the same time Steinberg and Barnett were busy busting the bomb, they were also under investigation by their captain (yes, another renegade) played by LaTanya, who was under investigation by Internal Affairs.

A crazy train is what it was. And a script without dialogue is like a train without tracks. Renegade train wreck? Yes, indeed.

I couldn't concentrate on the script for two reasons. One, it was a story that made concentration impossible. Two, I couldn't take my eyes off Al and Warren, improvising their brains out.

In many ways, they were polar opposites. Al was thirty-four, tall, painfully thin, and pale to the point of dead. Warren was sixty-three, short, black, bald, and overweight. Al couldn't hold a real-life human job for more than eight weeks. Warren was a night-shift doorman in an upscale, Third Avenue building, a job he'd held for forty-five years and counting. Al was a hopeless insomniac, unable to sleep for more than two hours a night, fifteen restless minutes at a time. Warren could sleep standing up, like a cow, a skill he had taught himself after decades of opening doors for tenants who had either returned home very late or had left the building very early and never bothered to learn his name.

But in one all-consuming way, they were remarkably similar, living different but parallel lives, fraternal twin sons from different worlds coincidentally living in the same brownstone: Al in 5A, Warren in 4B.

Like Al, who had traded any semblance of normal living for a life of late-night, artisanal hacking (Al was the Picasso of hacking), Warren had an interest so absorbing, so captivating, so monopolizing that it had years upon years ago ceased being an interest, ceased even being a passion, and had become the blood pulsing through his veins, the focus and meaning of his life to the exclusion of all social mores, niceties, and interactions.

Warren was, all at once, a world-class coin, currency, and stamp collector, which, as he told me day after day after day, made him one of the very few men on the East Coast who was concurrently a numismatist, a notaphile, and a philatelist. *Watch your mouth, Warren*, was my usual response.

No one, except Al, was allowed in Warren's apartment, including me. It was only because I'd needed his notaphile expertise on my last case, my Industrial Douchebag case, that I had been granted access, and 4B had been eye-popping to say the least.

Warren had removed the walls separating the first three rooms of his railroad flat, and the one huge, remaining room had been fantastically transformed into the *Library of Warren*, a cross between the Library of Congress and the combined research offices of the coin, currency, and stamp curators of the Smithsonian Institution.

To say Warren was unconventional, eccentric, and idiosyncratic would be to understate his special brand of bizarre. Throw in his unpermitted, unlicensed, and illegal rental car company, Warren Rental Car, a fleet of three identical, decade-old, stripped-down Toyota Corollas, and you had a man unmatched in terms of personal peculiarity. Except for Al, I mean, who ran neck and neck with Warren in the competitive categories of unnatural, unusual, unsuitable, and unorthodox human behavior, which is why they were each other's only friends—despite the fact they couldn't stand each other.

"Where did you learn how to act?" I said to both of them.

They were rehearsing the scene in the second hour where the renegade mad scientist implants the renegade drug dealers with Chinese DNA that makes them martial arts masters.

"Drama club. West Orange High School," Warren said, blending a genetic cocktail that would inexplicably allow Al and Charlie to fight like Steven Seagal and Chuck Norris— before they got old. Seagal and Norris, I mean.

Like Al, Warren had lived in the House of Emotional Tics for many years before I became the resident manager, but in the two-plus years I had known him, I'd had no idea he'd been in his high school drama club, or that he'd gone to high school, or that he'd lived in New Jersey, for that matter.

"I did improv at Fordham my freshman year, before I dropped out," Al said in his renegade drug dealer voice.

After Elliot Morgan stuck a .357 in my mouth, I thought, finishing Al's sentence in my head.

"Improv is easy," Warren said, staying in renegade mad scientist mode and injecting Al with the Chinese DNA. "Acting is hard. I played Willy Loman, who was sixty-three, same age I am now, it just so happens. Let me tell you, I made an impression."

"On yourself, my fat friend," Al said to Warren, pretending to feel the formula run through his veins. "You still act just like him—bellicose, bitter, and burnt out."

"Testy, testy, Al," Warren said, watching Al become the Karate Kid. "Maybe you could improvise getting a good night's sleep so you're not cranky the next day."

In the grip of Warren's DNA injection, while performing some kind of kung fu ballet under the elm tree, Al improvised flipping Warren off with double birds and, still in character, said, "Maybe you could sit on it and rotate."

I knew it was a very bad, terrible, awful idea. That went without saying. It was an idea way outside the box, so far away from the box, in fact, that I couldn't see the box, couldn't recall the box in the first place. What box? It was an idea built on soft and shifting sand, an idea so untenable, unimaginable, unworkable, and unreal in the real world, so absurd on its face, so improbable and impossible that it would be potentially dangerous if put into practice. And yet...

"I have an acting job for both of you," I said.

"We don't do charity gigs," Al said.

"It's a paid performance," I said. "Any interest?"

"What kind of time commitment are we talking about, McCall? There are only so many hours in a day. I'm already cast in *Kung Fu Fu*, and there's my Third Avenue job and the rental cars, and in case you've forgotten, I'm one of the very few men on the East Coast who's concurrently a numismatist, a notaphile, and a philatelist."

I knew it was a rotten idea when I watched them acting through the window in my kitchen. And I knew it again when I took my front row seat at the picnic table in the backyard beside the elm tree. It was the worst idea I'd had in a long parade of bad ideas, some of which, believe me, were horribly bad.

But it's the only idea I have, I thought.

"Watch your mouth, Warren," I said.

19

———

PIECES TO PUT TOGETHER

On Wednesday, Adam had introduced me to everyone on the staff as Danielle Sullivan, the redheaded management consultant, so on Thursday afternoon I wore a black wig, blue contacts, faded Levi's, and an Eli Manning football jersey and spent four hours at Blue Bar waiting for Stanley Stein. Blue never made an appearance, and neither did Griff. Adam was there, and he didn't recognize me. No one recognized me.

I started with a beer at the first-floor bar, ordered another beer and a sliced steak sandwich on homemade sourdough at the second-floor bar, drank a third beer at the third-floor bar, and then bounced from floor to floor to floor until four o'clock, when I grabbed a cab to the D-Cup for a *Psychedelic Sunday* rehearsal. Stanley never showed up.

After rehearsal, I went back to Blue Bar as a hazel-eyed blonde, swapped my Eli Manning jersey for a classic Broadway Joe jersey (a gift from Jimmy), added a New York Jets baseball cap, and played the floor-to-floor-to-floor-waiting-for-Stanley-Stein game until two in the morning. Blue and Griff were both in the house. Adam had gone home before I got back. Blue left at midnight. Griff closed. Again, nobody knew who I was. And, again, Stanley was a no-show.

Which was just as well because I didn't have a clue what I was going to do if he had shown up. I'd spent four hours during the day and another six that night waiting for the bookie, thinking about how to catch him in the act, and I'd come up empty—just like the half dozen detectives who'd tried before me. And now no one was trying to catch him. The grandfather had been grandfathered in, as if unlicensed gambling was illegal in Manhattan except for Stanley Stein.

I was thinking these thoughts as I got into bed at three in the morning, thinking I might never get a leg up with this case. But as my head hit the pillow, I had an itty-bitty epiphany: *If I can't catch Stanley, maybe I can catch one of the gamblers who sit beside him. Maybe I can catch Griff in the act.*

Back at Blue Bar on Friday, blonde again, with green eyes, dressed as a bonds trader, as I was coming down the stairs from the second floor, I passed Stanley on his way up. He wore a blue suit with a blue fedora, a stack of newspapers under his arm, unassuming, unpretentious, old granddad on his way to have an Old Grand-Dad. I continued down to the first floor, looked at the Wall of Champions for sixty seconds, and then went up the stairs to the second floor and walked to the bar. No Stanley.

I climbed the stairs to the third floor, the games floor, and saw Stanley seated at the bar, toward the back of the building, near the pool tables, the foosball tables, the eighteen-foot Grand Champion shuffleboard table, and the tournament dart board. There was an empty stool to his left, which struck me as impossible since the place was loud and alive, completely packed. How in the world could two empty barstools magically appear on whichever floor at whatever bar the bookie decided to have a beer when there wasn't another empty seat in the house?

I checked the time. Twelve thirty. I had a meeting at Lowry

Lowe with Tommy and his attorney at four o'clock, so I set my phone alarm for three thirty, in case nobody was gambling today and I fell asleep watching Stanley Stein read the paper for three hours. Then I moved to the opposite end of the bar and ordered a beer.

A bartender brought Stanley a beer the bookie never ordered, and a dead ringer for Dick Vitale took the empty stool. Twelve thirty-two, and someone was gambling.

Stanley greeted the Dickie V doppelgänger as if he were an acquaintance, someone Stanley only knew from Vitale's bombastic college basketball commentary. I couldn't hear a word of what they said, but I had a view of their exchange. Stanley glanced at him a couple of times, nodded a couple of times, and interjected something a couple of times. Just two guys shooting the shit while ESPN dissected every American and National League division playoff game in a never-ending loop of pregame predictions and postgame analysis on a dozen different flat-screens. After a few minutes, Dickie V's long-lost twin shook Stanley's hand and walked across the room and down the stairs.

I meant to follow him, but I was frozen. *What in the world?* I said to myself. *A three-minute discussion, a handshake, and that's it? How can that be it?* By the time I finished the thought, Dickie V was gone.

It took Stanley twenty minutes to read *The New York Times*. He saved the sports for last. Before he could finish his first box score, a buxom brunette took the seat to his left. After a few minutes of chatting, of Stanley glancing at her from time to time and nodding his head, they shook hands, and the woman walked away. It was one o'clock.

This time I followed her. She was half a flight of stairs ahead of me. We went down to the second floor and then down to the first floor.

This is stupid, I thought. *She's leaving. She knows him from some improbable past in which he was her pharmacist or science teacher. She just stopped by to say thanks for prescribing that acne cream or for teaching her the basics of biology. She didn't bet on a game. No way she bet on a game.*

Not that women don't bet on games. Adrenaline is adrenaline. Women feel the same mad rush as men when the chance to win big money is on the line.

And then the buxom brunette didn't leave. She got to the first floor, turned right, went past the hostess desk, and walked all the way to the back of the building, to the ladies' room. I watched her go in, took a breath, and went in after her.

There were three stalls opposite three sinks. The room was well lit. There was memorabilia on the walls and a flat-screen television on a swivel arm—so you wouldn't miss a touchdown when you were peeing.

Two young women were at the sink, reapplying lipstick. They were friends and dressed in the same trying-too-hard-to-look-like-you're-not-trying-too-hard style. The buxom brunette was in the middle stall. I recognized her shoes. I took out my lipstick and looked in the mirror. The young women left the ladies' room. The toilet flushed, the middle stall opened, and the buxom brunette came out, washed her hands, and left.

I didn't say anything to her. I didn't know what to say. *"Hey, big boobs, did you just place a bet with Stanley Stein?"* was in my head, but that kind of question could have escalated into a bad scene at the end of which I'd have been exposed, Stanley would find another bar, and Griff would get away with embezzlement on my watch.

I stood at the mirror, mad at myself for freezing, for not having a plan in place, and the stall to the left opened and a brown-haired businesswoman in a blue skirt and matching blue jacket moved to the mirror beside me—an accountant taking a long Friday lunch, a residential real estate agent starting her weekend early. We shared that small smile in the mirror professional women sometimes share in the ladies' room, and the brown-haired businesswoman went back into the bar.

I made my way up to the third floor, where Stanley was eating a sliced steak sandwich on homemade sourdough and reading the sports section of the *Daily News*. An overweight man who looked like a plumber or an electrician or someone in some kind of union that built things was seated on the stool to the bookie's left. Stanley stopped eating and shook the plumber's hand, and the man walked across the room, right past me, and down the stairs. It was one fifteen.

I casually followed him down to the second floor, where he went into the men's room at the far end of the building. I had the beginning of an inkling of an idea that something was wrong with this picture but no sense of what it was.

The plumber was in the bathroom for less than five minutes and then came out and sat with his buddies who were pounding beers and eating sliced steak sandwiches on home-made sourdough. His lunch was waiting for him. He had ordered his food with his pals on the second floor, said hello to Stanley Stein on the third floor, and returned to his table just as his plate arrived. *How the hell did the plumber know the bookie was on the third floor?* I thought. *And how could he time his bet to his freaking lunch?*

I went back to the third floor. Stanley was at the bar, and a blonde battleship was seated to his left. For the first time, I noticed a wiry black guy across the room by the Grand Champion shuffleboard table. He wore a suit with no tie. I noticed him because he had noticed me. He wasn't staring at me, but he wanted me to know he was aware of me. I acted like I didn't catch his vibe, as if there was no vibe for me to catch, as if I was just another sports fan on the third floor—like him.

I didn't have time to figure out the wiry black guy because the blonde battleship walked past me, headed for the stairs. I let her go, feeling the wiry black guy's eyes on my face. When the wiry black guy finally looked away, I slipped out of the room and went down the stairs. I didn't know which floor the blonde battleship had gone to, maybe she'd left the bar completely, but I stopped on the second floor and hurried to the ladies' room. As I stepped into the bathroom, the blonde battleship came out of the end stall. I turned to the sink and washed my hands. She washed her hands too and then went back into the bar.

What the hell is happening here? I said to myself. And then the middle stall opened and the brown-haired businesswoman came out and washed her hands at the sink right next to me. Our eyes met in the mirror, and there was a moment, a split second, where she thought she recognized me from the first-floor bathroom and didn't like that fact at all, that I was now in this bathroom too. It wasn't panic. It might not even have reached a level of concern. It was simply an unpleasant note she'd taken, something to be discussed with someone sooner rather than later. We didn't share that small smile this time, and she walked out.

It was one twenty-five when I got back to the third floor. Griff was sitting next to Stanley Stein. The wiry black guy was staring at me. No pretense this time. He'd figured out I was following the folks who'd sat next to the bookie, and he wasn't happy. *He's with Stanley*, I thought, though the two of them never acknowledged each other.

I didn't think the wiry black guy would shoot me in the middle of a full house, and I didn't think he'd grab my arm and casually escort me out of the bar either. On demand, I can send out a vibe that says, *If you put your hands on me, I will break your nose in a hundred pieces, so you better think goddamn twice about it.* I sent that vibe out, and it hit the wiry black guy in the chest and surprised him, and he thought twice about his next move. And because I was a professional actor, I did it without breaking my bond trader character, as if I wasn't even aware the wiry black guy was staring at me.

Griff sat with Stanley for half a minute more and then left the room and went down the stairs. I went after him. He stopped at the first floor and went all the way to the men's room. I knew what I had to do. I just couldn't get my feet to move.

The first floor was a zoo—two hundred sports fans, two dozen flat-screens, a dozen servers, four bartenders, and three hostesses creating a sonic roar of sports and music and beer and sizzling steak. The place was electric.

I took Jimmy's credit card-sized digital camera out of my purse, pushed open the door to the men's room, and went in. There was one guy at the urinal, head turned to the TV, no one at the sinks, one man in the first stall, and another in the middle stall. I went into the last stall—the handicap stall—locked the door, climbed up on the toilet, and then stepped up on the handicap support bar bolted to the stall wall so that I could look down into the middle stall.

Griff sat on the toilet, pants up, counting a stack of cash. He slid the money under the dividing wall into the first stall where another man (who I couldn't see, of course) lifted it and slid a pack of matches to Griff in return. Griff took the matches and stood up.

I got pictures of the whole exchange. How good I didn't know. But I got them.

As Griff stood, I dropped my head and stepped back down onto the toilet so he wouldn't by chance see my shoes on the floor. I heard him flush the toilet in the middle stall and, through the gap in the door, got the narrowest view of him washing his hands.

When he was gone, the toilet flushed in the first stall, and a man I couldn't make out in my sliver of vision washed his hands and left the bathroom too.

I couldn't put the pieces together yet, but at least I had pieces to put together.

I climbed down from the toilet and put the camera in my purse as my cell phone buzzed. I looked at the caller ID: Logan. I answered it.

"McCall," I said.

"Logan," he said.

"What can I do for you, Detective?" I said.

"You can get your ass to the Thirteenth," he said. "Jack Lowe is missing."

20

IT REALLY IS MY SHIT PILE

Lew Logan was having a banner day in the worst possible sense. He'd been up all night investigating a double homicide in which one of the victims was a key witness in another homicide he was also investigating, and the other victim was the guy Logan liked for the original homicide, which meant the detective was either back to square one on the first homicide or completely off the board for both of them. Plus, he had a major mustard stain on his shirt from a hot dog disaster at lunch and a hemorrhoid that was making him miserable. And, oh yeah, Jack Lowe was missing.

I knew Logan had a hemorrhoid because it was the first thing he'd said to me when I got to his desk on the third floor of the Thirteenth.

"I don't know what's worse," he said. "The pain in my ass in my ass, or the pain in my ass at my desk. Hemorrhoid goes away at long last, so I guess you're worse."

"How do you know Jack Lowe is missing?" I said.

"His wife called me, his partners called me, his doorman called me, his personal trainer called me. Nobody's seen him since Wednesday morning. He doesn't answer his phone, his texts, his emails. He's not where he's supposed to be—at the office, the courthouse, his apartment, the gym. He's nowhere. Off the goddamn grid."

"He could be alive."

"Or he could be dead. That's the thing about working homicide. They could always be dead."

His mountain of paperwork, the Logan Range, was particularly precarious today, with cliffs and ravines that would scare even a seasoned secretary.

"Why did they call *you*?" I said, knowing why they'd called him.

"Because I stuck my nose in the middle of your shit pile."

"It's not my shit pile," I said, thinking, *It really is my shit pile.*

"Course not. You got nothing to do with this mess."

"I didn't ask him to text me his next target."

"But he did. He killed your father, and you started tailing him and made a little game out of it."

"It's not a game."

"It is to him. And now I'm playing too. You told me Monday, I went there Tuesday, they called me first thing Thursday, now it's Friday, and, as advertised, one of the Lowry Lowe partners is likely rope-tied to a chair with his eyes blown out the back of his goddamn head."

I hated the sound of that because that was how they'd found Jimmy in the Monument Life elevator—tied to a chair with dark holes in his face. Since he'd been murdered, picturing him that way had made me stop breathing, made my heart stop beating, made the world fade to black. Now that Logan had brought it up, I could feel myself falling down the wormhole of empty sadness. Hard to know how long I was falling.

"I'm talking to you, McCall. Have you heard from him since Sunday?"

The Thirteenth came back into the light, and Logan was

dipping a handkerchief in water, trying in vain to remove the mustard from his shirt.

"No. You'll need club soda for that," I said. "They called you Thursday morning, the wife and the partners?" I had to handle this conversation with care or Logan would know I'd stuck my nose in deeper than him.

He nodded as if he'd known all along about the club soda and pushed back from his desk. "And the doorman and the trainer. By all accounts, Jack Lowe was a particularly punctual person, never late for anything. When he missed an early evening training session without so much as a phone call, the trainer got worried. He called the partners, and they were already worried—he'd missed a couple client meetings too. The partners told the wife, and she was more worried than they were. And with the death threat hanging over them like a blood moon, they called me, one by one by one."

"Did they give you anything, the partners and the wife?" Again, I was careful how I asked that question—conscious of my tone of voice, aware of my body language. I had to sound and look like I was asking standard questions anyone in my situation would ask and not sound and look like I was prying into a case I was already up to my neck in.

Logan cocked his head to the side. I was right on the line. "Anything like what?"

"Anything that would help you," I said like the amateur I was.

"Basic bullshit background," he said. "Friends and family, clients and associates, haunts and hangouts. All of which were dead ends I drove down yesterday, and none of which I'm sharing with you."

"Then why did you call me?"

"Because when I get back, you're going to text the killer a message from me, and we're going to find out where the fuck Jack Lowe is."

"Back from where?"

"Lunchroom," he said, standing. "Club soda."

He walked away, and my brain was swamped with a tsunami of thoughts. Wave after wave came pounding through my head. Wave one was Christopher Lowry.

McDreamy. When I'd asked him (as Emily Baynes) which partner he thought the death threat was directed at, he'd said Jack. Why did he say that? Truth and passion? Butcher-blade affair? What made him think someone wanted to murder Jack Lowe? Who did he think that person was? If it was true, then that person had hired the corporate killer who'd murdered my father. Where could I find that person? What else did McDreamy know about Jack Lowe?

Wave two was Lisa Lowe, the Italian Bombshell, Jack's wife. She'd said the death threat was meant for Michelle. Did Lisa not know what Christopher Lowry knew? Why hadn't Lisa thought the threat was aimed at her husband? Or was she less truthful about her answer? Lisa had to know something that would lead me somewhere.

Wave three was Michelle Lowry, the Swedish Queen, Christopher's wife. She'd said Lisa was at the top of the killer's list. She and her husband were distant and cold to each other, and I'd sensed something bad brewing there. Maybe it was Jack. Maybe it was Jack's behavior and Christopher had blurted out the truth and Michelle had intentionally misdirected me.

Wave four was Jack, the particularly punctual McSteamy. What had he done to piss someone off to the point where that person had hired a high-priced corporate assassin to tie him to a chair and blow his eyes out? And dead or alive, where the hell was he? Where the hell was Jack Lowe?

Before that last wave hit the shore, I got a text from a number I didn't recognize. I looked at my phone and read the text: *Hello, Emily. Jack Lowe here. I'm in Connecticut. Red Maple*

Horse Farm. Sunday night, 11 p.m. Show and tell. Come alone. All's well that ends well.

What in the world? I thought.

I knew Jack Lowe had my cell number. It was in Emily Baynes's Lowry Lowe file—easy peasy to put in his pocket. But why would he text the Texan? Why not text Lisa or Michelle or Christopher, who'd said Jack's neck was on the chopping block? Why not text Logan, who had been to the firm on Tuesday— the day before Jack went off the grid? Was that why Jack had disappeared in the first place? Was he hiding because he knew someone wanted him dead? Had Logan's Tuesday warning spooked him into running to Red Maple? Had no one thought of looking for Jack at Red Maple? Why not?

Shit, I thought.

Or what if it wasn't Jack Lowe texting me from Jack Lowe's phone?

Double shit, I thought.

"Here's the message I want you to send," Logan said, sitting at his desk with a bottle of club soda and a dish towel from the lunchroom. "'Detective Lew Logan of the Thirteenth Precinct is tired of me not sharing your number with him. He's sitting me on the sidelines for aiding and abetting a serial killer, so you won't be able to play with me anymore. But he says you can play with him. He says he's fun too. So if you're not afraid to run with the big dogs, text me back and ask for Logan. He wants to talk to you about Jack Lowe, wants to know where he can find him, and wants to know where he can find you.'"

Throughout his dictation, Logan worked on the mustard stain, which doubled in size and now looked like he had some kind of infected wound leaking yellow puss.

"That's not a text, Logan. That's a novella," I said.

"Say it any way you want," he said. "Just say it. I want him to know you're off the case and I'm on it. Got me? You're off this case, McCall. I don't want you anywhere near Jack Lowe. If you try to find Jack Lowe, I will arrest you for obstructing an ongoing investigation. Stop talking about Jack Lowe, stop thinking about Jack Lowe, stop wondering where he is and what the hell happened to him. Do you understand? Forget you ever heard the name Jack Lowe. Am I clear?"

I nodded my head with frustration—a stellar moment of acting, I must say—lifted my phone, and replied to Jack Lowe: *Be there or be square.*

I spent another minute pretending to type in Logan's lecture, hit Send as if I were texting the killer, looked at the detective, and said, "One more question. Are you going back to Lowry Lowe?"

"Not today," he said. "They got a meeting at four o'clock with a Texas tart and a computer geek who are ripping each other new assholes for a hundred twenty million dollars."

I know, I thought, checking my watch. *Time to go.*

21

FUCK THE FIFTH

I did not tell Logan about Jack Lowe and Red Maple Horse Farm. Instead, I grabbed a cab to 30 Rockefeller Center and found a first-floor restroom. As I made myself into Emily Baynes, I caught my own eyes in the mirror and barely recognized myself looking back. It wasn't the red wig or green contacts or Texas twang. Beneath the character costume, I'd become the kind of person who consciously, intentionally, and willingly withholds information from the police during an ongoing investigation, just like Jimmy knew I would—*Jimmy's Rules of Private Investigation for Kate, Rule Number Ten: lying is a part of the job. You have to lie every day, sometimes all day. You have to be a champion liar to crack your case. You have to do it, but you never get used to it.*

On the elevator up to the sixty-second floor, I realized my father was right. I would never get used to it. I even said it out loud to myself. "I'll never get used to it."

All my life, I'd been a law-abiding citizen—a single, song-and-dance mother of one. Yes, I'd followed an offbeat, off-balance, off-Broadway path, but all along the road I'd been as honest as the day is long. I'd paid the rent. I'd put food on the table. I'd been a truth teller, a straight shooter. That person was gone now. In her place was a lying liar telling lies to the homicide detective who'd arrested her once for murder, once for hooking (don't ask), and once for reckless endangerment. That I knew what I'd become and also knew I wasn't stopping anytime soon seemed surreal to me.

But then again, since Jimmy had been murdered in late July and I'd inherited McCall & Company and become a private investigator, the dial of my life had been permanently set on surreal. *The Harriman Affair*, the Industrial Douchebag, Ken Curry, the cops in the Town of Orangetown, the Barrington twins, Logan arresting me three times, and Fu saving my life four (maybe five) times were each and all surreal with a side of surreal. But nothing that had happened to me since my father's death, nothing I had seen or heard or dreamed or thought or said or done could match the surrealistic explosion that was Al Cutter and Warren White in the Lowry Lowe conference room.

Al was Tommy Baynes, murdering freak-geek husband of Emily Baynes. Warren was Lee Crouch, Tommy's attorney.

On Wednesday, after they'd agreed to the gig and I'd told them my plan, I'd said Al should look like an eccentric software genius and Warren should look like his lawyer. Who knew they were wardrobe overachievers? To the Lowry Lowe performance, Al wore a tennis warm-up suit, blue with white stripes (like he was the zombie version of Roger Federer), a matching tennis hat, and blue tennis shoes. Warren wore a brown pinstripe suit with a brown shirt and a brown tie. He must have been inspired by Al's matching ensemble because he wore a brown fedora on his bald head. The curious thing about Warren's costume was that all the various browns were the same tone as his skin, so it was hard to tell where Warren ended and his suit began.

"It'll be a goddamn dark day in Dallas before I give you a hundred twenty million dollars, Emily," Al said.

"We have attorneys, Tommy," I said. "We're not supposed to talk to each other."

"We're sitting across the table like it's a dinner party with your bloodsucking lawyers," Al said. "How can I not talk to you?"

It was true, which is the best kind of acting. Al and I were sitting directly across the conference table from each other. Warren was next to Al. Lisa Lowe was next to me. Michelle Lowry was at one end, and Christopher Lowry was at the other end, as if they were the parents and we were the unruly children.

I was surprised Lisa came to the meeting. Her husband had been missing since Wednesday, the day after Logan had told the four partners about the Friday death threat. Shouldn't she be focused on finding him? Shouldn't she be an emotional mess, too concerned, too distracted to sit in on something as tedious as the Baynes settlement? Didn't she have partners who could handle this one given the circumstances?

"Mr. Baynes," Lisa said, "insulting your wife's attorneys doesn't change the precedential fact that she was as responsible for your financial success as you were. She's entitled to half the estate you accumulated together."

"Did she code the program that made me two hundred forty million dollars?" Al said. "No, she did not code the program that made me two hundred forty million dollars. Did I code the program that made me two hundred forty million dollars? Yes, I coded the program that made me two hundred forty million dollars. She's entitled to what I give her. And out of the goodness of my heart, I'm giving her twenty million."

"You don't have a heart," I said.

"You fucked my cook," he said.

"Though we won't be entering that into the record," Warren said, putting his hand on Al's arm as if to remind him how that story ended. "Both Mr. and Mrs. Baynes made mistakes during their marriage. We don't see that particular episode as relevant to the settlement."

"We do, Mr. Crouch," Michelle said. "We think Mr. Baynes's behavior following his wife's affair is entirely relevant and worth exploring in front of a judge, if necessary."

"You brought up the cook?" Al said to me.

"No, you did," I said.

"You know what I mean. You told them about Seabury," Al said.

"Yes, we know all about the late Mr. Seabury," Christopher said.

"I plead the Fifth," Al said to my lawyers.

"Yes," Warren said, looking a little confused, "under advisement from his attorney, Mr. Baynes pleads the Fifth Amendment of the Constitution of the United States of America, so help me God."

And right at that moment, I could feel it slipping away. Pleading the Fifth was not something we had discussed at our rehearsal on Wednesday. It had never come up. We were off script, so to speak—not that there was a script, per se, in improvisation. But there were key words to track, conversation threads to look for and follow to their orchestrated ends, discussion clouds to sail through, schematics to be aware of, outlines to echo, chords to play, notes to sing. And none of those included pleading the freaking Fifth.

I had thought it just might work—Al playing Tommy, Warren portraying his various-shades-of-brown attorney. I'd known it was outrageous and risky and ill-advised, but I had thought if they could keep their characters in character and follow the overarching shape of the performance from one end to the other as I had mapped and charted, I might learn which partner knew what had happened to Jack Lowe. I had thought it just might work. And it *had* worked—right up until pleading the Fifth.

Their focus split between the large legal fee and Jack's disappearance had left the Lowry Lowe partners distracted enough to let Al and Warren and me momentarily slip through their regular reality window. But now the window was closing.

"This isn't a court of law, Mr. Baynes," Michelle said. "It's a settlement negotiation. You can't plead the Fifth."

"Pleading the Fifth is nonsensical," Lisa said. "I don't understand."

"What kind of attorney are you, Mr. Crouch?" Christopher said, implying he knew Warren wasn't an attorney at all. "What the hell is happening here?"

Warren and Al looked at each other with panic in their eyes, as if suddenly coming upon their own closing reality window. Any minute they would fall out of character, look at me, and tell the partners I'd paid them to do it. In which case my cover would be blown, Logan would be called, my son would be informed, and I would be screwed or arrested or both. I had to do something, and I had to do it now. I jumped to the end of the outline and ran for the end zone.

"I'll tell you what's happening here," I said to the partners. "My husband thinks having an affair justifies killing a man." I drilled Al with my eyes, trying to pull him back into the game like a *Star Trek* tractor beam. "Don't you, Tommy?"

Al blinked and looked at Warren. "Fuck the Fifth."

Warren blinked and looked at the partners. "Yes, under advisement from his attorney, Mr. Baynes would like to fuck the Fifth Amendment of the Constitution of the United States of America, so help me God."

We were still alive, but just barely.

"What in the world are you talking about?" Michelle said.

"You're not an attorney. And you're not Tommy Baynes," Christopher said to Warren and Al.

"Who are these men, Emily?" Lisa said. "What's going on here?"

"Tommy thinks if your wife or husband has an affair, it can make you murder somebody," I said, answering the second question and ignoring the first.

"Fucking right that's what I think," Al said. "I know what it did to me, seeing you and the cook. Probably did the same thing to these bloodsuckers."

"What's that supposed to mean?" Michelle said.

"Your history of extramarital affairs is part of the public record," Warren said. "If you introduce my client's violent past, we're going to introduce yours."

"What are you talking about?" Christopher said.

"The Friday death threat," Al said.

"I might have mentioned it," I said.

"One partner fucked another partner they weren't married to, and one of the other partners put a contract on the partner who fucked that other partner," Al said. "That's why it's Friday and one partner's gone missing."

"I might have mentioned that too," I said.

I could feel the temperature rise in the room, feel the tension build. I had the sense that whatever happened next was a long time coming.

"I know you're sleeping with Jack," Lisa said to Michelle. "Or you were until you found him fucking your paralegal."

"I knew it too," Christopher said.

"So you hired someone to kill him?" Michelle said, pointing at her husband.

"That was Lisa," Christopher said, pointing at Jack's wife.

"Or you," Lisa said, pointing at Michelle.

"It's like HBO GO," Warren said, falling out of character.

And yet the partners' palpable undercurrent of anger, disgust, and resentment did not translate into the Sturm und Drang normally associated with illicit affairs and contract death threats. There were no outward histrionics—no hand wringing or hair pulling or rending of garments. Instead, there were fingers pointing in accusation, voices dripping with animosity.

And yet, in that oddly underplayed moment, I'd learned which partner was sleeping with which partner and also learned that they all believed one of them had hired the same man who'd murdered my father to kill Jack Lowe. I was almost there.

"All that's left is which one of you hired him," I said out loud instead of inside my head and, oh yeah, without my Texas twang.

The partners stopped pointing at each other and pointed at me instead.

"I thought so," Michelle said.

"So did I," Lisa said.

"What happened to your accent?" Christopher said.

"Private investigator," Michelle said.

"Of course she is," Christopher said.

"I want her arrested," Lisa said.

"Call that homicide cop," Michelle said to her husband. "That's what she's doing here."

Christopher glared at his wife and at Lisa and then looked at me. "Whoever you are, you're too old for the idiot pretending to be your husband."

"I told her that," Al said.

"Me too," Warren said.

"Shut up," I said to them.

"I never believed he'd go for you," Christopher said.

"Told her that too," Al said.

"Ditto," Warren said.

"Shut up," I said to them.

"So that's bad casting," Christopher said. "And I have friends and family in Fort Worth. Your accent's awful. So even though it's hard to believe, given these two morons, your acting is even worse than your casting."

"Told her that many times," Al said.

"Too many," Warren said.

"Shut up," I said to them.

Then Christopher stood and started around the conference table toward the door, a route that took him behind Lisa and me. I pushed my chair back and blocked his path.

"What are you doing?" Christopher said.

"Answering my critics," I said, and I got up and punched him in the face, a brutal shot that broke his nose and sent him sprawling to the floor.

"Oh shit," Christopher said, bleeding all over himself.

"Got a rude right cross, though," Al said.

"Hell of a haymaker," Warren said.

"Get out," I said to them, and they both jumped up and ran from the room.

I followed them to the doorway but turned back to the partners and addressed them collectively. "Do the words *Red Maple* mean anything to you?"

22

AN ENJOYABLE EVENING OF
PLAYOFF BASEBALL AND COLD BEER

It was the beginning of the end for *Blood Song and Dance*, meaning we were closer to the final curtain than we were to opening night. After tonight's and tomorrow night's performances, there were three more weekends. Six more shows. And while I was looking forward to popping out of a painting and cavorting across the D-Cup stage as a singing-and-dancing bisexual hippie goddess from somebody's bad acid trip, I knew I would miss being a singing-and-dancing heartsick vampire biting New Yorkers in the neck and gallons of fake blood spurting stage left and stage right and upstage and downstage and sometimes backstage, when the tubes malfunctioned.

As usual, the house was full. New York is a city of some nearly nine million people. And Dennis and Posey had tapped into a loyal, sub-sub-sub-subset of several thousand who enjoyed ludicrous musicals absurdly told but passionately performed, enthusiastically voiced, and energetically danced. The D-Cup wasn't a large theater, but it wasn't a little black box either. It was small enough to be intimate but big enough to hold ridiculous rocking musicals that shook the windows—not to mention the audience's grasp of reality.

One recent reviewer nailed it in two words: *harmonic chaos*.

I kept those two words in mind throughout the Friday night show, and then kept them in mind after the show while putting on a brunette wig and hazel contacts and a long skirt and Frye boots and a silk blouse and a leather jacket, and then continued to keep them in mind during the cab ride to Blue Bar, and then still kept them in mind when I saw Griff and Adam in the lobby at the hostess stand, where they didn't recognize me as Danielle Sullivan, and finally kept them in mind when I found Stanley Stein seated at the second-floor bar, the kitchen floor, drinking a beer and reading the papers, an empty stool to his left. Harmonic chaos. My life.

Game one of the National League Championship Series was on almost every flat-screen—Cardinals against the Dodgers—and the place was buzzing. Full house.

Jimmy had loved baseball, and so I had loved it too. He'd had a bar in every borough, and when a big game was on TV, he would pick one of those joints for some superstitious sports reason or another, and I would meet him there for a beer and a burger, and we would watch the game, and I would keep score because Jimmy had taught me how and liked it when I did, and we would be together, and that's what I had wanted since I'd been a little girl—to be with my dad.

But I couldn't follow baseball this year. I had lost Jimmy, and the heart had gone out of the game for me. It would come back one day, maybe next season or the season after that, but right now it was too soon, the loss was too raw, the pain too present.

The wiry black guy, wearing a suit with no tie, stood at the end of the bar, as if he had nothing to do with Stanley, as if he were here for baseball and beer. He had made me earlier today, when I'd followed the gamblers after they'd chatted with the bookie, when I'd caught the brown-haired woman in a business suit in two different ladies' rooms and then caught Griff exchanging money for a matchbook in the men's room.

He had made me then, the wiry black guy, so I had to be sure he wouldn't make me now. I caused a little commotion snaking my way through the crowd, just enough of a scene so the wiry black guy had to notice me crossing the room on my way to the empty barstool. He acted like he wasn't paying attention, but he saw me and didn't recognize me from Tuesday, when I was a blonde with green eyes. I was good to go.

My plan was simple. I would play an old customer who was back in town and wanted to bet on the ball game but didn't know how it happened in this joint, didn't know how Stanley made his magic. I would make him believe he knew me, even if he couldn't exactly remember me. I would paint a picture of our past and place a big enough bet so that he'd be predisposed to find me familiar. I would convince him I belonged on the empty stool to his left. I would conjure up a hazy gray recollection of me that would seem real to him, and he would take my bet and tell me how it worked, and I would tell him who I really was, and I would have him dead to rights, and he would confess that Griff was gambling Blue Bar money.

I felt sure none of the half dozen undercover cops who'd tried and failed to bait the bookie had ever taken this tack. I was certain none of them had been accomplished actors. Acting was my edge. I was an attractive brunette with hazel eyes looking for a little action. He was a seventy-five (Six? Seven? Eight?)-year-old bookie, recollections of gamblers gone by not as clear as they once were. I would look into his eyes and help him create a memory of me. We would be old friends talking old times in two minutes. *It's going to work*, I said to myself.

I arrived at the bar and sat on the stool beside the bookie. "Hello, Stanley. Good to see you again."

He turned his head and glanced in my direction. In all my

life, I had never, not once, seen eyes like Stanley Stein's. They were cold and calculating, like the lens of a camera, collecting and cataloging images without emotion, without effort, without error. For the record, they were brown.

He looked at me for five full seconds. "We've never met," he said.

"Sure we have," I said. "You don't remember. It was a few years and a lifetime ago. It was—"

"It was never," he said, cutting me off. He was sure of it, knew it for a fact. There was no chance we had met and he'd forgotten. Zero chance. This was not a discussion we were going to have. He was not going to let me paint him a picture of our time together back in the day because there was no back in the day for Stanley and me. We were going to have a different discussion.

His sideward glance never left me. His eyes kept clicking away—click, click, click. It was unnerving enough to be called out on my first sentence, but his eyes had whacked me way off balance. I had seen the eyes of many übersmart, even genius-smart doctors and lawyers and entrepreneurs and writers and musicians and actors and artists and scientists and professors and captains of industry. Stanley's eyes weren't smart like that. They were a different kind of smart. They were all-knowing in the sense that they knew everything they knew with uncompromising certainty.

"I've sat next to you—" I said.

"Not one time, sister," he said. "You're either a cop or a private investigator. But you're not a cop because the cops know I'm not doing anything but having a drink and watching a ball game. So that means you're a PI. And there are only two things in the world I hate more than PIs. Want to know what they are? Broadway show tunes. And fucking Broadway show tunes. How can anyone listen to that idiot shit? Who the hell breaks into a fucking song in the middle of their fucking life? I hate that. The only thing worse than Broadway show tunes or a PI is a PI singing Broadway show tunes. That is a nightmare I could never endure."

I took a moment to be profoundly offended, seeing as how I *was* a PI who sang Broadway show tunes and had loved musical theater since seventh grade, when I'd played Kim MacAfee in *Bye Bye Birdie*. "Tell me how you really feel about it, Stanley."

"No problem. You're a second-rate PI, you measured me, you got it wrong, and now you're interrupting what was an enjoyable evening of playoff baseball and cold beer. You got five seconds to get off the stool or I'll introduce you to Harold, and I want you to believe this with all your heart, sister: you do not want to meet Harold."

The wiry black guy moved down the bar toward Stanley and me.

"The black guy is Harold?" I said.

"Jiu jitsu grand master, MMA middleweight champion, nasty-ass Navy SEAL, deep-cover Special Ops killer."

"He left all that behind for you?"

"I pay better than they do."

I took the photograph of Griff exchanging Blue Bar cash for a matchbook in the men's room out of my purse (I'd stopped at home before heading to the D-Cup to print it) and put it on the bar between Stanley and me. The bookie looked at the picture, and his eyes went click-click-click. He lifted his hand, hardly waved it, and Harold stopped dead and started back to his end of the bar.

"Evidence," I said.

"Of what, the managing partner buying drugs in his own bathroom? Buying a blowjob? Making change for a sports fan got no toilet paper? Evidence of nothing, sister, that's what I'm looking at," he said.

"Evidence is in the eye of the beholder," I said as I put the picture back in my purse. "I see Griff paying off your man in the men's room for a bet he made at the bar."

"When I was a kid, everybody said, *'You got gumption, Stanley.'* Lucky for me, I had more than that. I don't know how lucky you are, sister, but you got gumption. I'll give you that. Now get off my stool and go home to your hobbies before my mood goes in the toilet."

"That's insulting, Stanley."

"You're insulted?"

"Go home to my hobbies? Yes, I'm insulted." I took out my phone and snapped a picture of the bookie at the bar and then turned and took one of Harold, who was headed toward us again.

"What the—" Stanley said.

"And because I'm insulted, I'm going to sit here all night. And if Harold so much as breathes on me, I'll scream bloody murder. You don't think there are cops and lawyers in here? I do. In fact, I'll bet there are. Want to take *that* bet, Stanley?"

Stanley drilled me with his eyes and waved Harold to a halt. "You want a piece of me? Is that it?"

"I don't want you at all. I want Griff. He's betting Blue Bar money, and you're going to give him to me or I'm going to take you down with him."

He looked into his beer and said, "Gumption."

"Excuse me?" I said.

"Girlfriend," he said. "Find his girlfriend." Then he turned to me, subtly signaled for Harold, and said, "Now get the fuck off my stool."

I stood, smiled at Harold, and said to Stanley, "If it's an enjoyable evening of playoff baseball and cold beer, why do you need a bodyguard?"

"I got a reputation attracts lunatics like you."

"Makes sense," I said.

"Next time I introduce you to Harold," he said as I walked away.

I gave him the finger without turning around.

"Gumption," I heard him say.

23

I DIDN'T REALIZE THE PRACTICE OF TAI CHI INVOLVED SMIRKING

I woke up six o'clock Saturday morning with a headache—especially bad news because I didn't fall asleep until four. I didn't fall asleep until four because Stanley Stein had messed with my mind. Which is why I had a headache.

And Fu. I had a headache because of Fu too.

Stanley first. Throughout my acting career, meaning for most of my life, I had been objective about my performances. As much as I hated to admit it, there had been musicals in which I'd missed the mark, didn't quite catch my character, never found my true voice, couldn't walk the walk in a way that lived up to my own acting expectations. Whenever that happened (not often, thank goodness), I'd been straight up with myself.

Conversely, when I'd perfected a performance, nailed my character in song and dance and heart and soul, and the audience had stood and cheered, I'd been honest about that too. I never hesitated to congratulate or castigate my acting self. I'm paraphrasing the Santa song, but I knew if I'd been bad or good. And I'd been boffo with the bookie.

So why hadn't it worked? How could he have seen through

me with such certainty, with such speed? It wasn't my performance. It was something else. And wondering what it was had kept me up until four in the morning. And what was that bit about Griff's girlfriend? Who the hell was she? What did she have to do with anything?

As far as Fu, I hadn't seen him in a few days, but something he'd said on Tuesday while fixing the lobby light had stuck with me, irritated me, like dirt in my eye. Part of it was that Fu had been right about the Lowry Lowe partners screwing each other literally and figuratively—that he'd been right and knew it before I did.

I was a competitive person by nature. Growing up in Queens, my sister, Marilyn, and I were always going at it. From eating Cheerios to drinking chocolate milk to running down the street to jumping rope to playing cards to saying our prayers to brushing our teeth to getting dressed, anything and everything was a race, a game, a contest of wills. It wasn't a fair fight because Marilyn was six years older than me. When she would win, which was usually, she had a way of rubbing it in that drove me crazy. To this day, my skin got hot when I thought about it. I loved my sister, even though I couldn't stand her, and wanted to win every little game, every little challenge, every little moment to show her how much. She loved me the same way. We tortured each other daily to prove it.

And then she moved to Cleveland when I was twelve and that hot blood went away—until I met Fu, the only person besides Marilyn who could make me crazy with his smirky tone of voice. I was three years older than Fu, so he was like my little brother, the two of us twisting daggers in each other's backs to show how much we cared.

So, yes, that Fu had figured out Lowry Lowe first sucked a few eggs no doubt. But it was something he'd said while getting in the last word—just like my sister used to do—that had burrowed under my skin.

"May not need now," he'd said. *"But need soon. Can't do without Fu."*

Can't do without Fu. I didn't like needing Marilyn when I was a kid, even though I did. And I didn't like needing Fu now that I was a grown-up, even though I did. I'd inherited a brash independent streak from Jimmy, and being a single mom at seventeen, wanting to validate and verify I could take care of myself and my son, had made it worse. I knew I needed help, but I didn't like to admit it. I was Irish. Sue me.

Eyes at half-mast, brain foggy with dream state, legs not wanting to carry my sleepy weight, I zombie-walked through my closet and dining room into my kitchen, looking for a glass of water and three aspirin. Through the bars on my kitchen window, in the dim daybreak, I saw Fu in the backyard doing tai chi while Jerusalem Joe looked on from his perch.

Fu moved with elegance, grace, and dignity. Seeing him glide and slide through the postures without effort belied the fact that he was one part bulldozer, one part hurricane, one part stone-cold killer, and one part Fred Astaire.

I put on sweatpants and a sweatshirt and went outside. The Indian summer of September was gone. Fall was here. I sat on a rusted patio chair and watched Fu. My eyes closed. I might have dozed off for a minute. The parrot woke me up.

"Who invited you, sad sack?" Joe said.

"Your bird has anger issues, Fu," I said.

"Joe not angry," Fu said. "Joe funny. Joe comedian."

"Kiss my ass, girlfriend," Joe said to me.

"He doesn't like women," I said.

"Joe like women," Fu said.

"Ten laps, lard ass," Joe said to me.

"Joe not like you," Fu said.

And then the famous Fu smirk. I didn't think it was possible to smirk doing tai chi—wasn't the point to calm the soul, to open the heart, to let love flow, to become one with the universe? I didn't realize the practice of tai chi involved smirking. I could feel my skin flush. *I'm the one who needs tai chi*, I thought.

"I don't want to talk about Joe," I said.

"What want talk about?" Fu said.

"Jack Lowe's been missing since Wednesday," I said. "Yesterday, Logan called me in to see if I knew anything, and while I was sitting in the Thirteenth, he texted me."

"Why he text you?" Fu said. "You sit right there." Smirk.

"Heck of a job, Brownie," Joe said to me.

"Lowe, not Logan. Jack Lowe texted me," I said. "You can't be a dirtbag doing tai chi—you'll screw up the universe."

"What Jack Lowe say?" Fu said.

"He's in Fairfield, Connecticut, at a horse farm—Red Maple Horse Farm," I said. "He wants to meet me there tomorrow night at eleven. He said it was show-and-tell and I should come alone. He said all's well that ends well."

"Fu say trap."

"I know it's a trap. You think I don't know it's a trap? I knew it was a trap before you knew it was a trap. Of course it's a trap."

"Fu know first."

"I knew when I got the text yesterday. Friday. You heard about it right now. Check the calendar. It's Saturday. No way you could know first. It's physically impossible—by the laws of physics—for you to know first. You don't know anything about physics. You're not a physicist. You're a mob assassin."

"Fu go Red Maple tomorrow. Get car from Zombie. Go Connecticut. See Jack Lowe."

"Don't do that. Don't make the plan. I make the plan."

"Good luck with that," Joe said.

"Fu drive," Fu said.

"You don't have a license. If we get pulled over, there goes the plan, which you don't make because I make the plan because I knew first because I'm the PI."

"You got no chance," Joe said.

Shit. I had come down here to tell Fu about Jack Lowe and Red Maple Horse Farm and to ask him to come with me to Connecticut, and he'd beaten me to the punch. And he'd done it on purpose because he knew it annoyed me, and I had let myself get annoyed, which annoyed me all over again.

"You PI?" Fu said.

"Yes," I said.

"You make plan?"

"Yes."

"Tell Fu plan."

"Tell Fu plan?"

"Tell Fu plan."

"The plan is I get the car from Al, and you come with me to Red Maple because I think it's a trap."

"Sound like Fu plan." Smirk and double smirk.

"Heck of a job, Brownie," Joe said to me.

I stood up. Sometimes that's all you can do. "You are the most impossible person I have met since my sister."

"What sister name?" Fu said.

"Marilyn," I said.

"Introduce Fu Marilyn. Marilyn like Fu. Fu make new friend."

"I am not introducing you to my sister. Get that out of your skull. You and Marilyn are not going to be friends. She lives in Cleveland."

"Fu go Cleveland Sunday. Meet Marilyn."

I walked right up to him. He kept on tai chi-ing. "You are not going to Cleveland Sunday to meet my sister. You're going to Connecticut because I'm walking into a trap, and I need you to come with me in case someone has to save my life."

He held his pose but moved his eyes so they met mine. We looked at each other for five seconds and had a whole conversation about what we meant to each other, how grateful I was he'd saved me four (maybe five) times, how thankful he was to have something purposeful to do with his life besides change light bulbs and mop floors and take out the trash, how I needed him even though I didn't want to, how he needed to be needed during his exile to the House of Emotional Tics. "Fu come Connecticut," he said.

Maybe he smiled or maybe I imagined it. Either way, I turned and started back to the brownstone. "Sunday night. We leave at ten."

"That what Fu think," he said. Smirk, smirk, smirk.

I looked back at him, but his tai chi pose had turned him away from me. So I looked at Jerusalem Joe instead.

"I thought it first," I said to the bird.

"So long, sucker," the parrot said.

24

WHAT THE HELL HAPPENS WHEN I'M A BLONDE?

KNOWING SLEEP WAS NOT IN THE CARDS, I SAT ON MY SOFA TO consider the conversation I'd just had with Fu and promptly passed out. I woke up at noon, went for a run around the reservoir, which did nothing to clear my head, which said something about my state of mind, put on the Wanda Ward wig and green contacts, packed my bag, and went to Blue Bar as redheaded management consultant Danielle Sullivan.

Blue was back in town (he'd been gone Friday) but was not in the building, though he was expected shortly. Griff was off until tonight. Stanley Stein was also absent, possibly taking bets at some other watering hole. Adam Stoker was the douchebag on duty.

I went from floor to floor, keeping up the appearance, the ruse, that I was here to supercharge the Blue Bar revenue stream, talking to the staff about in-house procedures and processes, asking how, in their humble opinions, the operation could be streamlined, hoping something secret would slip into the conversation.

Most of the staff knew me by now and answered my questions with varying degrees of cooperation—depending on their relationship with Griff and Adam, who had poisoned the Danielle Sullivan well from day one. Many wanted to know if they'd be listed as efficient or inefficient in my final report. If they were nice to me, I said job security was in their immediate future. I told the assholes to freshen up their resumes. No one shared any hush-hush Blue Bar business that might have tied Griff to embezzled cash to Stanley Stein. No one said anything about Griff's girlfriend.

I worked my way down to the dungeon and knocked on Mary's open door. "Hi. Got a minute for me?"

She looked up from the pile of paperwork on her desk, gave me a bright smile, and waved me in. "Yes, of course, come in. Happy to see you."

She stood as I entered, crossed to me, and took my hands with her hands. "Excuse my mess. I just got back from Pennsylvania this morning. My grandson, Marcus, turned eighteen yesterday, and my daughter, Julia, planned a party," she said, gesturing to a photograph of Marcus in his high school football uniform on the field after a game, surrounded by family and friends. "And when my daughter plans a party, oh my—Katy, bar the door. Marcus is a straight arrow. His mother, she's my wild child."

She laughed like Doris Roberts and gestured for me to have a seat at her small conference table. As I did, she shut her office door and said, "Don't want any little birdies bothering us." Then she sat in the chair next to me. "How can I help you, Danielle?"

I put the picture of Griff exchanging money for a matchbook in the men's room on the table between us. "I can prove he's gambling with Stanley Stein, but I can't prove it's Blue Bar cash."

She lifted the photograph, nodded to herself, and said, "I knew it."

"Yesterday, I sat next to Stanley at the bar," I said, "and showed him that shot."

"Oh my," she said. "What happened? What did you say?"

I didn't mention Stanley's eyes or his knowing beyond a shadow of a doubt that he had never once met me despite my convincing performance to the contrary. Instead, I said, "I told him I didn't want him, that I wanted Griff, and that if he, Stanley, didn't help me, I would take him down too."

"You said that?"

"I said that."

"What did he say?"

"He said I should find Griff's girlfriend."

"His girlfriend?"

"You said you knew where the bodies were buried. I need you to dig that one up."

She smiled, took a key from her desk, and unlocked a wide file cabinet that stood against the wall that separated her office from Blue's office. "I know just where to put my shovel."

I smiled too. "I was hoping you'd say that."

"I've never met any of his girlfriends," she said, flipping through file folders. "No one has. Not Adam. Not even Blue. He doesn't bring them here. He keeps his private life private. The *rumor* is he has half a dozen. The *fact* is he has at least one."

"Facts are my friends."

"Then you should like this one."

She pulled a file folder from the cabinet and sat again at the conference table.

"On Monday," she said, "the day you started, Griff had me cut a check to Barbara Bloom."

"The famous Fifth Avenue florist?"

"Five hundred fifty dollars for thirty-six long-stem roses in a fancy vase."

I shook my head in wonder. "I assume the flowers are solid gold?"

"One would think. Anyway, I follow and file every check to confirm service has been rendered and payment has cleared the bank."

I could feel my pulse rate rise as it dawned on me. "You have the receipt."

"I wouldn't be much of an inside man if I didn't."

She opened the folder, flipped through the papers, and pulled out a copy of the cashed check stapled to the Barbara Bloom receipt. "The roses were delivered to Diane Swain. Between Madison and Fifth on 68th Street."

My heart skipped a beat, maybe two. "Diane Swain?"

"Do you know her?"

"Not personally. Was there a note?"

"That's the good part." She handed me the receipt.

I read the note out loud. "'Happy birthday, lover. Can't wait to see you tonight. Dave.'"

She made me a copy of the receipt. I put it in my purse, told her how grateful I was for her help, and left her office, on my way to the D-Cup for the Saturday night performance of *Blood Song and Dance*.

Except the light was on in Blue's office, which was right next to Mary's office, meaning he was in there. It had been off when I walked down the hall earlier. (All the dungeon doors had frosted glass panels, which was how you could tell if the lights were on or off.) I stopped in front of the closed door, took a breath, and realized that when I'd been going floor to floor, playing the staff, keeping up the ruse that I was trying to find efficiencies while *really* trying to get the goods on Griff, what I was *really, really* doing was playing myself. The whole time, it turned out, I'd been looking for Blue.

I could feel the heat on my neck. *Jesus, get a grip*, I said to myself and started to walk past the door. I never made it. I stopped and knocked instead.

"Come in," Blue said from inside the room.

I opened the door and stood in the doorway. He was seated at his desk. His face lit up when he saw me. I think mine lit up too. Or maybe that was the heat moving out from my neck to my cheeks.

Apparently, Blue had bought all the office furniture at the same time because he had all the same furniture that Mary had —except for a massive, heavy-duty, block-of-steel gun safe that said *Winchester* on it. The safe was six feet tall, four feet wide, and three feet deep. It backed up to the wall between his office and Mary's office. It had to weigh more than a minivan.

"I feel like I haven't seen you in days," he said.

"Two," I said.

"Two what?" he said.

"Days," I said. "We saw each other Thursday. Today's Saturday."

"Feels longer," he said.

He told me he'd been in Tampa visiting his sister, who'd just had her third child. She was married to an ophthalmologist, and they lived a swell Florida life, Blue said. I told him my father's Uncle Mike lived in Tampa too. In late July, at the reading of Jimmy's will in Shavelson's office, my father left his Volvo to Uncle Mike, although he left the keys to Mike's wife, Bonnie, because Mike was a drunk. *Sober up, Uncle Mike*, Jimmy had said in his will.

When the conversation turned to Griff and the missing money, I stepped into Blue's office and shut the door, hearing Mary's voice in my head: *"Don't want any little birdies bothering us."*

I told Blue about following customers into the restroom, and then following Griff into the restroom, and then taking the photograph, and then sitting next to Stanley Stein. And then I put the cash-for-matchbook photo on Blue's conference table.

He came around his desk and stood next to me, and we both looked at the picture. I didn't know what Blue was thinking, but I sure as hell knew what I was thinking, which was, *Oh my God, he smells good enough to kiss.* He had on a leather bomber jacket and some kind of aphrodisiac aftershave that blended into a manly, musky, leathery, early-morning-country-lake smell that made me swoony.

"Stanley told me to talk to Griff's girlfriend," I said, and for some reason my voice was low and husky.

"He never talks about his relationships," Blue said, and for some reason *his* voice was low and husky too. "I don't know who he's seeing."

"Diane Swain," I said, turning to him. "Mary found her for me."

"Of course she did," he said, turning to me too. "She knows where the bodies are buried."

We were very close to each other. I looked up into his eyes —blue on blue—and realized my heart was pounding. I could hear it. And then I realized it wasn't just my heart I heard. It was his too. "And she has a shovel," I said.

"Kate..." he said, his voice fading, his lips moving toward mine.

"Danielle..." I said, my voice fading too.

"Whatever..." he said, and he kissed me.

I knew I shouldn't kiss him back. I could hear Jimmy's voice in my head. *"You'll get close to your clients, Kate, close enough to kiss them. But don't. Don't ever kiss a client. The one sure-as-shit way to crap your case is to get romantically involved with a client. Trust me. I know."* I kissed him anyway. Big-time.

The kiss ended.

"We can't do this," I said in a whisper.

"Too late," he said in a whisper.

And then we kissed again, deeper this time, more intense. I put my arms around his neck. He pulled me closer. It was the kind of kiss where clothes come off and sirens scream and fire-works light the night. Finally, our lips came apart, but we did not separate. My arms were still around him. His arms were still around me.

"I've been thinking about you for two days," he said.

"I can tell," I said. "You put it all in that last kiss."

"No," he said. "I saved some for this one."

And then we kissed again, gentler this time, with emotion that surprised me and made me weak in the knees.

"That's not fair," I said, still holding him.

"All's fair," he said, somehow knowing what I meant, which in and of itself wasn't fair.

"You're my client," I said, pulling away, straightening myself, and gathering my things. "I'm your PI. I have to talk to Diane Swain so I can stop Stanley Stein and get Griff out of your register, which is a hard-enough string of things to do if I'm *not* hot and bothered. Except now, thanks to you, I have to do all that knowing, one, you're as attracted to me as I am to you, two, you kiss like a house on fire, and three, you're probably going to ask me out, and I'm probably going to say yes, and we're probably going to find out we like each other, and then this whole client-PI relationship thing is going to be a sexual mess and a half. And that's with me wearing a red wig and green contacts. What the hell happens when I'm a blonde?"

I knew I sounded like a flustered, flummoxed, and infatuated fifteen-year-old. I couldn't help it. At that moment, I *was* a flustered, flummoxed, and infatuated fifteen-year-old—smitten, seduced, and swept off my feet. I opened the door, stopped in the doorway, and looked at him—those eyes, that face, those hands, that kiss. "Well?"

"I'm okay with that," he said. And then he smiled, and my heart soared, and I thought, *I'm in big trouble now*.

"I have to be a vampire," I said. And I left Blue Bar for the D-Cup.

25

CONGENIAL COMRADES IN ARMS

JIMMY ONCE TOLD ME HE'D TIED HIS CLEATS, UNTIED THEM, retied them, untied them, and then retied them before every game he ever pitched—right shoe first three times in succession and then left shoe three times. He said he'd done it that way once by accident—before he was good at tying shoes—and then thrown a two-hit, complete-game shutout. He was eight at the time, and he'd never prepared to play nine innings any other way ever again. *"It's not ritual, Katie,"* he'd told me. *"It's religion."*

Athletes can be ritualistic to the point of incredulity. Actors can be just like that only more so. And no actor could be *more* more so than Roger Platt.

Of all the Schmidt and Parker Players, none was more particular about his pre-play preparation process, more idiosyncratic about his idiosyncrasies, than Roger.

Roger was always, every single time, the first actor to arrive at the theater. He couldn't be the second actor to arrive. Not even once. He *had* to be the first. His routine, which I knew by heart, began with twenty minutes of meditation that allowed Roger, as he said, to empty himself of his *physical world* and fill himself with his *theatrical world*. Meditation was followed by serious stretching, which was followed by intricate vocal exercises, which was followed by detailed makeup application, which was followed by rigorous facial calisthenics, which was followed by decisive line review, which was followed by "The Wearing of the Wardrobe," which was followed by and followed by and followed by and followed by until curtain. Each aspect of Roger's ritual had exacting subrituals of its own —absolute orders of things, precise positioning of things, habitual application of things—too many to mention.

I knew Roger's ritual routine by rote because I was always the second actor to arrive. And by always, I mean every time. I wasn't proud of being theatrically superstitious, but I couldn't help it either. I *had* to be the second actor in the theater before every show. Period. My ritual had become part of Roger's ritual, and his had become a part of mine. He had to be first. I had to be second. Once we were both in the house, our preshow preparations could begin in earnest. We were theatrically tied together by virtue of our entwined rituals.

Roger and I had co-starred in several D-Cup productions and had spot-on, spot-free theatrical chemistry. Our real-world chemistry had spots for sure but was good enough for us to be friendly without actually being friends. That was fine for me and for Roger too, meaning it was as fun for me to act and sing and dance with him as it was for him to act and sing and dance with me, and that was enough to carry us into the real world as congenial comrades in arms.

And as congenial comrades in arms, Roger had recently helped me, along with Dennis and Posey and Chloe and the other Schmidt and Parker Players, with my private investigations.

"Roger," I said, "if you're not busy tomorrow afternoon, I'd like you to make a house call with me. It's for the new case I'm working."

"I knew you'd ask," Roger said.

"You did?" I said.

"Absolutely," he said. "I'm your big stick, your coup de grâce, your ace in the hole, your key to the castle. Who are we this time? Doctors, lawyers, Indian chiefs?"

Know-it-alls. Jesus. "Real estate brokers," I said.

"Perfect. Nobody sells bricks-and-mortar like Roger Platt," he said.

We sat side by side at the long makeup counter in the D-Cup dressing room, one of my most favorite places in the world, me to his left, him to my right. As we always did, we spoke to each other in the mirror that ran the length of the counter while we applied our makeup. Small, bright bulbs spaced a foot apart lit the mirror. Industrial lights overhead lit the rest of the room. The counter had mismatched yard-sale chairs for a dozen actors. Soon, the rest of the Schmidt and Parker Players would fill the space.

"We're not selling bricks-and-mortar," I said. "We're selling ourselves as exclusive brokers for a new residential building in Brooklyn."

"Better yet," Roger said. "Exclusive is my middle name."

Roger was talented, but not as talented as he thought he was. His tragic flaw, his hamartia, was his ego—he was too cocky for his own good—and while working on my last two cases (meaning my first two), it had cost him a couple of times he would never forget. During my workman's compensation case, Roger had taken a swinging, flying iron teapot to the side of the head, and during my stolen identity case, he'd been pepper-sprayed in the eyeballs at point-blank range.

"Who's the lucky developer to get Roger on board?" he said.

"Diane Swain," I said.

"Which one?" he said, and I knew exactly what he meant.

In the 1960s and 1970s, residential real estate developer Sam Swain had made hundreds of millions of dollars building tens of thousands of garden apartments throughout Queens, Brooklyn, and the Bronx. He'd married a socialite named Diane Mason, who became Diane Swain, and they'd had three daughters, each of whom they named Diane because Sam so loved his wife—as if Sam were somehow the George Foreman forerunner. To clarify things for the public, the girls went by their middle names: Diane *Marie*, Diane *Rose*, and the youngest, Diane *Grace*.

Sam died young, and Marie and Rose married and moved away—one to Chicago, the other to Seattle. Diane Mason, Sam's wife, stayed in New York and ran the family business, and Diane Grace stayed with her and became a developer like her father and a socialite like her mother. Wild-child Diane Grace had never settled down and at age forty-two was still a gossip-rag, society-page stunner—and was now Griff's girlfriend.

"The youngest one," I said. "Diane Grace."

Roger applied eye shadow and nodded knowingly, as if the whole thing were already a done deal. "She's going to love me."

Narcissists. Jesus.

Roger was fifty-two years old and had been married and divorced twice due to his lifelong love affair with the stage. He was nearly six feet tall and fit as a fireman from delivering thirty-pound boxes of frozen shrimp to restaurants and groceries across Staten Island, one of three part-time gigs that paid his rent so he could pursue his passion: musical theater. Roger was also a janitor in a midtown Manhattan high-rise and a used-car salesman in Queens. None of those jobs meant anything to him. He was as much an actor in the center of his soul as I was.

"It's not a romantic mission," I said. "We have underlying business."

"Ulterior motives," he said. "My specialty. What are we fishing for this time?"

Everything was Roger's specialty. "The managing partner of

a big-league sports bar is embezzling cash to pay his debts, betting the money with a big-time bookie."

"Been there, done that," Roger said.

He'd been everywhere and done everything. Just ask him. On second thought, please, don't ask him. "Diane Grace is his girlfriend. After we convince her we're the best brokers in Brooklyn—"

"Get in her good...graces." He laughed at his quip. Roger thought he was the funniest, cleverest actor on way-off-Broadway.

"—I'll slip her boyfriend into the conversation and see if I can get her to confess that she knows what he's doing and she's as worried about him as we are."

"You sure you don't want me to ease the boyfriend in? It might be better for the performance if I do it. The broker-in-charge, so to speak."

Men. Jesus. "I'm going to take the lead, Roger. It's my case."

"I'm your wingman?"

"Co-star status, absolutely."

"Paying gig, correct?"

"Like the last two cases, correct."

"What's the name of our Brooklyn brokerage firm?"

"Haskins Milo."

"I'm Milo?"

"Theo Milo. That's you. I'll email you our business back-story tonight."

He rolled the name around his tongue. "Theo Milo. Theo Milo. I like it. Who are you?"

"Leanne Haskins."

"You don't think Milo Haskins has a better ring to it?"

"Wingman, Roger."

"Co-star status, got it. Equal billing though, right? Same card?"

Actors. Jesus.

26

A WHEELHOUSE YOU HAVE TO SEE
TO BELIEVE

BETWEEN HGTV'S *SELLING NEW YORK* AND BRAVO'S *MILLION Dollar Listing*, the high-handed pomposity, vanity, pretention, nerve, and blustery swagger of the Big Apple residential real estate brokerage business had become accepted, expected behavior. Over-the-top, in-your-face confidence was now an essential part of the sales team skill set—resume de rigueur— and was also a key component of my plan to nail Dave Griffin.

In the cab to the D-Cup, after kissing Blue in his office (and kissing him and kissing him), I'd Google searched Diane Swain and discovered she was interviewing A-list Brooklyn brokers at her majestic East 68th Street townhouse in a big-ticket, high-end, invitation-only cattle call beginning at nine o'clock Monday morning. Which is why Roger and I were standing at her front door at three o'clock Sunday afternoon.

The townhouse was five stories of limestone magnificence, complete with curved, ornate balustrades, wrought-iron railings, and six-foot windows that let in every ray of October sunshine.

To become Theo Milo, broker extraordinaire, Roger wore a gray pinstripe suit with a royal-blue shirt and ruby-red tie. To personify Leanne Haskins, Theo's partner in realty, I'd chosen the black business suit I'd worn in a late-late-night local cable television commercial I'd shot a few years back for a casket company called Cozy Coffin. That was really their name. I'd played a mortician selling an elderly client a Cozy Coffin that wouldn't break the bank. Unfortunately, the old actor died during the commercial—while she was in the damn casket. The ad ran for two weeks at two in the morning before the local cable company realized the woman was actually dead and pulled the spot off the air. I wore a chestnut-brown, shoulder-length wig with hip, heavy bangs and brown contact lenses. I chose stylish tortoise-shell glasses to complete my broker ensemble.

My plan was to use brains, balls, and bravado to convince Diane Grace to invite Roger and me to her cattle call—tomorrow morning, nine o'clock. I'd stayed up late after the Saturday night performance of *Blood Song and Dance*, written a real estate outline for our Sunday Swain matinee, and emailed it to Roger early this morning. If our pitch was successful and we were added to the list of auditioning brokerage firms, then when we were in front of her as Theo and Leanne, we would sell ourselves like there was no tomorrow—and then casually mention that we knew Griff. We would say we knew he was in trouble—embezzling and gambling—and that if Diane Grace knew it too, well, then we would tell her what we knew, and she would tell us what she knew, and we would help her help Griff out of the ditch he'd dug for himself.

It wasn't much of plan, but it was all I had.

We stood at the townhouse door and rang the buzzer. A security camera was twelve feet in the air and pointed at the doorway. We were on TV. I knew she was home, or at least someone was home (maybe Griff?) because I'd been watching the place since noon.

"Yes?" It was a woman's voice, fuzzy through the speaker.

"Good afternoon, Ms. Swain," I said. "My name is Leanne Haskins. This is Theo Milo." Roger smiled and gave a confident thumbs-up to the camera. "We're the founding partners of Haskins Milo, an up-and-coming, full-service, residential boutique brokerage firm specializing in one-of-a-kind, upscale properties. Our offices are in Brooklyn, and your outstanding, new Williamsburg building is right up our alley."

"The correct colloquialism is *in my wheelhouse*, Ms. Swain," Roger said confidently to the camera while flashing the A-OK sign. "And I've got a wheelhouse you have to see to believe."

"We're aggressive, we're confident, we're persistent, we're success-driven, and we would very much like to be included on your interview list for tomorrow morning—"

"Unless you'd like to see us now, Ms. Swain. Time is money, there's no time like the present, and time keeps on slipping into the future," Roger said.

Typical Roger, I thought. *Too far, too soon, too fast, too much.*

"What is your name again?" Diane Grace said.

"Leanne Haskins," I said. "Tomorrow morning would be—"

"Not you. The handsome young man with time on his mind," Diane Grace said.

"Theo Milo," Roger said. "At your service, Ms. Swain. And thank you for calling me a young man. Looking forward to returning the compliment up close and in person."

Roger looked away from the camera and winked at me. It was a cocky wink that said, *Look at me. I haven't even met her yet, and I have her in the palm of my hand.* I'd seen that same wink twice in the last three months: once before he got cracked in the head with a cast-iron teapot and once before he took a canister of mace in the face.

I turned so neither of us was facing the security camera and said softly, "Dial it down, or we'll never get this meeting."

"Relax," he said, "and watch me work my magic."

I turned back to the camera and hit the speaker. "We can be

here tomorrow morning at eight thirty, Ms. Swain. If you give us ten minutes, we'll give you—"

The buzzer sounded, the door clicked open, and Diane Grace said, "Come to the second floor and convince me you're the best brokers in Brooklyn."

27

REALTOR RAZZLE-DAZZLE

THE MANSION WAS OPULENT WITH A CAPITAL *HOLY SHIT, ARE YOU kidding me?* The large parlor on the second floor was breath-taking—marble and granite and oak, impossibly expensive Tiffany lamps, grand and gorgeous American antique furniture from centuries past, handwoven rugs that cost more than a house in the suburbs, original artwork in ornate gold frames, a fireplace big enough to park a compact car, and a mint-condi-tion, Steinway grand piano that had to be one hundred and fifty years old.

Roger and I waited in the parlor for Diane Grace to make her grand entrance. I expected her to be worldly, shrewd, and privileged. I expected her to be more beautiful than me, more stylish than me, and younger than me by three years.

What I didn't expect was that when Diane Grace made her grand entrance, it wouldn't be Diane Grace. But it wasn't. It was her mother, Diane Mason, Sam's wife, now seventy-eight years old. Still stunning, her hair was a sophisticated silver gray, styl-ishly cut so that she looked like the American Ambassador to Somewhere Beautiful. She was certainly dressed that way—international designer labels from head to toe. She was nearly eighty, don't get me wrong, but she looked damn good for her age.

"I'm Diane Swain," she said, crossing the room, hand extended, eyes focused on Roger. "Confidence excites me, Mr. Milo."

Roger and Diane shook hands for what I thought was two seconds too long, and then she turned her attention to me.

"Pleasure to meet you, Ms. Haskins," she said. "I assume you handle marketing and management and Mr. Milo meets the public."

And just like that, she had me backpedaling and off balance. She'd measured me without my even knowing she'd taken out her yardstick and created instant leverage in our negotiation. Sam had taught her well.

We shook hands, and I said, "I think Theo is possibly the best building representative I've ever seen, so, yes, you're right, Diane. I run the shop, and Theo closes deal after deal after deal. We've got both ends covered."

By using her first name without being invited to, I had re-leveled the playing field—at least so I wasn't free-falling on my ass in front of her.

She invited us to join her in a cozy corner of the parlor, sat on an antique settee as if she were a duchess, and gestured for us to begin.

Over the years, I had worked as a residential real estate receptionist several times, so I knew the lingo. Competitive market analysis, Multiple Listing Service, title insurance, assumable financing, contingency clause, earnest money, curable defects, and planned unit development...I threw them all into the mix with Realtor razzle-dazzle.

Roger followed my lead, and our theatrical chemistry clicked. We had energy. We had passion. We had experience. We had knowledge. We were the best brokers for the new Swain building in Brooklyn. Diane Mason even said so, applauding us when we were done. She appreciated our persistence, commended our confidence, and respected our resolve. She also said she owed it to tomorrow's invitees to follow through with their interviews but not to worry: though the ink wasn't dry and the deal wasn't sealed, it was fait accompli that Haskins Milo would be selling dwellings for Swain Properties.

Assuming, that is, Theo—Roger—was available for drinks that evening.

Huh? I thought.

Aside from the bizarre factoid that the imaginary Haskins Milo Brokerage Company had won their first contract, the whole thing was surreal for three reasons, more probably, but three that occurred to me without trying. Reason one: it was totally unexpected that we would be invited inside the swank Swain townhouse on the spot—we were here to join tomorrow's cattle call; today wasn't part of the plan. Reason two: it was totally unexpected that it was Diane Mason and not Diane Grace who'd invited us in and then hired us—it was the mother's Williamsburg building, not the daughter's, my mistake for Google searching Diane Swain instead of Diane Grace Swain. Reason three, and this is the one that was skewed on a skewer: Diane Mason was hot for Roger.

I mean sexually. I mean she wanted to have sex with him. It was the look in her eye, the hand on his knee, the lecherous smile on her seventy-eight-year-old lips. Having sex with Roger was practically a contract clause, for God's sake. Roger had seen the signs the same as I had and, to his credit, had stayed in character and, more or less, assented without saying so to some seventy-eight-year-old bump and grind after a few Sunday night cocktails. The show must go on, after all.

She moved us to the bar—leading Roger by the hand—to celebrate our bravura matinee and poured bourbon neat (Pappy Van Winkle 23!) in gorgeous crystal tumblers that had to cost four hundred dollars each, and I thought, *It's now or never.*

"I have to admit we were surprised to find you here, Diane," I said. "We thought the Swain building in Brooklyn belonged to Diane Grace. This is her townhouse, isn't it?"

"This is my townhouse. Diane Grace owns a loft in SoHo," she said.

"But she uses this address for deliveries and such, is that correct?" I said.

"Not that I'm aware," she said. "I don't understand the question."

"It's just that we were sure Diane Grace lived here," I said. "It turns out we have a mutual friend, and if she did live here, if it were her townhouse, if it were her Williamsburg building, if we had seen *her* today, we would have mentioned our mutual friend and expressed our concern about him, something we were meaning to do."

Her radar turned on and tuned in. I saw her ears perk up, her eyes narrow.

"I'm surprised you and my daughter would have a mutual friend," she said. "Who could that possibly be?"

"Dave Griffin," I said. "From Blue Bar. We know she's dating him."

She wasn't as good an actor as I was. Her cheeks flushed, and she couldn't hide it. "So that I can pass it along to Diane Grace, what, exactly, is your concern?"

"We heard he's embezzling money from the bar and betting it big with a bookie to pay off a dangerous debt," Roger said.

"If it's true, he's in trouble, and we'd like to help him if we can," I said. "Maybe your daughter knows about it. Maybe he's confided in her."

"And then maybe she's confided in you," Roger said.

Diane Mason put her four-hundred-dollar tumbler on the bar, moved to a priceless, Early American, antique chest, and with her back to us, took something from the top drawer and froze.

I looked at Roger as if to say, *What the fuck?*

He put his hand up as if to say, *I got this.* And then he tapped his right palm with his left index finger to remind me that he had her in the palm of his hand.

Cocky, cocky, cocky, I thought.

"Diane, really, it's okay," Roger said as he crossed the parlor to where her back was turned. "We'll have a few drinks, we'll talk it out, no big—"

Except when he was ten feet from her, she spun around and shot him point-blank with a Taser.

The probes exploded out of the electroshock weapon at a hundred miles per hour, sliced through Roger's royal-blue shirt with ease, dug deep into his skin like fishhooks, and with Roger's flesh and bone completing the circuit, delivered fifty thousand volts of electricity in the blink of an eye.

Roger screamed in unbearable pain, lost all control of his muscles as the high-voltage power hijacked his central nervous system, and fell to the ground in a stiff, spasmodic fit.

I watched him twitch in pain and felt like I was in shock too —admittedly, not the kind or level of shock as poor Roger. After five seconds, I recovered sufficiently to follow the probes from Roger's chest back down the copper wires to the Taser in Diane Mason's hand. Her eyes were already focused on me. I thought about punching her in the nose, but before I could pull myself together, she ejected the spent Taser cartridge, clicked in a fresh one, and aimed the thing at me. Roger, she knew, was out of the game.

"Dave told me you might come," she said. "He bought me this Taser and told me the lizards from Trenton could crawl through the tunnel anytime."

"What are you talking about?" I said, realizing Roger needed assistance and hurrying to him while he groaned on the ground.

"My daughter's not dating Dave Griffin," she said. "I am."

She might as well have shot *me* with the fucking Taser. "*You're* dating him?"

"Not dating him, exactly. Paying him for sex."

"You're paying Dave Griffin for sex?"

"Don't sound so shocked. It's the twenty-first century. He's young and virile, and I'm rich and ready to roll in the hay. He doesn't need to embezzle money. I give him plenty of it. He bets it at his bar, and I get laid. Everybody wins. Wait until you're seventy-eight before you judge me. You want to screw some old-timer who needs a pill to get it hard? I don't. I'm still hot to trot, and I want a man who can keep up and keep it up."

The flowers were for her, Diane Mason, not Diane Grace, I thought.

"Why don't you just pay off his debt?" I said, helping Roger to his feet. His legs were Jell-O. His eyes rolled like loose marbles.

"Because then the ride's over, and I'll need a new horse."

"I volunteer," Roger said. "Just don't Tase me, bro." He laughed, albeit weakly, at his own joke, which was how I knew he was going to be fine.

"That ship sailed, handsome," she said. "Not to mention you're a tad too old for my taste. Now run back to Trenton and tell your boss his business is with Dave and not me, and next time he sends a couple of yahoos here, I'll have a shotgun instead of a Taser."

"Jesus," I said, helping Roger wobble across the parlor to the door. "Are all old rich people as sick as you?"

"The horny ones," she said.

As I led Roger down the stairs and out onto East 68th Street, I wasn't thinking about I'll-need-a-new-horse Diane Mason Swain, and I wasn't thinking about don't-Tase-me-bro Roger Platt. The one and only thought in my mind was this: *It's not Dave Griffin with his hand in Blue's register. And if it's not Griff, then who is it?*

28

IF PAST IS PROLOGUE

I WRANGLED ROGER TO THE CORNER OF 68TH STREET AND FIFTH Avenue and hailed a cab. The worst was over, but it looked like he had thrust three fingers into a high-voltage outlet. His eyes were glassy and his legs lurched and leaned and waived and wobbled, and I swear it smelled like his hair had been burned, although I could have been imagining that last one. I asked him if he was okay, and he answered with AC/DC, which he sang with as much heart as a Tased man could muster, which seemed appropriate to me given the intensity of the electric surge that had recently rocked his body.

"My nerves are shaking, my bones are quaking, my mind is aching, and I'm not faking it..." His voice lost power after that, though he had enough energy left to laugh and say, "I'll be here all week, folks. Don't forget to tip your waitress." He told me he hadn't felt like this since he'd eaten three grams of hash when he was a young buck, and for that reason he'd choose getting Tased over getting pepper-sprayed or cracked in the head with a cast-iron teapot any day and twice on Sunday. I pointed out that today was Sunday, and he said, "Maybe only once, then."

A checker pulled to the corner. I put Roger in the backseat, gave the cabbie sixty bucks, and sent Roger to his sister's house in Jackson Heights, his crash pad when used car sales were slow, shrimp deliveries were thin, janitorial hours were spare, spending money was tight, and rent went unpaid.

I spent the rest of Sunday doing my usual Sunday things. I washed my clothes, paid my bills, cleaned my house, read my lines, and went to Raul's, where I started with the speed bag and thought about horny Diane Swain and her gambling gigolo, Dave Griffin. That was a curveball I never saw coming. *Swing and a miss*, Jimmy would have said.

"Wait until you're seventy-eight before you judge me," Diane Swain had said. *But even then*, I thought, *even at seventy-eight years old, who am I to judge someone else's sex life?* Oh sure, the mental image of Diane and Griff shaking the sheets made me retch in my throat, but my love life was as screwed up as anyone's. When it comes to the horizontal mambo, people feel what they can feel, do what they can do, and get what they can get. Don't they? Isn't that what Journey said in "Any Way You Want It"?

And then I stopped hitting the speed bag and let an epiphany wash over me. *You're taking love-life lessons from Journey, you idiot. No wonder you're a mess with men.*

I moved to the wall of mirrors and did ten rounds of shadowboxing, meaning move and duck and move and slip and move and jab and move and hit as if I were in a real ring in a real fight—three minutes on, one minute off, three minutes on, one minute off, three minutes on—for ten brutal rounds while counting my punches and watching my feet in the mirrors, that niggling, ubiquitous Journey song still playing in my head. Damn you, "Any Way You Want It."

In the second minute of round four, my brain bounced to Blue. I hadn't been deeply involved with a man in a good long while. I'd gone on plenty of dates, don't get me wrong, and had flings that were fun and a few unfortunate one-night stands I was still expunging from my memory banks (don't judge me until you're forty-five and single), but I hadn't had a meaningful emotional connection, a smoking-hot, blood-boiling bond, a love-is-blind-and-so-am-I relationship with a man in years. *The Harriman Affair* changed that for me, and then right after that there was Peter Mills, the rock star/triathlete/real estate broker who was, cough-cough, considerably younger than me, and both of those heat-seeking hookups had thrown me for a loop.

Which is why I was gun-shy about Blue.

Where was my head? Could I trust my own romantic judgment? If past is prologue, then how could I tell the difference between a real romance and the no-calorie, caffeine-free imitation? I was in no condition to think this through. My mind was preoccupied, wrapped up in a case I couldn't crack. I couldn't hear the Music of Love, forget sing along. The sonnets of my heart might as well have been written in Swahili. I couldn't feel the road beneath my feet, much less the wind beneath my wings.

But I *could* still feel the heat on my neck, Blue's arms around me, my arms around him, his lips on my lips. Oh yes, I could still feel that. I could see my reflection in his beautiful eyes. I could feel our hearts beating when we were close, his body against mine. I could imagine myself falling for him and him falling for me. Hadn't we been doing that all week? We were so easy together, so honest with each other. At least *I* thought so. And Blue had made me feel as if he thought so too. It was so good. Too good. Good enough to get lost in.

I'm in the deep end, I thought, *and I have to get to the side before I go under.*

And with that thought, it was settled. I would swim to safety, solve my case, and move on with my life. It was the smart, sensible, and professional thing to do. I would stop before I started. Later on, I would worry about the romantic aftershocks—such as they always were in my life.

I went to the heavy bag, hit it hard, and cleared my mind. In the open glade appeared Red Maple Horse Farm.

Oh right, Red Maple Horse Farm.

Tonight, at eleven o'clock, I was scheduled to walk straight into a trap in the horse country of Connecticut. When that kind of thing slips your mind, it's possible you need to reorder your priorities.

Red Maple Horse Farm was located on Catamount Road in Fairfield, Connecticut, about an hour and a half north and east of the House of Emotional Tics. Earlier in the week, I had mapped out the way there so Fu and I could park the White Whale half a klick from the horses. It was an easy trip: Cross County Parkway to Hutchinson River Parkway, left at the fork to 684, to 202, to 7, and then local roads to the farm.

Fortunately, the public records at the Fairfield tax assessor were online, so a few quick clicks and the deed for Red Maple Horse Farm was on my screen. Jack Lowe was not listed on the deed, which is why, I reasoned, his partners had not mentioned the place to Logan after Jack went missing—they didn't know about it. The name on the deed was Kristina Hannon. Who the hell was she? I went diving through a dozen Web screens and discovered Kristina Hannon was Jack Lowe's mother—Hannon was her maiden name. She had purchased Red Maple Horse Farm three years ago. So it was his mother's place? Was that the connection? I called the Fairfield tax assessor's office, said I was an IRS criminal investigation special agent, scared the daylights out of a young clerk named Deborah, who, I said, would soon be a suspect if her cooperation was not forthcoming, and discovered, with some digging by Deborah, that Jack Lowe had paid the Red Maple taxes since the deed was transferred to his mother's maiden name.

Why in the world would McSteamy pay the taxes on his mother's horse farm? His mother was a super-successful divorce attorney in her own right. The taxes on Red Maple would be pocket change to her. So did she buy him the place? The farm was a million five. Jack Lowe could handle that number with ease. Did he buy Red Maple using her name without telling her? Why would he do that? And why would he keep it secret from his partners, from his wife? And why choose his horse farm for a late-night rendezvous after vanishing into thin air? Why vanish in the first place? I would ask him all this and more in person in about six hours.

I went home, showered, ate the other half of what I casually called "Heaven Between Two Slices of Beautiful Bread"—chicken cutlet, fresh mozz, and pesto from Faicco's on Bleecker Street—set my alarm, closed my eyes, and took a two-hour nap.

There was no point wearing the red wig and green contacts. For all intents and purposes, Texan Emily Baynes was as dead as worldwide weatherwoman Wanda Ward. So I pulled my hair back in a ponytail, put on black jeans, a black sweatshirt, and black Nikes, packed Jimmy's six-inch restorer's pry bar and his automatic Colt .45 pistol—my pistol—in a little black backpack, and met Fu at Warren's White Whale, hoping that after eleven o'clock I wouldn't be as dead as Emily and Wanda.

29

IT WAS AN INVITATION IS WHAT IT WAS

IT WAS A NINETY-MINUTE RIDE TO RED MAPLE, AND AFFAIRS OF the heart were on my mind. I wanted to ask Fu if he'd ever been married or in love or tied somehow to a significant other —partly because I didn't like to drive and none of Warren's Toyotas had a radio to distract me from the fact that I was driving, partly because I was forever curious about my smart-aleck, Chinese mob assassin handyman, and partly because I was sick of wallowing in my own romantic stew. It was true I knew worlds more about Fu now than I did even three months ago—the fact that he could speak more than six words of English for one thing, that he could bake and decorate cakes like Duff Goldman for another, that he made bird movies in China for yet one more, and that his childhood story had an astounding start: once upon a time, Fu never knew his mother, was abandoned by his father, and was raised by a shifu to be a stone-cold killing machine. But I didn't know a thing above or below or deeper or wider than he wanted me to know.

Anyway, I couldn't ask him anything because he had his iPod plugged into his ears, and he listened to Italian opera at high volume from the moment we left East 83rd Street to the moment I turned the Toyota onto Catamount Road.

I killed the lights, pulled the White Whale off the dark, stone wall-lined, two-lane road into the even darker shadows, and pointed through the windshield to the gated entrance of Red Maple Horse Farm, about a quarter mile farther up Catamount.

"That's it," I said to Fu. "Fourteen acres, manor house, three barns, detached garage, big garden shed, two fenced paddocks, one fenced riding ring, and four fenced pastures. I'll take the —" I turned to look at him, and he was gone.

"Fu here," he said, outside the car and tapping the driver's-side window.

My heart practically jumped through my chest. "Jesus, Fu," I said, rolling down the window. (None of Warren's old-model, stripped-down Toyotas had electric windows or electric locks or electric anything.) "Don't do that."

"Fu go," he said, already running up the dark road toward Red Maple. He wore black from top to bottom.

"Where?" I called after him without trying to raise my voice at all—sort of a yelling whisper.

"Into night," he said, and then he leapt over the stone wall like a cheetah or a gazelle or a cheetah chasing a gazelle and vanished into a Red Maple pasture.

"Fucking Fu," I said to myself, thinking there was no way anyone would believe how fast and graceful and balletic and powerful and violent one extra-large Chinese man could be.

I followed Fu down Catamount, over the stone wall, and into the pasture, but I didn't see him anywhere. He had disappeared, as he'd said, into night.

There was just enough moonlight to see the silhouetted barns and buildings in the distance, maybe a football field away. Was it a two-acre pasture? A three-acre pasture? Four? Five? More? Less? I couldn't tell. Estimating Connecticut horse country acreage in the middle of the night turned out to be something I sucked at. It was far enough away for me to have time to become conscious about how nervous I was, I'll tell you that.

I stayed low and started for the manor house. My heart beat faster with each step I took. I had no idea why I stayed low— maybe because people did it in the movies or maybe so Jack's horses wouldn't freak out that some middle-of-the-night intruder was intruding in their pasture in the middle of the night. Except there were no horses. The pasture was empty. *Why are there no horses?* I thought. *It's a horse farm. Don't horse farmers leave their horses outside overnight to do whatever it is horses do in dark pastures until daybreak? Or do they bring them into the barn because of wolves? Jesus, are there wolves in the wilds of Connecticut? Shit, I hate the idea of wolves in the wilds of Connecticut. I hate even thinking about the idea of wolves in the wilds of Connecticut. Where's a fucking horse farmer's horse when you need one?*

The point is I knew I wasn't in Montana. The point is I knew there weren't wolves in the woods on Catamount Road in Connecticut. The point is your head does funny things when you're crossing Jack Lowe's pasture in the middle of the night on your way into a trap.

I reached the fence at the far end of the field and went to my knees. There was a large barn—a farm barn, with tractors and bales of hay and other gear, down a gravel road to my left and a smaller barn beyond that. To my right, the gravel road led to another big barn, a horse barn. The manor house was straight ahead. It was a classic New England Colonial (originally built in 1810, according to the deed). It was white with black shutters and two stone chimneys—postcard picturesque. The house was dark.

I took Jimmy's Colt—my Colt—out of my backpack. I didn't like guns. I had never liked guns. Guns scared me—they were heavy, they smelled like oil, they made a big bang when they went off, and if one went off in your direction, you might just die. Jimmy didn't like guns either, but he had one. *"You can't shoot someone before they shoot you unless you have a gun,"* he once said. *"That doesn't mean I'm a hothead lug nut who wants to run around town shooting the shit out of Cheyenne. It means I don't want to get shot."*

I didn't want to get shot. Exactly.

The wide gate was unlatched. I pushed it open and went through. The air was cold on my face. Not see-your-breath cold, but cold enough to know winter was on the way. I stood in the grass at the edge of the gravel road, took a breath to steady my nerves, and then moved across the road to the house. The gravel crunched beneath my feet, which is a sound you don't often hear in New York City. In the quiet, horse country night, it sounded incredibly loud to me, like I was cracking concrete with a jackhammer, and I cursed Jack Lowe for not paving his damn driveway.

I circled the manor house, peering into windows, as silent as I could be. There were no lights on inside. Not one solitary lamp. I went around the back of the house. On the far side, I could see the detached garage and the big garden shed. No lights there either. I continued down the front of the house. Nothing. No sounds, no lights, no evidence of anyone inside. I arrived back at the gravel road and looked toward the farm barn and the barn beyond that. Both buildings were completely dark. The Colt was heavy in my hand. My breath was fast and shallow. I looked down the road in the opposite direction and saw lights on inside the horse barn.

Shit, I thought. *Were they on from the beginning? Did I miss them in the deafening roar of the crunching gravel? Or did Jack just turn the freaking lights on right now? Why the hell are the lights on in the horse barn all of a sudden?*

Because it was an invitation, that's why.

I heard Tom Bodett's voice in my head: *We'll leave the light on for you.*

Fuck you, Tom Bodett, I said to myself, and then I took it back because I liked Tom Bodett and would stay in any motel, even a Motel 6, where Tom was leaving the light on for me.

I walked on the grass and moved cautiously toward the horse barn. It was painted the same white with black trim as the other buildings and had black shutters on the sides. The huge front doors were closed. Each door had a window, and each window was lit up from inside the barn.

The thing about walking into a trap is you actually, physically, have to walk into it in order to walk into it, and my legs weren't going anywhere. I looked at the Colt. *Here we go,* I said to myself, and I pulled the front doors open.

The center aisle was very wide, maybe fourteen feet. The floor was hard dirt. There were twenty stalls, ten per side. There were horses in some of the stalls. I could hear them snorting and breathing and moving around.

Jack Lowe was seated in a chair three-quarters of the way down the barn and in the center of the aisle. Not all the lights in the barn were turned on, and he was in a dark patch, in the shadows. The double doors behind him were wide open.

"Hello, Jack," I said, pointing my gun at him. "I'm holding a loaded Colt, and if anything moves anywhere, I'm going to blow the shit out of it, including you."

He didn't answer. His feet were flat on the ground, and his hands were in his lap. *He's got a gun too,* I thought.

I stood in the doorway, afraid to walk into the damn barn. "I have a couple questions for you. The first one is, why is your mother's name on the deed? Well, maybe that's not the first question. Maybe the first question is, how come none of your partners, including your wife, how come none of them know about your horse farm? Actually, that's not the first question either. The first question is did you disappear on Wednesday because you hired a corporate killer to murder one of your partners on Friday? Yes, yes, that's it. That's the first question. Did you do that Jack? Did you hire someone to kill Lisa?"

No answer. I forced my legs to move and started down the center aisle, keeping one eye on the divorce lawyer and the other on the stalls. My chest was burning. My knees were weak. My head was spinning. I was a single mother in way over my head. But I was also an actor, and I refused to let Jack Lowe think I was scared of him. "Or maybe Christopher? What about Michelle? I know you were sleeping with her until she caught you sleeping with her paralegal. Yeah, I know about all that."

And still he said nothing. He didn't move a muscle. I stopped in the middle of the barn, under the solitary amber bulb, and the fear I'd been feeling turned into an overwhelming sense of dread.

"Oh, Jack," I said, and I took three more steps toward him and saw that he was tied to the chair, skin a pale, sickly blue, eyes open, dead as a dime. He was in a suit but was barefoot. There was no blood on him—he'd been suffocated somehow. I stared at him for a long moment in which I thought of my father, tied to a chair just like this (except with his eyes shot out), and my stomach went queasy. I wanted to vomit, but I didn't. I let the image of Jimmy rip through me like a cyclone.

Just as I came out the other side of that terrible picture but before I could turn around and get the hell out of the barn, something heavy hit me hard on the back of the head and there was a moment of deep pain, and then everything went black.

30

———

I HOPE YOUR HEART EXPLODES

First thing I thought was my head hurt. Then I thought I must have a bump on the back of my skull the size of a golf ball and wondered if my hair was soaked with blood. Then I couldn't get my eyes open and thought I'd try to open them again in a minute and reached up to see how bad the bump was and discovered I couldn't move my arms. That freaked me out, and I tried to stand up and couldn't move my legs. I forced my eyes open and saw I was sitting in a chair and that I was tied to the chair—arms roped to my sides, legs roped to each other— and the chair was placed twenty feet in front of and facing Jack Lowe, who was as dead as I'd first found him, face still that horrifying hospital blue, eyes staring vacantly into infinity.

"Good morning."

The voice was behind me. All I could see was Jack Lowe and the open barn doors beyond him and the dark night beyond that.

"How long was I out?" I said.

"Seven minutes unconscious. Twenty-two minutes back and forth."

"Why didn't you kill me?"

"I was waiting to see."

"See what?"

"If your Chinese friend made the trip."

Fu, I thought. "He had other plans."

"What a shame. For you, I mean."

I felt a hand on my shoulder, and it froze me solid.

"Probably for you too," I said. "I mean, he's cleaned your clock twice in a row. That has to burn your ass."

And then he came around me so I could see his back as he walked to Jack Lowe.

"I tend not to take these things personally," he said, circling around Jack so that he was facing me, Jack on his left side. "I'm a professional."

He was taller than me, maybe five ten or an inch more. And he was trim and fit. He wore a gray ski mask pulled all the way down, black pants, a black leather jacket, and gray leather gloves. In his right hand, he held Jimmy's Colt—my Colt.

"You're a murderer," I said.

"A service provider," he said, "for the masters and champions of business and finance. Ask Jack."

"I was going to," I said, "except now he's dead."

"There is that," the killer said, moving away from Jack Lowe to the second to last horse stall on my left, where a horse was sticking its muzzle through the top half of the open Dutch door. The killer stroked the horse. "He bought this farm in his mother's name. It was his love nest. He came here for extramarital rides in the hay, so to speak. It's worth a million seven."

"How do you know what it's worth?" I said.

"He offered it to me—lock, stock, and barrel if I let him live. He said he'd had it appraised for a million seven. I told him the money meant nothing to me. I'm exceptionally well compensated for my work. My net worth is fivefold more than his. I told him I'd buy my own horse farm if I wanted one, which I don't, by the way. I'm not a horse person per se, although I enjoy the trotters now and again."

"Jimmy liked the trotters," I said. "I went with him half a dozen times. He called it 'a guaranteed good day.'" My head hurt but not so much that I didn't recognize how surreal it was to be talking trotters with the man who'd murdered my father.

The killer nodded and patted the horse. "There's something hypnotic about watching these enormous animals—twelve hundred pounds of power and muscle—control their gait when what they want to do, what they were born to do, is run like a locomotive until their hearts explode."

"I hope *your* heart explodes," I said.

"You're angry at me for killing your father," he said.

"Cut these ropes," I said, "and I'll redefine anger for you."

He walked to me, stopped three strides in front of me.

"Your father was warned. He wouldn't stop. He was arrogant and crude and disrespectful. He said terrible things to me before I shot him in the eyes. Your father chose death. I gave him what he asked for."

My heart was pounding with grief and rage and violence and loss. Tears came to my eyes. I couldn't hold them back. "Fuck you," I said, crying now. "Fuck you, fuck you, fuck you, fuck you..."

I heard my voice dissolve into sobs. The killer stood right there, directly in front of me, and watched me weep. I knew he was going to kill me. I knew I needed to focus, but all I could think of was Matthew. It was my son's life that flashed first before my eyes, and I fell into a black hole of fear and pain and heartbreak and regret.

I don't know how long I was lost, but then I saw an image of Jimmy. We were at Yankee Stadium, sitting in the bleachers, keeping score, drinking beer, and I had the conscious thought that I didn't want him to see me this way—crying like a third-grade girl, snot flowing out of my nose, shoulders heaving. I don't know how, but I pulled myself together and caught my breath. *If I'm going down*, I thought, *I'm going like Jimmy's daughter.*

"Put the gun down, take the ropes off, and give me five minutes," I said. "I'll show you what my father was trying to say."

The killer nodded and smiled. "The apple didn't fall far from the tree. Your father said more or less the very same thing."

Then he walked to Jack and adjusted Jack's head, tilting it back so Jack's chin was pointing up or at least more directly at me. "What I like about you is you're not a link in the law enforcement chain of command. You're not married to mundane government incompetence. You're not part of an inept and predictable emergency task force passing the buck up and down the departmental ladder, paralyzed by fear of failure and lack of intelligence. It's routine for me to outsmart the establishment, and I admit I've been a bit bored this last little while. Can you blame me? When you're ten steps ahead of everyone in the game every time you play, it's easy to become complacent. And complacency is the enemy of excellence, and so it is my enemy."

I was no shrink, and I was in no emotional or psychological condition to even play one on TV, but even with his ski mask on, I had the sense that this corporate killer was pure id—all impulse, all gratification. He had no superego whatsoever. Zero. None. No sense of right and wrong. No part of his persona deciding what was rational or realistic, what was moral or immoral, what was good or what was evil. He was a complete egomaniac, possessed by delusions of extreme personal greatness.

"Which is why you were so entertaining at first—a breath of fresh air," he said, and he walked back to where I was sitting. The horse he'd been stroking lost interest and pulled back into its stall. Jack's head fell forward.

"Anything could happen with you," he said. "You were a wild card. And there's a certain excitement to that, no doubt. But all roller coasters eventually arrive back at the station, as they must. What I don't like about you is that you're not smart enough to hold my attention. You've become a distraction, and distractions are bad for business."

"The police know I'm here," I said.

"I hope so," he said.

"They're going to fry your ass and I'm going to...wait...you hope so?" I said.

"I do," he said. "I want the Connecticut Keystone Cops to catch me this time—because it won't be me. It will be you."

I looked at the killer, and then I looked at Jack Lowe, and then I looked at the killer.

"Think," he said. "Be the Little Engine That Could."

"The eyes," I said.

He smiled and nodded and then walked back to Jack and lifted Jack's chin again. The blue tint of Jack's dead face made me nauseous, and I felt like I could puke any second, although that might have been the truth of the moment dawning on me.

"Yes," he said, holding up the Colt. "You shot Jack Lowe in the eyes, and then you shot yourself in the head with the same gun, this gun, your gun. Jack's farm manager will find him in his chair and you on the barn floor this morning at seven a.m. —because you never really told the police you were coming here—and *he* will call the local police after he stops hyperventilating, and the local police, when they're done tripping all over themselves, will declare it the perfect murder-suicide, and they'll bring in Detective Logan, who will admit to himself that he knew it was you all along. Which will be wonderful for him until the next time I work, at which point I'm hopeful Logan will realize what a troglodyte he truly is."

"Logan's no caveman. You don't know him. You've never met him."

"You're wrong, of course. I've met him many times. Do you think it's an accident he's the detective of record for my events?"

And then there were police sirens in the distance.

"And in true wild card fashion, you really did call them," he said.

"Maybe I did. Maybe I didn't. It's hard to remember. Let's wait until they get here and ask them."

"Let's not," he said, and he stepped to my right side and put the Colt to my head. I could taste the salt from my tears in my mouth. I strained against the ropes, but it was hopeless.

And then there was the sound of a horse galloping toward the barn.

"Do you hear that?" I said.

He must have heard it because he lowered the gun and walked toward Jack and the rear of the barn. The sirens were louder now—still in the distance but coming toward Red Maple.

Just as the killer reached Jack, a massive black horse thundered out of the dark night and into the barn like a locomotive, which is what the killer had said they were born to do, *and Fu was riding the horse bareback.*

The killer lifted the Colt to shoot Fu or the horse or something, but there was no time to fire, only time to get out of the way before he was trampled.

But he couldn't get out of the way. The horse was far too fast and sideswiped him hard and sent him careening across the barn like a rag doll. In that same split-second collision, the Colt .45 went flying deep into one of the horse stalls.

And then the horse was running right at me, and Fu reached down like a rodeo cowboy and lifted me into the air, chair and all—*with one arm*—and the horse galloped out of the far end of the barn and into the night.

We went through an open gate into a pasture, and I heard the sirens getting louder behind us, and then I heard two gunshots, and then I puked and passed out.

31

WE STILL TALKING ABOUT MY MOVIE?

When I woke up, Fu was driving the White Whale to the House of Emotional Tics. I was in the backseat, splayed like a drunk. I sat upright and put on my seatbelt. We were on the Cross County Parkway. It was after midnight. And yet there were cars all around us. Where the hell were all these people going at one in the morning? Probably zero of them, I imagined, were on their way back from a horse ranch where they'd nearly been murdered. Probably that was just me.

Fu had his earbuds in and was listening to Italian opera at decibels generally associated with jet engines and KISS concerts. It didn't seem safe to me that he was driving without being able to hear the traffic zipping past us on the parkway, but it also occurred to me that I might not be the best judge of what was safe, seeing as how about an hour ago I'd willingly walked into a trap, been knocked out and tied to a chair, and then had Jimmy's gun—my gun—pointed at my head by the man who'd murdered my father. Safe? Unsafe? How the hell would I know?

Fu found a parking spot on 81st between First and York. We walked back to the brownstone in silence. There were so many things I wanted to ask him—what took him so long to ride to the rescue, for instance—but everything hurt, including my pride, and I just wanted to crawl into bed and think things through. Fu went upstairs to give Al the car keys, and I went to my front door, where LaTanya had taped today's *Kung Fu Fu* call sheet. Rehearsal time was eight forty-five a.m. It was one forty-five a.m.

I never made it to my bed. I sat on my sofa, gave myself ten minutes to reconcile Red Maple and recalculate the whole Lowry Lowe equation, and fell fast asleep.

LaTanya buzzed my buzzer at eight forty-three. I stumbled to the intercom.

"Where you at, McCall?" LaTanya said. "You ready for your close-up?"

She was a whirlwind of a woman. One part Queen Latifah, one part Whoopi Goldberg, one part Tina Turner, and one part Clair Huxtable (if not Phylicia Rashad) when Cliff had done something to tick her off—a force to be reckoned with under any circumstances.

We moved into the House of Emotional Tics on the same day two and a half years ago. She lived in apartment 3B. To make money, she drove a cab, a yellow Volvo station wagon, for which she owned the medallion with her brother, Anthony, a six-foot-eight inch, three hundred fifty-pound behemoth known by all as Mountain.

"Two minutes," I said into the intercom.

"That's all you got," LaTanya said. "After that, you late. And if you late—"

"You infuriate," I said. "I know, I know."

"Infuriate, complicate, constipate, obfuscate, incinerate, obliterate, annihilate, adulterate, disintegrate, and debilitate," she said.

"Are you done? Because now I only have one minute," I said.

"Fifty-nine, fifty-eight, fifty-seven, fifty-six..."

I clicked off, threw on jeans and a sweatshirt, brushed my teeth, and was out the door in three minutes. LaTanya and Fu were waiting for me in the lobby, sitting next to each other on a little bench near the stairs, across from the mailboxes, reviewing the script.

She was every minute a match for Fu in terms of hard-headed eccentricity, audacious personality, and undaunted ideology.

We became fast friends after Jimmy and I recovered her stolen Volvo one week after it was taken on the very day we both moved into the brownstone. The fact that we returned it with the scumbag thief in the backseat was icing on the cake—especially for Mountain, who introduced himself to the scumbag in a big way.

She was forty-nine years old. Long, beautiful dreads, flawless skin the color of dark chestnut, sharp brown eyes that could burn a hole through your heart or lift your spirit to the clouds, whichever was called for, and a personal encyclopedia of opinions on romance to be taken with a pound of salt, seeing as how she'd been married three times—once for three weeks, once for three days, and once for three hours.

As the saying goes, she did not suffer fools gladly.

We were rehearsing the scene in *Kung Fu Fu* in which LaTanya's character, Captain Rashida Jewel, corners Fu and me in the brownstone lobby. There was no scripted dialogue, just the shape of the scene—LaTanya interrogating her renegade detectives regarding their whereabouts last night.

"You want to tell me where you were, or you want to hand in your badge and your gun? Up to you, Fu," LaTanya said. Captain Jewel had exactly the same tone and temperament as LaTanya. Go figure.

"What am I, chopped liver?" I said. Fu and I stood in the

middle of the lobby while LaTanya walked a loop around and around us. "Why isn't it up to me?"

"Because you can't be trusted with your own car keys, Barnett. That's why," LaTanya said to me.

"And he can?" I said, pointing at Fu. I wasn't particularly acting.

"Fu have more trust in one finger than you have in whole body," Fu said.

"Good. I like it. Keep it going," LaTanya said, dropping out of her actor character and into her director character, which, again, were exactly the same in patois and personality. "There's a world of bullshit between you two. Tension is the key to the Hollywood character castle."

Fu smirked at me. Which was impressive acting on his part because he was smirking at me as Detective Steinberg and also as himself.

"You want to know where we were?" I said to LaTanya. "I'll tell you where we were. We were in Connecticut, at a horse farm, tracking a killer."

"Fu say trap," Fu said to LaTanya. "Fu right. She wrong."

"I wasn't wrong. I knew it was a trap too," I said. "You weren't the only one who knew it was a trap."

"Did you get the killer?" LaTanya said, thinking the horse farm trap was part of the improvisation and acting like a NYPD captain trying to get to the bottom of things with her renegade detectives.

"Close but no cigar," I said. "I was tied to a chair, and Fu saved my life by galloping into the barn on a horse, lifting me up, and riding into the night like Buffalo Bill."

"Where you learn how to ride a horse, Steinberg?" Captain Jewel said to Fu. "They sure as shit got no rodeo in China."

"Exactly," I said. "What the hell with the horse, Fu?"

"Shifu teach Fu ride. When leave Shaolin temple, join Chinese circus. Ride horse. Do many trick."

Chinese circus trick rider? I thought. *Fine. Why not? I'll just add that to the file titled "Things About Fu That Blow My Mind."*

"Was that before or after you were in the mob?" I said.

"Fu run from Shaolin temple when mob come," Fu said. "Join circus. Then mob find Fu."

"And that's why you a renegade cop," LaTanya the director said. "Because you were in the mob. Good work, Fu. Go with it. Your co-star is on fire, McCall. Try to keep up."

"Did you know I was knocked out and tied up?" I said to Fu.

"Fu know," Fu said. "Fu watch."

"Fu watch? *Fu watch?*" I said. "He had the gun at my head. What were you waiting for?"

"Not bad, McCall," LaTanya said, still directing. "Good passion. Good emotion. Keep it real."

"More time talk to killer, more learn," Fu said. "What learn?"

"That's what I want to know, Barnett," Captain Jewel said. "What the hell you learn with a gun to your head?"

I'd learned the killer liked horses, trotters to be specific. I'd learned he was wealthy, or at least that he'd made a pile of cash and could afford to buy a horse farm in Connecticut if he wanted to, which he didn't. I'd learned his ego was as big as Boston, a button I would push later. I'd learned that he knew Logan, that they'd met many times, that Logan was an emotional component of the cases as far as the killer was concerned, that the killer had orchestrated Logan's involvement as the detective of record, and that it was personal for the killer with Logan. And I'd learned that I had made a deep enough impression that I'd become a distraction, a gnat in the night.

"If I can be annoying enough," I said to Fu, "then I can get him to make a mistake."

"Fu say good," Fu said.

We nodded at each other like renegade cop partners speaking a code their renegade captain couldn't crack.

"What you mean *good*, Fu? She already annoying enough...wait," LaTanya said. "We still talking about my movie?"

Just then the brownstone front door buzzer buzzed. Through the frosted glass door, we could see it was two uniformed NYPD police officers.

Fu and I shared a look. He knew why they were here. So did I.

"Fu stop," he said, gesturing at the cops.

"No," I said. "Go downstairs. Stay out of sight. Now, Fu—go, go." I had kept him out of the loop with Logan so far, and I wasn't going to let him in yet.

Fu nodded, though he didn't like it, and hurried down the basement stairs at the back of the lobby.

The officers buzzed again, laying into it this time. "What the hell they want?" LaTanya said.

I started for the door. "Me," I said.

32

THE LYING QUEEN OF LIARS

WE WERE IN A SMALL INTERROGATION ROOM ON THE HOMICIDE
floor, the third floor, of the Thirteenth Precinct, 21st Street
between Second and Third. "We" consisted of me, Logan,
Matthew, and Mel Shavelson, Jimmy's attorney, who somehow
appeared—like a skin rash—whenever I was arrested, which,
including today, if you were counting, was now four times since
the end of July.

"At six o'clock this morning, when I arrived at Red Maple
Horse Farm in Fairfield at the request of the local police department to add my expertise in murders where the eyes of the
victim are shot out of their head, I admit to having a moment of
nausea while standing in front of the late Jack Lowe," Logan
said. He was leaning against the one-way glass, legs crossed,
hands in his pockets, eyes drilling me. "Understand, McCall,
that I have seen a thousand murders over the course of my
career, and so murder, in and of itself, even unspeakably
violent, shoot-your-eyes-out murders, like those of your father
for one, Dr. Stone for two, and Bill Webb for three, even horrific
deaths like those do not so much as register on my intestinal

radar, as far as feeling nauseous is concerned. In fact, I can eat a beef burrito and investigate a homicide with the heat of the hot sauce still in my mouth. So we can safely assume it was not the late Jack Lowe, per se, that made me sick to my stomach. Do you know what it was?"

I was seated at the table with Shavelson, who was as disheveled today as he'd been every day since the reading of Jimmy's will. My son stood near Logan, leaning against a file cabinet.

"The Colt," I said.

"Bingo," Logan said. "They found your father's gun—your gun—in a dark corner of a stable, hidden under the hay."

There was steam coming out of Matthew's ears, he was that hot. But he was a professional prosecutor, so he kept his public persona as cool as he could. But a mother knows when her son is burning.

"The gun could have been there under any number of circumstances, Logan," Shavelson said. "Its presence alone does not signify guilt or even complicity in the crime."

I had my private investigator license in the first place because Jimmy had made me get it and keep it current so I could help him with surveillance and PI paperwork and other monotonies that he couldn't or didn't want to do alone. Especially surveillance, which, as Jimmy would say during the sixth or seventh hour of sitting on a city bench or in a parked car or in a corner booth of a greasy spoon, could suck the soul out of a pope.

While we were on surveillance, Jimmy would sometimes tell me about his lawyer, Mel Shavelson. I never believed the stories. I thought my father was making the man up out of whole cloth, a crazy character creation to kill the time. He *had* to be fiction because no real-life person could actually *be* Mel Shavelson. It wasn't until I was summoned to Shavelson's office, after Jimmy was murdered, that I'd experienced the overweight, out-of-shape, Scotch-drinking, chain-smoking, etiquette-ignoring human hurricane of physical, personal, and professional chaos face-to-freaking-face.

"Shove it, Shavelson," Logan said.

"Shove it, Shavelson," Matthew said.

"Shove it, Shavelson," I said. "What are you even doing here?"

"I have a government mole who alerts me when my clients have been arrested," Shavelson said, grabbing a Pall Mall from his suit coat and letting it dangle from his lips. He already had a pack of Winston sitting on the table and two packs of Marlboro in his briefcase—forget that smoking is illegal indoors and that we were in a police station. I had once seen him smoke all three brands at the same time while drinking Johnnie Black on the rocks at ten in the morning. "I got the call when they took you in and grabbed a cab to defend you. As a reminder, client pays transportation fees."

"I'm not your client," I said.

"That's what Jimmy used to say," Shavelson said.

"You think I killed Jack Lowe?" I said to Logan.

"I think that is a distinct possibility," Logan said. "I will know by the end of the day—as I have requested and received a rush through ballistics—whether you are charged with murder or with obstruction of justice or with excessive stupidity, which will accompany either charge, no doubt."

"We plead in advance to excessive stupidity," Shavelson said.

"Shove it, Shavelson," Logan said.

"Shove it, Shavelson," Matthew said.

"Shove it, Shavelson," I said. "I didn't kill him, Logan. You know I didn't."

"No, I absofuckinglutely do *not* know that, McCall," Logan said. "You were in the fucking barn with the fucking Colt."

"Have you completely lost your mind, Mom?" Matthew

said, sounding a lot like Jimmy. "If the ballistics come back a match, you're in serious trouble."

He was right. Serious trouble would be scratching the surface.

I had no idea if the killer had found the Colt after Fu sideswiped him with the galloping horse and the gun sailed through the air into the stable. I remembered hearing two gunshots before I puked and passed out. Even then I knew Jack Lowe had lost his eyeballs, but was it the Colt?

"For chrissake, McCall," Logan said, crossing the room and leaning over the interrogation table. "I want the goddamn truth, or I swear I will lock you up for the rest of your goddamn life."

"It's finally time to tell the truth, Mom," Matthew said. "Anything you know. *Everything* you know."

Jimmy had told me he always knew when it was finally time to tell the truth. He'd said it was a gut feeling he got when the pressure was about to blow the lid off. I looked at my son and at Logan and even at Shavelson, and it sure seemed like the lid was about to blow—there was steam shooting every which way —but my gut didn't feel the feeling. Instead, my gut was telling me to share as much truth as was needed and not a bit more. Not that my gut could be trusted, of course.

"Yes, I was in the barn with the gun," I said. "The killer kidnapped me and took me there. He was going to frame me for Jack Lowe's murder, even though Lowe was dead in the barn when I got there. He was going to shoot me in the head and then shoot Lowe in the eyes—with the Colt. But then a horse came galloping out of the night through the middle of the barn, and the killer got whacked, and the Colt went flying, and I escaped before he could kill me. That's the truth with a capital *T*."

Okay, maybe not a capital *T*. But there were threads of truth interwoven in that lie, which, as every actor knows, is what makes a lie work—you find the slender reed of honesty in a foggy swamp of deception and make the entirety of the lie about that one thin reed. I'd left Fu out of the story and fabricated the kidnapping component, but the rest rang true because it was true—somewhat true.

I wasn't proud of being a liar. Until I'd inherited Jimmy's business and became a private investigator, I was freaking George Washington when it came to telling the truth. It's why my son was so unhappy with me—because in only three months I'd morphed from the Honest Mom of Matthew into the Lying Queen of Liars. *I might not like myself for being dishonest with the police and my son and even Shavelson*, I thought, *but I'll like it better than being arrested for murdering Jack Lowe.*

"Unabashed bullshit," Logan said.

I knew Logan would say that. If the notes of a symphony were composed of truth and lies, Logan could hear a single subterfuge from a third-row violin buried in an otherwise brazenly truthful operetta.

"The old unabashed-bullshit approach," Shavelson said. "Not a winning prosecutorial plan when it's my client's word against, let's see, no one's."

"Unless the ballistics match the Colt," Matthew said. "Then it's your client's word against the only immutable fact before the jury."

"I'm not his client," I said to Matthew. "I'm your mother."

My son made a face that implied I had embarrassed him, and also made him feel ashamed and furious and sick to his stomach, which broke my heart. What mother wants her son to be ashamed of her? Jesus, I hated my job right then.

"I'm not your client," I said to Shavelson.

"That's what Jimmy used to say," Shavelson said.

After that, there was legal talk that I lost interest in because my mind was jumping ahead, and then Matthew left for court, and Shavelson left to go wherever it was Shavelson went on Monday mornings, and Logan escorted me to the holding cell. He took my purse and locked me inside, and we spoke through the bars.

"I'm assuming you deleted the text messages?" he said.

"From the killer? Yes, I deleted them. His number too. Phone's in my purse. You can check for yourself," I said.

He nodded that he would and turned to walk away.

"The killer knows you," I said.

He stopped dead in his tracks. "Excuse me?"

"When I was in the barn, tied up, looking at the late Jack Lowe, waiting to have my brains blown out, the killer called you a troglodyte, and I said, 'Logan's no caveman. You don't know him. You've never met him.' And he said, 'You're wrong, of course. I've met him many times. Do you think it's an accident he's the detective of record for my events?'"

"You're full of shit," Logan said, but I knew he believed me. It was more that he didn't *want* to believe me.

"I could have thrown you under the bus when my son said it was time to finally tell the truth, to spill anything, everything I knew. But I didn't, Logan. You know why?"

"Enlighten me."

"Because I'm close, and I can get him, and I'm going to get him, and you're going to let me. You're going to help me. That's why."

He was quiet for thirty thoughtful seconds. "You didn't kill Jack Lowe."

"No. Everything was true, more or less true, except for the kidnapping. That was a lie."

"The horse galloping into the barn and sideswiping the killer?"

"True. Ninety percent true."

"Just enough truth-to-lie so the story as a whole cannot totally be disproven."

"I hope so."

He nodded. "*Hope so* won't help you this time, McCall. You better get down on your knees and pray to the Holy Mother of Jesus that that sick motherfucker didn't shoot Jack Lowe with your gun."

33

FUCKING FUCKED UP FOR
EVERYONE INVOLVED

I WENT INTO THE HOLDING CELL AT TEN FORTY-FIVE A.M. I SAT there—with nothing to do but think about my life—until ten past midnight, when Logan let me out.

The ballistics did not match. I imagined the killer was shaken after his run-in with Fu and the horse and shot Jack Lowe's eyes out with his own gun as the sirens got louder, the cops closed in, and time ran out.

"I'm giving you the Colt," Logan said as he signed my release form, "because it was not fired, and the lab was unable to lift readable prints. And I am not at this moment charging you with a crime because in addition to your gun not meeting the threshold of evidence, you have deleted your text messages with the killer, and so your phone has no incriminating qualities either. Instead, I am holding the obstruction of justice charge in abeyance. The paperwork for this charge has been completed and is awaiting activation, which will send you into court, where I will impugn your character, meaning lack thereof, before the judge to the best of my ability, which, after decades in this dog pound, is prodigious, whereby you will spend the next six years in a state penitentiary wishing you had given me the killer's contact information in the first place."

"Thank you, I think."

"Do not thank me, McCall. Do not misconstrue this as a gesture of kindness. I do not like you. You have forged an emotional bond with the serial killer who murdered your father, and you have dragged me into that ill-conceived relationship in a way I find, let's see, what's the phrase, fucking fucked up."

"I didn't drag you in. He said he'd met you many times. I'm the messenger."

"And what if he was lying to you and you are passing this off as truth because *you* believe it to be true and so it seems true but cannot be discerned as actually true or simply true in your misdirected mind? What then? Then I am forced to internalize this as a false fact and act accordingly, which may not be in my best interest because it may be, in fact, false. Case in point, my releasing you with your gun, which, given your proclivity to put your life in danger, is fucking fucked up for everyone involved."

"He wasn't lying. I can tell the difference. I'm an actor. The guy knows you, and you know him. So who is he?"

"Do you have any idea how many liars, losers, and lowlifes I have encountered over the decades? Let's estimate one of each per day. Which adds up as follows: five workdays per week for fifty weeks, two hundred fifty days times three degenerates is seven hundred fifty scrotums, scumbags, and dickwads per year times thirty years is twenty thousand-plus maniacs, morons, and murderers. Where do you suppose I start to find the one you're dating?"

"We're not dating."

"You fooled me. And worse, you fooled him, not to mention yourself. The next time there won't be a horse galloping out of the night to save your ass. The next time you will be dead. So since putting you in prison for your own protection is now at the top of my to-do list and since I am unable to accomplish said task if you are deceased, you will report to me daily as to your communication with the killer. The first day you interact with him without me is the first day you begin your journey to jail. Now get the hell out of my precinct. Jesus Christ, does your brain not work at all?"

It was just like Jimmy would have said it.

I caught a cab outside the precinct. On the way home, I texted the killer with the following thought in mind: if my mission was to crawl under his skin and into his head to cause his ego to cloud his judgment so he would make a mistake so I could catch him, if that was my mission, then I was just the woman for the job. Ask my sister. I'd spent my childhood becoming a Grand Master of Annoyance by practicing on her. If Marilyn hadn't moved to Cleveland when I was twelve, I was headed for the record books. A *Ripley's Believe It or Not* annoyer, that was me.

And the most annoying thing I could do to the egocentric asshole who murdered my father, I figured, was to stay on his case—to hunt him and track him and taunt him and to keep hunting and tracking and taunting him and to tell him over and over that I was on his tail and would never stop. Jesus, it was annoying just thinking about it. He'd had enough of me after the appetizer. He'd made that clear. So now I would give him the all-you-can-eat buffet.

Surprised by your unprofessional performance, I typed into my phone. *Expected more. Thought you were better. How's your head? Has to hurt after being face-planted by a thousand pounds of horse. Though I bet your pride hurts worse than your head. Wanted to let you know I'm going to nail you for Jack Lowe and the others. I'm going to do it for Logan, I'm going to do it for my father, and I'm going to do it to demonstrate you're not special.*

I hit Send with no idea if he'd get the message or not. He might have changed his number and moved to San Fernando or San Bernardino or San Leandro or some San somewhere west. But I didn't think so. I thought he wasn't done with me either.

34

IS THIS PUBLISHERS CLEARING HOUSE?

By the time I got back to the House of Emotional Tics, updated my case notes, drank a glass of Pinot gris, got lost in a mindless movie, and fell into bed, it was four in the morning. The front door buzzer woke me at nine thirty. I don't know what time it first went off, but whoever it was must have been trying to get me for a while because they were leaning on the button.

I'd been dreaming about winning the Publishers Clearing House sweepstakes, about how happy I was that the cash-for-life prize would allow me to quit being a private investigator, leave my life in the dust, move to the Caribbean, and spend the rest of my days in the surf, sand, and sun. There were colorful balloons in the dream and an oversized check with my name near the number one million, as in dollars. My eyes three-quarters closed and my head still holding the dream, I zombie-walked my way to the living room intercom. "If this is Publishers Clearing House, just mail me my money," I said. "Is this Publishers Clearing House?"

"No, this is Blue. Let me in, Kate. I have news."

I buzzed him in. It wasn't until I unlocked and opened my

door that I realized I'd just fallen out of bed. *Oh God…I'm a sleepwalking mess*, I thought.

It was too late to do anything about my appearance because Blue stepped into my apartment, and I smelled leather and musk and didn't know what the hell to do next.

"I woke you," he said, taking me in.

When autumn arrives, I sleep in football jerseys (last night was the Broncos) that just cover my butt—with nothing underneath—and I could see him looking at my legs, which made me self-conscious, though not because of my legs. I had good-looking legs for a forty-five-year-old woman. Granted, they weren't the legs of a thirty-year-old strawberry blonde asking Blue to sign a menu, but they were strong, and they had a nice shape, not too much cellulite, and I had shaved them recently, so they were smooth.

No, the reason I was suddenly self-conscious was because of the *way* Blue was looking at my legs…and not just my legs. The way he was looking at all of me. I had seen that look before—in his office, on Saturday, when we kissed like there was no tomorrow.

"You have news," I said, trying to take my mind off how handsome he was, how good he smelled, how hot the back of my neck was getting.

"Griff quit yesterday," he said. "I tried to get you, but you didn't answer your phone."

"I was in jail," I said.

"You were what?"

"Not important now."

He nodded, took off his leather jacket, and dropped it on my couch. I could feel myself swooning. It was just Sunday, at Raul's, that I'd told myself I wasn't going to do this, that I wasn't going to get involved, that I wasn't going to fall for him, that I was in the deep end and had to swim to safety before I went under. Two days ago. Jesus.

"It's not him," Blue said, taking a step toward me.

"I know. I went to see Diane Swain on Sunday. Griff has sex with her for money and then bets the cash at Blue Bar with Stanley Stein. I would have told you Monday, but I got arrested. How do *you* know it wasn't him?"

I took a step toward him. The heat was racing through me now, down my back, and legs and arms, across my chest. My face was flushed. I could feel it.

"Money was missing this morning," he said. "And it couldn't have been Griff because he met me at a coffee shop early yesterday and told me he was done. He's marrying Swain, and she's paying off Trenton. He never went to Blue Bar. It's been someone else all along."

He took another step toward me.

"Who?" I said, taking another step toward him.

"Mary overheard Adam tell one of the cooks that he only needed a hundred thousand more to open his own place, and he knew someone who could quadruple his money Wednesday night, so all he really needed was twenty-five grand."

We were standing right in front of each other. I could reach out and touch his chest. And I did. I couldn't stop myself. Our voices were low and husky.

"What's Wednesday night?" I said, looking into his blue-blue-blue eyes.

"Playoffs," he said, gently stroking my face. "American and National."

"Stanley Stein," I said, putting my arms around him.

"Stanley Stein," he said, putting his arms around me.

"How much was stolen?" I said, kissing him.

"Twenty-five grand," he said, kissing me.

And then we kissed again and kissed again and kissed again, just like in his office but with more fire, more urgency. These were sex kisses, plain and simple.

"Did you come here to make love to me?" I said, unbuttoning his shirt.

"Maybe," he said.

"Are you going to?"

"Yes."

"Good."

And then he pulled my jersey up over my head, threw it on the couch next to his jacket, and lifted me up like we were newlyweds ready to cross the threshhold.

"Where's your bedroom?" he said.

"Down the hall."

He kissed me and carried me through my closet into my bedroom, and we made love most of the morning.

It's hard to say if one particular morning of sex is the best morning of sex you've ever had in your life. I'd had great mornings of sex (miserable mornings of sex too), so instead I'll say that making love to Blue was like being in the middle of an earthquake, a hurricane, a volcano, and a typhoon at the same time. I'll say it was hot and heavy and passionate and perfect. *Phenomenal* is a word that comes to mind. He was remarkably strong and self-assured and yet gentle when he had to be, when I needed him to be. Did I mention the sex was phenomenal?

When we were done, we did the spooning thing and just stayed like that for a long time, very quiet. On the one hand, I knew I shouldn't have done it. *Don't sleep with your client* is pretty much the first rule of every business on Earth. Accepted practice. Standard procedure. Company policy. Common sense. I wished I had some.

On the other hand, life is short. We were uncommitted consenting adults. I was attracted to him. He was attracted to me. We'd been flirting for a week. What was wrong with following through on a flirt if the opportunity presented itself? It wasn't like I had sex with every professional athlete who looked like a movie star and hired me to be his private investigator. It wasn't like I had all that much sex, period. Before *The Harriman Affair*, in fact, I hadn't slept with anyone in months and months. That being said, I liked sex. And I especially liked it with someone who was smart and caring and kind to me. If he was gorgeous and rich and famous as well, then those were perks.

"You told me you knew the difference between the you people think they know and the you *you* know," I said, spinning around to face him.

"This is me," he said. "This is Steve." And then he kissed me.

"This doesn't change anything," I said, thinking, *This changes everything.* "You're my client. I'm your PI. Don't treat me any different."

"No sexual mess and a half," he said. "I won't."

"Good."

"Just one thing?"

"What?"

"Can you wear the red wig next time?"

I punched him in the arm. *So glad there's going to be a next time*, I thought.

35

I'LL DENY I EVER SAID IT

I KISSED BLUE GOOD-BYE AT MY FRONT DOOR AND HAD HALF A mind to get back in bed and bask in the intimate afterglow, but it was eleven thirty in the morning, and the other half of my mind knew I had work to do. I poured myself a cup of coffee, toasted a bagel, sat at my kitchen table, and picked up my phone.

"Lowry Lowe," the receptionist said.

"Lisa Lowe, please," I said.

"One moment..."

I already had a direct line to the killer—I'd texted him today, in fact, at half past midnight on my way home from the Thirteenth, so I didn't need Lowry Lowe to find out how to contact him. What I needed was to get under the killer's skin and into his head in such a way as to annoy him to the point of carelessness. If I could find out which partner put the contract out on the late Jack Lowe, then I could put Logan in the middle of the case. That would make Logan happy and piss off the killer. A twofer I couldn't pass up.

"Lisa Lowe's office," her assistant said.

"May I speak to Mrs. Lowe?" I said.

"I'm not sure she's available. Who's calling?"

Screening calls. I thought so. I also thought she might not be in the office—her husband had been murdered Sunday night. There were tears to shed, arrangements to arrange, and affairs (so to speak) to put in order. On the other hand, I also *also* thought she would be behind her desk conducting business as usual. For all I knew, *she* had hired the killer to murder her husband—like Christopher had said before I broke his nose.

"Jessica Gibbs from Keller Williams," I said. "I'm an equestrian real estate specialist in Fairfield County. I'd like to talk about her late husband's Connecticut horse farm—if she's available, of course."

"Hold on, please."

It took less than a minute.

"This is Lisa Lowe."

"Mrs. Lowe, my name is—"

"Jessica Gibbs from Keller Williams. You're an equestrian real estate specialist in Fairfield. You want to talk about Jack's horse farm. I'm listening."

"I knew your husband," I said. "My condolences."

Silence. She was measuring me—and measuring herself—considering how much grief to demonstrate on the phone to a woman she didn't know. I could picture her, the Italian Bombshell, with her killer body and her sun-kissed Mediterranean skin and her supermodel mole, wearing a tailored Armani suit and sitting at her modern walnut desk, the panorama of Manhattan stretching out into infinity all around her.

"How did you find me?" she said.

Ah, no grief whatsoever.

I told her I'd been involved with Jack's purchase of the property and so knew about his law firm, had heard about his death, and knew that he was married and that his wife was his partner in the firm. I had a private buyer in hand, I said, and wanted to reach out to her before the equestrian vultures descended.

"Whether or not you're on the deed, Mrs. Lowe, you have a legitimate claim to the property," I said. "I'm in the city for a closing. Are you available for a late lunch?"

Silence again. "Yes, I'm available."

"How about three o'clock at Totto Ramen?"

"Which one?"

"West 52nd Street."

Universally considered one of the top five authentic ramen joints in the city, the West 52nd Street Totto Ramen is located in the basement of a ratty brownstone. Minimalist doesn't begin to describe it. Picture an ancient, narrow, abandoned, beat-up Greek diner with an unadorned counter, a row of bare tables, empty brick walls, and nothing else and you pretty much have it. And then the Totto crew took over with huge pots of paitan. The line starts forming at eleven a.m. By mid-afternoon, the crowd thins a bit before the dinner line starts. The menu is small, and the ramen is sublime and affordable, which is why the line starts at eleven.

There were three Totto Ramen joints in Manhattan. I'd been to all of them with my father many times, but Jimmy loved this one best because it was down and dirty, nothing fancy, no frills, just like him. *There's no bullshit in that basement, Katie,* he'd say to me. *"It's the perfect place for paitan."*

Lisa Lowe was already in line when I arrived at three. There were a few people ahead of her. To grease the conversational skids, sake was part of my plan, so I decided to record our lunch conversation in the event I couldn't recall what we'd said. I took out my phone and hit the red button. What the hell, I was a Realtor. My phone was supposed to be attached to my hand twenty-four hours a day, seven days a week.

She was exquisite. I'd seen her at the settlement last Friday, when I'd been Emily Baynes and Al and Warren had been my husband and his attorney, and she was even more beautiful than I remembered. At the end of that meeting, Christopher had said it was Lisa who'd hired the killer to take out her husband. We would soon see.

"Mrs. Lowe, I'm Jessica Gibbs," I said, walking up to her and putting my hand out. I'd Google searched Keller Williams in Fairfield County before speaking to Lisa and found an actual broker named Jessica Gibbs on the Realtor roster. Meaning if Mrs. Lowe decided to see if Jessica actually worked there, I did —or, well, she did.

"Lisa," she said, managing a thin smile and shaking my hand. She could have stepped directly onto a movie set as George Clooney's Italian bombshell co-star—black pantsuit with black boots and a black leather jacket with a black fur collar. Stunning.

"Jessica," I said. I wore a short blonde wig and gray contact lenses and the blue business suit I'd worn in *Death by Turkey*, a micro-budget indie feature about a Thanksgiving family reunion where everybody is murdered by the evil brother no one knew existed because Mom had hidden him away due to a prophecy she'd heard in a dream she'd had when she was a stripper on Staten Island and so on and so forth until everyone dies a bloody, gruesome death in contrived fashion at the actual dinner table. Yes, it was poorly conceived, written, and produced. Yes, it was unwatchable. I'd played the Realtor girl-friend of the mortgage banker brother who never knew about his evil sibling. I died by suffocation. The evil brother choked me with a turkey leg, shoving the greasy thing down my throat until I asphyxiated. Acting at its finest. My mortgage banker boyfriend was forcibly drowned in the gravy boat. He did ten takes. I felt his pain. The film was absurdly underfinanced and was never completed—thank God.

We made small talk about the Fairfield County equestrian real estate market and the value of Red Maple Horse Farm. We conversed about the private buyer, a hedge fund manager who was gobbling up beaucoup acres and wanted his name kept out of the deal. I told her the hedge fund manager was offering one seven, close in sixty days, contingent upon the inspector's report. The line moved, the party of three disappeared down the steps into the basement, and we were next.

I said it sounded like she'd never been to Red Maple. She said she hadn't. I wondered why her name wasn't on the deed, and she said it was because her husband had purchased it without her knowledge. I acted surprised and asked her why she thought he'd done that. "Man cave," she said, bone dry.

I asked if she knew what had happened to her husband, how he'd died, and she said he'd been murdered. I acted shocked. "Murdered?" I said. "Who in the world would want to kill Jack?"

And then two people walked out of the restaurant and up the stairs, and the hostess signaled it was our turn. Lisa didn't answer the question.

We sat at a table along the wall. I could reach out and pretty much touch the back of the man eating at the counter right in front of us, that's how tight it was. It was loud too. You couldn't overhear anyone's conversation, even if you were trying, which you probably weren't because you were busy slurping noodles a mile a minute.

We both ordered the Spicy Paitan with pork. I ordered two Asahi drafts and two Nigori sakes and said, "We should have a toast to Jack."

So the drinks came, and we toasted Jack, and I asked her about her practice, and she told me about divorce law, and I ordered two more sakes, and she asked me if I was married, and I made up a sad story about being separated and heading toward divorce, and I ordered two more sakes, and she asked me if there was significant money involved in the transaction, and I said my soon-to-be ex-husband was a radiologist and so, yes, there was significant money on the table, and she offered to represent me, and I ordered two more sakes and thanked her profusely, and our food arrived, and we talked about Red Maple Horse Farm and comparable properties, and we slurped noodles, and I said, "You mentioned it was a man cave, and I know I'm out of bounds here, but I'm going back to that because there's a rumor running around the horse crowd that Jack was having an affair, and I'd like to stop that stuff in its tracks because any rumor is a bad rumor in the real estate business and—"

"Revenge affair."

Exactly what Fu had said. "Excuse me?"

"He was having a revenge affair."

Maybe it was the sake, or maybe there was some kind of emotional connection to her husband, but her face was the slightest bit flushed.

"I don't understand," I said.

"I had an affair with Christopher, one of the partners—"

"You don't have to tell me this."

"I want to get it off my chest," she said, downing her sake. "I'll deny I ever said it, so it's fine."

"Good for you," I said, downing my sake. "I'll deny you ever said it too."

We both laughed.

"Jack found out and had an affair with Christopher's wife to even the score. Except Jack's affair ruined that marriage, and Christopher is a very bad loser. Dangerously bad."

"Didn't Jack's affair ruin your marriage?"

"Our marriage was ruined the day we said, 'I do.'"

"I don't know what to say," I said, and I meant it— wonderful acting on my part.

"Most people don't," she said, and she reached out and put her hand on my arm. It was either a gesture of friendship or pity. I honestly couldn't tell. Probably they were the same thing to her. "Not everyone lives life full speed full time in the fast lane. But we do—four partners in the same firm going hot and heavy on the high wire with no net. Except we all rolled over, and one fell out, and there were three in the bed." And then she leaned in to let me know this next bit was confidential. "Christopher and Jack started the firm together. Michelle and I joined later. In the formation documents, it says if any subsequent partners, meaning me and Michelle, should die, cause of death irrelevant, the founding partners, Jack and Christopher, inherit those shares of the firm. And if either of the founding partners should die, the surviving founding partner inherits all the shares, period. So who in the world would want to shoot Jack in the eyes? What's the saying? Follow the money? I suggest following Christopher's Porsche. It's a 918 Spyder going one eighty-five down Madison Avenue. But be careful. The thing about Christopher is he has no brakes. I'll take one eight, all cash, no contingencies, close in thirty days."

And then she stood and walked to the ladies' room. I wanted to think about the "no brakes for Christopher" bit, but before I could get that thought going, I got a text from *The Number*.

Back to work at Lowry Lowe this weekend—apparently professional enough to earn an encore—and you're invited to my command performance, time and place to be revealed before curtain. Early reviews are in: special from the first refrain.

36

PLANS ARE TRICKY LITTLE DEVILS

I said good-bye to Lisa Lowe without mentioning her life was at risk, without coming clean about being a private investigator, and without admitting I'd seen her husband at Red Maple—tied to a straight-back chair in the barn, dead as da Vinci, skin a suffocated shade of blue.

"I'll counter and be in touch," I'd said, climbing into a cab.

On the way down to the D-Cup, I called Logan's cell phone, got his voicemail, and told him I'd heard from "his friend." I knew that would piss him off, but I owed him one for locking me up most of Monday. (I'd inherited the Irish payback gene from Jimmy, who'd always settled his scores.) I read Logan the killer's text verbatim and told him I had not yet replied. "Thought you might have an opinion about that," I said. I did not mention my lunch with Lisa Lowe.

As the bell rang and the elevator groaned its way up to the theater, I considered ordering my thoughts but realized I'd need more time to straighten out those emotional pretzels than a three-floor ride to rehearsal would allow, so instead I wrapped my mind around Venus, Johnny Jedry's acid-induced incarnation of a hippie goddess, who steps out of a painting looking for lesbian love on a Sunday afternoon at the Met in the turn-on-tune-in-drop-out times of the late 1960s.

We were *supposedly* rehearsing act 1, scene 8—the scene before the scene where Venus (me) kisses Jedry (Chloe) while the jealous Adonis (Roger) watches from the wings in the Greek gallery. Before the epically epic kiss brings statues to life in lap-dancing frenzy, Venus and Jedry walk through the museum and share their feelings, including their mutual desire to expand their sexual horizons in gender-bending fashion. Mortal and immortal passions at play, the professor and the goddess hold hands as they stroll through the American Wing to the Greek Gallery, and, Dennis said, "Therein lies the problem."

Exactly. For me, holding hands meant the kiss was coming, and though we'd locked lips a dozen times since *Psychedelic* rehearsals had begun, I still couldn't get comfortable kissing Chloe. When I'd mentioned this after rehearsal one day, hoping, I suppose, that the moment could be rewritten into something other than an epically epic kiss—a romantic look, perhaps, or a warm embrace, Posey had said, "It's called acting, Kate." To which I'd said, "I know, I know." And Dennis had said, "Where the heart leads the lips soon follow." To which I'd said, "I get it, I get it." And Chloe had said, "I'm tripping, Kate. We're not really kissing." To which I'd said, "In your mind or in the play or in real life?" To which she'd said, "What's the difference?" To which I'd said, "Okay, well, then, fuck it."

But for Dennis and Posey, the holding-hands problem was something else altogether. The writer and director had decided that Venus and the professor holding hands would be reason enough for Adonis, secretly following them, to dive betwixt and between the unlikely couple, which would mean Venus and Jedry would never reach the Greek gallery, the gloriously glorious Kiss of All Kisses would not occur, the statues would not come to life, the lap dance would not escalate into the orgy, and the first act would never end. (As if anyone in the audience would willingly suspend their disbelief enough to concentrate on character motivation.)

A distraction was what the script called for, Dennis said, something to sidetrack the Greek god in the American Wing so he falls behind the goddess and the professor and catches up only just in time to witness their kiss.

So Posey had written a distraction that went something like this: as Venus and Jedry walk past the painting *Washington Crossing the Delaware*, the twelve-and-a-half-foot by twenty-one-foot massive masterpiece by Emanuel Leutze, George Washington himself skips off his skiff and waylays Adonis. Later, of course, George strips down to his white wig and participates in the second-act orgy, but for now, the first president of these United States wants the Greek god of beauty and desire to tell him how to brighten his smile. Posey had even written a quick song, a ditty called "The President's Pearly Whites," that George sings to Adonis until the god gets past him and hurries on to the Greek gallery.

I said *supposedly* because though we had the amended script and the new song, we weren't *actually* rehearsing the distraction because the distraction had not yet arrived, meaning the actor playing the distraction had himself been distracted by traffic.

While we waited for George Washington, Roger distracted us from the distraction of the distraction's distraction by regaling Dennis, Posey, and Chloe with the story of my Blue Bar embezzlement case, something I had not had the time or opportunity to do yet.

Everything I had shared with Roger to prepare him for his role as a real estate broker he pantomimed for Dennis, Posey, and Chloe. What he embellished or extemporized, I corrected with truth and fact. Blue, Griff, Adam, Mary, Stanley Stein, and Diane Swain all had roles in Roger's retelling, which was as it was, except that Roger rephrased the part of his Tasing in such a way as to imply that his heroism in the face of being shot with high voltage had somehow solved the case, which was not nearly as it was.

As I expected, Dennis, Posey, and Chloe were enthralled by the particulars while at the same time envious they had not been offered parts in the Blue Bar "play," as it were, meaning all three of them had been involved in my first two cases and were disappointed they had not been cast in my current case. I sensed hurt feelings too.

"So that's it?" Posey said. "Roger was large and in charge, and Diane Swain gave up Griff, and Stanley Stein stumbled, and Blue Bar lived happily ever?"

"Not exactly," I said.

"Which part, exactly, is inexact?" Dennis said, eyebrows rising as if new roles were just now coming online.

"You're not exactly large and in charge when you're Tased," I said, looking at Roger. "You're more of a quivering bag of flesh and bone."

"That's fine," Roger said, backpedaling. "I'll concede it was...shocking, if you admit my recuperative powers were impressive."

"I'll give you that one," I said.

"Fair is fair is fair," Roger said, nodding at the group, recovering his manhood, and reestablishing his co-star billing all at the same time. "You're looking at the new and improved me. I'm supercharged."

"What about Griff and Diane Swain?" Chloe said. "Did she give him up?"

"She married him," I said, thinking about it for the first time since Blue told me this morning.

"Excuse me?" Dennis said.

"Well, not yet," I said. "But they're getting married and she's paying off the Trenton tribe so her hubby will be debt-free.

She'd been giving him gambling money all along. He was never betting Blue Bar bucks."

"Go back to the part about them getting married," Posey said, making a face that said, *What in the world?*

"My guess is she shocked herself as much as she shocked Roger—"

"Supercharged," Roger said, flexing a bicep.

"—at the prospect of having to find a new young buck," I said, "and so she circled the wagons and traded Trenton for a husband."

"So you cracked the case with Stanley Stein?" Dennis said.

"Stanley didn't blink. Plus, Griff quit Blue Bar Monday morning, and there was money missing Monday night. It was never him."

"So we're still in the game," Posey said out loud instead of under her breath. "I mean, whoever's gambling house money—"

"—is still at the table," Dennis said, finishing her sentence as if they'd been married for decades, which they had, but adding enough excitement to his voice to let us all know he was as ready for action as she was.

"It's Adam," Chloe said.

"Of course it's Adam," Posey said.

"Has to be Adam," Dennis said.

"It was always Adam," supercharged Roger said.

"What's our plan?" Dennis said, assuming the plan included them.

"We have no plan," I said, and the realization of it bummed me out big-time.

"There's no plan?" Posey said.

"There's no way to catch Adam stealing the money," I said. "I've been through the books backward and forward and sideways and upside down. I've checked every register and computer printout and bank statement and deposit slip. I've spoken to every bartender and waiter and cook and hostess, and I can't catch him stealing the money."

The elevator bell rang. George Washington was on his way up.

"But we could catch him betting it at the bar," Chloe said. "That would be something."

"I thought that too," I said. "So I caught Griff in the act and had the pictures to prove it and put them in Stanley's face. I thought Stanley would see the jig was up and he would crack and give me Griff on a silver platter to save his own ass. I had them both dead to rights. I threw a brick in Lake Stanley Stein, and it didn't make a ripple. I have no idea what to do next. Dead end. I can't even *find* square one."

They could hear the hopelessness in my voice. I could hear it too. I would have to tell Blue that I'd struck out looking.

And then the elevator arrived, and George Washington stepped into the theater. As he crossed the D-Cup to the stage (where we were standing), Dennis put his hand on my shoulder and said, "Plans are tricky little devils, Kate. You can't try too hard to catch one. You have to let them come to you. When you least expect it, that's when they appear. Trust me. The plan is coming. And when it shows up unexpected, you're going to stop the proceedings and say, 'Ladies and gentlemen, I have a plan.' And then we're going to help you because we're your ace in the hole."

"Your leg up," Posey said.

"Your upper hand," Chloe said.

"Your best bet," Roger said.

"Thanks," I said to them. "But I'm down three runs, and it's the bottom of the ninth, and there's nobody on base, and there's two outs, and I have two strikes and a migraine."

And then rehearsal began, and the focus was on George Washington, a Schmidt and Parker Player named John Hitt, who was a hale and hearty sixty-eight-year-old actor with white hair and what appeared to be wooden teeth, a casting coup if it was true.

I tried to put the case out of my mind and focus on the moment at hand, but all I wanted to do was go back to the House of Emotional Tics, crawl into bed, and give up. I would have done it too—quit the case, quit the PI business, quit everything—but *Jimmy's Rules of Private Investigation for Kate, Rule Number Five* popped into my head: *Find a reason to care about the case. It's business, but it's personal too. That's the kick in the ass that keeps you going when everything else says, "Call it a damn day and go home."*

Everything else was saying just that: *Call it a damn day and go home.* Except I *had* found a reason to care about the case: Blue. It *was* personal now, about as personal as it could be. And thinking about how personal it was made me think about Blue in my bed this morning, and thinking about Blue in my bed made the storm clouds clear just as George Washington skipped out of his skiff and intercepted Adonis, and I stopped the proceedings and said, "Ladies and gentlemen, I have a plan."

37

DENIALS AND STONEWALLS AND ALIBIS AND MISDIRECTION

WHEN I GOT BACK TO THE HOUSE OF EMOTIONAL TICS, TWO things were waiting for me in the lobby: Wednesday's call sheet for *Kung Fu Fu* and Detective Lew Logan. I must admit I was caught off guard. I wasn't expecting the call sheet.

"You got my message?" I said to Logan, grabbing the call sheet and putting my key in the door.

"Fuck yourself, McCall," he said. "That asshole is not my friend."

"Ah, good, you did get it," I said.

He would never say so, but I saw the corners of his mouth form the beginnings of a smile. He was Irish too, after all, and so I felt sure he appreciated the need to settle scores.

"What do you want?" I said.

"Bottle of beer would be good," he said.

I had a six-pack of Sam Adams in the fridge. I gave Logan one, took one for myself, and sat at my kitchen table. Logan leaned against the counter. We did not toast each other.

"After receiving your voicemail, I went to Lowry Lowe and met with the three surviving partners, individually and collectively," Logan said. "I informed them of this most recent death threat and suggested they consider making immediate and extended out-of-town travel arrangements, for business or pleasure or family or any fucking reason that would put them someplace other than here, because due to the lack of specific, death-threat logistics provided by my source as pertaining to the particular partner being threatened, for instance, and also, for instance, the open-ended nature of the death-threat timeline and location, meaning anytime this weekend in any fucking place anywhere, meaning no relevant, actionable information whatsoever, the NYPD could not and would not provide personal, around-the-clock protection."

"What did they say?"

"Individually or collectively?"

"Either. Both."

"Collectively, they agreed that they, the surviving partners, would not vacate the city nor upset the normalcy of their lives, as if their lives were normal in any goddamn regard, despite their dead partner's demise, because running scared was not in their nature and because of business obligations, meaning divorces in the balance and money on the line, and because of personal preferences, meaning safety in numbers as opposed to safety in South Buttfuck, Nowhere, and because of other nonsensical bullshit that I have thankfully forgotten."

"Individually?"

"Denial, stonewall, alibi, misdirection."

"Misdirection?"

"Each attorney was pleased as pie to point at their partners, in the event I was seeking a suspect."

I thought of Lisa Lowe pointing all the arrows at Christopher Lowry. "You don't think it's one of them?"

"I think it's all of them. But I have a bad feeling for Lowry."

"Which one?"

"Both. They have history."

"History?"

"Six years ago, Christopher Lowry was peripherally interrogated for conspiracy to commit murder."

"He was?" *How did I miss that?* I thought.

"Big-bucks-banking divorce. During the proceedings, someone unsuccessfully tried to murder the CEO, who brought charges against his soon-to-be ex-wife. Lowry was the wife's lawyer. He was questioned by the police as a possible accomplice, seeing as how he was illicitly involved with the wife at the time."

"The wife being Michelle Lowry?" I knew that but didn't want Logan to know I knew it.

"What does she win, Don? The charges were summarily dropped under suspicious circumstances, meaning the CEO was found dead in his Bergen County backyard pool shortly thereafter, meaning if you don't succeed once, try, try again. It remains unclear whether or not the eyes of said CEO were still in his head when they found him floating."

I had read about Christopher having an affair with Michelle while she was still the banker's wife, and then representing her in the ensuing divorce, and then marrying her after the settlement. That was part of the public record collected and included in Al Cutter's Lowry Lowe folder. But I didn't know anything about the conspiracy-to-commit-murder addendum. Lisa Lowe hadn't mentioned anything about that. *It could be Michelle or Christopher*, I thought.

"How come nobody knows about this?" I said.

"You mean how come you don't know and I do?"

"No. Maybe. Yes."

"Because you are an amateur, and I am a professional, and because Christopher and Michelle Lowry were Teflon. Nothing stuck. The whole thing was buried at the bottom of the Grand Canyon. A murdered CEO was bad business for the bank. So his death went down as an accidental drowning."

"How did you find out?"

"Lisa Lowe told me."

Freaking Lisa Lowe, I thought. "So you think it's him?"

"Or her, or both of them, or any of them. What in the goddamn hell do I know?"

He pointed his empty bottle at the fridge. I finished my beer and got us another round. He stayed put at the counter. I leaned against the sink, maybe four feet from him, and thought about my lunch with Lisa. She'd made it clear to Connecticut horse farm Realtor Jessica Gibbs that Christopher Lowry had both personal and professional motives. So why hadn't she done the same for Logan? Had she seen through me, somehow known I was the PI who'd played the Texas tart? Was she setting me up? She was telling me (Jessica) that Christopher Lowry had it in for Jack Lowe—and maybe for her and Michelle too. But, again, she hadn't told Logan any of that.

And yet Lisa Lowe *had* told Logan the conspiracy-to-commit-murder story. Why hadn't she told me that one? And why hadn't she told Logan about her affair with Christopher and Jack's revenge affair with Michelle? Why hadn't Lisa told Logan about the original partnership deal or Christopher's Porsche flying down Madison Avenue with no brakes?

Or maybe she *had* told Logan and *he* wasn't telling me. I knew I couldn't trust Lisa Lowe—or any of the partners—but I couldn't trust Logan either.

"You read me the entire text?" Logan said.

"Word for word."

"And you didn't text him back?"

"Thought you might like to weigh in, like I said."

It was too late for me to stand on ceremony as far as communicating with the killer. I had originally thought letting Logan into the conversation would scare the killer away. But now that I knew the killer and Logan were buddies, that ship had sailed.

Logan nodded. "Last time he told you where and when."

"He's challenging me."

"So it's a game?"

It wasn't a casual question. It was the kind of question cops ask in the interrogation room. The kind of question Logan had asked me before.

"I don't think so," I said. "He's a super-psychotic egomaniac. Smarter, better, faster than everyone else. He needs to show me I'm no match for his genius. He gave me less hoping I could keep up. Maybe he'll give me more later. He thinks I'm the Little Engine That Could."

"Or couldn't," Logan said, taking a notepad out of his pocket. He flipped it open and made little checks and cross-outs as he flipped through the pages.

"What's that?" I said.

"A list," he said.

"Of what?"

"Names of people I've met who could be the killer. I narrowed it down to ninety-three. I'm crossing off anybody who couldn't possibly be a super-psychotic egomaniac. Notice I'm leaving your name in place."

"You think I go around shooting people's eyes out?"

"Not particularly. But you are somehow always present in the lead-up and the aftermath, not to mention the middle. And I am proven wrong every day, and so your name is on the list."

"I'm not an egomaniac."

"You are an actor."

"Thank you. And I'm definitely not super-psychotic."

"Again, you are an actor."

"And again, thank you." I got us each another beer, and we both sat at the table.

"The first steps have been taken to create a task force to catch this asshole," he said. "In case it's you, don't say I didn't warn you."

"Don't tell me. Tell him," I said, taking out my phone.

"You going to share his number?"

"No."

He made a note in his pad.

"Stop doing that," I said. "What do you want to say to him?"

He took a long hit of his Sam Adams and said, "'You fucking pussy.'"

"Jesus, Logan. Don't piss him off any more than he already is."

"You're right. Try this. 'You fucking rat-fuck pussy. This is your old friend Lew Logan getting ready to shove a task force up your rat-fuck asshole.'"

"Oh, well, yeah, much better."

He dictated a novel, and I dutifully typed it into my phone. It was the longest text I had ever seen. In it Logan talked about my relationship with the killer and how that was ultimately foreplay because what the killer really wanted, Logan knew, was a piece of the police detective because there would ultimately be no satisfaction in beating me—literally or figuratively—because I was a rank amateur with pathetic skills, poor judgment, and negligible history, meaning the killer had known Logan for years and had only known me since the end of July, when he'd murdered my father. There was a paragraph about picking on someone your own size, meaning the killer should pick on Logan and not me. And there was a chapter about the task force that was forming to find and fuck with the killer's future.

"'And so I am offering you an opportunity to engage the locomotive instead of the Little Engine that can't get out of her own way—'" Logan said.

"Hey," I said.

He waved me off. "'McCall is out, and I am in. Time to run with the Big Dog. What are you afraid of, you puny fuck? That I'm smarter than you? You already know I am. And you know where to find me. But where do I find you?'"

He gestured at my phone. "Hit Send."

I hit Send, and we sat at the table for a minute, and then I said, "So what are you doing this weekend?"

"You hitting on me, McCall?"

"Not in your wildest dreams."

"There is a God."

"Ouch, Logan. What, I'm not your type?"

"Not in your wildest dreams," he said, and took a hit of his beer while trying to hide the beginnings of a smile. Some scores are settled faster than others.

Believe it or not, it was a warm moment in the sense that Logan had again reminded me of my father, who busted my chops relentlessly, often while trying to hide his smile.

"I meant what are you doing about Lowry Lowe," I said. "The killer said his encore was this weekend."

"Nothing. Same as you. This whole goddamn thing is built on quicksand. No evidence except bodies without eyeballs. No hair, no blood, no fibers, no DNA, no leads. I've got nothing. And if I've got nothing, you've got less. So stay out of it. Next time I catch you in the middle of anything labeled Lowry Lowe, you're going to jail."

"I've met the guy, Logan. I've got more than nothing."

He took out his list and made notes.

"Stop doing that," I said.

38

CUFFS IN THREE, TWO—

IT WAS WEDNESDAY NIGHT IN THE MIDDLE OF OCTOBER AND THE jam-packed, wall-to-wall crowd at Blue Bar was crazy for Major League playoff baseball, sliced steak sandwiches on homemade sourdough, and cold craft beer. Game three of the National League Championship Series was on every flat-screen television. Game four of the American League Championship Series was on deck. The place was supercharged (like Roger!) with high-octane, jet-engine, sports-bar adrenaline. If you'd never liked baseball your entire life, you would have changed your tune tonight.

I was on the third floor, the game floor, standing beside the eighteen-foot Grand Champion shuffleboard table, watching Dennis and Posey challenge two bleached blondes from Brooklyn who were on the lookout for Blue. I knew that because I'd heard one of them say, "I saw him on the second floor. I could get lost in those blue eyes."

Trust me, girlfriend, I thought; *you have no idea.*

At one of the pool tables, Roger and Chloe had teamed up to play two Lenox Hill lawyers in a spirited game of eight ball. The truth is I didn't know if they really were lawyers—or from

Lenox Hill—but they looked like lawyers, though pretty much everyone looked Lowry Lowe lawyer-ish to me these days.

Every seat on the third floor was taken, as was every seat at the bar. Except, of course, for the barstool beside Stanley Stein, which was intermittently occupied by a steady stream of the bookie's best friends, each of whom sat beside Stanley for a nod and a wink and then vacated the barstool and set off to find a random restroom, where they would exchange cash money for a matchbook.

As was standard for Stanley, the bookie wrote down exactly nothing—not a number, not a word, not a jot, not a scribble. And business was brisk. I'd counted twenty-two gamblers since I'd found him having dinner and reading newspapers at the third-floor bar. Who knew how many he'd met before I'd arrived? Even if Stanley's "bathroom attendants" were keeping written records of the money they'd collected, they weren't in on the actual bet or knew who placed it. The actual bet and the person who'd placed it was information known only to Stanley —and each particular gambler, who had no knowledge about any of the other gamblers and their particular bets. Someone had to keep track of who was owed what and when and why— but who was doing that job?

Not Harold, that's for sure. Stanley's personal, jiu jitsu grand master, MMA middleweight champion, nasty-ass Navy SEAL, deep-cover, Special Ops killer bodyguard with no patience for private investigators kept his distance from the bookie and the bets while keeping an active eye on the room overall. As usual, Harold was positioned at the far end of the bar.

The whole thing was maddening to say the least, which was maybe why the cops had grandfathered Stanley Stein into the reluctantly accepted, illegal fabric of the city.

Anyway, none of that was the foremost thought in my mind.

The foremost thought in my mind was, *Thank you, General George Washington.*

At yesterday's rehearsal, when our first president jumped out of Leutze's wall-sized wonder and intercepted Adonis so that Venus and Professor Jedry could continue on to the Greek gallery and consummate their lusty lust with a kiss, the plan had come to me fully formed as a "since-then" proposition: since catching Adam Stoker and Stanley in the act or immediately thereafter would not prove Adam was guilty of gambling stolen Blue Bar cash, then intercepting Adam *before* he reached the bookie was the next and only remaining step in my embezzlement-busting equation.

I was dressed like a sports fan—faded blue jeans, black Converse sneakers, black sweater, New York Yankees baseball cap—but wore green contacts and a black wig pulled back in a ponytail because the last time I was in Stanley Stein's close orbit I had been a blonde, and I didn't want Harold blowing my cover.

Unexpectedly, I found myself enjoying the game. I had thought it might take more time for me to find my way back to baseball, since it had been a pastime I'd shared with Jimmy all my life and I couldn't think of one without the other, and thinking of my father since his murder at the end of July had left me feeling empty and lost and sad beyond measure. Since the end of July, in fact, thinking about baseball and Jimmy had torn me apart.

Anyway, I *was* thinking about Jimmy, a wonderful memory of us sitting sky-high at the top of the upper deck behind home plate at Yankee Stadium, drinking cold beer and eating peanuts, watching the Bombers battle the Birds, me keeping immaculate score, Matthew busy with a friend who'd tagged along, and my father telling me I was doing a good job, that I could keep score with the best of them. And then he'd said I was doing a good job across the board, meaning he was proud of me as a person, as a daughter, as a single mother, as an assistant PI, and, yes, even as a way-off-Broadway actor. And I remember glowing inside. Right there in the upper deck. *Glowing.*

But this time, drinking Allagash White on draft (one of Jimmy's favorites) and watching Major League Baseball and remembering my father lifted my heart instead of blowing it to smithereens, and I raised my glass ever so slightly and turned my eyes to the ceiling, looking through it to heaven somewhere, and ever so softly said, "This one's for you, Jimmy."

And then Adam Stoker appeared in the doorway.

Dennis, Posey, Roger, and Chloe were watching me while they played shuffleboard and eight ball, waiting for me to signal that the douchebag had arrived. I put my beer down and mouthed the word *showtime* in each of their directions, and they followed my eyes and spotted him, and we all casually moved into position.

As he crossed the third floor to the bar, Adam stopped to say hello to half a dozen people who recognized him and were probably angling for a free round of beer because why else would anyone say hello to that arrogant prick. Even when he stopped to chat, Adam's eyes went to Stanley. He was waiting for the barstool beside the bookie to be vacated. He was waiting for his turn to parlay twenty-five thousand stolen Blue Bar dollars into one hundred thousand so he could finance the opening of his own bar somewhere else sometime soon.

And then the thin man on the barstool shook Stanley's hand and walked away, and Adam moved in, thinking, I imagined, that he would soon have enough dough to open his own place.

When he was ten feet from the empty barstool, Roger and I stepped in front of him—physically stating there was no way he was getting through us to Stanley.

"Adam Stoker," I said, showing him my badge from the Schmidt and Parker Players production of *Cop on a Hot Tin Roof,* a musical send-up of Tennessee Williams's 1954 Pulitzer Prize-winning classic drama that featured a NYC family of police offi-cers instead of Southern cotton planters. Yes, it was hilariously bad.

"Who the hell are you?" Adam said.

"You don't ask the questions today, Mr. Stoker," Roger said, showing Adam his badge from *The Federal Bureau of Song and Dance*, a ridiculous D-Cup musical about a government law enforcement agency created to bring in the bad guys with singing and dancing instead of guns and shoot-outs. You haven't really experienced musical theater until you've seen Al Capone do the samba.

"Come quietly, Mr. Stoker," Posey said, showing him her badge from *Last Cop on the Beat*, an incoherent D-Cup musical about the end of New York City policemen patrolling their neighborhoods on foot. One beat cop, played by Roger, bucked the new order by singing and dancing through his neighbor-hood beat to prove a point that eluded everyone in the cast and everyone in the audience. Posey played Roger's mother, and Dennis played his father. I played Roger's sister. Every familial emotional moment was conveyed with a song. Good times.

"Or I'll cuff your hands behind your back and drag you across the room like the arrogant little shit you are," Chloe said, holding up handcuffs and her badge from—*Jesus*, I thought, *I don't know where the hell Chloe's badge comes from.*

"Cuffs in three, two—" I said.

"Okay, okay," Adam said. "Where are we going?"

"That's a question, Mr. Stoker," Roger said, taking Adam's arm and leading him across the room.

We encircled Adam as if we were bodyguards, putting our hands up to keep the crowd at arm's length. Admittedly, we were the most unlikely law enforcement team ever assembled. But we were actors, and so people got the hell out of our way in a hurry.

We hustled Adam through the doorway and down the

stairs. Between the third and second floors, he was quiet and confused and concerned. Between the second and first floors, he got pissed off and demanded to know who we were and what we wanted and why he was under arrest and what the hell was happening.

"Those are all questions, Mr. Stoker," Roger said.

"What's happening, Adam," I said, "is the government has you dead to rights."

"Dead to rights for what?" Adam said, more nervous than he wanted to let on.

"You're going to like living in jail, Mr. Stoker," Roger said. "You can ask questions all day long and no one gives a damn."

I could see Adam was surprised when we reached the first floor and didn't exit the building but instead went down the stairs again to the basement. And he was more surprised when we escorted him into his office (Griff's old office) and shut the door behind us. And he was even more surprised when he found out what the charges were.

But the biggest surprise was still to come.

39

SERVE AND VOLLEY

TO THE DUNGEON DECOR DE RIGUEUR—EXPOSED BRICK WALLS, stained oak floor, wraparound maple desk with matching credenza, leather guest chairs, small conference table, file cabinets, bookshelf—Adam had added an industrial floor lamp that swiveled and bent and adjusted to whatever task was at hand.

And since the task at hand was interrogating Adam Stoker, Chloe had positioned the floor lamp in such a way that it shined across the conference table from where Adam was seated, burning bulb directly in his face—like every bad cop show on TV.

It would have been a hilarious scene in a wackadoodle D-Cup musical except for the fact that it was real life and not fiction, and we were impersonating state and federal law enforcement officers, a felony in all fifty states.

"Congratulations, Mr. Stoker," Roger said, "you've hit the much-coveted law enforcement trifecta: NYPD, DEA, and FBI."

"A list of letters that add up to a decade in a distant prison," Posey said.

"We all want a piece of you," Chloe said, "so either you start singing or I go first. And believe me, the FBI has sharp teeth."

"What's left after the FBI's done, the DEA is going to rip to shreds," Dennis said. "In case you were wondering."

Roger and I were NYPD, Dennis and Posey were DEA, and Chloe was FBI. Against my better judgment, I'd allowed everyone to choose their own code name for the interrogation (last names only), and the group decided their names should be associated with tennis equipment companies. Did I mention it was against my better judgment?

"I didn't do anything wrong," Adam said.

"We're way past right and wrong," I said. "We're up to crime and punishment."

"Backhand down the line for a winner, Dunlop," Roger said to me before turning to Adam. "Your guilt has already been decided, Mr. Stoker."

"What are you talking about...backhand? Guilty of what?" Adam said.

"You tell me, Stoker," Posey said. "And I volley like Venus Williams, so don't test me."

"Volley?" Adam said.

"Special Agent Wilson has an overhead you'll never forget —" Dennis said.

"True that, Special Agent Prince," Posey said.

"—meaning it's your turn to talk the talk, Stoker," Dennis said.

"I...I don't...talk about what?" Adam said.

Dennis and Posey had taken up tennis back when Margaret Court was the queen of the Sport of Kings. The D-Cup couple still played mixed doubles in Brooklyn once a week to relieve the stress of creating chaotic musical theater and, apparently, to prepare for bogus Department of Justice interrogations should they arise out of thin air.

"The cook gave you away, Adam," I said, thinking this whole

tennis thing was a terrible idea. "We know you're opening your own place. We know you need a hundred grand to cross the finish line. And we know that tonight you're gambling twenty-five thousand at the bar with Stanley Stein to quadruple your money."

I reached into his sport jacket, grabbed a thick envelope out of his pocket, and dumped a stack of bills onto the conference table.

"What cook?" Adam said, the first edges of concern slipping into his voice.

"Don't sweat the cook, Stoker," Chloe said. "He's in witness protection somewhere in Wisconsin or Wyoming or wherever. You'll never find him."

"Easy on the witness protection, Agent Slazenger," I said to Chloe. I'd seen her run off the rails too many times to trust her with a discussion about witness protection, a conversation that could go in any direction anywhere in the world if left unchecked.

"Ten-four, Dunlop," Chloe said. "It's just with sweaty little lobbers like this, I want to smack a topspin forehand in his face."

Chloe had played second singles on her high school tennis team in Akron, Ohio, back before she'd moved to New York, become an actor, dropped acid, changed her chemical composition, and lost a few marbles.

But Chloe wasn't wrong. Adam Stoker *was* a sweaty little lobber, in the sense that he was little, he was lobbing lies left and right, and he actually was sweating bullets, which meant he was hiding something, which I took to be guilt—although it could possibly have been the floor lamp burning his face off. I considered the floor lamp for half a second and then let it go. It was guilt, absolutely. I could taste it. Adam Stoker was guilty of Blue Bar embezzlement. A bit more pressure applied in the proper places and he would fall right into my pocket, and the case would be solved.

"Twenty-five large cash money is a big number for a bar manager, Adam," I said. "Where'd you get it?"

He stammered and stuttered, and his eyes went wide, and he blinked a hundred times. "What...what do you mean? I...I...I saved it."

"Foot fault, Mr. Stoker," Roger said. "Even the baseline judge on the far court could see that one."

"Foot fault?" Adam said.

"What Detective Head means," I said, "is we know you're lying."

Yes, Roger was Detective Head. He'd gone first and had actually chosen that name, saying it gave his character an underlying lust to know the truth. We all knew it was really because he had a filthy mind and just liked hearing people say the word *head*.

Roger's second wife had made him join a Staten Island tennis team and also sell life insurance sixty hours a week, which is why that marriage ended in divorce and also how Roger came to be a Walker Park singles quarterfinalist—a loss he still attributed to the hangover he'd earned celebrating getting to the quarterfinals in the first place.

"Second serve," Special Agent Prince said, moving right up against the conference table. "Where did you get the twenty-five grand?"

"What?" Adam said.

"Drop shot, Stoker," Special Agent Wilson said, moving hard up against the table too. "Move your damn feet."

"My feet?" Adam said.

"Racket up, Mr. Stoker," Detective Head said, leaning over the table.

"I...I don't understand," Adam said.

"Bend your knees, you little shit," Agent Slazenger said,

standing right beside Detective Head. "Do you understand that?"

"No...I...what?" Adam said.

"There's twenty-five grand on the table," I said. "And there's twenty-five grand missing from the Blue Bar bank account."

"I didn't take the money from Blue Bar," Adam said.

"We know you did," Head said.

"No, I didn't," Adam said.

"You're going to jail," Wilson said.

"I didn't do it," Adam said.

"The cook says you did," Prince said.

"It's not true," Adam said.

"Tell your high school coach to stay out of the girls' shower," Slazenger said, and everyone looked at Chloe as if to say, *Huh?*

I moved right up to the conference table too so that all five of us were three feet from Adam, who was melting under the Department of Justice pressure and also under the hot, harsh light of the floor lamp. It was time to serve and volley.

"Here's the way this is going down, Adam," I said. "You're going to give us Stanley Stein and return the twenty-five grand, and we're going to forget the embezzlement charges."

"I didn't embezzle the money," Adam said.

"Cuff him, Slazenger," I said to Chloe, who pulled out her cuffs and slammed them hard on the table, which once again begged the question, *Where in the heck did Chloe get real handcuffs?*

"Stand him up, Head," Chloe said to Roger.

"I love it when you say my name," Roger said, and he reached out and roughly stood Adam up and pulled his arms hard behind his back.

"Wait, stop," Adam said as Chloe got her cuffs ready.

"Sailed it long on ad out," Posey said.

"Game, set, match," Dennis said.

"I stole the money from my neighbor," Adam said, spitting out the words, voice full of fear.

"You what?" I said.

"Stole the money from my neighbor," Adam said, and I think there were tears in his eyes, or maybe it was sweat. "He's a drug dealer. He lives across the hall. His name's Ricky Cordoba. You should arrest him. He plays Latin music twenty-four hours a day, every fucking day. I can't sleep, so I tell him to turn it down. He tells me he's going to sic his dog on me. He's got a little fucking Chihuahua. I hate that fucking Chihuahua. It looks like a rat. Its name is Tito. He's a fucking Chihuahua named after Tito Fuentes, who plays fucking Latin music. I hate Latin music, and I hate that rat-dog, and I hate Ricky. He's a bully. He's always picking on me. If I see him in the hall or if I'm getting my mail or doing my laundry, he threatens me, tells me to mind my own business and keep my mouth shut about his drugs and his guns and his life or else, and then he plays that fucking music, and I can't sleep."

"You didn't steal the money from Blue Bar?" I said.

"Ricky has guns and pills and pot and drugs and stacks of cash all over his apartment," Adam said. "I see it when he opens the door when I tell him to turn down that fucking music, his little fucking dog barking at my ankles like a snapping turtle."

"You stole the money from Ricky?" I said.

"I broke into his apartment and took twenty-five thousand dollars, and I killed his dog," Adam said.

"You what?" I said.

"I hit it with Ricky's baseball bat just to shut it up. And then I kept fucking hitting it until it was dead. Okay? I stole the money from Ricky and killed his dog. I didn't steal the money from Blue. I stole it from Ricky Cordoba. And, yes, I was going to bet it at the bar with Stanley Stein. Okay? There you go.

Stanley Stein is taking bets at Blue Bar, and I'll testify to it in court."

And then he sat back down at the conference table and wept, only pausing to show us pictures of the Cordoba break-in and dog murder he'd taken with his phone.

Dennis, Posey, Roger, Chloe, and I looked at each other with stunned expressions, mouths agape, lost for words.

Finally, Adam looked up at us—five of the most unlikely law enforcement officers ever assembled—and said, "So I gave you Ricky Cordoba *and* Stanley Stein, right? I'm off the hook for stealing the money and killing the dog?"

Adam's not the one stealing money from Blue Bar was what I was thinking, but what I said was, "Oh, Lucy. You got some *splainin'* to do."

"What?" Adam said.

And then I pulled off my black wig. I'd worn the red Wanda Ward wig underneath the black wig so I could become restaurant efficiency expert Danielle Sullivan and get the last word with Adam Stoker.

"I knew you weren't a consultant," Adam said, red and teary eyes shooting open with recognition. "You never had a card."

"It's in my car," I said. "I'll get it for you after I call Ricky."

40

LAST-MINUTE CHANGES TO THE DOCKET

THURSDAY MORNING BEGAN WITH A *KUNG FU FU* FIGHT-SCENE rehearsal that escalated into a brawl after Al landed a left jab on LaTanya's jaw. Since the movie was an existential exercise in improvisation, we thought LaTanya's counterattack was plot-driven characterization—good-guy captain subduing bad-guy drug dealer. But when blood flowed from Al's nose, we knew it wasn't acting, improvised or otherwise, and we pulled LaTanya off him and dragged them to opposite ends of the backyard and gave them ten minutes to cool their jets—an adult timeout—before picking up the scene from the first frame of the fight, which, in retrospect, was a terrible idea. Let's just say the rest of rehearsal was especially spirited and ended with LaTanya's chin adjusted a few degrees to the right and Al's bloodshot eyes set off in black and blue.

As was long-standing D-Cup tradition, with two weeks to go before opening night, Thursday afternoon's *Psychedelic Sunday* rehearsal was scheduled in a set-in-stone sort of way to be the first time the entire cast was off-book, meaning no scripts anywhere onstage, all lines committed to memory—holy crap, gang, time to get your shit together.

And as was also long-standing D-Cup tradition, only two of the Schmidt and Parker Players were ready to release their scripts, which resulted in what was also *also* a long-standing D-Cup tradition: actors panicking like parakeets, calling for lines like life rafts, forgetting their blocking, and drumming up a sense of dread that could stop a storm.

And in also *also also* D-Cup tradition, I was one of the two actors who knew their lines—Roger was the other one—so between the half dozen inspirational speeches by Dennis and Posey about an actor's responsibility to the play, to the producers, to the writer and the director, to the cast and crew, and to musical theater in the abstract, I had plenty of time to think about Christopher Lowry.

I felt sure that Christopher was hiring the man who murdered my father to kill his partners one by one so he could gain complete financial control of his law firm. That there was passion-fueled revenge in the mix (Jack Lowe's affair with Michelle Lowry had blown up Christopher's marriage) and a probable history of hiring killers (the murdered Bergen County banker) solidified my thoughts on the matter.

But Logan had made it clear that my imminent arrest was, well, imminent should I stick my nose near Lowry Lowe this weekend, any weekend, or ever, and Matthew would rocket through the roof of the Thirteenth Precinct if Logan put me in jail again, so I thought, *I won't go to Lowry Lowe after rehearsal. I'll go home. I'll. Go. Home.*

So when Dennis dismissed us, I grabbed a cab in front of the D-Cup intending to take it straight back to the House of Emotional Tics. But it was five thirty, Thursday afternoon, and the killer had texted me on Tuesday saying he was *back to work at Lowry Lowe this weekend*, and this weekend started tomorrow, and tomorrow might be too late, so instead of telling the cabbie 82nd and First I said, "30 Rockefeller Center."

I called Lowry Lowe to confirm Christopher was still in the

office, which he was, said I was a courthouse clerk with papers for him to sign, got cleared for admittance at the desk, took the elevator to the sixty-second floor, positioned myself by the elevator bank, just down the hall from the law firm, and checked emails that were never sent, replied to nonexistent text messages, and answered phone calls from imaginary business associates while waiting for Christopher Lowry to exit his office. *I won't get involved*, I said to myself. *I'll just watch and see if anything suspicious happens. I'll. Just. Watch.*

But if I do see something suspicious, I said in my head, *then I'll step in front of him and stop him in his tracks and ask why he'd hired a corporate killer to murder his partners. I'll confront him and challenge him before he gets on the elevator, but I won't get physical. I'll just talk. I'll. Just. Talk.*

My half-baked plan was to say I was an investigative reporter for the *National Enquirer*. (Which is why I just happened to bring along the fake *Enquirer* press pass I'd worn in a late-night body soap commercial—the point of which was to demonstrate how the soap could even wash the scum off a gossip rag writer. It aired once at three thirty in the morning and never again after that.) I would tell Christopher I was an *Enquirer* reporter, and I'd taken a tip from a text, and I was investigating and writing a story about a playboy divorce lawyer who murders his partners via corporate assassin. *And if he doesn't come clean, the son of a bitch*, I thought, *I'll just deck him with a right cross. I'll. Just. Deck him.*

So in my mind I had gone from heading straight home to punching Christopher Lowry in the face in front of the elevators. Proof positive, if you needed any, that surveillance, no matter how long it takes, ten minutes or ten hours, is the devil's workshop. When your brain can go anywhere, that's exactly what it does.

While I was considering reconsidering being there in the first place, the Lowry Lowe door opened, and Christopher stepped into the hall with a group of people—lawyers, clients, associates—and started toward the elevators. He had tape across his nose where I'd hit him with a haymaker, but he was still drop-dead gorgeous. He was in the middle of the group. Surrounded on all sides. There was no way for me to get to him, to cut him off, to put my hand on his chest and stop him mid-step, so he went right by me. Or maybe he went right by me because I froze. That could have been it. My heart was pounding. I think my knees were shaking. And then the elevator door was closing, and Christopher was getting away, and I unfroze at the last moment, stopped the door from shutting, and followed him into the elevator.

There were seven of them and me. They chatted and laughed on the way down, making small talk about a court case in Queens they all agreed was hilarious, and then the door opened on the first floor, and we all filed out, and I trailed them outside and across the concourse into One Rockefeller Plaza, home of Morrell Wine Bar & Café, one of the city's most famous wine watering holes. At the door to Morrell, the group said so long, farewell, *auf Wiedersehen*, good-bye, and went different directions. Only Christopher went into the bar. I went in after him.

Morrell is magnificent by any measure—sleek, modern, and ultra-hip, with an incredible menu and the best by-the-glass wine list in North America, featuring one hundred and fifty high-end wines by the glass. It was super-swank and popular with corner-office business executives, international tourists with money to burn, and fast lane divorce lawyers in the midst of murdering their partners.

Christopher moved through the crowd to the bar, where the better half of their busted marriage, Michelle Lowry, was waiting for him.

I found a spot at the end of the bar, ordered a twenty-dollar glass of Russian River Valley chardonnay, and watched the soon-to-be-divorced divorce lawyers have an intense and unhappy conversation.

My silenced phone buzzed before I swallowed my first sip. I didn't usually answer calls in busy bars, and I didn't recognize the number, so I let it go.

The same number called back immediately. I let that one go too.

But the third call from the same number I answered. "Kate McCall."

"Private investigators shouldn't be screening calls when they're tailing targets. It could be someone with a tip for the taking."

The bar noise made it hard to hear but not impossible, so I knew who it was. I had committed that voice to memory. It was the man who'd murdered Jimmy.

"Call Logan," I said. "He wants to talk to you more than I do."

"No, he doesn't. I didn't kill *his* father."

I stopped breathing. My voice vanished. At the other end of the bar, Christopher and Michelle were shaking their heads and arguing with incredulity and anger.

"Are you enjoying your wine?" he said. "Looks like a chardonnay from here."

I nearly fell off my stool. *He's watching me*, I said to myself. *He's watching me right here, right now.* "I was until you called. Oh, and we traced this number. Logan's got you now. Matter of minutes, asshole."

I was bluffing, playing for time. As casually as I could, I glanced around the room. He was here, but where? It was a full house, and half the crowd was on their phone. It seemed like everyone was a talker, texter, surfer, or gamer. *What the hell is wrong with people?* I thought. *Doesn't anybody ever turn off their fucking phone?*

"Logan has nothing. I'm calling you on a phone I took from

that idiot at the end of the bar—see him?—so this number won't be good again after right now. And I'm texting at the same time on the untraceable number you know. Can you guess who I'm texting?"

I checked the end of the bar. Some guy in a suit was frantically searching his pockets and his briefcase, telling his date that his phone was gone.

"One of the Lowrys," I said to the killer.

"Both of the Lowrys."

Jesus Christ, both Christopher and Michelle had taken a time-out from their heated conversation to look at their phones and type a reply.

"Last minute changes to the docket," the killer said. "It's how lawyers live...and die, it turns out. Tell Logan to turn on his task force. He's going to need it."

"You tell him."

"No can do. You're my Logan middleman now, my NYPD go-between. I can only imagine the depths of your discomfort at being put in this position, and that pleases me...your frustration and distress. You're so close to me but still so far away."

"Where are you, you fucking coward?"

"In front of your face, Little Engine. And there's the bell. See you next class."

And then he hung up. I looked around the room and then back at the bar, where Michelle took what was left in her wineglass, tossed it in Christopher's face, and walked away. Christopher said something to her back and went the opposite direction.

I knew what I *wanted* to do. I wanted to run after Christopher, grab him by the throat, and choke the truth out of him. But I knew I had to get to Michelle first and tell her Christopher had hired an assassin to kill Jack Lowe and now to kill her.

As I put twenty-five dollars on the bar, a man sitting across the room with his back to me stood up and followed Michelle out the door. Black leather jacket. Black gloves. Black ski hat. Same height and shape and size as the man at Red Maple. Was it him? It was. It had to be. He was right. I was so close but still so far away.

Shit, I thought, and I followed them both out the door.

41

LATE FOR CLASS

THEY HAD A HEAD START AND A HEAD OF STEAM, MICHELLE IN the lead and in a hurry, the killer less than half a block behind her, and then me another half block behind him. We were on East 48th Street cruising east. I had to walk like I meant it just to keep pace. We crossed Fifth and then Madison and then Park, where I missed a light and fell farther behind and almost got leveled by a limo as I was trying to catch up.

Michelle crossed Lexington, the killer closing in, me still half a block back. Just past a Hyatt, on the north side of 48th, was a handsome apartment building with a corner café that had sweet sidewalk seating—flower boxes and awnings and wrought-iron fences. The Swedish Queen went past the café and into the building. The killer went in right behind her.

I called Logan as I crossed 48th Street to the building's revolving doors and left a voicemail about following the killer and Michelle to this address, including the part about an impending murder in process, and then I revolved myself into the lobby and, straight ahead, saw Michelle in an elevator car, waiting for the door to slide shut. Just as it did, the killer slipped into the same car. Then the elevator door closed, and they were gone. I glanced at the doorman, moved to the elevator, and watched the LED floor lights blink from floor to floor. Michelle and the killer got out on six. I hit the call button.

"Can I help you?"

It was the front desk guy. He hadn't recognized me and wasn't happy that I'd called for an elevator without clearing it with him first. He was young, maybe twenty-three or twenty-four. His nameplate read Kyle. It was a classy enough building that the front desk guys wore blue suits and red ties and not doorman uniforms. The suit, apparently, gave Kyle courage I felt sure he didn't have when he wasn't the front desk guy. I sized him up and down. He was an inch or two taller than me and skinnier than me by a lot, which pissed me off, I must admit. I put out a vibe that said, *I could kick your skinny ass, Kyle, so back the fuck off right now.*

He took a step away from me, so I knew he'd caught the vibe. "Everyone has to check in at the front desk."

"Not everyone. Isn't that what you meant to say?" I pulled my fake *Enquirer* press pass out of my purse—along with my phone and a fifty-dollar bill. "Look, Kyle. I appreciate the fact you're just doing your job, but so am I. All I need is a picture of a door on the sixth floor. So unless you want to see your building on the cover of the *National Enquirer* tomorrow morning side by side with your happy head shot..."

I snapped a close-up and turned my phone so he could see it.

"...you're going to mosey into the mailroom so you can swear under oath you never saw me and let me take a two-minute ride on the elevator. No one will ever know I was here, and you'll be fifty bucks to the good."

I put the fifty in his hand. He looked at it and then looked at me. "A hundred bucks to the good. Isn't that what you meant to say?"

"Yes, it is, Kyle," I said, and I took another fifty from my purse and smiled like Kyle and I were going to be best buds from this moment on, like he had beaten me at my own *Enquirer* game and I was fine with it, like I even respected him for it.

He pocketed the money. "I'm checking mail for the next two minutes," he said, and he smiled back at me like we might meet later for a drink and turned to walk away.

"One more thing," I said, stopping him. "Michelle Lowry?"

"Shit," he said. "I knew it."

"She's having an affair with a married congressman. Guy's a dirtbag."

"So is she. 605. What's your name?"

"Sharon Miller."

"Kyle O'Connor. Nail them both to the wall, Sharon."

"Will do. Thanks, Kyle."

And then he went to the mailroom. I hit the button, the elevator door slid open, I stepped in, punched floor number six, and checked my purse for Jimmy's Colt.

On the way up, I held the gun in my hand. *I'll never get used to it*, I thought. No matter how heavy you imagine a gun is going to be, it's heavier than you think, although it could be the weight of the idea of the permanent damage it can do that makes the damn thing so burdensome.

The elevator door opened, and I stepped onto the sixth floor. A brass sign pointed 601-605 to the left and 606-610 to the right. It was a wide hallway, beautifully carpeted, with fancy wall sconces spaced every twenty feet or so. There were only ten apartments on the entire floor, meaning the apartments were extra large, meaning when you live in a high-end building like this one, with wide hallways and fancy sconces and extra-large apartments within walking distance to Rockefeller Center, you shelled out multiple millions for your four-bedroom abode.

I arrived at apartment 605 and didn't know what, exactly, I

was supposed to do. Stop the killer from murdering Michelle Lowry, of course. But, specifically, what the hell should I do now that I was standing here?

I could wait for Logan, couldn't I? No, I couldn't. Waiting for Logan was out of the question. Michelle Lowry could be dead before he even received my message. I could grab Kyle and tell him the truth and drag him up here and have him open the door with his master key. Scratch that. Just like Logan, precious minutes would be wasted and Michelle might be dead and the killer gone by the time we got back. I could knock on the door, really pound on it to startle the killer and scare him off. Negative. He could just keep killing her and then maybe escape through a window on an exterior ledge. Why not? It happened like that all the time on TV.

My only option was to get into apartment 605 and shoot the killer myself. But could I do it if I had to? Could I pull the trigger given the moment at hand? Was I the kind of human being who could take the life of another human being? Was that how I was raised? Was that how I raised my son? Who the hell was I now that the pressure was on? It was an enormous question, as wide as West Virginia. I shook my head with confusion. There was no way I could reason it through standing here in the hallway, the Colt in my hand. No way I could find the answer in the ether of the atmosphere in the next two hours, forget the next two minutes or two seconds.

And then a voice in a dark corner of my head said, *Screw that noise, McCall. This is the son of a bitch who held your own gun to your own head. This is the crankshaft who murdered your father. Could you do it? Hell yes you could. You could absolutely blow his fucking head off.*

All those thoughts flew through my brain in the time it took to blink my eyes.

And then I heard screaming inside apartment 605.

I checked the door. Locked.

I went into my purse and grabbed the six-inch restorer's pry bar I'd inherited from Jimmy at the reading of his will in Shavelson's office. I never thought I would use it, but when it came in handy unlocking a file cabinet during my workman's compensation case, I started carrying it around (like Kyle carried his master key) in the event I encountered a locked lock I needed unlocked...like right now, in fact.

I put it in place and applied pressure. Nothing.

Come on, I said silently, looking up and down the hall.

The screaming stopped. She was dead. And then she was screaming again, fighting for her life. If I couldn't get the door open, she would lose that fight forever.

I applied more pressure—*come on, goddammit*—adjusted the angle of the pry bar, applied more pressure—*come on, come on*—readjusted the angle, applied more pressure—*shit, shit, shit* —readjusted the angle, applied more pressure—*come on, you stupid motherfu*—click, the lock popped open.

I threw the pry bar back in my purse and grabbed the Colt in the same motion that I pushed the door open and went inside.

It was a large, gorgeous space, professionally decorated from end to end and top to bottom. I wanted to stand back and let the feng shui flow through me, but my feet followed the screaming down a hallway to a closed door. I kicked the door open, flew into the room, and found Michelle Lowry on her bed, on her hands and knees, getting the bejesus fucked out of her from behind by the guy who'd followed her out of the wine bar.

I recognized him now. His name was Casey, Carson or Corey, I couldn't recall, and he was one of the young Lowry Lowe lawyers I was introduced to when I was Emily Baynes from Austin and there was one hundred twenty million bucks in the balance.

Michelle and her boy toy looked at me with absolute shock,

stuck together like dogs in heat, breathing hard, eyes blinking, unable to bark.

I was as blown away as they were. But I pointed the Colt at them and held up my bogus press pass and opened my mouth without having the slightest idea what words would come out. "*National Enquirer.* Nobody move."

And then I heard my phone buzz. Someone was texting me. I put my press pass in my purse and took out my phone. (So now I had the Colt in one hand and my phone in the other.) It was a message from the killer. *Late for class, Little Engine.*

Shit, I thought, and then I looked at Michelle and Casey-Carson-Corey and took a photo of them on the bed, still stunned, and said, "Stay where you are or the gossip goes viral."

And then I took off through the apartment, ran down the hall to the stairwell—I couldn't risk waiting for the elevator—flew down the stairs and across the lobby, and sprinted west on 48th Street back to Rockefeller Center. Somehow, I called Logan on a dead run. His voicemail picked up yet again—didn't he ever answer his freaking phone?—and I said, "Logan, forget the apartment building on 48th and Lex. Go to Lowry Lowe. I'm on my way. Lowry Lowe, Logan. Hurry."

I caught the lights just right, so it only took me fifteen minutes to get back to 30 Rock. Logan was in the lobby when I arrived, accompanied by four uniformed officers. He cleared me with building security, and we all took the elevator to the sixty-second floor. A guard unlocked the Lowry Lowe front doors, and we hurried to Christopher's office, where we found him seated behind his desk, rope-tied to his black leather chair, dead as de Gaulle, horrible holes in his head where his eyes used to be.

42

____

WRONG ABOUT BEING WRONG

Within the hour, Lowry Lowe was swarming with cops. There were uniformed policemen and homicide detectives what felt like every five feet. Someone somewhere in the upper levels of police power had decided that having a high-priced corporate assassin who shoots the eyes out of his victims as a way of signing his kills on the loose in the city of New York was, at last, unacceptable.

On orders from Logan, the police fanned out through 30 Rock and the rest of Rockefeller Center. Logan stayed in Christopher's office. Not surprisingly, so did Christopher.

Three CSI officers, two men and a woman, dusted for invisible prints, used some kind of infrared laser to look for a dried droplet of blood, went through every desk drawer, every file cabinet, and every inch of the floor, the walls, the doors, and the windows with a fine-toothed comb, searching for a strand of hair, a fiber of clothing, a partial piece of DNA—anything that might get their investigation off the dime.

The woman, a forensic wizard named Wadzinski, focused on the dead body still rope-tied to the chair. She spent considerable time examining Christopher's now empty eye sockets, using a multitude of small-blade scalpels and other surgical tools. She wore high-tech magnifying gear so she could find and capture microscopic evidence, a pinhead on a pinhead. She'd set up bright lights to eliminate the possibility of shadows.

If *anything* incriminating was left behind—a speck of a scrap of a scintilla of a crumb of a grain of a mite of a molecule —one of these three NYPD professionals would find it, bag it, and tag it to the killer.

Logan ran point. Everything went through him. He made notes in his notebook when cops reported back to him and handed out new marching orders as needed.

My marching orders were to stay put, keep my hands in my pockets, and shut my mouth until Jesus got here. Literally, that's what Logan said to me. "McCall, you stay put and keep your hands in your pockets and your mouth shut until Jesus gets here."

I could tell the CSI team wasn't having any luck by their whispers of frustration, the shaking of their heads, and the fact they hadn't bagged a single freaking fragment of evidence. I could see the irritation on Logan's face too. I shared that feeling. We both knew they weren't going to find anything.

After about fifteen minutes, a young, handsome, Hispanic detective came into the room, and Logan looked at me and said, "Now we're saved. Get over here, McCall. Let me introduce you to Jesus."

I crossed the office, careful not to trample anything CSI related, which, in this case, was everything in the office.

Logan looked at the detective and gestured at me. "This is Kate McCall. She's an amateur private investigator can't get out of her own way trying to find the fuck who murdered her father, who happens to be the same goddamn killer who shot this poor asshole's eyes out. She is the human equivalent of a kidney stone, and dead bodies without their eyeballs follow her like a family of ducks on a lake. She is not my friend. And she is not your friend. If you remember this, your life may not be ruined, though there are no guarantees as far as McCall ruining your life."

And then he looked at me and gestured at the detective. "This is Detective Jesus Carrera"—he pronounced it *Hey-Seuss* —"but I call him Jesus, as in Son of God, because he's thirty years old and was resurrected from being a juvenile delinquent, which is what he was in his previous incarnation, to being a homicide detective, which is what he has been for all of one year. So naturally, in their infinite wisdom, the NYPD has decided he is the perfect partner for me now that Harriman has left the building."

We shook hands.

"Kate," I said.

"Jesse," he said.

"How's he doing so far?" I said to Logan.

"Worse than you," Logan said.

"They're ready for you in the conference room," Jesse said to Logan while gesturing at the CSI team. "How's it going in here?"

"What do you got, Wadzinski?" Logan said to the wizard, who was scraping for clues under Christopher's fingernails.

"Less than zero," Wadzinski said without looking at Logan. "It's like no one did this, like Mr. Lowry appeared in this chair out of thin air, like this murder happened without a murderer, like Mr. Lowry's eyes shot themselves out. There's no incriminating material. No markers whatsoever. This guy just doesn't make a mistake."

"Cause of death?" Logan said.

"Pre-autopsy assessment is asphyxiation," Wadzinski said. "He blew the eyes out after."

"Keep looking," Logan said. "Everybody makes a mistake in the end."

The conference room was packed with police, maybe a half dozen detectives and twice that many uniformed officers (men and women, various ages and ethnicities). Logan stood at the head of the table and addressed the crowd. Jesse stood nearby. I found a piece of wall, leaned against it, and listened to Logan. But I couldn't stop my mind from wandering out of the conference room and back to Morrell.

"Wadzinski says cause of death was asphyxiation," Logan said.

"He always does the eyes?" one of the detectives said.

Logan nodded and shook his head at the same time. "We have been and remain on absolute radio silence regarding the eyes. Friends, family, surviving spouse, associates, reporters, insurance, legal, medical—full blackout. No one knows, and I want to keep it that way. I don't want the media creating a copycat, but yes, he always does the eyes. 'Hello, is it me you're goddamn looking for?' Thank you, Lionel fucking Richie."

I was going to get into his head and under his skin and unsettle him to the point where he'd get careless and make a mistake, I thought, *and instead he'd gotten into my head and under my skin, and I'd made the mistake. He'd been in the wine bar. He'd watched me order a Russian River Valley chardonnay. He'd called me on the fucking phone and challenged me to follow him out of Morrell and to his next hit. He'd known all along that the boy toy had been waiting for Michelle to finish with Christopher. He'd set me up and messed with my mind, and I'd followed the wrong Lowry.*

"Time of death was one hour ago, give or take," Logan said, "and there's no physical or even metafuckingphysical evidence in the late Lowry's office, except for the fact that he was murdered somewhere between the sixty-second floor and Morrell, which means I want every fucking inch between here and there torn apart. On top of that bag of bad news, I want to know everywhere he went the last two days, everything he did, everyone he talked to, and everyone *they* talked to, where *they* work, who *they* work with, and where all *those* fucking people were the last two days. Every step between the wine bar and the law firm is a crime scene, and every person in Lowry's orbit is a suspect..."

He played me to play Logan, I thought, *and I'd done just that, and then Logan told him about the task force, which is what he'd wanted in the first place: a challenge. Now he'll be more meticulous than ever. He'll never make a mistake. And it's my fault. Logan and Matthew were right. I have no business in this business. It's time to get out. Time to walk away. Time to tell Logan I'm done with investigating anything private, and, God bless America, I'll tell him as soon as he finishes addressing the task force.*

I actually stopped leaning against the wall and stood straight up, intent on tapping Logan's shoulder and telling him my PI days were in my rearview mirror.

"I want to know how this cocksucker moves a dead lawyer past security on a Thursday evening in the middle of October," Logan said, "and accesses an office on the sixty-second floor, where he ties the dead lawyer to his own fucking chair without anybody in the fucking building suspecting a goddamn thing is amiss. I want to watch every 30 Rock security film for the last two days, every angle, every screen, frame by fucking frame..."

But then I thought, *Wait a minute, hold the phone. Now I know, or at least think I know, that one of the Lowry Lowe wives has been contracting the killer to murder her partners, and that by itself can be considered a kind of mistake, meaning by narrowing the field to two names instead of three, the killer himself has made my chances of waylaying the lawyer who hired him, and in the process uncovering his identity, better than they were when my chances were one in three. I was wrong about being wrong. He didn't exactly tilt the odds in my favor, but he evened the field to fifty-fifty. Now all I have to do is figure out which wife to waylay.*

And then the meeting ended, and a riptide of detectives pulled Logan away, and everyone left the conference room except me, and I didn't tell him about my rearview mirror.

43

SOMETHING OF A SETBACK

I didn't call Ricky Cordoba to tell him Adam Stoker had killed Tito Fuentes, Ricky's Chihuahua, with a Louisville Slugger, though Lord knows I'd wanted to. I was carrying enough baggage and didn't need to add responsibility for Adam's murder to the load I already lugged through life. Ricky possessed pot and pills and drugs and guns and stacks of cash, of which Adam had helped himself to twenty-five grand, but his most prized possession was the pooch. If I'd phoned in the anonymous tip that Adam, Ricky's across-the-hall neighbor, had stolen his money and grand-slammed his dog, then that would have been the end of Adam. Although Stoker was an MBA, so I imagined he was smart enough to know that by now he should be somewhere off the grid in Alaska. To which the only response was: good-bye and good riddance.

I did have one Adam Stoker regret: I never got to punch him in the nose.

Those were the thoughts in my head as I walked down the stairs to the Blue Bar offices on Friday at noon. I wore the red Wanda Ward wig and the green contacts because though Griff and Adam were out of the picture, I had not yet uncovered who *was* in the picture, and so I was still on the case as Danielle Sullivan, which is how the Blue Bar staff still knew me. I didn't want any of them to know me as me. Not yet.

I was meeting Blue for lunch. I hadn't seen him since Tuesday, when we'd made love all morning, and that seemed like a long time ago.

I'd wondered several times over the last three days whether sleeping with Blue had been a mistake—or even a big mistake. There were reasons galore on the mistake side of the ledger. For God's sake, I'd had to buy a second ledger just to get them all down. On the not-a-mistake side of the ledger, I had only come up with one reason: I liked him. That can sometimes be reason enough, don't get me wrong, but was it reason enough this time? Or was this time another spectacular Kate McCall romantic misfire?

I could feel my heart pounding as I knocked on Blue's office door. Jesus, I was nervous. I wanted it to be real. I wanted it to be true. I wanted him to like me as much as I liked him. I felt fifteen years old. The light was on in Blue's office, but the door was locked. I knocked again.

"He had to run out for a few minutes, Dani. Told me to tell you he'd be right back." It was Mary, standing half in her doorway and half in the hall.

"Hi, Mary," I said.

"Hi, stranger," she said. "Come into my office. I have news."

In her own words, she was my inside man, so I crossed my fingers in hope that her news was about my Blue Bar embezzlement case—a jump start to get me going again because I was stalled out on the Road to Nowhere with a dead battery and no cables. She shut the door behind us as we went into her office, and I thought, *Yes, she doesn't want any little birdies bothering us.*

I sat at her small conference table, and she grabbed an envelope off her desk, and I thought, *Yes, yes, she has evidence only an inside man could uncover.*

She opened the envelope and removed a stack of photographs, and I thought, *Yes, yes, yes, she's got pictures of someone with their hands in the cookie jar.*

She took the seat beside me, smiled like the Cheshire cat, and said, "I was in Allentown, and my oldest grandson got engaged, and we were all there to see it happen. It was wonderful, Dani. Take a look."

This was her news—her grandson's engagement. Not a break in the Blue Bar case.

She showed me every picture half a dozen times at least. Her oldest daughter, Alyssa, had two boys and a girl. The oldest boy, Gregory, was in his last year of pharmacy school, and he'd proposed to a young woman named Alexandra, who everyone called Alex, who was also studying to be a pharmacist. They'd grown up on the same street and had dated since middle school (and shared the same affection for prescription drugs, apparently). They were, Mary said, each other's *romantic destiny.*

They were graduating together in the spring and getting married the spring after that, but they wanted to make it official before they finished pharmacy college because, well, that's the way they'd planned it back in high school.

Gregory put on an elaborate proposal that involved the renting of their old high school gymnasium, the inviting of both families in their entireties, the corralling of the high school marching band, the trucking in of every peony in Pennsylvania (Alex's favorite flower), and the blowing up of every balloon in the Lehigh Valley. Alex thought she was going to see a concert at their alma mater and was super surprised to arrive at her very own marriage proposal. The stands were filled with both families, and everyone screamed and cried as Gregory got down on one knee at midcourt, and the whole affair was perfectly perfect—except for the absence of Mary's late husband, which had made Mary cry a little, though they became tears of joy again pretty quick.

Mary showed me the pictures of her younger sister and her sister's children, the math genius professor and the rich one who'd started his own car-detailing business in community college and dropped out to make a fortune Turtle Waxing automobiles. Mary's children were just as accomplished as her sister's children, although Alyssa was talking about taking a long leave of absence from her big, important job at the bank to be a painter or a sculptor or a glassblower or something artistic.

And Mary was over the moon about her grandchildren and the nephews and nieces and cousins and uncles and aunts and brothers and sisters, who were all fabulous in their own ways. She showed me their photographs, and each one came with a story—success stories of school and sports and work and vacations and holidays and reunions and family life in the Lehigh Valley.

Her pride in Gregory's proposal was palpable, and I wondered if I would one day feel that same sense of unbridled joy when Matthew proposed to Insufferable Nina. Probably not, I imagined, since Obnoxious Nina and I detested each other with the intensity of a solar storm.

But the real issue for me was the phrase Mary had used that was now ringing in my ears: *romantic destiny*. Was there such a thing? Were we all blessed with the same amount of romantic destiny at birth, or did some people get more than others in the way pro athletes are given more talent in their sport, like Blue with baseball, for instance.

More to the point, was I anybody's romantic destiny? Was anybody mine? Could Blue be my romantic destiny? Isn't that kind of life-changing, emotionally cataclysmic moment of awareness consequential enough that I would have sensed it if it had happened to me? I mean, if it *was* Blue, wouldn't we *both* have recognized our romantic destiny from the beginning or at least after we'd made love on Tuesday? When, exactly, does romantic destiny display itself—right off the bat, during the seventh-inning stretch, or in the second game of a day-night doubleheader?

Had this been my issue with relationships all along, my inability to recognize my own romantic destiny?

And just how far back in time did my blind spot go? When they were sixteen, Gregory and Alexandra were planning their wedding after they finished pharmacy school in the future. When I was sixteen, I was planning to be an actor and got pregnant. Had I missed my romantic destiny when I was a teenager? When I was in my twenties? My thirties? Forties? Had I missed it Tuesday?

Holy shit, I thought; *what a confidence shaker.*

I had to admit I was a little envious of the newly engaged couple. Not because I wished I was engaged (although there had been a bit of that in the mix for decades), but because I wished Mary was *my* grandmother, as excited and proud and filled with love and happiness about my life as she was for Gregory and Alex.

Jimmy was dead, his few surviving relatives lived a thousand miles away or more, and I had no family in New York with me. *If I did have family in New York*, I thought, *I'd want it to be Mary, my inside grandma.* Doris Roberts as Aunt Bee.

Anyway, it wasn't just the mystery of my romantic destiny I couldn't solve.

"It's not Adam embezzling the money," I said as Mary scooped up the photographs.

"Oh my. Are you sure?" she said.

I told her the story of interrogating Adam in his office, how he'd stolen the money from Ricky and beaten Tito with a baseball bat for good measure.

She agreed this was something of a setback. I knew that because she said, "This is something of a setback."

"Who else has access to the money?" I said. "There has to be someone."

There *was* someone. It wasn't Griff, and it wasn't Adam, and it couldn't be Mary because Mary had the checkbook but, by security design, no access to the actual cash money. We looked at each other. She was thinking what I was thinking, *The someone couldn't be the someone because the someone was Blue.*

"That is a crazy thought," Mary said.

"The craziest," I said.

"Why in the world would he steal his own money?" she said.

"He wouldn't," I said. "I've never once seen him talk to Stanley Stein."

"Because that would be too obvious," Mary said.

"Of course it would," I said.

"So he might have someone else bet the money for him," she said.

"Who?" I said.

"You tell me," she said.

Jesus Christ, what the heck was happening in this conversation? It was ridiculous to even consider Blue embezzling money from Blue Bar. And yet my mind was racing for an answer. Several employees had on one occasion or maybe two, when they were off the clock, sat beside Stanley and then run to a restroom to place their bet. But none of them had access to the kind of money that had been embezzled.

But then a vision appeared in my mind's eye. It wasn't a name so much as it was a color: red. There was a cook who was also a bartender, a utility player who'd do anything to help the team. His name was Eric Miller, he was a redhead, and he'd been gambling plenty with Stanley Stein since I'd first arrived in the bar.

44

YOU CAN'T UNTHINK A THOUGHT

My father was at his philosophical best when we were on a stakeout, an extended form of surveillance in which one sits for hours, days, or weeks waiting for some unlucky loser to cheat on their spouse or hot-wire a car or bust their parole or break the boundaries of a recent restraining order. It is a form of boredom so protracted and painful that PIs have been known to experience out-of-body hallucinations leading to psychosomatic revelations resulting in life-changing affirmations.

Case in point, once when we were on a particularly prolonged stakeout, waiting for some psycho to steal her neighbor's mail, Jimmy told me about another PI on an unremittingly tedious stakeout, also (coincidentally) waiting for some psycho to steal her neighbor's mail, who had a revelation that he was meant to be a milkman in Big Sky country. The next day, the guy quit being a PI, moved to Montana, and bought a cow.

That is often the kind of thing you hear on a stakeout—but not always. On one memorably mind-numbing occasion, Jimmy said this: *"Katie, here are two pearls of PI wisdom you need to remember for the rest of your days. The first one is 'Everybody's radar is on all the time, but you don't know what they're listening for. The second one is 'You can't unthink a thought.'"*

Both pearls came to mind during my lunch with Blue.

We took a table on the second floor, near the open kitchen. We both ordered sliced steak sandwiches on homemade sourdough and Defender IPAs from the Brooklyn Brewery. The sandwiches were excellent, as always, and the Brooklyn Brewery kills it every time.

Blue Bar was packed, and playoff baseball was already in the air, though the games didn't start until later tonight. Usually, the weekend didn't get going until happy hour, Blue told me, but when you threw National and American League championship games into the mix, then the party started at lunch and all bets were off—*except with Stanley Stein*, I thought.

And thinking that thought reminded me of pearl one: everybody's radar is on all the time, but you don't know what they're listening for.

Blue was distracted from the moment we'd met at the table, meaning his radar was dialed way up—and I had no idea what he was listening for. It wasn't me, that much I could tell. I wasn't feeling any sort of romantic destiny, but I also didn't have the sense that he was over me either. The fact that we'd made love on Tuesday was just not on his mind at the moment, even with me sitting right next to him. So what was?

I didn't want him to be listening for the sounds of his own embezzlement, but that idea had come into my head, and I had thought about it, and that reminded me of pearl two: you can't unthink a thought.

"I have to tell you about Adam," I said.

"He's gone," Blue said.

"Dead?"

"Oregon, maybe Washington. He left me a voicemail at two in the morning. He was already on the road. Said he was on his way to the Great Northwest and was never coming back. You have any idea what that's all about?"

"I do."

I told him the story about Ricky and Tito and the money and the baseball bat.

"So it wasn't him," Blue said.

"No," I said.

"And it wasn't Griff."

"It wasn't Griff."

"That's not good because money was missing this morning. And if it wasn't Griff and it wasn't Adam, then who was it?"

I didn't answer. Partly because I didn't know the answer and partly because I thought the answer might be him.

"How much this time?" I said.

"Twelve thousand," he said.

"Lot of money," I said.

"Hey, Blue. Sorry to interrupt."

It was Eric Miller, the redheaded utility man. He was wearing a shirt and tie, a sport jacket, and dress slacks, which meant today he wasn't a cook or a bartender; today he was a dead ringer for Fred and George Weasley. Yes, those Weasleys, from *Harry Potter*, Ron's red-haired, troublemaking twin brothers. With a different twist of fate, in fact, Eric Miller could have been one of the Weasley triplets. Instead, he was working at Blue Bar and betting with Stanley Stein whenever he had money, which was more often than not, now that I was thinking about it.

"You've met Danielle?" Blue said to Eric, gesturing at me.

"Several times," Eric said. He nodded a little. Or maybe he didn't nod at all. I nodded half as much as he did to let Blue know I knew Eric as well.

"Eric's my new general manager," Blue said. "And my new bar manager too."

On the one hand, I was stunned. On the other hand, the

pieces were falling into place. I didn't want to think that thought, but I did. And now I couldn't unthink it.

They had a quick conversation about the cook taking Eric's place, then the new general manager didn't nod good-bye, and I didn't nod good-bye back, and then he was off to do general manager things.

"That was fast," I said.

"I need someone now," Blue said.

"Why him?" I said, and though I'd tried to say it as innocently as possible, I knew there was a hint of inflection, a tinge of tone, that put a pinpoint of private investigation into the words.

"What do you mean?" Blue said, just slightly narrowing his eyes.

And for the first time since I'd met him at Fu's party for Jerusalem Joe, I could see Blue's line.

Everybody has a line, a virtual boundary, an ethereal mark on the ground you can't cross or step on or even go near without invoking a reaction of disappointment or shock or anger or revulsion or resentment or suspicion or violence or worse. It's common courtesy not to go anywhere near another person's line, and most of the time most people don't—why in the world would you want to piss off or push away someone you like or love? (Someone who might just be your romantic destiny?)

The problem is you can't know what someone else's line is all about—why *that* line is *their* line—until you get too close for comfort. And since you also can't know *where* their line is, when it's suddenly right in front of your face, there's a good goddamn chance you're going to step on it or over it, and that is a bad idea because the line could be about secrets you weren't supposed to know and probably don't want to know, meaning some secrets are not meant for sharing. And so it's subconscious, normal human nature to avoid another person's line at all cost. For private investigators, however, sneaking up to someone else's line is just another perilous part of the job.

I hated sneaking up to Blue's line. There was something special between us. We'd both felt it from the beginning. So if the Blue Bar embezzlement case turned out to have nothing to do with Blue on the bad end, then I would be sad as hell if sneaking up to his line ruined our relationship—and if it did turn out bad, then that would be even worse.

But I couldn't unthink my thought, and so I had to go gently enough to make it seem as if I weren't going at all.

"I mean, he told me he's only worked here a year," I said.

"Give or take."

"That's enough time to make him your GM?"

"He knows the bar, he knows the kitchen, he's a good kid."

He was hardly a kid. Eric Miller had to be thirty-five years old. "Where's he from?"

"Trenton. I met him through Griff. He worked at one of Griff's bars. More than one, I think."

"He's part of the Trenton crew?"

"Was part of the Trenton crew. It's fine, Kate."

"Dani. If the premise is someone's stealing your money and betting it with the bookie at your bar, how can that be fine? You know he bets with Stanley Stein, right?"

"Everybody bets with Stanley," Blue said.

"Is he here?"

"Stanley? I hope so. I could use the money."

That's where it ended. After that, we talked about other things—a trip he was planning to San Diego, boxing's best heavyweight champions (he had memorabilia from it seemed like all of them), my *Blood Song and Dance* performance later tonight (he promised to see it in two weeks, on the last Saturday of the run, our annual Halloween costume party performance), the food, the traffic, the coming winter—anything other than

Eric Miller, Adam Stoker, Dave Griffin, Stanley Stein, and stolen money.

He didn't want to talk about it? Okay, neither did I. But I didn't want to talk about it because I was torn between my feelings for him and my personal predisposition, inherited from my father, for solving a case in which he might now be implicated. The question was, why didn't Blue want to talk about it?

Was it because *someone* had been stealing him blind for weeks and weeks and so far, despite hiring a private investigator, there was still no way to know who it was, or because *he* was the one embezzling and betting his own cash and the clues were starting to point his way, which was unbelievable in the sense I didn't want to believe it, or was it because he didn't know how to tell me that sleeping with me was a mistake he wished he could take back? That last one gave me a sick, empty feeling in the pit of my stomach.

After lunch, he walked me outside to hail me a cab. One pulled to the curb, and Blue kissed me good-bye. It was an electric kiss, meaning electricity was sparking all over the place when our lips met. How could two people kiss like that, with freaking electricity coming off their lips, and not be sharing a romantic destiny?

I got in the cab, and no matter how hard I tried, I couldn't unthink my thoughts.

45

NOT MY TURN FOR AN ALL-TOO-EASY ONE

A THOUGHT OCCURRED TO ME DURING THE SECOND ACT OF THE Friday night performance of *Blood Song and Dance*. It was during the scene in which my character, cabaret-singing vampire Farina LeBleu, jaded with jealousy, opens the neck of Nancy North, a risqué, rival nightclub singer who's hot for Roger's character, piano-playing maestro Orlando Bilzi, because Orlando is Farina's true love, and she must have him for herself. The fact that Farina mixes Nancy's blood with vodka and adds a wedge of lime is beside the point, which is that while drinking the cocktail for brunch, I realized, as if for the first time, that only two characters remained for Farina to kill: Orlando and Mariah Muldoon, the lesbian lover of lady vampires, Chloe's character.

But this realization was *not* the thought that occurred to me, though it did lead me to recognize that the deadly game of Last Lowry Lowe Lawyer Living was down to the final two attorneys, and so the next round would be the final round, and the man who murdered Jimmy would be gone again, maybe this time for good.

But this recognition was *not* the thought that occurred to me, though it did lead me to admit that no matter how or how hard I pressured Michelle Lowry and Lisa Lowe, neither one was going to give me any guidance as to which one had hired the killer who had murdered their husbands—or shed any light as to who the next victim would be.

But this admittance was *not* the thought that occurred to me, though it did lead me to understand that if I were going to catch the killer and, in the process, save one of the Lowry Lowe women from getting her eyes shot out, I would have to lean on someone else with access to inside information.

But this understanding was *not* the thought that occurred to me, though it did lead me to recall that Michelle Lowry's boy toy's name was not Casey, Carson, or Corey; it was Carter. Carter Ringwald.

But this recollection was *not* the thought that occurred to me, though it did lead me to consider the fact that Logan had his task force looking everywhere but at Carter, so I would lean on Lowry's boy toy because there very well might be a clue somewhere inside him, since he was fucking Michelle at the same time he was working for her and had to have seen something amiss or heard something suspicious while they were flirting in her office or screwing like dogs in heat in her boudoir. And since there very well might be, meaning there very probably was a clue inside him, all I had to do was break him wide open and let the clue fall in my lap.

But this consideration was *not* the thought that occurred to me, though it did lead me to think the thought that occurred to me, which was this: if I was going to break Carter Ringwald wide open, then Charlie Nye would be my hammer.

I chose Charlie over Fu because my Carter caper called for a Staten Island mafioso vibe, and Fu wouldn't look Italian if you dipped him in a vat of Armani. And even though Charlie wasn't Italian either, he definitely wasn't Asian, so that was a start. Fu, of course, had a seriously imposing physical presence, but Charlie had a special kind of crazy that, given a certain staging, could crack Carter like an egg.

As far as the Carter caper was concerned, what Charlie had going for him was a violent nature. The threat of imminent, explosive violence was part of his aura. The sense that his heart held a predilection for physical violence was in his eyes. The possibility that he used excessive violence as a way to carry a conversation was in his body language. The idea that extreme violence directed specifically at you was at the end of his next sentence or maybe in the middle of the sentence he was now saying was in his soul. His own mother had told him he was violent.

He'd done an insane stint in Afghanistan and another in Iraq as a mechanic in the vehicle pool, hot-wiring Humvees in the middle of the desert under enemy fire with bombs underfoot. It was, he once told me, grad school for car thieves. And so he became one—a car thief, I mean.

After the army, he got caught stealing a Porsche in Pittsburgh and went to prison. He did the time and moved to Ohio, where he was arrested and convicted for breaking and entering a bedding business in Bowling Green. At his sentencing, the judge tacked on two years for the accompanying assault and battery charge and said he'd wanted to add up *all* of Charlie's previous assault and battery charges that hadn't held but couldn't corral enough Gorilla Glue in the Buckeye State to make them stick.

He got out of jail, moved to the Big Apple, got arrested for grand theft auto, and was living life in an upstate lockup when the city of New York offered him immediate early release in exchange for services to be rendered now and far into the future—the services in Charlie's case being towing illegally parked cars and cars with piles of unpaid parking tickets to auto prison. Charlie took the deal and moved into the House of Emotional Tics.

He lived in 2B. He was fifty years old. Like Fu, he had been shot and stabbed on several occasions and had the scars to prove it. He had badass tattoos, some from his time in the army and some from his extended stays in prison. He had gray hair and gray eyes. He played poker and screwed hookers.

The only reason Charlie Nye wasn't killing a dozen people a day was weed. He was a prodigious pot smoker—and a small-time dope dealer too. And lately, he'd been a farmer as well, growing a row of reefer plants in the backyard behind a line of scrubby bushes.

The weed chilled him out and mitigated his violent streak, though I always had the funny feeling, maybe because I had seen it surface, that violence was lurking under his skin. With Carter Ringwald, I was counting on it.

Friday night, when I got back from the D-Cup, I went to the intercom and buzzed Charlie, who was buzzed, and told him I had a rush job for tomorrow, needed his help, and would pay him accordingly. I told him the plan, and he said he was on board, and then he forgot what the plan was, and so I told him again, and he said he was on board.

Then I called Al, who was trading flip-flops for flatware for floorboards in Florida. I told him the plan, that I had a role for him too, and that Charlie was already good to go, and Al said he wanted more money than I was paying Charlie because Charlie was a three-time ex-con and dope-smoking loser, and Al was a paragon of virtue.

"I'm paying you both the same," I said.

"What part of 'This is his brain on drugs' are you missing?" Al said.

"The part where I tell Charlie you want more than him because he's a three-time ex-con and dope-smoking loser?"

"If you tell him—"

"He'll beat you like a drum. Yes, I took that into consideration."

"You are a miserable human being, McCall."

"At least I am a human being."

Charlie found an unattended, I mean illegally parked, jet-black Lincoln Town Car with tinted windows at seven a.m. Saturday morning and towed it to a garage on East 82nd Street, around the corner from the House of Emotional Tics, where one of the garage guys looked the other way for a bag of free weed.

And Al hacked into Carter Ringwald's digital calendar, so we knew where the boy toy lived, where he was going, and what time he was leaving to go there.

It was all too easy, which gave me a bad feeling in the pit my stomach. But then I thought, *Hey, maybe I deserve an all-too-easy one; maybe it's my turn for something to be all too easy for a change,* and I started to believe it, and the feeling went away.

Ringwald lived at the corner of Columbus and West 66th Street. He had written in his digital calendar that he was meeting Michelle at the gym at ten a.m., Saturday morning, so we double-parked outside his building, flashers flashing, and waited for him.

I wore the black wig with heavy bangs and black contact lenses that became my character in the original D-Cup musical *Tony Loves Toni*, which told the tale of a mafia don dying of loneliness because his heart was surrounded by a wall of stone —literally, it was a medical phenomenon, a wall of stone surrounded his actual heart, and no one, including Dennis and Posey, could explain it. In the play, the don meets a bank teller while robbing a savings and loan and falls in love for the first time in his mafia life.

I had played Toni Gardino, the beautiful bank teller from Brooklyn. Roger had played Tony Franzetti, the downtown don. Needless to say, through the magic of song and dance,

Toni's love breaks down the stone wall around Tony's heart— another mysterious medical miracle—and the couple sings and dances their way to a new life, in which they open an Italian dinner theater on the Jersey shore and live happily ever after.

Charlie wore a black suit with a black shirt and a black tie and black sunglasses and looked like Tommy Lee Jones in *Men in Black*. Al wore dark slacks and the kind of two-tone, wiseguy shirt that Paulie Walnuts wore on *The Sopranos*.

I sat in the backseat of the Lincoln. Al was my driver, good casting on my part because he worked the graveyard shift for a limo outfit a few times a week to help fill the endless sleepless nights that were his life. Charlie was my muscle, my man on the street.

At nine forty-five, Carter came out of his building. He was dressed casually and carried a large Nike gym bag. He was a handsome young divorce attorney having a passionate affair with a partner. He was making good money. He lived in an upscale building in an upscale neighborhood. Life was good for Carter Ringwald.

But it was about to get less good.

I rolled down the window and called out to him. "Hey, Carter, got a minute?"

He looked at me, confused. Did he know me? He *must* know me. I knew his name, for Pete's sake.

"Come on, Carter. I'm double-parked over here," I said with Italian inflection.

He walked toward the Lincoln. I opened the door as he took his final steps to the sedan.

"Do I know you?" Carter said.

"You should," I said. "I'm your worst nightmare."

And then Charlie, my Man in Black on the street, came rushing up behind Carter and, all in one motion, grabbed him hard and rammed him right into the backseat of the Lincoln as

I slid over to make room. Charlie pushed in behind him and shut the door.

"What the hell is this?" Carter said. "Who are you? Let me out of this car."

"Sit tight, Molly Ringwald," Charlie said, stoned on his own product.

"I'm not Molly Ringwald," Carter said.

"You look just like her. You could be her brother," Charlie said.

"You do look like her," Al said from the front seat. He had dark shades too.

"I don't look anything like her," Carter said.

"Twin brother from a different mother and a father with the same last name but not the same father as the other father of the different mother," Charlie said. "Think about it."

"Who the hell are you people?" Carter said.

"I'm Toni Gardino," I said. "I'm a client. Christopher Lowry is—was—my attorney. His wife is representing my husband, Anthony Gardino. That's right, Carter, mafia hit man Tony Gardino and his beautiful wife, Toni Gardino. It's in all the papers—mafioso love affair on the skids. Now my lawyer is dead, and you're fucking my husband's lawyer, and I want to know what you know."

I took a moment to congratulate myself on using a piece of my theatrical past to solve a crime in my PI present. The moment didn't last long because the doorman of Carter's building, an African American bodybuilder banking a few extra bucks opening doors on 66th Street, had seen Charlie force Carter into the Lincoln and was walking toward us with concern and purpose.

"I've never heard of you or your husband, and I'm getting out of this car right now," Carter said.

"Lock the doors, Christopher," I said to Al. I'd given Al and

Charlie names from *The Sopranos*. Charlie was Junior. "Carter's not going anywhere."

Al locked the Lincoln just as the doorman tried to open the back door.

"Let me out," Carter said. He was trying to sound angry, but now there was fear and panic in his voice.

"Relax, Molly Ringwald," Charlie said.

"Stop calling me that," Carter said, and he started to struggle. Charlie struggled back, and so did I.

Outside the Lincoln, the doorman was pulling on the door and signaling for help.

"Get out of my way, asshole," Carter said to Charlie, and he reached for the door and started to climb over Charlie to exit the sedan.

But Charlie's fist came flying forward fast, and I saw he was wearing his brass knuckles before I had a chance to tell him to stop.

Crack. The brass knuckles hit Carter flush in the face, a high-speed collision that bashed Carter backward onto me. Blood was pouring out of Carter's busted nose, which was splattered all over the place.

"Jesus, Junior," I said.

"He called me an asshole. I had to clock him," Charlie said. "My mother taught me that. If someone calls you an asshole, you clock him."

"Your mother said that?" I said.

"Now you know where I get it," Charlie said.

Carter was stunned, seeing stars. And then he focused in, saw his own blood, and said, "Oh my God, I'm bleeding. Oh my God, oh my—" And then his eyes rolled back in his head, and he passed out, stone-cold unconscious.

"What the fuck?" Al said from the front seat.

"What do you know?" Charlie said. "Molly Ringwald's a hemophobe."

"Hemophobe?" I said.

"As in hemophobia," Charlie said. "Irrational fear of your own blood. If I've seen it once, I've seen it a hundred times."

If anyone had seen someone faint from the sight of their own blood a hundred times, Charlie Nye would be that person.

"What do we do now?" Al said as a crowd gathered around the Lincoln.

"Dump him on the sidewalk," Charlie said.

"Too late," I said. The doorman had walked behind the car and was taking a picture of the license plate on his cell phone. People were knocking on the windows, pulling on the handles, yelling at the car. "Time to go, Christopher."

"Where?" Al said, putting the Lincoln in gear and pulling away.

"East 83rd Street," I said.

"We're kidnappers now?" Al said.

It was a big damn question that required some thought on my part. There was the moral issue of dragging Al and Charlie, not to mention myself, across the boundary of being bad boys and girls to being felons firmly in Wrong-Side-of-the-Law Land, which meant there was Logan to consider, and my son too. I'd wanted Charlie's *threat* of violence to crack Carter in the car, but Charlie's *actual* violence had reared its brass-knuckled hand and now Carter was unconscious. With the clock ticking, all I could do was go with the premise that a thing happens because it happens, and in this case, it just happened to happen because that's how it happened, meaning we weren't actually kidnapping Carter because we never intended to take him. It was serendipitous.

Shit, I thought. *Definitely not my turn for an all-too-easy one.*

"We're not intentionally kidnapping him," I said. "We're accidentally kidnapping him. You got something on your mind, now's the time."

He caught my eyes in the rearview mirror. He *always* had

something on his mind. And it was usually money, meaning more of it for him.

"Accidental kidnapping's an extra two fifty," Al said.

Of course it is, I thought. "Fine," I said. "Charlie?"

Charlie wiped his bloody brass knuckles on Carter Ringwald's pants and said, "About fucking time we accidentally kidnapped somebody."

46

WHOSE CAGE IS THIS?

There was a room in the basement of the House of Emotional Tics, across from the laundry and down the hall from Fu's apartment, that we'd used as a storage and workshop space until the arrival of Jerusalem Joe, at which time it became what Fu liked to call "Joe's Apartment" and what I liked to call "Joe's Rent-Free Apartment."

It was ten by ten, had one wall with hardware store shelving, one wall with a janitorial slop sink with mops and brooms and buckets, and one wall with a built-in tool bench, including a pegboard on the wall above the bench with all types of tools hanging from all kinds of hooks.

Before Joe came to town, the room had been filled with unlabeled boxes of various shapes and sizes holding unknown House of Emotional Tics shit from years gone by. Fu had cleared away everything stacked on the shelves and everything else piled on the floor—where the boxes had gone was a mystery—so there would be enough space for Joe's custom-made, phone booth-sized cage, his massive perch, and other parrot paraphernalia and Fu collectibles that now filled the shelves. The tool bench was left intact because though the tools had always been considered property of the house, they now belonged to Fu, meaning nobody was allowed to touch them—as if anyone would enter Joe's Rent-Free Apartment to touch a tool while Joe was in there.

Charlie and I carried Carter from the car to the house as if the boy toy was passed-out piss-drunk, Carter between us, arms slung over our shoulders. We lugged him downstairs to Joe's Rent-Free Apartment and put him in Joe's cage, seated on the floor, slumped to the side, hands bound to the bars. Fortunately, Joe wasn't home.

Charlie said he needed a smoke, which meant get stoned because he pulled a joint from his pocket, and that left me alone with Michelle Lowry's affair du jour. I looked at poor Carter Ringwald, a prisoner in a parrot cage, and was hit by a wave of empathy.

When I was seven years old, before my mother got sick, my sister dragged me against my will from our living room into our bedroom, where she tied my wrists to the legs of the desk Jimmy had built from a kit a client had given him for wrecking the nose of a mechanic who'd replaced the engine of their new car with the engine of an old car (instead of changing their oil) without telling them. A new engine (and a new nose, no doubt) immediately followed the beatdown.

Anyway, Marilyn kidnapped me because she'd thought the boy across the street had told me something secret. Marilyn had a crush on the kid and wanted to know what I knew, assuming I knew anything in the first place. In fact, the boy *had* told me something secret, and I finally folded and spilled the beans—the boy liked my sister, but he liked another girl more—and Marilyn let me go after she stopped crying.

My sister had tied me to the desk with ribbon, so I probably could have escaped at any time, but I didn't because I was seven, and I imagined the ribbon was rope soaked in saltwater for several seasons. (Or maybe I subconsciously craved the attention, since Marilyn hardly knew I lived in the same house.)

Anyway, I felt bad for Carter, though not so bad to let him go before I found out something secret.

He came to ten minutes after we locked him up, got his bearings—he was in a cage, tied to the bars, busted nose, big headache—and said, "Where am I?"

"Abandoned basement in Bayonne," I said.

"I hate New Jersey," he said, looking around the room.

"Join the club," I said.

"Whose cage is this?" he said, checking out his temporary lodging.

"Does it matter?" I said.

"I guess not," he said. "My nose is broken."

"You think?"

He was quiet for a minute, and then he looked at me for the first time since he'd regained consciousness. "Congratulations. You can add assault and battery to your kidnapping charge, which is a federal offense, in case you didn't know. You're going to prison for twenty-five years."

"Unless we murder you and burn your body. Then those charges go away."

Did I just say that? I thought. *Oh my God, I love acting.*

"This sucks so much," he said.

There was a stool at Fu's tool bench. I carried it to the cage and sat down in front of Carter. "Sucks worse for me."

"There's no way this sucks worse for you."

"Much worse."

"I'm the one who's kidnapped. I'm the one in the fucking cage. I'm the one with the busted nose. I'm the one in the fucking abandoned basement in Bayonne. How could this suck worse for you?"

"For one thing, Carter, in case you haven't noticed, I'm in the fucking abandoned basement in Bayonne too. How's that for a complete waste of my time? For another thing, now I have to deal with kidnapping you, or maybe murdering you, on top of the rest of my messed-up life, which includes my damn divorce, which was worse than World War I when I had a lawyer who was *alive*. Now that I have a lawyer who's goddamn dead, which means no lawyer at all, my divorce is going to be like a meteor colliding with Earth and killing the fucking dinosaurs. For still one more thing, hello, my lawyer was murdered by a hit man hired by my husband's lawyer—who you happen to be screwing. On top of all that, I have to sit here and listen to you whine about your life. Me, me, me, me, me…Jesus Christ, Carter, give it a rest, why don't you?"

Oh my God, I thought. *I love acting so much.*

"I've never heard of you or your husband," he said.

"Then you are living under a rock," I said. "And I know what's hiding under there with you."

"What are you talking about?"

"I'll show you mine if you show me yours."

"What does that even mean?"

"It means I think Michelle Lowry, or maybe Lisa Lowe, hired a professional corporate killer to murder Christopher Lowry and Jack Lowe before that. It means I think you saw something in the office or heard something in Michelle's bedroom about who hired who to do what to who. It means if you don't tell me what I want to know, I'm going to tell somebody something about someone and someone's going to do something about somebody."

Oh my God, I thought. *Nobody loves acting more than I do.*

"I don't know anything about any of that," he said. "And even if I did, I wouldn't tell you. I play poker. I know when someone's bluffing. You've got nothing."

"I've got your digital calendar."

"What?"

Ah yes, there it was—the tender tone of abject terror. "Your digital calendar. I hacked into it. Jesus, Carter, you must lose a lot of money."

"What are you talking about?"

"Poker. You must lose your shirt. You can't catch a bluff worth a damn."

"I mean what are you talking about hacking into my calendar."

I took some printed pages from my pocket. "I mean I know about Bethany."

"Oh no…"

I didn't think anyone could sink lower than the bottom of a parrot cage, but Carter proved me wrong. I think he knew what was coming next. I think he knew I knew he knew. "You're getting married in March in Miami. It says so right here. You got the first two weeks blocked out and labeled: *Wedding Week One* and *Wedding Week Two*."

"No, no, no…"

"I'm betting Bethany has no idea you're fucking Michelle Lowry five months before your wedding."

"This is the worst day ever."

"Not yet."

"What do you mean?"

I took out my phone. "I'm going to call your fiancée and tell her about Michelle. Then I'm going to tell her she should know better than to marry a divorce lawyer, though I think she'll figure that out on her own. What the hell is it with you divorce lawyers? Anyway, *then* it will be the worst day ever. That's what I mean by *not yet*."

I started to dial Bethany's number.

"Stop, please…" Carter said, cracking wide open.

"Why should I?" I said.

"I heard them argue. Michelle and Lisa. Lisa was furious because Michelle changed the Lowry Lowe partnership agreement behind Lisa's back. They were fighting over who controlled the shares, the money, the firm, now that Jack and Christopher were gone. That's all I know. That's all I heard. Please don't call Bethany. Please..."

And then he started to weep. It was pathetic, and yet I still didn't feel all that bad for him. He was the one who got caught cheating on his fiancée. If I hadn't busted into the bedroom when he was fucking his senior partner, he might have gotten away with it. But I was trying to catch Jimmy's killer, so I did bust in. *Tough luck, Carter*, I thought.

Charlie walked in just then, smelling like an ounce of something profound, and I said, "Time for Carter to go home."

"You get something?" Charlie said.

"Something secret," I said.

Charlie nodded, took his terrifying switchblade out of his pocket, and snapped it open in a way that scared me half to death.

Carter stopped crying and watched Charlie walk toward the cage, one eye on the knife, the other eye on the crazy-violent, stoned man who'd broken his nose.

"What are you doing?" Carter said.

"Pulling your plug, Molly Ringwald," Charlie said, and he cut Carter's arm just enough so the boy toy could see his own blood.

Carter screamed at the pain, looked at his bleeding arm, and blacked out.

47

MAYBE I COULD NIP THIS
KIDNAPPING THING IN THE BUD

AL DROVE THE LINCOLN BACK TO THE SAME SPOT CHARLIE HAD towed it from—just to mess with everybody's mind—and left Carter slumped behind the wheel, bandage on his arm where Charlie had drawn blood.

We'd all worn latex surgical gloves our entire time with the Lincoln (and with Carter), so there would be no prints for anyone to find—except Carter's—should the boy toy call anyone to find them. Although I imagined that when Carter woke up from his hemophobic nap, he wouldn't be telling anyone what had happened and, in fact, would invent some other tall tale to tell his muscle-bound doorman because if he let even a little truth out of the bag, then the rest of the truth might follow and Bethany would be history.

Carter's accidental kidnapping took two hours, top to bottom, which was either impressive or unimpressive for a kidnapping—serendipitous or otherwise—although I had no idea which one, since I'd only been involved in the one kidnapping so far.

Anyway, it was noon, and I had to be back at the D-Cup at four o'clock for a *Psychedelic Sunday* rehearsal, followed by a dinner break, followed by the Saturday night performance of *Blood Song and Dance*. So I had time, which was a good thing because I needed to reconcile what the hell had happened with Carter.

Not what had happened—I knew *what* had happened. I'd been flip with Al and Charlie in the Lincoln, things had gone east when I'd wished they'd gone west, Carter had gone south when I thought he'd go north, a crowd had gathered around the Town Car, and in a New York minute I'd decided that, yes, we were accidental kidnappers. But now, in the light of day, with time on my hands, I needed to think about what it *meant*.

What I meant by what it meant is this: Jimmy, in his forty-five years of being a professional private investigator, had never once, not a single time, ever kidnapped anyone—accidentally or on purpose. And after three measly months on the job, I had.

To filter that fact through the chaos already running roughshod in my head, I went for a run around the reservoir, shadowedboxed ten rounds in front of the full-length mirror in my walk-through closet, showered, made myself an omelet with sautéed mushrooms, onions, roasted red peppers, Italian sausage, and fresh mozzarella from Faicco's on Bleecker Street, and updated my case notes while I inhaled my preshow meal.

Nothing helped. No matter how I thought it through, whether I was running or boxing or showering or cooking or eating, I couldn't get past the primary problem, which was *Jimmy's Rules of Private Investigation for Kate, Rule Number Nine: the last thing in the world you'd ever do is the next thing in the world you have to do.*

With Jimmy's Rule Number Nine as my misguided guide, I'd bent the law a dozen times, broken it more than that, been arrested on multiple occasions, kissed women like I'd meant it, lied like there was no tomorrow, drugged a psychopathic COO, pissed off the police, embarrassed my son, put myself and my friends in honest-to-God danger, and generally abandoned all semblance of normal, law-abiding living. When it came to my brief but inglorious time as a PI, I'd been a hot mess. Now I was a hot mess who kidnapped people.

Maybe I could nip this kidnapping thing in the bud, I thought, *if I put my mind to it.*

So in the cab down to the D-Cup, I put my mind to it, and it occurred to me that my father must have had exceptions to Rule Number Nine. He'd had exceptions to all his other rules. Why would Rule Number Nine be different? It wouldn't. He had to have crafted a list of exceptions. *Had to.*

And so as *Psychedelic Sunday* rehearsal began, I started my own mental list, which I titled, in my head, *Kate's Exceptions to Jimmy's Rules of Private Investigation for Kate, Rule Number Nine: the last thing in the world you'd ever do is the next thing in the world you have to do.*

I had time to think it through because we were rehearsing the scene early in act I where Roger and I, as Adonis and Venus, first pop out of the painting after Chloe's character, Professor Johnny Jedry, sings her solo, "Can't Count the Colors," as the acid she drops in the cab kicks in.

All Roger and I had to do was stand still and wait for our cue to exit the painting and join Chloe in a Posey original called "Here Comes Venus—And Adonis Too," a boozy, barroom rocker in which all the other paintings in the gallery joined in for the chorus. It should have taken three and a half minutes, the length of Chloe's song, to get us out of the painting, but Chloe was struggling with the singing (and with the dancing and acting that went with it), and on top of that, she had questions about what the lyrics meant in the moment, not to mention in the universe past, present, and future, and so Dennis had some directing to do.

During the directing, I started my mental list: *Exception Number One: I will never kill anyone who isn't trying to kill me first.*

As soon as I put the mental period in place, I laughed with

relief. *Screw you, Rule Number Nine, I thought. You're not ever getting me to kill someone who's not trying to kill me first. It's not the next thing in the world I have to do no matter what you say.*

I admired Exception Number One from all angles and then put my mental pen in place to continue the list. *Exception Number Two*, I wrote in my mind, and then...crickets. I couldn't come up with Exception Number Two. I thought of all the things I wouldn't do next in the world even if they were the last things in the world I would ever do, but the truth was I had already done all of those things, meaning besides murdering someone who wasn't trying to murder me, anything else that was the last thing in the world I'd ever do was, in fact, the next thing in the world I would have to do—including, holy shit, kidnap someone.

But Jimmy had drawn the line at kidnapping, hadn't he?

Well, maybe not. Maybe kidnapping someone had never come up in Jimmy's long, storied career. Maybe if kidnapping had come up, and if it had been the last thing in the world he'd ever do, maybe then it would have been the next thing in the world he would have done.

That was the reason he'd never kidnapped anyone, I thought. Jimmy would have kidnapped someone if he'd had to. He'd just never had to.

Surrendering to that line of thought loosened the logjam, and I finally admitted to myself that kidnapping Carter had not been entirely accidental. It had started out that way, but when Al asked me if we were kidnappers, after Carter had passed out at the sight of his own blood, I'd said we were—and that was not an accidental answer.

And if I was willing to accept Carter's kidnapping was, in part, intentional, then I also had to accept it had worked, meaning I'd kidnapped Carter to learn something secret, and he had told me something secret because he'd been kidnapped, and nobody likes to be kidnapped.

Kidnap anybody, I said to myself, *and there's a damn good chance they'll tell you something secret just to get un-kidnapped.*

As I finished thinking that thought, Chloe finally, mercifully, completed her song and dance in one clean take, and our cue was cued, and Roger and I stepped out of the painting and into the play.

I had the next line, and it was my full intention to deliver it. I'd rehearsed it dozens of times. I knew the line. I *owned* the line. I knew what the line meant in the moment, not to mention in the universe past, present, and future. So I fully expected to step out of the painting and say the line. But I opened my mouth and what came out was this: "I'm going to kidnap Stanley Stein."

48

AH, SURVEILLANCE

"*THAT'S YOUR PLAN?*" ROGER SAID.

"That's my plan," I said.

"You can't plan *that* plan without us," Posey said.

"*That* plan was written for us," Dennis said.

"We're perfect for *that* plan," Chloe said.

"You should call *that* plan 'The Schmidt and Parker Players Kidnap Stanley Stein and Make Him Talk Plan,'" Roger said.

"You're not listening," I said. "Kidnapping is a federal offense, which means honest-to-God jail time if we get caught, which is why *that* plan is a *me plan* and not a *we plan*, meaning you're sitting it out, meaning you're not doing it, meaning I don't want you doing it, meaning it's risky, it's dangerous, it's dumb, and I can't ask you to do it because the guilt will kill me if you get caught."

"You're not asking us, Kate," Dennis said. "We're asking you."

"We're insisting," Posey said.

"Okay, good, great, fine. So show of hands," I said, "who's not doing it?"

"If *that's* your plan, you'll need a full cast of characters,"

Roger said. "It's not a one-man-band kind of plan. First things first—you'll need a supercharged leading man, and I happen to know one waiting in the wings. One thing, though...it is a paying gig, right?"

Actors, I thought. "It's not a gig," I said. "It's kidnapping."

"It's not kidnapping," Chloe said.

"Excuse me?" I said.

"Kidnapping is when you grab someone off the street or out of their bed or from their car and take them somewhere else and keep them there instead of where they were. What we're doing is not technically kidnapping," Chloe said. "It's babysitting."

"*We're* not doing anything," I said.

But they all agreed *we* weren't technically kidnapping Stanley Stein; *we* were babysitting him, and I couldn't talk them out of the *we* part, and so the whole idea went from being a certain kind of private investigator nonsense that slipped out of my mouth to a specific kind of private investigator nonsense that involved a D-Cup cast of characters kidnapping a New York bookie in the privacy of his own home.

"We're all our brother's babysitter in one way or another," Chloe said. "So *that* plan sounds reasonable to me."

Everyone bought into Chloe's brother's babysitter bit, and I thought, *When Chloe is the voice of reason, you know you're in deep dirt.*

And when you're in deep dirt, the only way out is to keep moving, so after the Saturday night *Blood* show, instead of going with the cast to our nearby neighborhood Mexican joint for chicken enchiladas and Tecate in cans, I went back to the House of Emotional Tics to take care of business.

I crossed the lobby to the intercom and pushed the button for 5A.

"What?" Al said. His voice was scratchy through the

speaker, though not scratchy enough to hide his palpable frustration at still being awake after all these years.

"It's Kate. I want to rent the White Whale. I'm on my way up."

"No can do, McCall. I'm in the middle of a monster deal."

"Open the door, hand me the keys. It'll take five seconds."

"Five seconds is a lifetime in a deal like this. I'm moving Frisbees in Fresno for faucets in Fargo for flip-flops in Freemont for fishhooks in Fairbanks, and Fargo is freaking at the feasible faucet fallout. Jesus Christ, McCall. Get your priorities straight."

"On my way up."

"You are a miserable human being."

I got the keys from Al and was parked across the street from Blue Bar by eleven o'clock Sunday morning.

Ah, surveillance. Where brain cells go to torture themselves to death, I said to myself as I settled in for the long haul.

The American and National League Championship games were not until tonight—both series, as predicted, were tight and going the distance—so Stanley most likely wouldn't get to Blue Bar until later in the afternoon (if he got there at all), but then again he might do lunch instead, or even a day-night doubleheader of lunch *and* dinner. Who could tell with Stanley Stein?

I didn't want to miss the bookie when he arrived because I needed to know how he traveled. And I didn't want to miss him when he left because following Stanley home, no matter how he moved around the city, was an equally important part of the process.

I needed to know about Harold too. Because if Stanley and his military muscleman were attached at the hip—traveling together, living together—I would have to flush my kidnapping plans down the toilet, which is where they probably belonged in the first place, along with the rest of my spitting and sputtering PI life.

Ah, surveillance. Where self-doubt meets self-loathing, I thought.

I intended, as I often did when I had twelve hours of nothing to do but sit in one place and look at a door, to fill the day by balancing my checkbook, writing letters to friends far and wide, catching up on emails, scanning the trades for auditions, updating my case notes, and trying out an adult coloring book to see what the fuss was about.

But I knew my good intentions would be swept aside by a typhoon of self-reflection, and I would actually spend the day staring into space wondering how in the hell I had become a forty-five-year-old, single, private investigating actor sitting in a stripped-down, decade-old Toyota Corolla waiting for Old Uncle Bookie to bounce into Blue Bar. I mean, how in the hell had I turned into the woman I was?

I knew I would spend hours considering Michelle Lowry and Lisa Lowe, trying to figure out which one had hired the corporate killer to murder their partners and take control of the firm. Whoever it was, there was still one partner left to kill. How would I ever get a handle on who was who and which was what now that Logan had taken the wheel with a task force?

And thinking about Logan meant I would also be thinking about my son. Matthew had not spoken to me since Monday, at the Thirteenth Precinct, with Logan and Shavelson, after Logan had been to Red Maple Horse Farm, where the Connecticut police had recovered the Colt in a far corner of a dark stable.

Matthew and I had never gone a week without speaking to each other in...*ever*. We had spoken practically every day since he could speak, for Pete's sake. I knew in the Thirteenth he was mad at me, and I also knew it was my fault for being stupid and careless, but how could I have been *so* stupid, *so* careless that my own son couldn't even talk to me anymore? I would call him today, while I was wasting time in the White Whale, and try to repair the mother-son damage I had done. What a fool I'd been since becoming a PI! What a fraud! What a fuck-up! What a failure! What a...*shit*.

Ah, surveillance. Where self-regret meets self-deprecation, I thought.

I looked at my watch. It was five minutes after eleven. Five minutes into it, and I was already a basket case. Eleven hours and fifty-five minutes to go.

Eric the Red arrived at eleven fifteen. Blue Bar utility man Miller was the new number two, and so he now had a key to the street-level office door, which was where he entered the brownstone.

Miller had two memorable attributes: his red hair and the fact that he'd never struck me as the sharpest knife in the drawer. He seemed to be a living, breathing example of failing up. He wasn't an idiot. He was shrewd in his own way. But he wasn't number two material either. So why was he the new general manager?

Maybe because he was the kind of guy who, if someone said, *Hey, Miller, go put this ten grand on the Dodgers with Stanley Stein, don't tell anyone where you got the money to make the bet, and good things will happen for you*, then he would go ahead and make the bet and keep his mouth shut. Maybe that's why he was the new GM.

Miller's promotion couldn't have been an off-the-cuff kind of thing. Blue was smart enough to know Miller wasn't smart enough to be his general manager. So maybe Blue had hired me and pointed me toward Griff and Adam, hoping that my investigation would get rid of them—which it did—so he could install Miller as his main man.

What had Griff said that day Adam and I passed him on the stairs? He'd told Adam to *put it on Blue's tab*. Maybe those two guys had teamed up because they suspected (*or knew*) Blue was stealing house money and betting it with Stanley, and they didn't like it because their bonuses were based on overall Blue Bar performance, and if big money was missing, then the bottom line numbers would be a train wreck, and their bonuses would be collateral damage. Maybe Blue had to get rid of them to shut them up and put Eric the Red in prime Stein position—and maybe I had helped him do it.

Blue arrived at eleven twenty and stopped at the bottom of the main entrance stairs to sign autographs and chat with three attractive young women who, even from across the street, looked to be fawning all over him.

The bar opened in ten minutes for Sunday brunch. Since there were big games on tap, the place would be jam-packed all day long. I wondered if Blue was thinking about that while he signed his name and chatted with the women. I wondered if he was thinking about Eric the Red. I wondered if he was thinking about me.

I'd only known Blue for two weeks, but this time that was enough time to open my heart and connect. We'd liked each other from the first day we'd met, and then we'd talked and talked, and then we'd kissed like crazy, and then we'd made love last Tuesday, and we'd both felt something deep and real, and now we were finding out just how far that feeling could go.

But if Blue was embezzling his own money—and using me to do it—we were done. If he wasn't, we were at the beginning of something very special. And if Stanley Stein had anything to say about it, I would know which was which soon enough.

Harold arrived by cab at four forty-five. The brown-haired businesswoman I'd seen twice in the ladies' room arrived at four fifty. I felt sure the bookie's man in the men's room arrived right around then too, but I'd only seen a sliver of him through a closed toilet stall door and so wouldn't recognize him if we were face-to-face.

Though hundreds and hundreds of sports fans were

already inside—a three-floor full house—I imagined that Harold had secured two stools at one of the bars and that an army of folks with money to burn was waiting for their bookie to begin taking bets.

Stanley did not let them down. At five o'clock, a checker dropped him off in front of the bar. He wore a brown suit with a brown fedora and carried three newspapers—just another day with a cold craft beer and a sliced steak sandwich on home-made sourdough and all the sports he could read while catching a ball game on TV.

I did not listen to the games. I did balance my checkbook, write letters to friends far and wide, catch up on emails, scan the trades for auditions, update my case notes, try out an adult coloring book to see what the fuss was about—no fuss for me; I didn't like coloring books when I was a little girl, and I didn't like them now—and call my son to mend fences. I'd left Matthew a voicemail at four o'clock and waited for a call back that never came.

At eleven forty-five p.m., the brown-haired businesswoman left the bar and caught a cab. Five minutes later, Harold followed her out of the brownstone and down the stairs and strolled off into the night in the opposite direction. Stanley came through the door at midnight. He stood in front of Blue Bar and waved down a checker. I put the White Whale in gear and followed that cab.

We took the park across town to the FDR, went through the Queens-Midtown Tunnel to 495 East, got off at Woodhaven Boulevard, turned onto Alderton and then onto Fleet and then onto 70th Avenue and then onto Ingram, a tree-lined street with wide sidewalks and fine Forest Hills homes—beautiful brick Colonials and lovely Tudors. There were expensive cars in the driveways. The neighborhood was nicely landscaped.

Two and a half blocks down on the right-hand side was a tidy, two-story Tudor. It looked like the home of a retired

Citibank financial analyst and his real-estate agent wife, or a cosmetic dentist and his adorable family, or the owner of a successful Manhattan wine shop, or a senior corporate accountant in a bustling midtown firm. It did not look like the home of an infamous New York bookie.

But it was. Stanley got out of the cab, walked to the front door, took out his key, and went inside. It was twelve forty-five. Without traffic, in the middle of the night, it had taken forty-five minutes to get here. Stanley Stein was a commuter.

I watched the lights go off in the Tudor, drove the White Whale back to the House of Emotional Tics, slept for five hours, and was parked again down the block and across the street from the bookie's house by nine a.m., Monday. All was quiet, so I called Lowry Lowe and made an appointment to see Michelle Lowry on Wednesday afternoon.

At three-thirty p.m., a checker pulled to the curb in front of Stanley's place, and the bookie, wearing a blue suit, black shoes, and a black fedora, came outside, climbed into the cab, and was driven away. I followed them into the city, to Manny's on Second, another terrific sports bar, located between 92nd and 93rd on, as you might imagine, Second Avenue.

Nobody had to tell me what Stanley was doing in there. I had it pretty well figured out. I felt sure Harold had already secured two stools at the bar and that the brown-haired businesswoman and whoever the hell was collecting the cash in Manny's men's room were already in place. Stanley stayed all afternoon and well into the evening and was back in Forest Hills by midnight.

I followed him Tuesday too—same routine, except this time he went back to Blue Bar. Each night, Stanley took a checker home to Ingram Street. And each night Harold and the rest of Team Stein found their own ways home. I didn't care where they lived, so long as it wasn't with the bookie. Especially Harold. Stanley's well-paid handyman had a talent for breaking bones in other human beings with his bare hands, so it was important that any bones involved in the proceedings not find themselves in Harold's hands. But Harold didn't live with Stanley. I thought it might even be possible that Team Stein had no idea where the bookie lived in the first place. Stanley Stein was smart as a whip, clean as a bean, impossible to trace. No lines led to the bookie because that's the way he'd planned it. The police had been stonewalled for years. There was no way to arrest him.

Fortunately, I wasn't going to arrest him.

49

IT'S NOT MY BIRTHDAY, YOU IDIOT

On Wednesday, I parked the White Whale on Kessel, one block down and two blocks over from Stanley's Ingram Street Tudor. It was ten a.m., one of those mid-October mornings that reminded everyone just how sucky winter would be when it got here in full force any freaking minute—cold, gray, damp, depressing.

But I was a ray of summer sunshine, the brightest birthday singer Forest Hills had ever seen, dressed in my merriest colors, wearing my happiest smile, delivering good cheer and well wishes to front doors across the boroughs. I exited the Toyota, reached into the back, lifted a gift-wrapped birthday present off the seat, grabbed a dozen birthday balloons tied together and floating around the Corolla, locked the car, and walked to Stanley's house.

At the entrance to his front path, I closed my eyes, took a breath, steadied myself, renewed my resolve, marched confidently to Stanley's door, rang the doorbell twice, knocked three times, and put on a smile that could power Poughkeepsie.

A minute later, I heard someone unlocking the lock and

unchaining the chain. My heart was pounding. My legs were shaking. Talk about live theater. What if he recognized me from the bar? What if he was as certain he knew me now as he was certain he didn't know me then?

It had been almost two weeks since I'd sat beside him, wearing a brunette wig and hazel contact lenses, hoping to create a memory in his fading mind. That plan had been busted because Old Uncle Bookie's mind was anything but fading. (Truth be told, Stanley *had* given me Griff's girlfriend—now fiancée.)

So today I'd worn a shoulder-length blonde wig and blue contacts and big glasses, one last barrier between Stanley's click-click-clicking eyes and me.

The door opened, and there he was, wearing stylish slate-gray, pinstriped pajamas, a black bathrobe, and black slippers. He could easily have been wearing a morning fedora if such a thing existed. He was up and about but not yet ready to embrace the day. He hadn't shaved or showered. I had the sense I'd interrupted his breakfast. He looked at me with those merciless brown eyes, and I felt panic building in my brain. "Who are you?" he said without caring to hear my answer.

"Barbara Jurasek, from Broadway Singing Telegrams. And this is just for you on your special day: Happy birthday to you, happy birthday to you, happy birthday dear—"

"It's not my birthday, you idiot," he said, cutting me off.

"Oh, I'm *soooo* sorry. Maybe it's your wife's birthday. Is she available?"

"No wife here, sister. You got the wrong house."

"But this is the address they gave me. Is there anyone else home?"

"No. Now get the fuck lost," he said, running out of patience.

He started to shut the door, probably thinking I would walk

away and sing my song for someone down the street, but I moved forward as if he'd invited me inside, pushed the door back open, stepped into his foyer, and shut the door.

"What the fuck?" he said, and he reached into his pajamas and pulled out a gun. He was going to shoot me in his foyer with the gun he had hidden in his pajamas. *In his pajamas.* Did I mention the bookie had a gun in his pajamas?

But he was slow on the draw. Before he could pull the trigger, in one fast motion I dropped the box, let go of the balloons, and punched Stanley Stein so hard in the nose that I thought I might have killed him. He went down like a sandbag, crashing into an antique table, tumbling over it, falling to the hardwood floor face-first, antique table, Tiffany lamp, and other tabletop knickknacks smashing on top of him, not that he would know it —the bookie was out cold before he hit the ground.

I locked the front door, realized I was breathing like a runaway train, and thought it might be a good idea to put on latex gloves and reassess.

I had not planned on knocking his block off. I had planned on overpowering him—though I hadn't given too much thought as to how I was going to do that because he was in his seventies, and the overpowering him part was just going to happen. I was going to tie him to a chair and gag him, and that was going to be that. But Stanley had pulled a gun out of his pajamas—*his fucking pajamas*—and if some geezer, any geezer, pulls a gun on me, I'm pounding him into next week and asking questions later.

Which was what he had done and what I had done. The good news was that I'd told the cast I would bag the bookie myself and send smoke signals when the coast was clear. If I hadn't put my foot down about that, well, a vision of the Schmidt and Parker Players running down Ingram Street, holding gift-wrapped boxes and birthday balloons and screaming, "Run for your lives. He's got a gun in his pajamas," moved me out of reassessment mode into action mode.

I put Stanley's gun in my pocket, flipped him onto his back, grabbed him under the armpits, and dragged him across the front hall through the living room and then the dining room and into a large family room off the kitchen at the rear of the house.

Then I went back into the kitchen. Stanley's breakfast was on the table where he'd left it—oatmeal with fresh strawberries, black coffee, and rye toast burned to a crisp. I looked at his breakfast and wondered if he'd had the gun in his pajamas while he was actually eating, if he ate oatmeal every morning with the gun in his pajamas, or if he'd grabbed the gun off the counter when he'd heard the doorbell ring or what. *Jesus, Stanley*, I said to myself. *I think it's safe to eat breakfast in your own damn house without keeping a gun in your flipping pajamas.*

Then again, it had turned out *not* to be all that safe, so there was that.

I carried the bookie's breakfast chair into the family room, hurried back through the house to the foyer, grabbed the gift-wrapped birthday box I'd dropped when I'd decked him, and carried the box to the family room. I opened it, took out the ropes I'd packed, lifted the bookie onto the chair, and tied him tight across the chest, head slumped forward. Then I tied his wrists and his ankles. Then I went back to the box, grabbed a colorful scarf out of it, lifted his head, and gagged him.

Stanley's cell phone was on the kitchen table beside his breakfast. I picked it up and hit the button. It was locked. I needed his fingerprint, so I went back to the bookie and pressed his thumb on the button. The screen opened, and I scrolled through his contacts, looking for Harold. There he was. No last name. Just Harold. Like Madonna or Cher or Liberace or Lassie.

I went through Stanley's texts to see if he'd reached out to Harold yet today. He had not. I read through a dozen text conversations between Harold and Stanley to catch the cadence, the tone of Stanley's voice when he was texting.

Then I typed this message: *Sick in bed. Feels like flu. Staying home.* I hit Send and looked at the bookie, still unconscious, and waited.

Within two minutes, Stanley got a reply from Harold: *Need me?*

Not today, I typed. *Give me a few to get back on my feet.* I hit Send.

Be there Thursday at 5, Harold texted back.

Oh crap, I thought. *Harold does know where Stanley lives.*

So now, on top of breaking all kinds of laws that could send me to jail for a decade or two, there was a "ticking clock" hanging over my head.

Stanley started to stir, so I went back to the foyer and grabbed the balloons, which had floated up to the ceiling, and carried them to the family room, where I tied them to the breakfast chair. Then I moved the family room furniture out of the way, creating an open performance area, a Stanley Stein stage, so to speak, so the bookie would have a front row seat for the show.

If you had asked me back in early July, before Jimmy was murdered, if by mid-October I'd be kidnapping (fine, fine, babysitting) a top-three New York bookie in his very own Forest Hills home, I would have said you were nuts. Now *I* was nuts.

And yet here I was. And there he was, opening his eyes, getting his bearings, realizing he was tied to the chair in a serious way. He did not struggle. He did not scream. I imagined he knew it was pointless. He just stared at me, his eyes going click-click-click-click-click.

Then he turned his head to the side, saw the ribbons tied to his chair, followed them up to the balloons, and looked back at me.

There were plenty of places to begin with the bookie, but I decided to start by finishing the song I'd sung at the front door. "Happy birthday, dear Stanley, happy birthday to you."

And then I called the cast.

50

STRIKE UP THE BAND

They were parked a few blocks away on Fleet Street. Roger had insisted we create a code, so I said, "The bookie is in the bag," and Roger said, "Strike up the band." And then that's what I did. While I waited for Dennis, Posey, Roger, and Chloe to arrive, I sang Stanley Stein "Sit Down, You're Rockin' the Boat" from *Guys and Dolls*—a cappella, heart and soul.

When Stanley realized I was singing him a Broadway show tune, his eyes opened wide, and he pulled against the ropes for the first time since he'd figured out he'd been tied to his breakfast chair.

I sang the last notes, did a bit of Broadway dancing, and finished with a flourish in front of his face.

"I love *Guys and Dolls*, don't you?" I said. "Did you know it won the Pulitzer Prize for Drama in 1951, but because one of the writers was Abe Burrows, who was in deep dog-doo with the House Un-American Activities Committee, the award was vetoed, and the Columbia trustees just didn't give one out that year? A little Broadway fun fact for you, Stanley, to start your kidnapping off with a bang."

His eyes went click-click-click-click-click.

"I'm going to take your gag out," I said, "but if you scream, I'll put it back in. Not because anyone is going to hear you, they won't, but because you can't be screaming while we're singing Broadway show tunes for you, which is what we're going to do until you tell me who's stealing Blue Bar money and betting it at Blue Bar."

I took out the gag.

"I found you," he said. "Took a while because of the wig and the colored contacts and the glasses, but you got the same shape face and eyes, the same lips, same nose, same chin. Not close, you understand—exactly the same. You're the brunette with hazel eyes who sat at the bar and said you knew me from back in the day. I'm guessing you're the blonde with green eyes who followed my friends and took pictures without permission. I was right. You're a private investigator."

"A private investigator singing Broadway show tunes, Stanley," I said. "Your favorite combination."

"Harold is going to break every bone in your body," he said.

"Not until tomorrow," I said.

The doorbell rang. I put the gag back in Stanley's mouth and went to greet the cast.

"Surprise," they said as the door opened, though it wasn't precisely a surprise party. They were each disguised—Roger wore a fake mustache, Dennis had dyed his hair blond-blond-blond, Chloe wore a red wig, Posey had a spray-on tan that had turned her skin as orange as her clothes, which were as orange as an orange. They all carried gift-wrapped birthday presents so the neighbors, if they were watching, would think grumpy Stanley Stein had a few friends after all and was having a little birthday bash in his very own honor. Those same neighbors, if they were watching, would lose interest after that and would not consciously keep track of who came and went or when they did. Chloe and Posey, as directed by me, had brought birthday balloons, in addition to gifts, for a festive feeling. And Roger, overacting as always, had ad-libbed a bottle of champagne, which he held high while saying, "Let's get this party started."

I let them in, shut and locked and chained the door behind them, and escorted them to the family room where Stanley was a captive audience, so to speak.

The gift-wrapped birthday boxes were filled with costumes and props and sheet music. The cast looked at Stanley, bound and gagged in his front row seat, and set about the business of creating a musical revue the bookie would never forget.

"Stanley," I said, "these are some of the finest musical actors you will ever not meet." I gestured at the cast for them to introduce themselves. One at a time, they stepped forward with flair. Of course, they'd created code names.

"Rex Harrison at your service," Dennis said, tipping the top hat he'd taken from his gift-wrapped box.

"Carol Channing, or Stockard Channing, or even Channing Tatum, if you prefer," Posey said, holding up a white wig that gave her orange skin a space-alien glow.

Roger held up the trombone he'd packed in pieces in his birthday box and had already reassembled and said, "Robert Preston here, ready to lead the big parade."

And then Chloe said, "Pearl Bailey is in the house."

It was an odd name for an Ohio white woman—maybe the whitest Ohio white woman—to choose, even in the context of character code names for a Broadway show tunes kidnapping.

"Interesting choice, Pearl," I said.

"I'm black, and I'm proud," she said.

Stanley watched the cast, disbelieving this could be happening to him in his real, waking life and not in his worst nightmare.

I snapped him out of it. "Curtain in three minutes."

He made noises of disapproval through the gag and pulled against the ropes again as I led the cast into the kitchen for final instructions.

"Stanley has a landline in the living room," I said.

"My grandma has one back in Ohio," Chloe said. "It's attached to the wall. You spin the dial to call someone."

"She likes antiques?" Posey said.

"She likes to be connected," Chloe said. "Maybe Stanley likes to be connected."

"Maybe Stanley would like to be connected to your grandmother," Roger said.

"Focus, people," I said. "Do not, under any circumstances, answer the landline if it rings. And quadruple that warning when it comes to the front door. Do not open the door for anyone except me. Period. And if a tall, wiry black guy who looks like he could break bones with his bare hands comes knocking, stop what you're doing and run out the back door and across the neighbor's backyard and onto the next street before he swings around the house, which he will. His name is Harold. You don't want to meet him. I'm dead serious about Harold because I don't want you to be dead. Got it?"

They got it. I looked at my watch. It was ten forty. "Sing him every song from every musical that's ever been written. Call me when he cracks."

"Where will you be?" Dennis said.

"Lowry Lowe," I said. "A friend at the New York City Bar Association told me Michelle Lowry is being questioned for a possible ethics violation. After that, Blue Bar."

"Who do you know who works for the bar association?" Posey said.

"Me," I said.

51

YOUR LEGAL LOGIC MAKES IMMACULATE SENSE

MICHELLE LOWRY WAS STUNNING IN A ROLAND MOURET, double-wool crepe midi dress, cap-sleeve with a split neckline and a sheath silhouette. At about four grand, the dress on a Neiman Marcus hanger would be sublime, so on the Swedish Queen it was drop-dead gorgeous. She wore black, jeweled-bow, red-sole Christian Louboutin pumps for an easy thousand bucks; a yellow gold and titanium Cartier diamond watch for eight grand that was a timepiece of pure art; and a soft, classic pearl necklace with matching earrings that together had to be five thousand easy. Meaning her Wednesday afternoon ensemble was worth as much as some folks make in a year. The only thing missing was her wedding ring—surprising, since her husband had only been dead since last Thursday, or maybe not so surprising.

She was leaning against the front of her modern walnut desk, watching her assistant escort me into her immaculate office.

"Mrs. Lowry. I'm Marsha Friedrich, ethics investigator for the New York City Bar Association," I said. "Thank you for making time for me today."

She did not offer to shake my hand or welcome me in any way. Instead, she looked at me with icy eyes and nodded at her assistant, who immediately exited the room and shut the door behind her.

"You have me at a disadvantage, Ms. Friedrich," Michelle said, gesturing for me to take a seat on one of the modern leather sofas that formed a casually elegant sitting area in front of her desk. "I can't imagine why an ethics investigator would feel the need to meet with anyone at Lowry Lowe, let alone a partner."

After leaving Stanley Stein in the Broadway musical hands of the Schmidt and Parker Players, I'd changed clothes in the White Whale to become an ethics investigator for the bar association—a dark-gray business suit that made me feel ethical—but I'd stayed with the shoulder-length blonde wig, the blue contacts, and the big glasses I'd worn to sing the bookie "Happy Birthday."

The last time the Swedish Queen had seen me, she was getting screwed from behind by Carter Ringwald, and I had said I was from the *National Enquirer*. The time before that I'd been red-haired Emily Baynes from Austin, Texas, so I felt good about not being recognized, and Michelle gave no indication she knew who I was. So I sat on a sofa and thought, *So far, so good*.

"I can clarify that for you, Mrs. Lowry," I said. "We were informed by someone in your firm that, in an effort to consolidate power and control funds, you altered the Lowry Lowe partnership agreement without consulting the other surviving partner, Mrs. Lowe."

She did not flinch. She also did not sit on the sofa across from me. She continued to lean against her desk. "Are you going to tell me the name of the informant?"

"No, I'm not," I said. I imagined she suspected it was her boy toy, and I watched her lips to see if they silently said *Carter*. But she was a frozen fortress and gave me nothing. "However, on behalf of the bar association, I would like to offer my condolences for the deaths of your husband and for your partner, Jack Lowe. This has to be a time of great personal and emotional stress and heartbreak, and it's to be understood if professional mistakes were made in the immediate aftermath of these two tragic murders."

She offered me a thin smile that said she didn't give a shit about my condolences and said, "Professional mistakes?"

"The bar frowns on closed-door partnership amendments. We believe this kind of accusation, coming as it does from inside your practice, could compromise the firm's fiduciary responsibilities to its clients, if it hasn't already done so."

"Nothing could be further from the truth."

"Have you discussed the partnership amendment with Mrs. Lowe?"

"I'm not going to dignify that with an answer."

"Mrs. Lowry, under the historical circumstances, an exploratory conversation seems warranted."

She narrowed her eyes and walked around her desk, considering, I felt certain, how she was going to control this exploratory conversation. Her Roland Mouret had a sexy, full-back zipper. I imagined Carter Ringwald unzipping the thing before fucking his boss on the very sofa where I was sitting, and I thought I might contact Bethany as soon as I left Lowry Lowe and mention her fiancé's extracurricular activities.

Michelle took a seat behind her desk and removed something from her top drawer. "That's a peculiar turn of phrase, *historical circumstances*, seeing as my firm has no circumstantial history whatsoever with the bar association."

"I'm talking about *your* historical circumstances," I said.

She locked her jaw for a subtle second. If I hadn't been looking for a reaction, I would have missed it. But I was looking. And more than that, I was trying to knock her off balance.

"Explain that to me," she said.

I heard the undercurrent of anger and impatience in her voice. She was cold and controlled about it, yes, but I was an annoyance she wasn't expecting, and she was annoyed. Good. That's where I wanted her. *"When they're annoyed, they drop their hands,"* Jimmy used to say, using boxing lingo to make his point. *"And when they drop their hands, you can knock them out."*

"Of course," I said. "You were married to Mark Muller, the investment banker who was murdered in his Bergen County backyard. Is that correct?"

Her jaw locked again but longer this time and harder too. "An irrelevant fact of my past life that is none of your business or the bar's business or anyone's business."

"You left Mr. Muller for Christopher Lowry—your attorney at the time of your divorce—married him, and joined his firm. Your husband had an affair with Lisa Lowe, and then Jack Lowe had an affair with you, which ended your marriage to Mr. Lowry. Those are the facts, are they not?"

"*Personal* facts. Is the bar dabbling in marriage counseling these days?"

"There was suspicion at the time that a corporate contract killer was hired to murder Mr. Muller, your late ex-husband. And that same suspicion has been carried over to the murders of your current late husband and to Jack Lowe."

She tried to control her temper, the narrowing of her eyes, the flushing of her face. It was a challenge. I could see her working to keep the rising tide of emotion at bay.

"Are you accusing me of something, Ms. Friedrich?"

"I'm saying this kind of suspicion—corporate killers and murdered husbands and law partners—goes beyond ethics violations into the arena of criminal behavior."

"What do you want?" she said.

I have her, I said to myself. *Two minutes, and she's mine.*

"The truth, Mrs. Lowry," I said. "Maybe you both knew the

killer's name, but it was Mr. Lowry who hired him to murder Mark Muller. And then maybe Mr. Lowry gave the killer's name to Mrs. Lowe while they were having an affair, and then maybe *she* hired the killer to murder Mr. Lowe and Mr. Lowry. Maybe you altered the partnership agreement to protect yourself so Mrs. Lowe wouldn't murder you next. That is a perfectly plausible, eminently defensible series of circumstances, I'm sure you'll agree. I'm saying now is the appropriate time, what with an ethics violation hanging over your head, to set the record straight for the bar association before this devolves into a criminal investigation. If you know the name of the corporate contract killer, that will go a long way toward your exoneration."

She nodded as if she understood I was right.

She's going to tell me who he is, I thought, *and I'm going to nail the son of a bitch.*

"Lisa is the secretary of Lowry Lowe LLC," Michelle said. "*She* amended the partnership agreement without consulting *me*, and she has it locked in her desk."

She stood up and showed me what she'd taken from her drawer: keys. She was going to unlock Lisa's desk and get me the document to prove her innocence. Her next sentence would be the killer's name. She came around her desk and stopped across from me, in front of the other sofa, coffee table between us.

"Your legal logic makes immaculate sense, Ms. Friedrich," Michelle said. "But what makes no sense, what I can't figure out, is who you work for."

Uh-oh, I thought. "I'm an ethics investigator for the New York City Bar Asso—"

"Yes, yes, you're an investigator, but I'm afraid you have no ties to the bar, which makes you a *private* investigator. That was clear as soon as you opened your mouth. However, your questions don't circle back to a disgruntled, losing Lowry Lowe client or to a winning client's vengeful spouse. Frankly, your questions don't lead to anyone anywhere. Would you like to tell me who hired you?"

I knew I should stand up, say something, and get the hell out of there, but I couldn't get my legs to move—or my mouth, for that matter.

She walked to her door, opened it, stepped into the hall, and held up the keys. "That's fine. You think about it while I get Rockefeller Center security up here." Then she shut the door and locked me in her office.

52

NOT EXACTLY STANDARD
COURTROOM STRATEGY

She was calling Rockefeller Center security.

That was the *good* news.

The bad news was that for the second time in two weeks I'd been busted in the middle of my act. First by the bookie, who'd called out my routine at Blue Bar, and now by Michelle Lowry, who'd seen through my Marsha Friedrich like a screen door—as she'd just said before locking me in her office.

What the heck was happening with my acting? Was I having an off week? Or was this the beginning of some sad, slow fade? Was I an everyday player in a brief, midseason slump? Or was I a pinch hitter who was too old to play in the field and could no longer time a fastball or measure a curve? Were my best theatrical days behind me?

Or was it this particular audience?

It is a fact of the theater that an actor can give a bravura performance that brings down the house except for that one guy in the third row who just didn't freaking buy in. There is always that guy in the third row, the one too cold or too hard or too distant or too distracted to be swept away in the magic of the acting moment. Stanley Stein certainly fit that bill. And so did Michelle Lowry.

So no, I decided, it wasn't my career coming to the dead end of Talent Road. It was an unfeeling, unforgiving audience two times in a row. It was bad audience luck. I knew where I stood in the theatrical scheme of things: six rungs down the professional ladder from Gwen Verdon and Bernadette Peters and Patti LuPone and Betty Buckley and Idina Menzel. But I also knew I was on the same ladder.

And though it was true Michelle hadn't fallen for Marsha Friedrich hook, line, and sinker, it was also true my performance as an investigator for the New York City Bar Association had made her take the bait just enough to let it slip that it was Lisa Lowe who had changed the partnership documents and that the papers were locked in Lisa's desk drawer.

Which brought me back again to the good news: Michelle Lowry was calling Rockefeller Center security, meaning she was not calling the police, meaning I had struck a Lowry Lowe nerve, meaning Michelle didn't want the police digging up any more law firm dirt, meaning either Michelle had hired the killer to murder Jack Lowe and her husband...or she knew Lisa had done it.

Either way, I had to get my hands on the partnership documents. What had started as a story from the mouth of Carter Ringwald, delivered with desperation from the bottom of Jerusalem Joe's cage, had been substantiated by Michelle Lowry and was now potential proof positive that there was murderous motivation at work. I had to get those docs out of Lisa Lowe's desk. With the secretly amended partnership papers, I would have the leverage to extract the name of the man who'd killed my father from the surviving Lowry Lowe women. Assuming they didn't kill each other first.

More good news? Calling Rockefeller Center security had the added bonus of guaranteeing Logan would not arrive in an infuriated huff and arrest me yet again, which would concurrently create unwanted family drama and make my son's head explode.

Anyway, the first step to putting my hands on the partnership papers was getting the hell out of Michelle Lowry's office. So I took my cell phone from my purse and called Mel Shavelson.

"Shavelson," he said, answering on the first ring.

"It's Kate McCall. You in a cab?"

Horns honked. Middle Eastern music played in the background. He was definitely in a cab.

"On my way back to the office after yet another divorce mediation meeting," Shavelson said. "My soon-to-be ex-wife is raking me over the coals. She already took, let's see, everything, and now she wants the hair on my nuts. You can't take the hair on a man's nuts, McCall. You have to at least leave him his nut hair. One day, when you get married and divorced, you'll know what I'm talking about."

"I don't have nuts."

"Figuratively speaking."

"Where are you now?"

"48th and Eighth. Red light. I've got some kind of Pakistani music blowing my eardrums all the way to Pakistan. I told him to turn it down, but he doesn't speak English, although he understood me just fine when I told him my address. What the hell is it with me and Pakistani cab drivers? Just last week I—"

"Make a right, Shavelson. I'm locked in an office at Lowry Lowe."

"What the hell are you doing there?"

"I just told you. I'm locked in an office. Michelle Lowry is calling Rockefeller Center security to take me to Rockefeller Center jail. 30 Rock. Sixty-second floor. Tell your cabbie to make a right."

"She's not calling the cops?"

"No."

"I should have hired her to represent me. My wife wants my nut hair. Did I tell you that? Michelle Lowry would have at least saved the hair on my testicles."

"Jesus, Shavelson. It's not about you right now. Did you make a right?"

"Don't say anything until I get there. Client pays additional right-hand turns."

"I'm not your client."

"That's what Jimmy used to say."

Rockefeller Center security arrived first. There were two of them. A young one named Darren, who still had prepubescent acne though he was probably thirty years old, and his boss, a sixty-something-year-old bulldog named Chet.

I told them I wasn't saying anything until my lawyer arrived, and Chet said I wasn't under arrest yet, but he could make that happen in a matter of minutes if I didn't tell them what I was doing here.

"What I'm doing here, Chet," I said, "is being held prisoner by paid employees of Rockefeller Center, which will make me a millionaire by the time my lawyer gets done with you."

"Your lawyer?" Chet said.

"He's on his way," I said.

"I doubt it," Darren said.

"I paid for an additional right-hand turn," I said. "He'll be here any minute."

"Lawyers don't make house calls in the middle of the day," Chet said.

"Want to put twenty bucks on it?" I said.

"I'll take that bet," Darren said.

"Show me the money," I said, taking a twenty from my purse.

"The only person showing anybody anything is you showing me your identification," Chet said.

We argued back and forth about whether I had to show him my identification. Chet's argument included the need for increased security at Rockefeller Center and "all over the country, for Pete's sake, with all the bombings and shootings and whatnot," and then the office door whipped open and Shavelson blew into the room like a Tasmanian tornado—if such a tornado could be conceived as a chaotic storm of legal papers, unlit cigarettes, disheveled clothing, and unruly hair.

"I'll need both your names, phone numbers, addresses, Social Security numbers, driver's licenses, and Rockefeller Center ID numbers," Shavelson said, commandeering Michelle Lowry's desk, opening his briefcase, spreading out spreadsheets and legal-looking folders—and one pack each of Pall Mall, Lucky Strike, and Winston cigarettes.

Chet and Darren looked simultaneously confused and intimidated by the overweight, whirling dervish that was Shavelson.

"I'm Mel Shavelson," he said, handing Chet and Darren his business card, "and this is my client, who will keep her mouth closed the entirety of the time it takes me to remove her from your custody and sue you and this firm and the Rockefeller family for more money than even my soon-to-be ex-wife, may she burn in Bermuda, can imagine."

"On what grounds, Mr. Shavelson?" Michelle Lowry said, stepping into the room.

"These misguided men are profiling my client," Shavelson said.

"That is patently absurd," Michelle said.

"The state assembly passed legislation prohibiting law enforcement officers from engaging in racial or ethnic profiling," Shavelson said. "I'd say we have that in spades."

"Hey, wait a minute..." Chet said.

"But she's white," Darren said.

"The color of one's skin is not cause to put them through a

humiliating and unconstitutional search," Shavelson said. "And last time I checked, white was a color."

"That's not what I meant," Darren said.

"Because she was white, you assumed she was a private investigator with criminal intent," Shavelson said. "That is precisely the kind of behavior the legislation is intended to correct. You are the poster boys for miscreant law enforcement officers."

"They are not law enforcement officers," Michelle said.

"I think a judge might disagree," Shavelson said, "right before he awards my client damages, costs, and attorney fees that will make Warren Buffett blush. I hope you gentlemen have outside sources of income because Rockefeller Center will drop you like third-period French."

"I tend bar in Brooklyn," Darren said.

"My wife teaches fourth grade. No way we make it on one income," Chet said.

"You are mistaken, Mr. Shavelson, if you think your carnival act is going to scare me into letting your client walk away," Michelle said, looking at the security officers as if to say, *Buck up, you idiots.*

Shavelson looked at me and gestured at Michelle. "Do you know this woman?"

"Michelle Lowry," I said.

Shavelson nodded. "Your reputation doesn't do you justice, Mrs. Lowry. Hubba hubba."

Everyone's eyes shot wide open. Michelle's, mine, Darren's, Chet's. Wipe open.

"Excuse me," Michelle said.

"On rare occasions," Shavelson said, moving two steps closer to her in such a way that she took two involuntary steps back, "the chemistry of attraction moves from the ethereal to the corporeal in the blink of an eye and action is demanded."

What the hell, Shavelson? I thought. And I felt sure everyone else was feeling the same feeling, especially Michelle, who was the sole subject of Shavelson's creepy focus.

"Excuse me," Michelle said.

"We should hook up is what I'm saying," Shavelson said.

If our eyes had shot wide open before, now they popped out of our heads.

"We should what?" Michelle said, taking another step back. "You mean me and you?"

"Never judge a book, Michelle," Shavelson said. "I had an affair with my masseuse, and we raised the red roof in more than one Red Roof Inn, if you catch my drift."

"That is disgusting in every imaginable way," Michelle said, looking at me. It was the first time since I'd met her that we were in complete agreement.

"And ways you can't imagine," I said so Shavelson's come-on would come on as even grosser than she'd imagined.

Shavelson took another step toward her. She took another step away and looked at poor Darren and Chet, who, in all their Rockefeller Center security days, had never experienced anything like Mel Shavelson.

"How about you represent me in my divorce and see how you feel about it after you get to know me?" Shavelson said.

"Get out, Mr. Shavelson," Michelle said, "and take her with you."

Shavelson moved back to Michelle's desk and shoveled his shit back into his briefcase, took me by the arm, and hurried me toward the door.

"Next time I call the police," Michelle said to me as I walked by her.

I stopped on a dime, my face in front of her face. "You don't want the police poking around anymore than I do. Just tell me who killed Jack and your husband and you'll never see me again."

She leaned in and whispered in my ear. "The next time I see

you will be the last time I see you—the last time anybody sees you, until they find you in a sewer somewhere dark and dangerous. Consider that free legal advice."

In the elevator, I said to Shavelson, "Hubba hubba?"

"She's not the kind of woman you can scare with legalese," he said. "She's the kind you have to disgust into submission. Believe me, there are waves of them."

The thought of him disgusting waves of women into submission turned my stomach. "Not exactly standard courtroom strategy," I said.

"Works more often than you think."

"I think it probably works a hundred percent of the time."

"Except for my masseuse. It drove her wild with passion."

"Jesus, Shavelson. I have to eat dinner later."

We rode in silence for thirty seconds, and then I said, "Anyway, thanks."

"When a client calls," he said, "I'm Johnny-on-the-spot."

"I'm not your client," I said as the elevator doors opened.

"That's what Jimmy used to say," he said.

53

THE WHOLE SNEAKY ENVELOPE THING

I drove the White Whale back to the House of Emotional Tics, showered off the lewd layer of Shavelson crud that stuck to my skin like insect goop every time I saw him, put on the shoulder-length red wig with bangs and green contact lenses that made me Danielle Sullivan, Blue Bar's Big Apple-by-way-of-Bayonne management consultant, chose a black business suit that made me feel like a badass efficiency expert, and made myself a BLT. It was two o'clock, and I hadn't eaten anything since before I'd kidnapped Stanley Stein in his Forest Hills home.

I checked Stanley's cell phone, which I had taken with me, to see if he'd received any messages from Harold. He had not.

But just thinking about Harold raised the hair on my neck, so I called Dennis to remind him that Stanley's bodyguard was part of the picture and also to see if they'd had any luck cracking the bookie. But the bookie wasn't cracking.

"We're throwing everything at him," Dennis said with both desperation and determination. "Solos, duets, three-parts, quartets, comedies, romances, dramas. He's swearing a blue streak at us and howling in agony, but he's not breaking."

"Keep at it," I said. "He has to break. He's just a man. I'll be there later."

"Don't come until tomorrow morning," Dennis said. "We need more time. I've never seen anyone hate musicals this much. It's personal now, bigger than any of us. It's about the pride and joy and glory of Broadway. It's him or us."

I reminded Dennis about watching for Harold, but he was distracted and had to hang up because the four of them were set to sing "Let the Sunshine In," the closing anthem of America's mystical love-rock musical, *Hair*. Dennis said they were stripped to their underwear to make it feel like the real deal. "We'll get naked if we have to," Dennis said before he hung up.

It was four o'clock by the time I arrived at Blue Bar. I got settled on the second floor, the kitchen floor, sitting at the end of the bar so I could see the staff in the open kitchen and also the rest of the room as I ostensibly went through the day's lunch tickets, comparing the kitchen printouts to the register ring-ups, looking for irregularities, conjuring up new efficiencies. But really I was watching Eric Miller.

Blue's new general manager was reviewing inventory with Large Sarge, the daytime kitchen manager. His actual name was Julius Newhouse, apropos because he was the size of a new house: six-two, three hundred fifty pounds, arms like thick steel pipes, legs as big as a bison. He'd played nose tackle for Rutgers and been drafted by the Browns, but he busted his knee on the first day of rookie camp, came home to New Jersey, and went to work in a series of New York City kitchens. He'd joined the US Army Reserve along the way and had risen to the rank of sergeant, which is why everyone called him Large Sarge.

There were fifty or sixty customers still hanging around at the bar and tables, finishing up late lunches, getting early starts on Hump Day happy hour. Bartenders and waitstaff went about the business of closing out lunch and resetting for dinner.

I wasn't expecting anything of consequence to happen. Eric

the Red was going through his general manager paces just like Blue had hired him to do. I'd never seen Eric do kitchen inventory before, which was why I'd wanted to be here in the afternoon on Wednesday. I had to mark kitchen inventory off my nothing-ever-happens-on-surveillance list, and Wednesday was kitchen inventory day.

As I was giving up in my mind, Eric came out of the kitchen into the servers' work area in front of the kitchen. A long counter/island separated the dining room from the work area, which was called the alley. Another counter/island separated the alley from the kitchen itself.

There was a locked drawer in the alley island that belonged to the general manager. I knew that because both Griff and Adam had shown it to me. They'd kept papers and other random GM stuff in the drawer and sometimes locked the lunch receipts in there—if it was the middle of a shift, for instance, and they were clearing cash out of the registers and couldn't make it downstairs to the safe because the place was packed and the kitchen was crazy.

Anyway, Eric unlocked his drawer, paused for a moment, casually scanned the room to see if anyone was watching him, lifted an envelope, flipped through the contents as if he were counting money, scanned the room again, and then put the envelope in the inside pocket of his sport-jacket.

I had to give him credit. He was subtle and casual about the whole thing. He didn't want anyone to see him with the envelope, and no one did. He was calm enough about the whole sneaky envelope thing that I had the sense he'd done it before —maybe many times before.

But I had to give myself credit too. I'd witnessed the entire episode from the moment Eric had unlocked the drawer to the moment he'd put the envelope in his pocket. He'd looked right at me, and still he'd had no idea I was watching him.

If Eric hadn't counted the contents of the envelope, I might have let it go. But he *had* counted it. There was cash in the envelope. Now I couldn't let it go.

Large Sarge called the general manager into the kitchen. Eric the Red must have been distracted or overconfident or both because he made a monster mistake. He took off his sport jacket and left it on the island. Then he rolled up his sleeves and went into the kitchen to do inventory things with Large Sarge.

I knew I should take two seconds to consider the situation, a moment to measure my next move. *What's the plan?* I said to myself. *You need a plan.* But before my brain could think it through, my legs slid me off the barstool. I crossed the floor to the island, went behind it into the alley, stopped at Eric's sport jacket, reached into the inside pocket, and pulled out the envelope. My heart was pounding. I think I was holding my breath because I don't remember breathing.

I opened the envelope. It was filled with cash. And there was a note, a single slip of paper with something written on it. Not written. Typed.

Count it, I thought. *Count it now.* I took the money out and counted it—six thousand exactly in hundreds, fifties, twenties, and tens. Half the money missing last Friday. Had to be.

Then I read the note: *Dodgers over/under.*

Tonight was game six of the National League Championship Series—Dodgers and Cardinals at Busch Stadium. Game seven, if necessary, would be Friday night in Chavez Ravine. I felt sure I was holding Eric's game six bet in my hands. Although, I felt equally sure it wasn't really Eric's bet. The new Blue Bar GM had been pleasantly surprised to see the envelope in his drawer. If he'd put it there, why the hell would he have been pleasantly surprised to find it? He wouldn't have been. Someone else put it there for Eric to discover. Eric was making the bet for that person.

It was a big game. The Cardinals could close out the series, or the Dodgers could force game seven, and the odds were good that the bookie would be at Blue Bar tonight. And if Stanley didn't show, well, then he would definitely be at Manny's on Second, and Eric could grab a cab, make the bet at Manny's, and be back at Blue Bar in no time. Except the odds were bad the bookie would be at any sports bar anywhere because he would be tied up (literally), enjoying an evening of Broadway show tunes courtesy of the Schmidt and Parker Players, who might be performing in the nude.

There was still no way to confirm that Blue had put the envelope in the drawer except by confronting Eric with the facts, meaning the money and the bet. When, where, and how to confront him were questions to which I had no answers.

"What are you doing, Danielle?" Eric was standing ten feet down the alley, incredulous and furious. "Give me the envelope."

Just like that, when and where were moot. How was still open for discussion.

"Tell me who gave you the money, Eric," I said.

"Give me the envelope," he said, taking a step down the alley toward me.

"I know you didn't steal it from Blue Bar by yourself. You're not smart enough."

"Give me the envelope, Danielle." He took another step closer to me. He glanced around the room to see if we'd attracted anyone's attention. I didn't think we had because he kept coming. I put the envelope behind my back. Even if no one was watching us yet, I had the sense that would change in the next sixty seconds.

"You're just smart enough to sit next to Stanley Stein," I said, "put six grand on the Dodgers over/under, take your cut if they beat the spread, and keep your mouth shut. Although the jury's out as to whether you're smart enough to keep your mouth shut."

"Give me the fucking envelope."

"Someone's giving you embezzled Blue Bar money to bet with Stanley Stein," I said, "and I want to know—"

I didn't get to finish the sentence because he took three long strides in a heartbeat, grabbed me, and tried to rip the envelope out of my hand.

He was bigger than me and stronger than me, but he didn't anticipate that I'd be this much stronger than he'd thought I was and that I wouldn't be afraid of him and that I'd fight like a feral cat.

I kept the envelope out of his reach, and we wrestled in the alley. *I'll bet we've got people watching us now*, I thought.

We spun around and around, smashing into the islands on both sides of the alley, sending plates and glasses and peppermills and silverware crashing to the ground. He was frustrated and enraged. We were both breathing hard now. There was no way I was giving him the envelope. There was no way he was letting me keep it.

I had a moment of leverage and pushed us both up onto the top of the servers' island, where we rolled over and off the counter and fell hard to the dining room floor. The envelope went flying, and the cash exploded into the air. I heard shouting.

We rolled across the floor. He made a fist and swung at me. I moved my head just enough so he hit my shoulder and not my face. We rolled again, and I drove my knee into his groin. He pulled the red wig off my head. I hit him in the face.

And then I felt myself being lifted off the ground by the scruff of my neck, like a puppy, and at the same time being separated from Eric, who was being lifted by the scruff of his neck just like me.

Large Sarge held us both at arm's length. He looked at Eric and said, "You ever swing at a woman like that again in front of me, I'll take your damn head off."

Then he looked at me, at the Wanda Ward wig on the floor nearby, and back at me. I opened my mouth to explain, but Large Sarge said, "You best shut your damn mouth, Danielle, or whoever you are." And I did.

Then he looked at Blue, who was standing near us in disbelief. Blue looked at Large Sarge, then at Eric, and then at me. "My office, Kate," he said.

54

BOTH HANDS HELD BAD NEWS

For most of middle school and all the way through high school, I'd spent a fair amount of time in the principal's office. School just wasn't where I wanted to be. From seventh grade on, I considered myself an actor and not a student. I wanted to get busy with the beautiful business of being an actor, and I wanted to bail on the boring business of being a student. *I don't need to pay attention because I'm going to be an actor* is what I thought throughout math and science and everything else that wasn't reading or writing. The result of this miscreant mind-set was that I was sometimes less than well behaved.

And the result of my occasional bad behavior was that I was sent to see the principal on a somewhat regular basis. I dreaded sitting in the office waiting for the principal to make an entrance and set me straight about life and school and respect and being a productive part of the student body and the population in general. I dreaded knowing Jimmy would be called and there would be hell to pay when I got home.

Waiting in the principal's office, anticipating the bad news and hearing my father's frustrated voice inside my head, was the hardest part.

Anyway, that's how I felt sitting alone in Blue's office. I was dreading the drama, anticipating the emotional fallout.

Not counting Sunday's Stanley Stein surveillance, when, from across the street, I'd watched a group of groupies fawn over him at the bottom of the Blue Bar steps, I hadn't seen Blue since last Friday, when we'd had lunch on the second floor (where I'd just tangled with the missing Weasley triplet) and he'd informed me he'd promoted Eric the Red to both general manager and bar manager.

Wednesday, of course, was also the day I couldn't unthink my thoughts, and my thoughts were that Blue might be embezzling his own money and betting it through someone else with Stanley Stein.

I'd been worried at the time (and was *still* worried) that my relationship with Blue would end whether he'd been betting his own cash, in which case he'd be the guilty party, or if he had *not* been betting Blue Bar money, in which case I would be the guilty party for accusing him of the crime. It was a lose-lose proposition for me, which sucked eggs because I liked Blue. There was something special between us. We'd proved it again after lunch when we'd kissed at the curb and sparks shot from our lips.

I waited ten minutes before he arrived, plenty of time to twist myself into emotional knots.

"Have you lost your mind completely?" Blue said, shutting his office door behind him. He had the envelope in one hand and my Wanda Ward wig in the other. I'd forgotten Eric had pulled it off during our MMA match in the Blue Bar dining room. The servers had collected the cash, put it back in the envelope, and given it to Blue.

Both hands held bad news, but which was worse? The red wig represented my blown business-consultant cover. The envelope contained an actual stack of stolen Blue Bar money.

He put the envelope on his conference table. The wig was worse.

Which confirmed it was not a professional question, had I lost my mind. I had heard it in his voice. He wasn't asking if I'd lost my mind as his PI. It was a personal question, an emotional question. He was asking if I'd lost my mind as the woman he was seeing, the woman he was starting to care about in a way that might be, could be, kind of already was pointing him and me and us down the road to a deeper relationship.

A part of me wanted to quit the case right there, take that road, and never look back, just like many normal, stable, forty-five-year-old, single women would do when they've finally met a man who leaves them breathless. But I couldn't do it.

"Did you count it?" I said, pointing at the envelope.

"Yes," he said, holding onto the emotional part of the moment.

"And?"

"Six thousand."

"Last Friday you told me twelve thousand was missing. What a coincidence. Exactly half of it is in that envelope."

He looked away and put the wig on the table.

"Your new GM was going to bet it at the bar with Stanley Stein," I said. "Dodgers over/under."

He lifted the envelope. "You don't know whose money this is."

"It's not his money. He has no money. So whose money is it, Blue? You tell me."

Shit, I said to myself. I'd wanted to sound like his hardcore private investigator, and instead I'd sounded like his heartsick girlfriend.

He knew what I'd meant, but he asked me anyway. "What are you saying?"

"I'm running out of suspects."

"You think I'm giving him my own money?"

No, I thought. *That's crazy and impossible, and I don't believe it for a minute. Can we forget all this and hold each other and kiss like crazy for the rest of the day, for the rest of my life?*

"Are you?" I said, and I felt tears on my cheeks. I wasn't weeping or anything close to it, but I was emotional enough that my eyes were filled with tears spilling over and running down my face.

He saw the tears, and he softened his stance, his voice, and the look in his eyes. "I can't believe you're asking me that."

"Neither can I."

"You don't have to."

But you're the only one left with access to the money, I thought. *There's no one else.*

"Someone has to," I said.

"But not you," he said, coming across the office and taking me in his arms.

I wanted to be strong. *Pull yourself together*, I said to myself. *Act like a grownup. Act like Jimmy. Act like a private investigator.* But his arms were strong, and he smelled like musk and leather and love, and he kissed my tears, and I cried into his chest.

55

EVERY MINUTE SINCE I WAS NINE YEARS OLD

At nine o'clock Thursday morning, on my way to Stanley Stein's house, there was an accident on Woodhaven that took thirty minutes to untangle. While I sat in the White Whale, in traffic otherwise known as a parking lot, Blue called. Eric had quit after our dining room smackdown. I apologized for losing Blue yet another general manager, and he said not to worry, he'd already hired a woman named Justine Simonsen who had recently left her job as the assistant general manager of some sports bar in New Jersey.

"Just like that," I said.

"If you're not first, you're last," he said.

By the time I rang Stanley's doorbell, it was ten o'clock. Dennis, Posey, Roger, and Chloe had subjected the bookie to twenty-four hours of Broadway show tunes. They'd sang solos and done duets. They'd thrown in three-part harmonies and vaudeville barbershop quartets. They'd crafted a crazy cornucopia of Broadway ballads and rock-the-house, full-cast barnburners. There'd been dancing galore. Roger had led the big parade with his trombone.

They'd stripped down to their underwear for a full performance of *Hair*.

Stanley looked like he'd been in a street fight with a grizzly and had somehow lived.

"Has he eaten anything?" I said.

"Saltines," Dennis said.

"For the first few hours, he swore us up and down," Posey said. "Then he was dejected, then he was distressed, then he was despondent, then he was sorrowful, then he was suffering, then he was tormented, then he was agonized, anguished, and awful, and finally he was just sad, somber, and silent."

"He drank a lot of water, which made him have to take a leak every twenty minutes," Roger said. "That was not fun. One of the times he took a leak, he told me he'd rather kill a dog than listen to one more show tune."

"I don't think he likes musicals," Chloe said.

"Or dogs," Roger said.

"He didn't break?" I said.

"He didn't break," Dennis said.

I sent them home. From this point on, it was the bookie and the PI and the best of Broadway. From *Fiddler* to *Phantom*, *Rent* to *Wicked*, *Grease* to *Hairspray*, and *Cats* to *Cabaret*, I would curtain call Stanley Stein until he told me what I wanted to know or until five o'clock—when Harold had said he would check in on his boss.

But first we were going to have a little something to eat.

"Hello, Stanley," I said. I was wearing the blonde wig, the blue contacts, the big glasses, and the bright and sparkly birthday-singer clothes, so I looked a lot merrier than I was feeling. But I was an actor, and I had a job to do. "What a day. So many Broadway show tunes, so little time. You must be starving. I hope you don't mind. I made you oatmeal with fresh strawberries. I'm going to take your gag out and feed you. I think you should eat. You've got a long day ahead of you. I've got a big show planned. Of course, it could all be over right now if you tell me who's betting Blue Bar money at Blue Bar."

I took out the gag.

"When this ends, I'm going to kill you," he said. He was worn out, blown out, and burned out, so his physical energy was low, but there was enough gas left in his tank to fill the words with ample venom to kill a cow.

"I know. Now open your mouth and eat your oatmeal like a good bookie."

He was starving, so he opened his mouth, and I spoon-fed him oatmeal and fresh strawberries. When he was thirsty, I held a water glass up to his mouth so he could take the straw and drink.

We were quiet for a few minutes, and then I said, "How come you don't have any pictures, Stanley? Most people have pictures. You have none. Not one single photograph of anything or anyone. That's not normal."

I'd noticed that yesterday morning when I'd punched him in the nose and tied him to his chair, and I'd thought about it during the day. And the more I'd thought about it, the more unusual it seemed. In this whole wide world, who the heck had zero pictures of anything in their house? It had to mean something, though I had no idea what.

"None of your fucking business," he said.

"Hanging on the wall. Sitting on a table. Magnets on the fridge."

"I don't need pictures."

"Everybody needs pictures. Nobody can remember everything that ever happened to them, everyone they ever met."

"I can."

"Disneyland vacations? Holiday get-togethers? Graduations? Ball games? Birthdays? Where are your wedding pictures? You're not married?"

His eyes filled with sadness and something more: memories. I'd hit a nerve.

"You are married?" I said.

He locked his jaw. His face tightened with remorse and remembrance. He turned away from me. He was done eating oatmeal.

"You *were* married," I said. "Where is she, Stanley? What happened to her? Bookie business no good for marriage?"

If the show tunes had loosened him up a little, then maybe talking about his life would loosen him up half as much again, and if I could loosen him up enough, then maybe he'd let it slip who was ripping off Blue Bar. But instead he said nothing.

"We'll get right to it, then," I said. I went to the kitchen, put the oatmeal bowl in the sink, and walked back to Stanley. "I'm going to sing a few songs from *Bye Bye Birdie*, first musical I was ever in, seventh grade. You're going to hate it."

I moved my chair out of the way, took center stage right in front of him, and got ready to start my first song, "Put on a Happy Face." But before I could sing the first line, with the gray skies clearing up, Stanley said, "I wasn't a bookie when I was married."

He was exhausted. From the show tunes, yes, but also from living a life that somehow included no photographs of anyone or anything, nothing to remind him of the years gone by. "What did you do?"

"Sold life insurance."

"How long ago was that?"

He didn't have to think about it. The numbers were immediately present. "We met when we were sixteen. Got married at eighteen. She died at forty-eight, pneumonia of all things. I sold life insurance for ten more years after she passed. Forty years in all. Then I became a bookie."

"What was her name?"

"Christina D'Elia when I met her in Manhattan. Christina

Stein for the thirty years we were married, which is how fucking long she's been dead. Thirty years."

She'd been gone for three decades, and yet the emptiness in his voice made it seem as if she'd died three days ago. I wondered if thirty years from now I would feel the loss of my father the same way Stanley felt the loss of his wife. Jimmy had been dead since the end of July, almost three months, and sometimes it seemed like I'd lost him last week, like he had only just had his eyes blown out of his head.

"Thirty years is a long time," I said. "You should have pictures of her around the house. Remind you of the good old days. Cheer you up when you're feeling blue."

He was quiet for a minute, eyes closed, drifting through time. Then he looked at me and said, "I remember every breath we took together, every inch of her face, every time she laughed or cried, every word she said for thirty years, thirty-two if you count our courtship. I don't need pictures. It's all in my head."

It wasn't poetry—although it was one of the most romantic things I'd heard in a long time—it was a statement of fact. He'd said it as if it were true with a capital *T*, as if he actually remembered every moment of their lives together, as if it really were in his head forever.

"You mean figuratively, right?" I said. "You don't mean you literally remember every minute of your life."

"Every minute since I was nine years old."

"That's not possible. Who can do that? Nobody. You're a bookie. What are the odds that somebody can remember everything that ever happened to them since they were nine?"

"One in a hundred twenty-five million. More or less."

"Excuse me?"

"HSAM. Highly superior autobiographical memory. Hyperthymesia syndrome. Maybe sixty people in the world have it. I'm one of them. Except I have the best case ever, or the worst case, depending on your point of view."

I'd heard of it. The great Marilu Henner from *Taxi* had it, or something like it. Superhuman memory.

"I went to California ten years ago, after they first discovered it, or named it, or whatever the fuck social scientists do in California," he said. "I already knew I had it. Since I was nine, I knew. But I wanted to get tested. So they tested me, and they read the results, and they couldn't even fucking speak. I was off their charts. They couldn't measure me. Sixty people on the planet have hyperthymesia. Their memories are in kindergarten. Mine's a Ph.D."

"I'm sure they're smarter than that."

"It's an analogy. Memory doesn't make you smart. Some of the sixty with HSAM are idiots. Some are savants. Some are autistic. It's got nothing to do with IQ."

Maybe not with the other superhuman memory folks, but Stanley's IQ was *also* off the charts. Matthew had told me the bookie was worth twenty million dollars they could find and probably another twenty million buried so deep they would never find it. The problem, Matthew told me, was Stanley was much smarter than everyone trying to nail him. "It's not even close," Matthew had said. "You know the IQ for when you're a genius? Stanley Stein's IQ is higher than that."

"You didn't stay in California with the social scientists?" I said.

"So they could test me the rest of my fucking life? No chance. I told them they'd never see me again, came home, and kept being a bookie."

"All the things you could have been, you chose bookie?"

"I like ball games. Plus, I got a knack for odds."

I was as speechless as the California social scientists. And then a light bulb as bright as Broadway went off in my head. "That's how you do it. You don't write anything down because you remember it."

"Every bet, every game, every day for twenty years."

"And everyone who ever sat on the stool beside you. Jesus. That's how you knew you'd never met me."

"Don't tell anybody."

"No one would believe me."

"No shit."

And then we spent a minute saying nothing, me standing in the middle of the room, him sitting in his breakfast chair. I think it was eye-opening for both of us. For Stanley because he had shared personal information I was sure he'd had no intention of sharing. For me because I now knew how he'd stayed so far ahead of the police for the last two decades.

"I'm going to kill you when this ends," he said.

"I heard you the first time," I said, snapping out of it. "Let me get this straight. You have a superhuman memory, which means you can easily recall how much you hate Broadway show tunes, and you still won't tell me what I want to know so you don't have to hear them hour after hour after hour."

"You kidnap me in my own fucking house, I'm not telling you shit out of spite. Not even if you sing 'Suddenly Seymour' sixty times in a row."

Stanley Stein despised "Suddenly Seymour," the beloved ballad from the nationally adored musical *Little Shop of Horrors*, sung by the fabulous Ellen Greene playing the role of Audrey? He might have been the only person in America who didn't fall hard for the horror-comedy rock musical. *Little Shop* ran off-Broadway for five years at the Orpheum Theater in the early to mid-1980s and so captured the American imagination that regional and community theater companies across the country lined up (and still line up) to perform it for cheering audiences, who sing every word along with the cast, especially with Audrey, whose "Suddenly Seymour" brings down the house every time. I knew that because I had played Audrey in several productions over the years. I was no Ellen Greene, but I had pipes to be proud of and did the song justice. The musical moved to Broadway too, and Hollywood made a movie adaptation, which became a classic, though the real magic happened off-Broadway, as it often does.

"You don't like *Little Shop of Horrors*?" I said. "What the hell is wrong with you, Stanley? Everybody likes that show. I never met anybody who didn't like *Little Shop*."

"I hate that one the most. Dumbest piece of Broadway shit ever written. Idiot outer space alien plant comes to Earth and drinks human blood in a neighborhood of low-life losers who sing and dance about it because they got nothing else to live for. Had a niece one time made me take her to see it at some fucked-up local theater company in New Jersey. Thought I'd died and gone to hell."

For the second time in the last ten minutes, the bookie had told me something he should have kept to himself.

"You're right," I said. "Memory has nothing to do with how smart you are. Change of plans. Say good-bye to *Birdie*, and say hello to *Little Shop*."

I put the gag in, and his eyes went wide with anticipatory anguish. He'd figured out what was about to happen.

"'Suddenly Seymour' is four-and-a-half minutes long, give or take," I said, "and we've got six hours to go."

Stanley shook his head and yelled at me through the gag. He was better at math than I was and had fast figured out I could sing the song sixty times before Harold rang the doorbell. We would see who could last longer.

56

WE'LL ALWAYS HAVE HOBOKEN

There is a universal saying that all people in the universe say: "I can't get that song out of my head." Stanley and I gave that saying new meaning. We gave it meaning it was never meant to mean. I was entirely Irish on my mother's side and absolutely Irish on my father's side, so I could be stubbornly stubborn just falling out of bed. Not to mention I was Jimmy McCall's daughter, so I'd learned stubborn from the Hard-headed Heavyweight Champion of the World.

Stanley, apparently, went to the same school as my father. He howled in pain through his gag while I sang "Suddenly Seymour" for five hours straight. When I took time-outs, I played him the song on CD. I wasn't sure who suffered more. It was a toss-up. I had never wanted to stop singing a song to someone more than I'd wanted to stop singing that song to Stanley. It was killing me to sing "Suddenly Seymour" over and over and over and over at least as much as it was killing him to hear it.

The bookie was on the ropes, figuratively speaking, but I was out of gas and didn't have the creative power for a knockout punch. I had him where I wanted him and couldn't put him away.

And then, at four o'clock, when I simply couldn't sing it one more time, when I was ready to let Stanley win by decision, I had a moment of inspiration that filled my lungs with a second wind. I took out his gag. It was *mano y mano* from now to the end.

"Ladies and gentlemen and bookies," I said, "I'd like to bring out a good friend to us all. Mr. Bob Dylan."

"Don't do it," he said, horrified. "Don't even think about it."

He could feel it. I could feel it too. The end was near. The only question was *Would I run out of time before he went down for the count?* Harold, I felt sure, would arrive in one hour and ring the bell, expecting Stanley to let him in and tell him all about his flu-like symptoms.

There was no way for me to slow the ticking clock. All I could do was sprint to the end.

And so I sang him "Suddenly Seymour" as Bob Dylan, getting deep into the role of America's troubadour. And then I sang it as Johnny Cash. And then I sang it as Cyndi Lauper. And then as Bobby McFerrin. And then Bob Marley. Mick Jagger. Mickey Rooney. Aretha Franklin. Rod Stewart. Tony Bennett. Carly Simon. James Taylor. Carly and James doing a reunion duet of "Suddenly Seymour" on Martha's Vineyard.

He was so close, Stanley was, so close to breaking down, but he wasn't there. I needed more—one last combination to put him away.

And so I sang the song to the melodies of other famous songs by other famous singers. I sang the lyrics of "Suddenly Seymour" to the melody of "Me and Julio Down by the School-yard" in the persona of Paul Simon. I sang it to the melody of "The Night They Drove Old Dixie Down" in the style of the great Levon Helm. I sang it to the melody of "Hey Jude" in the voice of the cute Beatle, Paul McCartney—a fantastical creative challenge indeed.

And then it was four forty, and I was screwed. The doorbell would ring in twenty minutes, and I would race out the back and that would be that.

I had one more shot, one more song, one more singer. I sang the opening chords in their familiar rhythmic measure. Stanley's recognition was instantaneous.

"No," he said. "Not the Chairman. Not Ol' Blue Eyes. Please..." His voice disappeared in a black hole of despair.

And then I sang "Suddenly Seymour" to the melody of "New York, New York" with the sense and sensibility of Frank Sinatra.

"Hoboken," Stanley said softly. "Hoboken..."

Stanley and Frank were both born in Hoboken, New Jersey —a Hudson River waterfront city across from Manhattan. Matthew had told me Stanley was a big Sinatra fan.

"Stop," Stanley said. "Please. No more..."

I stopped. "Talk to me."

"I was born in Hoboken, little Jewish kid with the fucking memory of a supercomputer. All my friends were Italian. Fucking gang of Hoboken hoodlums like you've never seen. A ton of trouble. They're still my friends. Good guys, all of them."

"Mobsters, you mean."

"Businessmen," he said, nodding that they were mobsters. "Sinatra was born there too. He's the patron saint of Hoboken. My fucking hero. You just can't sing that fucking song like Frank."

"Little town blues," I said.

"Eric Miller," he said. "Redhead cook and bartender. New GM. He's been betting with me since Tuesday, June twenty-eighth. Cardinals at Cubs. Four grand on the over/under. Always bets the over/under. Paid out six grand."

"I know about Miller," I said. "I caught him with stolen

cash. The problem is he's not the one embezzling it from the bar."

"Not the sharpest tool in the shed," he said.

"So who's giving *him* the money?" I said.

Stanley dropped his chin to his chest.

"Vagabond shoes," I said.

He looked up. "Blue's into me deep. Big money. He's the safe bet."

I stopped breathing. I had expected it to be bad news, but hearing the bookie say it out loud, that Blue was the safe bet, took my breath away.

"What do you mean *deep*?" I said.

"I mean he's got a problem. Been in and out of rehab a couple times. Betting with me since he threw for the Mets."

My heart was breaking, and I could feel tears in my eyes, but I had to keep going. "What do you mean *big money*?"

"One day soon I'm going to own that bar. Last thing in the world I want to own, a fucking sports bar. It's like somebody else's kids. It's fine because end of the night you go home, they're not your problem. But if it's your bar...who the fuck wants that?"

And then we were quiet. Stanley was quiet because he was whipped. Still tied to his breakfast chair. Still wearing the pajamas he'd had on when I rang his bell and forced my way in, and he pulled a gun from those pajamas, and I knocked him out. I was quiet because I liked Blue, was close to him, had made love with him, and had never sensed, not one time, that he had a problem with gambling—a problem big enough for rehab.

How could I have missed that? Was I so lost in the swirl of our heat-seeking romance that I ran right by the fact my client, who'd hired me to bust a sports betting embezzlement scam, had a gambling addiction? I made a mental note to spend some serious time looking at myself in the mirror. *Jesus Christ*, I thought, *now he has to make his own bets.*

Although without knowing it, I'd apparently said it out loud too because Stanley shrugged and said, "Maybe not. He hire somebody to take Eric's place?"

"A woman named Justine Simonsen," I said. "She managed a sports bar in New Jersey."

Stanley laughed. "He don't have to make his own bets if Justine's in the game."

Something about the way he said it implied there was more to what he'd said than what he'd said. "You know her?"

"Sure I know her. She and Blue have history. They had a thing when he was with PIX. She was a bartender at a Third Avenue sports bar went out of business. He was there most nights I was there."

In the same second he'd said that sentence, my heart sunk into the empty pit of despair in my stomach. "You said a thing. What? A romantic thing?" I said, trying to sound like a private investigator and not a lovesick teenage girl.

"Gambling thing," he said. "Old flame too. They were both young and beautiful. I don't know the details of their love life, but they bet together, I know that. I know every bet they ever made."

I wanted to ask him a million questions about Justine and Blue. But my brain was melting, and I couldn't form words into sentences. So I was silent. He was silent too.

And that was dumb luck because if I'd started hounding the bookie for more information about the probably-was-romance-Third-Avenue-sports-bar days with Blue and Justine, then I wouldn't have heard the key in the backdoor.

I looked at my watch: four fifty. I had expected Harold to ring the front doorbell in ten minutes. I'd assumed the jiu jitsu grand master, MMA middleweight champion, nasty-ass Navy SEAL, and deep-cover Special Ops killer would be prompt by nature. But I had neglected to consider that ten minutes early was most likely right on time for a guy like Harold.

But what I had not assumed was that instead of ringing the doorbell, Harold would let himself in the back door because he had his own key—or knew where Stanley's key was hidden—and didn't want to wake the bookie, who, so far as Harold knew, was battling the flu or pneumonia or the plague or whatever.

I grabbed my purse and jacket and ran for the front door. As I darted past Stanley, I said, "We'll always have Hoboken." And then I was gone.

I didn't stop running until I reached the White Whale, parked three blocks away. I jumped in the Toyota, started the engine, and pulled away from the curb. It was only when the Corolla was moving that I allowed myself to look back and see if Harold was after me.

He wasn't. I imagined he was in the Tudor untying the bookie and helping him from the breakfast chair to a sofa somewhere. I felt sure they were having a discussion about killing me if they ever found me. I was glad I'd missed that conversation.

I think I felt relief—getting out of Stanley Stein's Tudor alive—but I couldn't say for sure because everything I was feeling was blurry and boozy and buried beneath the heartbreak I felt for Blue.

57

THE LOWRY LOWE MARITAL MERRY-GO-ROUND

T HE MOST MISGUIDED TELEVISION PILOT I WAS EVER IN WAS produced by a conman who had twice gone to prison for fraud. His name was Bill Garrity. He was a sixty-nine-year-old chain-smoking, pill-popping wild man. The name of the series was *Addams Family Flowers*. Bill told the cast and crew the show had come to him in a dream while he was in prison the second time. In the dream, Bill said, God had told him the show was his ticket to heaven, meaning, I supposed at the time, money, fame, power, and parties for the rest of his days.

The show in Bill's prison dream was a riff off the fabulous Charles Addams 1964 TV series *The Addams Family*. In Bill's dream, Gomez goes broke and the family opens a flower shop on the Lower East Side of Manhattan. *"Hilarity will ensue,"* said God in the dream. God said nothing about securing the rights from the Tee and Charles Addams Foundation before raising production dollars from trusting dupes and dopes.

So naturally, before we shot our first frame of film, the Tee and Charles Addams Foundation heard about the pilot and delivered a cease and desist letter to Bill. The producer opened the letter on the first day of shooting, had a coronary, and died on the spot—making it the only decease and desist letter I'd ever heard of.

So point number one is that I had been cast as the flower shop delivery girl (who falls in love with Pugsley) and still had my Addams Family Flowers delivery jacket and laminated ID on a lanyard.

Point number two is that when I was waiting for Michelle in the Lowry Lowe reception room on Wednesday afternoon, playing the role of New York City Bar Association ethics investigator Marsha Friedrich, a file clerk named Whitney was showing off her brand-spanking-new engagement ring to the receptionist and several other young and beautiful Lowry Lowe women. A hospital management man named Nat had proposed the night before, and Whitney was over the moon.

Remembering points one and two, I called Lowry Lowe first thing Friday morning, asked for Whitney the file clerk, told her I was Joanne from Addams Family Flowers, and said I had a personal midday delivery for her that she had to sign for and wouldn't want to miss.

Rockefeller Center security is on point. The only way past them is with a scheduled and approved meeting or with a phone call from the front desk to whatever office is the destination of choice. Without those prerequisites, packages go to the Messenger Center and are delivered in-house. Even with those prerequisites, bags are checked, IDs are scrutinized, and elevator passes are grudgingly granted.

But after a quick call to Whitney in the Lowry Lowe file room, a glance at my impressive Addams Family Flowers laminated ID, and a little rough and tumble through my backpack purse, I took the elevator to the sixty-second floor, holding the big bouquet in the snazzy vase I'd bought ten minutes ago at Rockefeller Center's Grecian Gardens Florist.

"Is Lisa Lowe in her office?" I said to the receptionist. "She went to law school with my cousin, and I wanted to say hello."

"Mrs. Lowe is at a mediation," the receptionist said, transferring calls and watching her computer screen. "She'll be back by twelve thirty."

"Oh well," I said. "Anyway, I've got flowers for Whitney in the file room. She's a clerk, I think. Got engaged, looks like."

Whitney burst into the reception area, trailed by two more young and beautiful file clerks, ran to the bouquet, found the card, and read it out loud to her friends: "'I can't wait to spend the rest of my life with you. Love, Nat.'" I had never met Nat, of course, but I'd assumed he couldn't wait to spend the rest of his life with Whitney and also that he loved her, so that's what I'd written on the card.

The file clerks were overwhelmed by the romance of it all and said so—to Whitney, to me, to the receptionist, to a passing Lowry Lowe attorney and his soon-to-be divorced client. The sheer size of the bouquet Nat had chosen was part of the thrill. It was so big, in fact, that it only made sense for me to carry it to Whitney's desk in the file/copy/mail room, which was fine with the receptionist because I would be escorted through the hallowed halls of Divorce Central Station by the file clerks.

As I put the vase on Whitney's desk, I removed the six-inch restorer's pry bar I'd inherited at the reading of Jimmy's will from the bottom of the bouquet and surreptitiously slid it in my pocket. I'd hidden it from the Rockefeller Center security guards because if they'd found it in my bag, they would have wondered what in the hell an Addams Family Flowers delivery woman was doing with a pry bar and, hey, while they were at it, who in the hell were Addams Family Flowers in the first place.

While the file clerks admired the bouquet of boundless love Nat sent to Whitney, I slipped out of the room and walked calmly through the office like I belonged there, like I had important Addams Family Flowers business to attend to somewhere down one of the Lowry Lowe hallways.

From visits to the law firm as Emily Baynes of Austin-by-way-of-Abilene, soon-to-be-filthy-rich ex-wife of Tommy Baynes, and ethics investigator Marsha Friedrich, I knew that Lisa Lowe's office was across the hall from Michelle Lowry's office and down the hall from the offices of their late husbands, Jack Lowe and Christopher Lowry. I checked my watch. Twelve fifteen. I had fifteen minutes before Lisa got back from her mediation.

I turned down Partner Row, which was more or less the main highway through the center of the office. There was hustle and bustle as lawyers and clients and everyone in their orbits finished phone calls and emails and left for lunch. Lisa's office door was shut. Right across the wide hallway, Michelle's door was closed too.

I stopped at Lisa's door, pretended to check a schedule or a text or something on my phone, and glanced up and down the hallway. I was just another invisible messenger making a Lowry Lowe delivery. I held my breath and turned the handle. The door was unlocked. I opened it, slid inside, and shut and locked it behind me.

Lisa's office looked like the inside of a Tuscan villa. There were warm accent colors throughout—modern-yet-old-world paintings, pottery, throw rugs, and pillows meant to soften the modern Lowry Lowe vibe. Michelle had made no effort to soften her professional space. You could hang meat in Michelle Lowry's office. You could drink red wine and watch the sun set over the Italian countryside, or at least over Manhattan, in Lisa's panoramic, sixty-second floor, Rockefeller Center windows.

I could picture Gina Lollobrigida or Isabella Rossellini playing a high-powered divorce lawyer hiring a high-priced corporate killer, murdering her partners one by one, and taking full control of the firm.

I quickly crossed the office to Lisa's large walnut desk, put my restorer's pry bar in place on her private file cabinet, and had four thoughts in rapid-fire succession.

One: *This is insane. This Lowry Lowe business—from top to bottom, back to front, and side to side, from living partner to late partner, from Emily Baynes to Marsha Friedrich, from Red Maple Horse Farm to 918 Spyder doing one eighty-five down Madison Avenue, from Carter Ringwald to Whitney the file clerk—this Lowry Lowe business is crazy from every angle, meaning there is no angle from which this Lowry Lowe business is not crazy.*

Two: *I am insane. I'm standing in one of the two surviving partner's private offices, pry bar firmly in file drawer, pretending to be an Addams Family Flowers delivery person, hoping to snatch unethically altered partnership papers in the hope of gaining evidential leverage (like the freaking pry bar) so I can pressure the partners and uncover the killer's name. In certain circles, that is the definition of insanity.*

Three: *I will open this file drawer and give the unethically altered partnership papers to Logan because I am in over my head, out of control, and dancing with danger. Logan has a task force, for shit's sake. I have the House of Emotional Tics.*

Four: *I am done with private investigating. After I turn over the partnership papers, McCall & Company will fade to black. For one thing, Matthew will kill me if I get arrested for doing something like I'm doing now—if he ever talks to me again, since he hasn't said one word to me in days, and I am heartsick over it. For another thing, I finally meet a man I like, and he turns out to be embezzling his own money from his own sports bar to fund his own gambling addiction, and I'm the one who has to catch him in the act. Heartsick meet heartbroken.*

Time to be an actor again. Time to be a mother again. Time to be me again, I thought. *Time to quit being a PI.*

With thoughts of immediate PI retirement in mind, I applied pressure to the pry bar. But I heard someone in the hallway jiggle the door handle and froze. Then I heard a key in the lock. I ran across the office to Lisa Lowe's coat closet, which was slightly ajar, hid in its darkest shadows, and stopped breathing.

Through the opening between the closet door and the doorframe, I had a straight and narrow view of Lisa's conference area—two gorgeous leather sofas and four leather club chairs perfectly placed between and around coffee tables and end tables and fabulous designer lamps. Instead of a standard conference table, Lisa had a living room to die for.

The office door opened and Lisa entered, followed by Michelle. I was once again struck by the stark contrast between them. The Italian Bombshell was resplendent, lustrous, and magnificent in Carolina Herrera. The Swedish Queen was exquisite, stunning, and statuesque in Dolce & Gabbana. Both women were supermodels posing as divorce lawyers. One of them was also moonlighting as a power-mad murderer. The other would not be alive for long. I had no clue which was which.

"First she was Emily Baynes, and then she was Marsha Friedrich," Michelle said in mid-conversation. She was in the living room area, so I could see her. She was turned to Lisa's desk, where, I assumed, Lisa was standing, out of my view. "She knew about the professional killer and wanted his name. She thought Christopher told you who the killer was when you were sleeping with him and that you contacted the killer and had Jack and Christopher murdered. She thought I amended the LLC agreement to protect myself from you."

"What did you say?" Lisa said. I still couldn't see her.

"I told her you amended the agreement," Michelle said.

Lisa stepped into the sitting area, where I could see her. "To protect myself from you?"

"So you could have it all in the event of my tragic death," Michelle said.

"I think you don't trust me," Lisa said, stopping directly in front of Michelle.

"That's funny because I think you don't trust me," Michelle said.

"I don't trust you," Lisa said.

They were two of the most beautiful, successful, confident, callous, and ruthless women in Manhattan, and they looked ready to choke the life out of each other. They had each said from the beginning that the death threat had been meant for the other one, and now it was only the two of them left. I had the sense that in the next thirty seconds I would find out who was right and who was dead.

"I don't trust you either," Michelle said, raising her hand to smack Lisa across the face.

But instead of doing that, instead of slapping the shit out of the Italian Bombshell, Michelle stroked Lisa's hair, pulled her head forward, and kissed her on the mouth. Lisa kissed her back big-time.

My eyes popped wide open. It was all I could do not to shout *What the hell?*

Michelle and Lisa kept kissing. Gently at first, but then with increasing heat and passion, arms around each other, hands going up and down and over and under, grinding their bodies against each other. The temperature in the room rose ten degrees.

From the beginning, I had hardly been able to keep up with the Lowry Lowe marital merry-go-round, which played like a late-night-cable episode of an X-rated *Love Boat* that guest starred a contract killer and featured a plotline that went something like this: McDreamy was married to the Swedish Queen, McSteamy was married to the Italian Bombshell, and all four young, wealthy, gorgeous attorneys were partners in the same high-priced, high-powered, high-wire, 30 Rock law firm. How high was the wire? McDreamy had an affair with the Bombshell, so McSteamy had an affair with the Queen, which ruined McDreamy's marriage. McDreamy was a super sore loser, so McSteamy was murdered at Red Maple Horse Farm, and McDreamy was suspect number one. Except McDreamy was himself murdered soon after McSteamy, and so the Queen and the Bombshell became suspects one and one-A by default.

But suspects one and one-A were currently sticking their tongues down each other's throats, having an affair of their own, and there was no way to know which one had called the contract killer to murder the men and which one was about to be murdered. I thought all that through in a half a second, though the clock had stopped ticking since Michelle and Lisa had locked lips.

As I was wondering what in the world I should do, my silenced cell phone vibrated in my pocket. Someone had texted me. I looked away from the sensual scene unfolding in Lisa Lowe's living room and glanced down at my phone to check the message, hoping my son was finally returning my calls and texts. But it wasn't Matthew.

It was *The Number*. The killer was texting me. I was stuck in the coat closet, Lisa and Michelle sucking face fifteen feet away, and the killer was texting me. *Listen up, Little Engine, time for the grand finale, in which we begin the workweek with the last late Lowry Lowe lawyer. Can you guess who it is?*

And then it hit me like a thunderbolt: *Yes, I can.*

58

GOING TO BE A MURDER AT THE END OF THIS ONE

I DID NOT GET CAUGHT IN THE CLOSET. A LOVELY LOWRY LOWE paralegal knocked in the nick of time, and Lisa and Michelle straightened themselves up, smoothed themselves out, and exited the office as if they weren't having an affair that would make Ally McBeal blush.

I slipped out like I'd slipped in and marched through the law firm as if my job here was done and all systems were go. On my way out, I saw Carter Ringwald in the reception area, and he saw me. He recognized me too, or at least thought he did. Anyway, the expression on his face said I was familiar to him in the worst possible way. He pointed at me and was about to say something along the lines of *Hey, I know you. You're the one who kidnapped me and tied me to the bottom of a parrot cage. It's her, everybody. She's the one. Call the police.*

He was standing at the entrance doors, tongue-tied and shocked to see me. I walked across the room, put my finger on his lips in the universal sign for *ssshhh*, leaned in, and whispered in his ear, "I'm watching you, Molly Ringwald. Breathe one word, I call Bethany." Then I left Lowry Lowe without looking back.

It was three o'clock by the time I returned to the House of Emotional Tics. I had to be at the D-Cup for the Friday night performance of *Blood Song and Dance* in two hours, but if I didn't dillydally, I would have time for a thirty-minute jog to clear my head.

But as I walked down the path to the front door, Edie and Ray Mazzone stepped out of the brownstone and stopped me dead in my tracks. Actually, it was what they were wearing that made my feet say *Nope, we're not taking another step until we find out what the heck is happening here.*

This was often the case with Edie and Ray, who had owned and operated a laundry business on First Avenue and 63rd Street for fifty years before selling out and retiring. Ray had run the back of the shop, inhaling dry-cleaning chemicals mixed with hot steam twelve hours a day, six days a week, fifty weeks a year for five decades. What brain cells he had left had been shaken and shuffled in loopy patterns that presented them- selves as unimaginable clothing combinations, meaning Ray Mazzone was dressing on a different plateau than the rest of planet Earth. He was seventy-seven years old and thin as a pencil. He'd recently discovered Viagra and swinging, much to the chagrin and consternation of Edie—and everyone else in the brownstone, who he peppered with updates regarding his impending sexual adventures, which we all hoped (no one more than Edie) would remain imagined.

Edie was seventy-five. She had run the counter of their dry- cleaning business. She was a bleach-blonde glamour girl then and now. And when I say glamour, I mean *glamourous*, I mean full-blown hair and makeup, I mean jewelry jamboree. Ball gowns, wedding dresses, and period costume clothing from one turn of the century to the next was her style whether she was headed to the Korean market around the corner or to fetch the mail in the lobby. She'd been dressed to the nines for Jimmy's backyard wake, for Pete's sake. I liked Edie. I liked Ray too, but there was just so much Ray a normal human person could absorb at any one given time.

Edie was wearing sunshine-yellow, vinyl, 1960s go-go boots and a rainbow-colored mod miniskirt that made her look like a bowl of Skittles. Her hair was pulled back by a bright blue headband. Ray was wearing green fly-fishing waders that came up to his chest, no shirt, and an African skull cap from Ethiopia.

"Hello, Kate," Edie said as we met near the bottom of the brownstone stairs. "We're walking to UPS."

"They got my membership package for the North American Swing Club Association," Ray said.

"I'm going to burn it as soon as we get home," Edie said.

"Are we expecting trout on Second Avenue?" I said.

"We came downstairs, and Fu was mopping the lobby with half of Lamoka Lake," Ray said.

"We didn't want to ruin our shoes, so we went back upstairs to change," Edie said. They lived in 2A, so it was only one flight.

"Looks like I'm going to get wet," I said, looking down at my feet.

"No, dear," Edie said. "Fu left a dry path to your door."

"To my door?" I said, going up the stairs. "Thanks for the inside info."

"I got your inside info right here," Ray said, pointing at his crotch as he walked down the path. "I'm not wearing anything under these waders. Swinging free in the breeze because I'm a swinger."

"Burning it as soon as I get home," Edie said. "Not to worry."

Ray said something else, but I didn't hear it, thank God, because I went into the lobby.

Fu was mopping the floor, just like Edie and Ray had said. He'd covered it with a sea of soapy water—except for a bone-dry path that led straight to my front door and a dry square patch in front of my apartment. I walked to my door. Fu met me there.

"What are you doing, Fu?" I said.

He held up the mop and smirked. "What look like?"

"Looks like you're mopping," I said.

"You smart," he said. "Must be PI."

"I mean *why*, Fu?" I said. "You were mopping the lobby when I left this morning, and now you're mopping again, and the lobby is a swimming pool except for in front of my door? Why is that?"

It was true. He'd been mopping the lobby when I left for Lowry Lowe dressed as an Addams Family Flowers delivery person. He'd cornered me and grilled me, and I'd told him about the secretly amended partnership papers and my plan to "borrow" them.

"You tell Fu," he said, making the dry ground smaller so that we were closer to each other.

"Fine," I said. I knew what he wanted to know. "I didn't get the partnership papers. But I got something else. I know who's next."

I told him about the flowers and the partners having an affair and the killer texting me about starting the workweek with the last late Lowry Lowe lawyer, and he mopped and listened and mopped and listened, and we were surrounded by soap.

"Tell Logan?" he said.

"Tried to," I said. "I called the Thirteenth on my way home. Logan's at a funeral in Minnesota. Gets back Monday. I left messages for him and his new partner, Jesse. By the time Logan gets into the city, it will be too late. He'll be collecting a dead body instead of stopping a murder."

"Why think not kill Monday?" he said.

"Because the creep said 'in which we begin the workweek with the last late Lowry Lowe lawyer.' He didn't say 'in which we begin the workweek with me murdering one of the last two Lowry Lowe lawyers.' She's already dead on Monday. He's going to kill her on Sunday."

"How know not sooner?" he said. "Today, next day?"

"Because when I was in the closet, after I got the text, I heard them talking about their weekend. They're going to Pennsylvania together to look at the leaves. They're gone tonight and tomorrow and tomorrow night. They come back to the city Sunday morning."

"That why Fu mop Friday," he said. "So Sunday Fu no mop."

That's where he'd been going all along. Fu kept mopping the floor in front of my door, making the dry box smaller.

"There's no way, Fu, absolutely no chance in the world, none, zero, that you could know in advance of me knowing that the murder would be Sunday, since I'm the one who got the text from the killer in the closet, and I'm the one who heard the lawyers say they were leaving for the weekend. Me, not you— me. There's no way you could know before I knew," I said.

"Fu know first," he said. Smirk.

Don't let him get your goat, I said to myself, and yet he got my goat, just like my sister used to do when I was a little girl and was helpless to stop her. No one could get my goat like Marilyn...except freaking Fu, who, in addition to all his other gifts, was also some kind of mystical goat whisperer.

"How, Fu?" I said. "Tell me how you knew first."

"Fu read tea leaves."

"I read some tea leaves too. You know what they said?"

"Fu know first?" Smirk.

"They said this is your childish way of saying you want to come with me on Sunday to help stop the murder."

"Fu know you say that before you say that. Fu know all."

"If Fu know all," LaTanya said from across the soaking-wet lobby, "then Fu know I was doing my damn laundry when he mopped the lobby floor with half the Hudson River. If Fu know all, then Fu know I can't cross this lake in my damn slippers. If Fu know all, then Fu know I would stand here holding my damn basket listening to you two bicker like babies about who was the first to know the prick who killed Jimmy would kill another Lowry Lowe lawyer on Sunday. If Fu know all, then Fu know nobody stopping any murder on Sunday without LaTanya."

She had come up from the basement and was holding a wicker basket full of folded clothes. She was wearing her legendary laundry outfit: Incredible Hulk T-shirt, baggy green sweatpants, and bunny rabbit slippers that were supposed to look like real rabbits on her feet (and kind of did).

"What is that supposed to mean, nobody's stopping any murder on Sunday without you?" I said to her. "Why do you want to come?"

"B-roll," she said. "First day of principal photography for *Kung Fu Fu* is a week from Monday, Halloween. If I can shoot you two running around like cops on a case, then I'm well on my way to winning the Academy Award for Karate before we officially film frame one."

The truth was I'd intended to ask Fu for backup on Sunday, not that I would ever admit it to him, but I had not expected the LaTanya tagalong. She'd been in some tough spots with me already, so I knew she could take care of herself, but I had a bad feeling. "We're talking about surveillance. Not exactly scintillating cinema," I said to her, thinking, *There's going to be a murder at the end of this one.*

"Going to be a murder at the end of this one?" she said.

"Looks like it," I said.

"Then let me shoot the shit out of you catching the killer and make Fu a movie star," she said.

"If you're shooting the shit out of *me* catching the killer," I said, "why are you making *him* the movie star?"

"Nobody knows," she said. "It's the magic of Hollywood. You in for Sunday, Fu?"

"Fu in," he said.

"Good," she said. "Me too, so mop me a damn path across the damn floor so I can go upstairs and pre-produce some pre-production."

"Fu magic movie star," Fu said, mopping himself closer to me, not LaTanya. "Want autograph?"

"Wrong way, Fu," LaTanya said.

"Fu you, Fu," I said.

"Fu you too," he said. The dry floor got smaller still. "Know next dead Lowry Lowe lawyer?"

"Yes, I do," I said.

"How know?" Fu said, still mopping.

"I'm a professional," I said. "It's what I do."

He mopped himself right next to me, closed us in, and looked deep into my eyes.

"My slippers are getting wet, Fu," LaTanya said. "Guess how much I like that."

"Prove know," Fu said to me.

"How?" I said.

"Tell Fu," he said.

"Fu you, Fu," LaTanya said.

"Fu you too," Fu said to her without turning to her. "If no tell, no know," he said to me.

This was how it happened with Marilyn too. We'd be going about our business and all of a sudden we would be in a toe-to-toe tête-à-tête. In all the verbal confrontations we'd had as kids, I'd never had the last word. It was always Marilyn. Now, she was older than me and bigger than me and stronger than me and more confident than me, so she could reasonably be expected to best her kid sister ten out of ten times—or a hundred out of a hundred. And she did.

After Marilyn moved to Cleveland and my life progressed, I

had my fair share of last words—but none with Fu. I'd never once had the last word with Fu. Not even for the first two years we both lived in the House of Emotional Tics when he only let on he knew six words. Even then he always had the last word. And once he became a big-time talker, forget it. I hadn't been close enough to a last word to get so much as a whiff.

But I had the sense that was going to change right now. Call it an ebb of the tide. Whatever it was, I could feel it in my fingertips.

"Who's the next dead Lowry Lowe lawyer?" I said. "That's what you want to know?"

"Tell him so I can cross this damn lobby," LaTanya said to me.

Fu smirked. "You not know," he said to me.

"Oh, I know, Fu. I definitely know who's next," I said. *It's happening right now*, I thought. *The last word will be mine.* "The question is, do you really want to know or do you *really* want to know?" *Tables turned*, I said to myself.

Fu cocked his head a bit and tightened his grip on the mop ever so slightly. "Must tell Fu now," he said, meaning he *really* wanted to know.

Of course, I had to tell him...but not until Sunday. From now until then, I had an unexpected Last Word Window. And I intended to climb right through it.

"If you *really* want to know now, Fu, read your tea leaves," I said, proving it was possible to be a professional forty-five-year-old woman and an immature grade school girl at the same time. I smirked in his face and walked across the wet lobby floor toward the front door.

I took three steps, and he said, "Fu know before you know."

"Oh for God's sake," LaTanya said.

I stopped on a dime. "No, you don't."

"Fu know first."

"How, Fu? How do you know first? How do you know before me?"

"Fu figure."

I walked back through the sloshy water onto the dry island of floor in front of my apartment. "You did *not* figure out who the next dead Lowry Lowe lawyer is. No way."

"Way," Fu said.

"Okay, Fu. Fine. You know first? You know before me? You know who it is? Tell me who it is," I said.

"Want to know who now, read tea leaves," he said, smirking like all get-out. And then he mopped his way across the floor.

"You out of your damn mind, McCall?" LaTanya said. "You walked into that like a blind man in a blizzard."

Shit, I thought. *Another last word bites the dust.*

59

LET'S FIND OUT WHAT THE HELL JUSTINE IS UP TO

LET'S FIND OUT WHAT THE HELL JUSTINE IS UP TO

A FUNNY THING HAPPENED DURING THE FRIDAY NIGHT performance of *Blood Song and Dance*. A group of ten, maybe twelve, girls in full Goth regalia who'd been to see the show a half dozen times over its run—the Goth Girls Gang, we called them—stood up during the first act and delivered dialogue with the actors and even sang the songs as if the D-Cup were hosting a rowdy midnight screening of *The Rocky Horror Picture Show*.

The Schmidt and Parker Players as a troupe did not know what to do, so throughout the first act, we went on like nothing was amiss, like it was just another night of *Blood Song and Dance*, where fake blood spurted at odd times and Chloe occasionally performed a character from another play. Indeed, we plowed through the plot, such as it was, as if the Goth Girls Gang wasn't co-performing the play with us.

During intermission, backstage was abuzz with debate. Should we stop the show and ask the Goth girls to exit the theater? Summon the police? Challenge them to a catfight in the alley?

Go with the flow was the final verdict, so we settled in, and the second act was a blast and a half. It might even have been our best full-cast performance yet. The Goth Girls Gang gave us the gift of theatrical vitality, vigor, verve, and vim. Some of them had wonderful voices and sang the songs in fine harmony. One of them knew every single line of my dialogue. I found myself playing off her performance, and I think she found herself playing off mine.

The audience had the sense they were in the middle of an off-off-off-off-Broadway magic moment and gave us two curtain calls—one for us, one for the Goth Girls Gang.

After the play, we all agreed it was a once-in-a-theatrical-lifetime experience, seeing as how there were only three *Blood* performances remaining and the Goth Girls Gang did not have tickets for tomorrow night's sold-out show or either sold-out show next weekend—our great, grand, Friday-and-Saturday-night, Halloween finales.

I thought about the Goth Girls Gang while I was hitting the heavy bag at Raul's early the next morning and then again on my way to Blue Bar around eleven. I'd been struggling with how to move forward with Blue and the missing money since Wednesday, when I'd caught Eric with what had to be half of the most recently stolen cash, had a rollicking wrestling match in front of a full dining room, and confronted Blue in his office afterward. Blue had not fired me. He'd simply said I didn't have to ask him the hard questions—he hadn't denied raiding his own register; he'd only said *I* didn't have to be the one to call him on the carpet for doing so. Was that an admittance of guilt? I thought so. And, oh yeah, by the way, he hadn't "broken up" with me either.

I had mixed emotions about the whole thing, to say the least. I imagined Blue was implying he liked me enough that he didn't want me to get hurt if he was embezzling his own money, and since he *was* embezzling his own money, then I should disentangle myself from the case so I wouldn't get hurt.

And that's where the Goth Girls Gang came into the picture. Not so much them, as weird and wonderful as they were, more the Schmidt and Parker Players' reaction to them, the go-with-the-flow approach that got us through the second act with flying colors.

I had the sense that go-with-the-flow was how I had to handle my Blue Bar case from this point forward. My guts were twisted like a Fifth Avenue pretzel. There was no way to solve the case and keep my relationship with Blue. If I forced things one way or the other, I might lose them both. I knew, of course, that losing them both was a distinct possibility no matter which way I forced what, but if I could go with the go-with-the-flow approach, I figured, an answer would appear.

And as I climbed the Blue Bar steps, that's what happened. *No matter how this ends*, I thought, *I have to face my son, my father, and myself.* If I let Blue off the hook because I liked him, because I'd slept with him once, because he could kiss like thunder, then I wouldn't be able to face Matthew, who was as straight a straight shooter as anyone, or Jimmy, who'd held himself (and me) to a higher standard—despite bending rules when rules needed bending, which was more or less every day. In the end, Jimmy always, every time, did the right thing, even when it wasn't to his benefit. I think that might be the definition of *higher standard*, come to think of it.

"*I don't want to nail him, Jimmy,*" I said to my father in my head. "*I like him.*"

"*There may be times your cases don't come first,*" he said. "*But I can't think of any.*"

"*So I have to nail him?*" I said.

"*He wants you to,*" he said. "*He's always wanted you to. He can't get out from under on his own. It's a call for help.*"

"I hate being a PI," I said.

"Give it time, Katie," he said.

"Because I'll get used to it?" I said.

"Because if you give it enough time," he said, *"you'll forget the ones that hurt."*

I introduced myself as a private investigator working for Blue to the trio of hostesses by the front door. I didn't bother wearing a wig or colored contacts. My cover at Blue Bar was blown during my midweek WrestleMania match with Eric. The hostesses looked at each other with faces that said, *Holy shit, she's the one who used to be Danielle who duked it out with Eric and lost her red wig and turned out to be a private investigator, which is what everybody thought she was anyway.* They told me Blue was out of town until Tuesday. They didn't know if Mary was in her office, which made sense because sometimes Mary used the street-level door so no one would know she was there because people were always bothering her about the books and the money, and sometimes she just needed to get her work done, she'd once told me. I let the hostesses know I was going downstairs to check for myself. None of them tried to stop me. I guess they'd heard I'd held my own with Eric.

Blue's office door was shut and locked, and the lights were off inside. Adjacent to his office, at the end of the hall, Mary's door was shut and locked and dark inside as well. But the first office—Griff's office, then Adam's office, then Eric's office—had lights on, and the door was ajar. I took a breath, knocked on the door, and stuck my head into the office. "Knock, knock," I said. "Are you Justine?"

She was seated behind the desk, reading register printouts. Unpacked boxes of papers and personal possessions were stacked around the office. One framed, grainy, black-and-white photograph blown up to poster size was already hanging on the wall behind her. In the photo, she was younger than she was now, and she was a bartender. Someone had stood on a chair and was shooting down at the bar. Customers at the bar were leaning in, looking up, and showing off fistfuls of cash. They were celebrating and drunk. Blue was in the photo. If the unpacked boxes were a sign she wasn't settled in, the photo was a sign she was definitely here. Did I mention Blue was in the picture?

"I am," she said, smiling without meaning it. "Who are you?"

"Kate McCall. I'm a friend of Blue's," I said. "New friend."

"Me too," she said. "Old friend."

I gestured at the photo on the wall behind her. "I see that."

"You're the private investigator," she said, coming around the desk as I stepped into the office.

"You're the new general manager," I said as we shook hands.

We were about the same age. Maybe she was a few years younger than me. And we were about the same size. Maybe she was a half-inch taller than me. She had shoulder-length blonde hair and gorgeous green eyes. She was curvy like me and in good shape too—athlete shape, same as me. She had a firm handshake and pretty smile. She was cool and confident. She wore blue jeans and cowboy boots and a black sweater. She could have walked off the set of *Coyote Ugly*. I had the sense she was a party girl and had lots of friends. I wasn't going to be one of them.

I congratulated her on the new job, and she talked about how sometimes the planets align and the lights turn green and the cards come up aces. It was the perfect time for her and Blue to hook up again, she told me, just like the old days.

She asked me about the embezzlement case, wondering if I was getting any closer to the heart of the matter. That's how she said it: *the heart of the matter*.

So Blue had not only told her that he and I were professionally involved, he'd also told her we were personally involved. Or maybe he hadn't said we were sort of seeing each other. The truth was it didn't matter if he'd told her or not. Women know these things. We have romantic receptors that pick up the subtlest signals. Stanley had said she was Blue's old flame? Guess what? I would have known it with or without the bookie's insider info. Did I mention Blue was in the photo?

I opened my mouth to deliver some kind of bullshit answer about the case and her cell phone rang. She moved to her desk, answered it, and then looked at me. "I have to take this, Kate. Can you excuse me, please? I'll see you around the bar."

I said I understood and that I would see her around the bar too. Then I stepped out of her office, back into the hallway, and closed her door...though not quite all the way. I stood to the side of the door, so she couldn't see me, and listened to her conversation. It's called eavesdropping in polite society. It's called *let's find out what the hell Justine is up to* if you're a private investigator.

"Hi there," she said. She was excited to hear from whoever it was. I had the horrible feeling it was Blue. "How's your trip? We still on for Tuesday? Great. What time do you get back?"

Definitely Blue, I thought.

"If you come straight from the airport, we'll just make it. Yes, Stanley will be here. Because I saw him at Manny's for AL game seven, and he said so."

World Series starts Tuesday night, I thought.

"How much do you want to put in play? Six grand sounds good. Well, the drawer's out of bounds thanks to Eric and the PI, who I just met, by the way. Relax, she has no idea. How about give me a stack of folders with the envelope in the middle. It'll look like work. Exactly. I'll be at the bar, third floor. Yes, seven forty-five. See you Tuesday."

I'll see you both Tuesday, I said to myself.

60

THERE'S A REASON THEY SAY IT IN EVERY COP MOVIE

WE SAT IN THE WHITE WHALE, FU IN THE MIDDLE OF THE backseat, earbuds blasting Italian opera. He had to sit in the middle to keep the Toyota from tilting too far to one side or the other. He wore his old-school Oakland Raiders sweatshirt with the sleeves cut off. Though he knew nothing about football, didn't watch or follow it in any football fan sort of way, the Raiders were his favorite team. This morning, before we'd left the House of Emotional Tics, I asked him why the Raiders. His answer was *"Just win, baby."* Anyway, he was in the backseat, and his opera was thumping, and his eyes were closed, and I had no idea what was in his head.

On the other hand, I knew just what was in LaTanya's head. She was behind the wheel, rewriting rewrites of rewrites of *Kung Fu Fu*, imagining anew the storyline, incorporating our surveillance and rescue of the last late Lowry Lowe lawyer into the movie's already convoluted plot points. I told her surveillance was generally death-by-boredom from beginning to end at which point nothing ever happens, and she said she would fix it in post and disappeared into her script. She was packing her pro-quality Nikon DSLR, what she called her "lean, mean, silver-screen machine." It was small and light and easy to use—perfect, she said, for chase scenes and fistfights.

"How does it do with three people sitting in a car all day?" I said.

She didn't think it was funny. "This ain't no comedy, McCall," she said.

Prior to the opera and the rewrites, we'd arrived on East 48th Street and Lexington Avenue at ten a.m., in case the Lowry Lowe romantic weekend getaway to the Pennsylvania Poconos ended early—a distinct possibility, I thought, what with one of the partners planning the murder of the other. There weren't any parking spots across from the sidewalk café, so I jumped out of the White Whale, and LaTanya circled the block for forty-five minutes. When a minivan finally pulled out into traffic, I stood in the middle of the empty parking space, protected it like a mama bear, flagged LaTanya down on her next pass, and waved her in like a ground controller at LaGuardia Airport.

Then I crossed the street, told the blue-suit/red-tie doorman (not Kyle) that my name was Rebecca Harrelson, that I was the sister of Bethany, who was engaged to Carter Ringwald, and that I wanted a word with Michelle Lowry, who was fucking my sister's fiancé. He told me Mrs. Lowry was out of town for the weekend. The doorman's nameplate read *Owen*. "Duh, Owen," I said. "She's with Carter." Owen said that he felt Bethany's pain and my pain too, and that as far as Mrs. Lowry was concerned there was plenty of pain to go around, but that he'd been on duty since six this morning, and they hadn't returned from wherever they'd gone. I asked Owen if my husband had stopped by to offer Mrs. Lowry a piece of *his* mind, and Owen said no. He also added that no one had been in or out of the building besides the usual suspects, meaning regular dog walkers, early-bird joggers, a marine who'd returned home from Afghanistan to visit his parents, and several tenants who'd gone to church or brunch. Other than that, Owen told me, it had been a slow and unremarkable Sunday morning. I thanked him, walked across 48th Street to the White Whale, and sat shotgun.

I looked at Fu and LaTanya, and they looked at me. It was ten past ten. We argued for the next five hours.

We argued about the smartest animal on Earth. LaTanya said it was a dolphin. Fu said it was a parrot. I took LaTanya's side, so then we argued about who was smarter, Jerusalem Joe or me. This led to an argument about who was the better PI, me or Fu. Which grew into an argument about who was a better actor, Fu or me. LaTanya came to my defense, pointing to my lifetime of musical theater experience, so that led to an argument about who was the better director, Fu or LaTanya. That argument lasted until we were hungry, so then we argued about what to eat for lunch and who should leave the car to get it. No one wanted to lose that one, so we settled on Jimmy John's and had them deliver to the Corolla.

It went like that all afternoon. We argued about music and movies and cars and clothes and pets and people and food and flowers—especially flowers. When he was first exiled by the Chinese mob to America, Fu had worked for a Chinatown florist before his relocation to the House of Emotional Tics, so he was a flower expert. LaTanya's grandmother was a florist, so she was an expert too. And my mother, Christine, worked at a flower shop in Queens before she got sick, so I wasn't taking a backseat to anyone in a flower fight. We were perhaps the three most hardheaded hardheads in the city of New York, and we were trapped in the prison-cell-sized confines of the White Whale.

And then we were bored of arguing, bored of one another, and bored of being bored, so Fu put in his earbuds and pumped up his Italian opera, LaTanya took out her script and rewrote the rewrites of her rewrites, and I reflected on Blue and Justine.

After not-so-accidentally overhearing Justine's phone conversation with Blue about betting six grand on Game One of the World Series with Stanley Stein at Blue Bar on Tuesday night, I'd called Dennis and Posey and put a plan in motion. It would be my biggest plan yet, a major production that would require calling in favors from a dozen way-off-Broadway theater companies, a "Cecil B. DeMille," Posey had called it at Saturday night's *Blood* performance. And now it was Sunday afternoon. The clock was ticking. Soon enough it would be Tuesday night, and I would nail Blue, and my heart would be broken.

As I put the period on that thought, a Town Car pulled in front of the apartment building, and Michelle Lowry, the Swedish Queen, exited the Lincoln, and went inside. I pointed her out to Fu and LaTanya and told them now we would see what we would see. As the doorman closed the door behind her, Detective Lew Logan called.

Logan was in the Minneapolis-Saint Paul International Airport, waiting for his flight back to New York. I asked him how the funeral went. "It's the land of ten thousand frozen fucking lakes, McCall. How in the fuck do you think it went?"

The conversation crashed downhill from there. He had just now received my voicemail—something to do with "the North Star State's frozen fucking phone lines," he told me—and wanted to make sure I kept my nose out of his business.

"Repeat after me, McCall. I am nowhere near this case," he said.

"I am nowhere near this case," I said, watching Michelle Lowry's apartment building door.

"Good," he said. "Now tell me how the hell you know Mrs. Lowry is the next name on the list."

I opened my mouth to explain it, and the marine who'd returned from Afghanistan to visit his parents exited the apartment building carrying an extra-large duffel bag slung over his shoulder. He was dressed in camo from head to toe. The duffel was camo as well. His camo hat was pulled down low. He wore dark sunglasses. A half-chewed cigar sat in the corner of his mouth. He was right out of central casting.

The second I saw him, I had an overwhelming sensation of awareness. *It's him*, I said to myself. *He put her in the bag*.

The marine waved down a cab, the cabbie popped the trunk, and the marine slid the duffel off his shoulder and laid it in there like there was a body inside.

I clicked off the call with Logan. I was distracted and didn't say good-bye. Maybe he'd think it was a frozen fucking phone line that disconnected us.

"Follow that cab," I said to LaTanya with heartfelt urgency while pointing at the marine as he shut the trunk.

"I like your spirit, McCall," LaTanya said without looking up from her script. "But *follow that cab*? That the best you got, girl? *Follow that cab*? What po-lice movie you ever see where someone don't say *follow that cab*? We trying to improvise, not plagiarize. You got to dig deeper in your ad-lib locker than *follow that—*"

"It's *him*, LaTanya," I said, grabbing her script and making her look at the cab as the marine climbed in. "He put her in the trunk. There's a reason they say it in every cop movie. Now, follow that fucking cab. Go, go, go."

Fu took out his earbuds. "Dead or alive in trunk?"

"She's in his duffel bag. I don't know," I said as the cab rolled past us, headed east toward Third Avenue.

"You for real with this shit?" LaTanya said. "This ain't my movie?"

"Yes, there he goes," I said. I think I was shouting by then. I'm sure I was.

LaTanya put the White Whale in gear, pulled out of the parking spot, nearly caused a three-car crack-up, and took off after the marine.

The cab caught the light at Third Avenue and turned left. We missed the light.

"Go through it, LaTanya. Go through it," I said.

"Tell me something I don't know," LaTanya said, already running the light.

"Don't lose him," I said. "There, there, he's making a left. Stay with him."

The cab turned left onto 49th Street. We were a few cars behind, but we made the turn too.

"Did you look at this antique piece of shit we in?" LaTanya said. "It's a damn lawnmower. Got no motherfucking horse-power at all. Got two goddamn hamsters on a wheel."

"Fu go faster than you," Fu said, smirking like the worst-ever backseat driver.

The cab went straight through the light at 49th and Lexington.

"Fu you, Fu," LaTanya said, finding Fu's eyes in the rearview mirror, pushing the gas pedal to the floor, and flying across Lex as the light flipped red.

"Fu you too," Fu said.

We cruised down 49th Street, heading west, two cars behind the cab, which turned right onto Park Avenue.

"Right on Park. Right on Park," I said, pointing at the killer's cab.

We caught the lights on Park and cruised uptown, Fu leaning forward, telling LaTanya how to drive, LaTanya telling him to zip it in language I can't repeat in public.

It's the perfect disguise, I thought. Who would stop and question a career marine? Excuse me, Sergeant Major, by any chance do you have an unconscious woman in that duffel bag by the name of Michelle Lowry? No one, that's who.

Yet the truth was I had no idea if she *was* unconscious. She could easily have been dead. Though my gut told me he hadn't had time to kill her. She'd only been inside for three minutes. He'd knocked her out, stuffed her in the bag, and carried her to the cab. Or he'd killed her quick. There was only one way to find out.

"He's turning onto 59th," I said. "Right, right."

"Got him," LaTanya said.

At Lexington, the cab went through the light and pulled to the curb in front of the entrance to the 59th Street subway station, under the big red H&M sign. We missed the light and were stuck on the other side of Lexington.

"Shit," I said as the marine got out of the cab, went around to the trunk, and lifted the duffel onto his shoulder. "We're going to lose him."

"Fu go now," Fu said, and he opened the back door, jumped out of the Toyota, and weaved his way through heavy traffic, horns honking, tires screeching, across Lex toward the subway entrance.

I jumped out of the car too and leaned back in the open door. "Double-park in front of the subway," I said to LaTanya. "Put your flashers on. Fuck it if we get towed."

"Don't beat his ass until I get there," she said as I shut the door.

61

HARD TO COMPREHEND IT
ACTUALLY HAPPENING AT ALL

Fu and I took the stairs two at a time, crashing into the 59th Street and Lexington Avenue subway station like an episode of *Law & Order*. We used our MetroCards (yes, Fu had a MetroCard) to blow through the gates, stopped dead center in the landing area, and did a three sixty. The marine was a minute or so ahead of us and nowhere to be seen, but he was definitely down here somewhere.

The 59th Street station is a major hub for the Lexington Line and the BMT Broadway Line, home to the 4, 5, 6 trains and the N, R, W trains. There are local and express lines extending four levels underground with long stairways and escalators connecting even longer platforms decorated with fifty-year-old, museum-quality mosaics and state-of-the-art digital signage (a four-story train station stacked straight underground, one of dozens beneath Manhattan!). There are crossunders and mezzanines linking the platforms, which are used daily by thousands of people—from grizzled New Yorkers to first-time tourists—going uptown, downtown, crosstown, and out to Queens.

On the platforms, competing street musicians play jazz,

rock, blues, hip-hop, rap, country, and classical for tips; artists sell originals and rip-offs; poets present the spoken word; crazed preachers bring down the wrath of God; homeless New Yorkers lurk in the shadows; vendors of all nationalities hawk genuine-imitation Indian rugs, faux Swiss watches, knockoff Italian jewelry, and not-the-real-thing designer clothing while trains roll in and out on every level seven days a week, twenty-four hours a day. This all happens with eye-popping intensity to an ear-shattering soundtrack. It is nonstop stimuli on steroids. Or, as New Yorkers like to say, just another day waiting for the 6.

We'd been on the main entrance/MetroCard level for maybe ten seconds. I had no idea what platform the killer was headed for, and there wasn't time to get in his head and figure it out. But I knew local trains ran more often, meaning more frequently, than express trains—or at least that's how it had always seemed to me—so I looked at Fu, said, "Locals first, follow me," and we took off down the stairs to the local Lexington line, the 6—Fu to the northbound side (Parkchester and Pelham Bay Park), me to the southbound side (Brooklyn Bridge-City Hall).

We flew past the first mezzanine and landed on what's called a *side platform*—two tracks in the middle, northbound and southbound platforms on either side of the tracks. There were a few hundred people on each side. Fu and I each sprinted the length of our platform, weaving in and out of the crowd, looking for the marine, for the duffel, for camo. I kept one eye on Fu, and he kept one eye on me. We arrived at the end of our platforms at the same time, looked at each other across the tracks, and signaled we'd found nothing. Then we dashed to the exits and hurdled down the stairs, deeper into the station.

We blasted through the crossunder and went down again to an *island platform*—two tracks on either side of a center platform for the N, R, W trains. The southbound trains head toward Coney Island-Stillwell Avenue, Whitehall Street-South Ferry, and Bay Ridge-95ᵗʰ Street. The northbound trains head toward Astoria-Ditmars Boulevard and Forest Hills-71ˢᵗ Avenue. There were at least a few hundred folks on the platform, maybe more, maybe three hundred. I had the same thought all New Yorkers have when they arrive on a particularly packed platform on the flipside of the weekend: *Where the hell are all you people going on a Sunday afternoon? Get a goddamn life already!*

We went as fast as we could through the crowd, weaving back and forth, from the north side to the south side and back again, tacking like racing sailboats until we reached the far side of the platform. No marine. No camo anywhere.

What the heck? It was possible the killer had arrived on his platform at the exact moment his train pulled into the station and was gone as we got there. But the platforms would have been empty when we'd arrived a minute later. And both platforms had been full of folks waiting for trains. *He's still here*, I thought, *on the last platform.*

Fu and I dropped down to the next level and across the mezzanine saw LaTanya, carrying her camera and running down the stairs from the other side of the N, R, W platform, the side where Fu and I had started. She'd been two minutes behind us. We met in the middle of the mezzanine.

"What the fuck with all these people?" LaTanya said. "Nobody in the city has a goddamn life?"

"Exactly," I said. "He's on the express. I take the north side. Fu takes the south side."

"I'm with Fu," LaTanya said.

"Why are you with Fu?" I said.

"Fu movie star," Fu said. "You co-star."

"He's got a point," LaTanya said.

"No, he doesn't. There's no point there," I said. "He has no point at all."

"Fu have movie star point," Fu said. "You have co-star point."

"Fu you, Fu," I said.

"Fu you too," Fu said.

We took off across the mezzanine—me headed for the north stairs, Fu and LaTanya (and her camera) headed for the south stairs. On my side, the Lexington express trains (the 4 and 5) went north to Woodlawn-86th Street and to Nereid Avenue and Eastchester-Dyre Avenue. On Fu and LaTanya's side, they went south to Crown Heights-Utica Avenue and to Flatbush Avenue and Bowling Green. The tracks were in the middle, between the north and south platforms.

I burst onto the northbound side, looked across the tracks, and saw Fu and LaTanya explode onto the southbound side. Then I looked out at the long platforms, north and south. There was a smaller crowd waiting for the southbound express train, maybe fifty or sixty people. There were about that many, maybe a few more than that, on the northbound side. And halfway down the northbound platform, *I saw the marine.*

He was standing ten feet from the edge of the platform. The duffel was over his shoulder. His dark sunglasses were still in place. His hat was pulled down low. The cigar was in his mouth. Just a career soldier home on leave. I looked across the tracks at Fu and pointed at the marine. Fu had seen the camo and was running to the other end of the southbound side so he could hit the exit, run up to the mezzanine, and then fly back down the stairs onto the far end of the northbound platform. All I had to do was push the Marine into Fu, and we would have him. Once and for all, we would have him.

I started down the platform toward the killer like I meant business. Maybe a little too much business because people sensed how serious I was and cleared a path to get the hell out of my way. But the hustle and bustle of people moving aside as I marched toward the marine caught his attention, and he saw me, and I saw him, and he knew who I was. He spit out his cigar and started to run the other way, toward the exit where Fu would soon appear and beat the killer into unconsciousness.

In the distance, I saw the lights of an express train rolling down the track, deep in the tunnel, on the northbound side, the track closest to my platform. And though I heard it before I saw it, I turned and spotted the headlights of the southbound train heading into the station too. The marine saw the trains as well, and then everything happened so fast it was hard to comprehend it actually happening at all.

Fu raced down the stairs from the mezzanine onto the northbound platform and sprinted toward the marine, who saw Fu coming, knew I was behind him, and realized he was trapped. The killer ran closer to the edge of the platform and, without breaking stride, *tossed the duffel out onto the track...with the train screaming into the station.*

The marine was just ahead of me, sprinting toward the exit at the end of the platform. We were all running hard. I was fifteen feet behind the killer, and Fu was fifteen feet ahead of him. We were like three speeding cars seconds from a head-on collision. I yelled at Fu at the top of my lungs and pointed at the duffel on the tracks.

Fu took a swing at the marine as they sprinted past each other, and though the punch didn't land, it threw the killer off balance enough for me to gain ground.

Without breaking stride, Fu raced past the marine and then past me to the edge of the platform, both trains pulling into the station on both tracks, and he leaped into space and onto the northbound track near the duffel. People were screaming like mad. I saw LaTanya across the tracks, still on the southbound platform, filming the whole thing.

As we reached the exit that led up to the mezzanine, I dove through the air and landed on the marine's back, and we crashed to the ground and rolled and wrestled like our lives depended on it. We rolled so that I was facing the tracks, me on top of the marine, and I saw Fu on the run grab the camo duffel with one arm and jump the third rail (660 volts!) as the north-bound train missed him by inches. The southbound train was bounding into the station at almost exactly the same second, and the trains passed each other like hyper-fast ships in the night. I had no idea if Fu made it out alive from between them because the trains were so loud I couldn't hear the screaming. Or maybe the screaming was so loud I couldn't hear the trains. Was everyone screaming in horror that Fu had been crushed with the duffel? Jesus Christ, was this really happening?

We rolled again, and I swung up at the marine and hit him square in the jaw, which knocked him back but didn't get him off me. I tried to punch up at him again or at least grab his glasses so I could see his freaking face, but he hit me hard in the solar plexus, an intentional shot that knocked the wind out of me big-time. As I gasped for breath, he jumped off me and was gone up the stairs to the mezzanine.

While I sucked wind on the platform near the stairs, people circled around to see if I was dead. Somebody told somebody to get a cop, and I wanted to tell them *no cops*, but I couldn't breathe, so I couldn't talk. Instead, I stared up at the crowd looking down at me and wondered if they were thinking New York was the craziest goddamn city on the planet because in the middle of some random Sunday afternoon they just saw some random woman fist-fight some random marine in some random subway station while some random Chinese man jumped in front of a train to grab some random duffel bag.

Anyway, that's what *I* was thinking. I finally caught my breath, got to my feet, and ran through the circle of gawkers and up the stairs to the mezzanine. I wasn't running after the killer. I knew he was gone. I wouldn't catch him now even if I kept running up the stairs and down the platforms and through the crossunders and across the mezzanines. I'd had him, and I'd lost him.

No, I was running up the stairs to the mezzanine because I had to hurry down the opposite stairs to the southbound platform, where I had no idea what the hell I was going to find.

Except both trains were still in the station. *Can't be good*, I said to myself. *They stayed in the station and busted their schedules to deal with whatever it is. And whatever it is, it can't be good.*

62

MAYBE SHE'S AN OPTOMETRIST

A CROWD OF SIXTY OR SO HAD FORMED A LAYERED CIRCLE NEAR the edge of the platform about thirty feet from the mezzanine stairway. The southbound express stood still with its doors open. Most passengers stayed on the train, jaded New Yorkers not giving two shits about the reason they'd stopped, and instead most likely wondering why they'd taken the express in the freaking first place. *Should have grabbed the goddamn local* is what they were probably thinking. I'd thought that thought a thousand times.

I approached the three-deep, shoulder-to-shoulder crowd and said the magic words that always part the sea: "Excuse me, I'm a doctor."

People moved aside, and I held my breath, thinking I'd find Fu in pieces: an arm here, a leg there, blood everywhere. But instead I found Fu on his knees beside the duffel, fiddling with the lock that kept the zipper zipped. LaTanya was nearby, filming him, filming the crowd, filming the trains.

Fu glanced up at me. "No get marine?"

"No get marine," I said.

"Fu get bag," Fu said.

"Yes," I said, kneeling beside him and putting my hand gently on his shoulder. "Fu get bag." I think there were tears in my eyes—of relief, of joy, of affection. He was the twin brother I never had—my Chinese mob assassin, smug, smirking, annoying-as-hell twin brother—and he was alive. Anyway, if there were tears, I wiped them fast.

"You going to show us what's in the bag, or are we going to stand here all day for no reason," said a heckler in the front row of the crowd. He was a thirtysomething, snot-rag, Wall Street asshole. Maybe a bond trader. Possibly a commodities broker. Definitely a douchebag. There's always one guy in the front row. The heckler.

Just then Fu jimmied the lock, ripped it off the duffel, and unzipped the zipper. The crowd gasped as first the face and then the body appeared: Michelle Lowry.

"Oh my God. Is she dead?" I said to Fu.

"You said you were a doctor," the heckler said to me and the crowd.

Fu put his face close to her face. "Not dead."

"If you're a doctor," the heckler said, "how can you not know if she's dead or alive?"

As with all snot-rag asshole hecklers, I did my level best to ignore him.

"She's been out a long time," I said to Fu. "She was in the cab, in the trunk. He carried her over his shoulder. He threw her onto the tracks. Is she drugged?"

"You don't know if she's drugged?" the heckler said. "You're the worst doctor I've ever seen."

LaTanya turned her camera toward the heckler.

"Don't film him," I said.

"Local color," LaTanya said. "An authentic New York loudmouth."

During that exchange, Fu took a closer look at Michelle Lowry. "Fu say drugged."

"What the hell drug knocks someone out like this?" I said.

"Oh, come on. She's not a doctor," the heckler said to the crowd. Some of them agreed with him, some were willing to give me more of a chance, and some were still stunned at the turn of events they'd witnessed on the Lexington express platform and didn't care if I was a doctor or not. They were absorbed by the body in the bag.

"Fu not doctor," Fu said.

"And you only play one on TV," the heckler said to me.

"At least she's alive," I said to Fu. "And she still has her eyes."

"Maybe she is a doctor after all," the heckler said to the crowd, mocking me. "Maybe she's an optometrist."

"Po-lice going to be here any minute," LaTanya said, still filming.

"What's the penalty for impersonating a doctor?" the heckler said.

LaTanya was right. The police were on their way, probably bounding down the stairs this very moment. All of this—an unconscious Michelle Lowry in a duffel bag in the middle of a subway brouhaha—would get back to Logan, and while the detective had heard past whispers about a large Chinese man helping me out of tight spots, he didn't know it was specifically Fu from the House of Emotional Tics. And I wanted to keep it that way. Same with LaTanya. The last thing either one of them needed was to be on Logan's shit list.

"Go now," I said to them both, "before they get here. Go, go..."

We looked at each other for moment, and then they took off down the platform.

Four police officers arrived thirty seconds later from the other direction. They were young and old, short and tall, fat and thin, black and white. And they were annoyed they'd had to run down the stairs all the way to the express platform. What the hell had been such a big damn deal that they'd had to *run*, for chrissakes?

As the cops got their bearings—the crowd, the stopped trains, the Swedish Queen in the duffel bag, the helter-skelter vibe on the platform—I subtly stepped away from Michelle Lowry, still drugged into oblivion, and stood in the front row of gawkers, half hidden by someone's shoulder, opposite the heckler.

"Can anybody tell me what the hell happened here?" the first cop (old, tall, thin, black) said, gesturing at the body in the bag on the platform as the second cop (young, short, fat, white) checked to see if Michelle was alive.

"He can," I said, pointing at the heckler. "He saw the whole thing. Said he knew the guy who put her in the bag and dropped her on the tracks. Hinted at it, anyway. He might be in on it. Seems like it. Definitely your best witness."

The third cop (young, tall, fat, black) moved beside the heckler. The fourth cop (old, short, thin, white) moved behind him so the heckler was boxed in.

"What? Wait. No. Wait. I didn't...I don't..." the heckler said, a whole lot less tough than he'd sounded just two minutes ago when he was riding my ass.

"I think he knows who this is too," I said, pointing down at Michelle Lowry. "He's got a Wall Street motormouth. Said no way the cops could solve this one. Big talker. Got a lot to say to everyone."

The first cop moved in front of the heckler. "You got something to say to me?"

"No, I mean...I have a meeting. I have to go," the heckler said.

"Yeah, you got to go. You got to go with us," the second cop said as I slid back through the crowd, out of the circle, and up the stairs to the mezzanine.

The rest of the Wall Street asshole's afternoon, I felt sure, would now be ruined: missed meetings, angry clients, multiple interrogations, detectives, police artists, and lawyers galore. I wasn't proud of wrecking his day, but what goes around comes around, especially on Wall Street. And anyway, it didn't bother me as much as having my father's murderer slip through my hands. That was killing me.

When I got to the street, two cop cars were parked where the White Whale had been, which meant either the city had towed it or LaTanya and Fu had gotten away clean. I would find out which was which soon enough. I wasn't in the mood to walk twenty-five blocks uptown—I wasn't in the mood to do anything but crawl into a hole—so I waved down a cab and took the easy way back to the House of Emotional Tics, where Fu was sitting on the front steps, Jerusalem Joe perched on his left shoulder.

He was reading the *World Journal* (Fu, not Joe), the leading Chinese newspaper in New York, while feeding the parrot seeds and nuts from a bowl on the step beside him. He was in the middle of the steps, though more to the left, so the only way up was to pass by Joe on the right, which meant there was no way up at all because without a baseball bat or a steel pipe in hand, it was unwise for anyone to get too close to the bird. But since Joe and I had undeniable mutual animosity, for me it was a suicide mission. So I stopped in front of Fu, which was what he'd wanted in the first place.

"Open Sesame, Fu," I said.

He didn't look up from the paper, didn't acknowledge me at all, just fed the parrot a cashew and kept reading. "Fu say sit."

"It's been a bad day. Slide over, and let me go home."

"Bad day you. Worse day killer."

"Worse day killer? Are you kidding? How do you figure that?"

"Lowry alive. Killer no get paid."

I opened my mouth to say *No fucking way* or *I let him get away* or *Get the hell out of my way*, but instead I said, "He won't like that."

It was true. Lisa Lowe wouldn't pay one dime for murdering Michelle if Michelle wasn't murdered. Meaning as far as collecting his big fat corporate assassin payday was concerned, the killer was shit out of luck. I'd denied him a victim, which, in addition to denting his bank account, was going to be hell on his ego. Plus, I'd smacked him in the jaw with an uppercut he'd remember into next week. And every time he felt that pain, he'd think of me, and how I'd been a step ahead, instead of a step behind, and had crashed his party, blown his cover, busted his blueprint, and punched his face. Sure, I'd had him in my hands and lost him, and that sucked more than I could explain, but *I'd* won this round, not him. Me. The Little Engine. Fu was right. The killer's day was worse than mine.

And yet still I was down about the whole thing. I sat on the steps and said, "Big picture, I'll never see him again. He won't give me another shot. I feel like I failed my father. I'll never get this guy."

"Killer call," Fu said. "No like lose last."

I nodded, hoping he was right. After a while, Fu said, "How know Lowry in bag?"

"Because I knew Lisa Lowe hired the killer," I said.

"How know that?" Fu said.

"Logan's going to ask me the same question," I said.

63

PUT YOUR PRETTY PRADA ASS BACK ON THE CHAIR

Logan surprised me Monday morning with a squad car and two uniformed officers whose marching orders were to transport me to the Thirteenth Precinct for a chat. That's what the officers said. Logan wanted to chat. Now, to me, a chat meant you chat, I chat, you chat, I chat until we're done chatting. But to Logan it meant chewing my ass out for forty-five straight minutes. He was pissed about me sticking my nose in his business, about me endangering the lives of innocent New Yorkers, about me wasting NYPD time on a know-nothing Wall Street asshole, and about Lisa Lowe not giving him one actionable answer since he'd brought her in an hour ago.

We were in the adjacent observation room, watching Jesse question the Italian Bombshell through the one-way glass. Jesse and Lisa were in the same interrogation room where Logan and Harriman had questioned me right after my father was found murdered in an insurance company elevator, eyes blown out the back of his head.

When Logan finally took a breath, I told him that it was *my* father who'd been murdered, so it was kind of my business too; that I hadn't endangered anyone and, in fact, I had *saved* the life of one New Yorker, Michelle Lowry; and that any time spent ruining *that* Wall Street asshole's day was time well spent, which Logan couldn't argue. Then I said I would nail Lisa Lowe for him if he gave me five minutes alone with her.

That led to a profanity-laced soliloquy that was stunning even for Logan. I had no idea there were so many colorful ways to describe me, and I was Jimmy McCall's daughter, so I knew bad words in lost languages. But Logan set the curse word bar at a new height. I couldn't see the bar it was set so high.

Then Jesse opened the interrogation room door and stepped into the observation room, shutting the door behind him. "I've got no chance with her," he said to Logan. "She's too fucking smart. If she doesn't want you to know, you're never going to know."

Logan nodded with frustration. He'd discovered the same thing after playing an hour of Twenty Questions with the Italian Bombshell.

"Give me five minutes, Logan," I said.

"When pigs fly on a cold day in hell while the pope shits in the woods and Macy's tells Gimbels all the fuck about it," Logan said.

"You're going to give me a gold star and take me off your shit list, that's how sweet it's going to be when I tie her up in a bow and hand her to you," I said.

Logan looked at Jesse, and they both looked at me. "I assume I'll learn how you knew it was her," Logan said, gesturing through the one-way at Lisa Lowe.

"Must-see TV," I said.

Logan shook his head and said with incredulity, "You are my biggest mistake of the year, McCall." Then he nodded at Jesse, who opened the door, and I stepped into the interrogation room with Lisa Lowe.

I had never seen her look more beautiful. She wore a dark-chocolate Prada pinstripe business suit and had matched it with an equally extravagant Prada bag. A Movado Sapphire bracelet watch, feminine and magnificent, adorned her right wrist. Three, delicate David Yurman gold bracelets bangled her left wrist. She still had on her wedding ring. The size of the diamond was only outdone by the splendor of the setting. Jack Lowe had done her a solid there, not that it mattered. She'd murdered him anyway.

My point is it wasn't shabby for a Monday morning interrogation ensemble. Indeed, it was hard to imagine anyone with this combination of sophistication, brilliance, power, wealth, prestige, and beauty ever sitting in this room before.

"I haven't spoken to enough detectives," Lisa said, turning to the one-way and talking through it to Logan, "so you send in the token female?" Then she turned to me. "I said I would cooperate, and I have. I rearranged my schedule to accommodate a few questions, and instead it's turned into a parade of police." Then she turned back to the one-way and stood up. "You're not going to charge me because you have nothing because I've done nothing, so let's agree we're finished here and get on with our lives."

"I'm not a detective," I said. "I'm a private investigator, and I have news you need, so put your pretty Prada ass back on the chair, and I'll tell you what it is."

She looked at me and narrowed her eyes. "I know you from somewhere."

"Yes, you do," I said in my best Texas twang. "Sit down, Lisa."

She sat. I sat across the table from her.

"Emily Baynes," she said. "Minus the red hair and green eyes."

"Austin-by-way-of-Abilene," I said.

"You broke Christopher's nose," she said.

"You had him murdered," I said.

She smiled, and I sensed pity, as if she were letting me know

I wasn't smart enough to play the game with her, that this was going to get ugly fast.

"Tell me that's your news," she said. "I would so enjoy suing you for slander. As I've repeated ad nauseam since arriving in this hellhole, I have no idea what you're talking about. Though I am curious why you're involved in this tragic narrative."

"I'm involved because the man you hired to murder your partners is the man who killed my father," I said.

"I'm sorry for your loss," she said without a shred of sympathy.

"I'm sorry you're going to jail," I said. "But before I prove to the detectives you're guilty of conspiracy to commit murder, I'm just so curious why you would do it."

"I didn't do it," she said.

"Power?" I said. "You were already more powerful than an aircraft carrier. Money? You have more money than Mariah Carey. Prestige? You're like the most famous divorce lawyer in the kingdom. I just don't get why you would hire someone to murder your husband, murder your lover, and murder Michelle. I mean, come on, are you kidding me? You hired him to murder Michelle? You were fucking her, for chrissakes. Is nothing sacred?"

Her jaw dropped open but only for a moment. She stood, indignant, glared at me, and then glared at the one-way. "This is outrageous. She has no evidence whatsoever to support anything she's said. All of this would be thrown out as meaningless hearsay in any court. She's a pathetic, no-name PI trying to score points with the police for reasons I can't imagine. Open the door, and let me out now."

"Save it for someone who gives a shit, Lisa. I'm just getting to the good part. Now sit down before I break *your* nose." I stood and held up a fist.

She wasn't used to anyone threatening her physically, I

could tell. Then she blinked herself back into defiance mode and took her seat. "What's your name?"

"Kate McCall," I said, and I took my seat.

"When I'm done with you, Ms. McCall, you will have nothing."

"When you're done with me, you're going to need a lawyer," I said, and then I looked at the one-way. "It *is* outrageous. I agree. And it's true, I'm a pathetic, no-name PI trying to score points with the police." I smiled at Logan and then looked across the table at Lisa Lowe. "But it's also true I have evidence. I was in your office on Friday, maybe quarter past noon, something like that. You got back early from your mediation and surprised me. I hid in the closet while you and Michelle got hot and bothered. Someone texted me—well, not just someone. Anyway, I got a text while I was in your closet, and I got distracted, but then I had my phone out, so I took some quick pics of you two on the couch. They're high-quality soft porn, let me tell you. Want to see?"

"No," she said, as I took out my phone. "I certainly do not."

I was bluffing. I never took any pictures. I was too blown away by Lisa and Michelle getting it on and by the text from the killer. She could have had me right there in the room, Lisa Lowe. All she had to do was say, "None of that is true; let me see those pictures right now." But she didn't because my performance was pitch-perfect. I believed every word of what I'd said and every second of saying it, and she did too. It was more true than not true, and I knew she knew it. I'd played the true part as the whole truth. I was an actor. It was what I did.

"I don't blame you," I said.

"And you think your invasion-of-privacy pictures—inadmissible, I might add—prove I hired some fantasy hit man to murder Jack and Christopher and Michelle?" she said half to me and half to Logan. "All they prove is that I enjoy the company of men *and* women, not exactly news you can use."

"I think it proves smartphones are a PI's best friend," I said.

She turned to the one-way. "I'm going to crucify you with your superiors, Detective Logan. Your career, such as it was, is over. That said, are we finally done here?"

"No," I said to Logan on the other side of the glass. "We're just getting to the good part."

64

BIG MO IN THE HOUSE

I could picture Logan on the other side of the one-way, shaking his head with disbelief that he'd let me in the interrogation room with his suspect. He'd already decided, I imagined, to lock *me* up if I let Lisa Lowe slip away.

"I don't know if you'll remember this," I said to Lisa, "because we'd had a ton of sake, and I can't remember shit when I've had a ton of sake, and I didn't remember *this* because I'd had a ton of sake until Logan's game-day speech to his task force, which was in your conference room after Christopher was found dead in his chair without his eyes."

"She's lying, of course," Lisa said to the one-way. "I've never had so much as a fountain drink with Ms. McCall in my entire life. She's a con artist, like all private investigators. Surely even you can see that, Detective."

"That would be true," I said, raising the register of my voice and altering my cadence and accent so I sounded like a Fairfield County Keller Williams Realtor specializing in equestrian properties. "Except I was also Jessica Gibbs, and we had lunch at the 52nd Street Totto Ramen two weeks ago. You told me not everyone lives life full speed full time in the fast lane? Ring any bells?"

There is a moment in every game where the momentum shifts in such a way that the outcome of the game itself resets and becomes clear no matter how one-sided the score had been up to the moment the momentum shifted. This was that moment. *Big Mo in the house*, Jimmy would have said if he'd been in the room with Lisa and me.

"Anyway, Logan said something in that meeting that I didn't think of until Friday when I was in your closet. Would you like to know what he said?"

The confidence in her eyes was draining, but she was keeping up appearances for Logan. "Did he say, 'Keep this amateur half-wit away from me for the rest of my life'?"

"Not right then, though he's said that many times to my face since my father was murdered," I said. "No, right then what Logan said was that his task force was on absolute radio silence, those were his words, regarding the eyes, you know, that the killer shoots them out of his victim's head as a way of signing the murder. Friends, family, surviving spouse, complete work, media, legal, medical blackout. Nobody but a select group of cops—and me, actually—knew about the eyes before that meeting, which was exactly eleven days ago, the day Christopher was found murdered in his Lowry Lowe office. Nobody else except you."

There was just the slightest bit of perspiration on her upper lip. If I wasn't sitting right across the table from her and leaning in looking for signs that she was breaking, I might not have seen it. But I was and I did.

"You can't prove that," Lisa said, looking at me and then at the one-way. "She can't prove that I knew anything about any of this at any time."

"I had the feeling we'd be drinking sake, and I didn't trust myself to remember everything we talked about, so I recorded our lunch date," I said, putting my phone on the table in front of me.

"You're bluffing," she said.

Too little, too late, Mrs. Lowe, I said to myself. "We were both three sheets to the wind, and you leaned in across the table and told me Christopher and Jack started the firm together. That you and Michelle joined later. You told me about the formation documents, who inherited what and when if someone got murdered, say. And then, and this is the good part, and then you said, 'So who in the world would want to shoot Jack in the eyes?'"

"Complete fabrication," Lisa said. "How dare you accuse me of—"

I hit Play, and Lisa's recorded voice filled the interrogation room.

"Christopher and Jack started the firm together. Michelle and I joined later. In the formation documents, it says if any subsequent partners, meaning me and Michelle, should die, cause of death irrelevant, the founding partners, Jack and Christopher, inherit those shares of the firm. And if either of the founding partners should die, the surviving founding partner inherits all the shares, period. So who in the world would want to shoot Jack in the eyes? What's the saying? Follow the money? I suggest..."

I hit Stop, and though Lisa Lowe said nothing, her silence meant she knew she was screwed.

"That was two days after I found your husband murdered at Red Maple," I said. "Maybe you can explain to Detective Logan how you knew Jack's eyes were shot out when no one else in the world knew anything about it."

Lisa swallowed hard, blinking herself into oblivion as all the bad mojo in her future crash-landed in her brain.

"Or maybe I can do it for you," I said. "You knew your husband's eyes were gone because you hired the killer to murder him, and the killer had said you'd know it was him because Jack would be dead with holes in his head where his eyes used to be. Which brings me back to why the hell did you do it? You had everything."

It took a moment, but then her eyes found focus somewhere not here, and her voice returned, though it sounded far away. "It was never about having everything," she said, mostly to herself. "It was about what it's always about when powerful people fly too close to the sun: more. It's always about having more." And then she looked at me, remembering, it seemed, that I was the one who'd caught her. "Though I'm sure that's beyond your common capacity to comprehend."

"You got that right," I said as I nodded and stood. "But here's something I can comprehend. The next words you're going to hear are *Lisa Lowe, you're under arrest for conspiracy to commit the murders of Jack Lowe, Christopher Lowry, and Michelle Lowry...*"

The interrogation room door opened, and Jesse stepped into the room with another detective, a woman I didn't know. Before they could arrest her, I looked at Lisa and said, "Oh, here's some news you can use. I stopped the killer before he murdered Michelle, so I saved you six figures, so you're welcome. Now you get nothing, and she gets more of everything—pain, heartbreak, loneliness, guilt, everything."

Logan was waiting for me in the observation room, arms crossed, shaking his head like Jimmy used to do when he was proud of me but still wanted to put me on a one-way flight to Finland.

"You never took those pictures," he said. "I could read your bluff from here. You're the worst poker player in the history of cards."

"Good enough to beat Lisa Lowe," I said.

He laughed out loud. It might have been the first time I'd ever heard him laugh like that. "That's a fact."

"Now factor in the further fact that *I'm* the one who gave the killer a black eye," I said, "and I have to ask: Am I off your shit list?"

"Yes, McCall. You're off my shit list," he said. "Now get your gold star and go home and stay home. This guy's going to lick his wounds and be back with a vengeance, and next time he won't play nice, so good job, good luck, good-bye, you're done."

He stepped to the interrogation room door and put his hand on the handle.

"I'm not done," I said.

He did not open the door. "You're definitely done."

"I'm the one he calls."

He was going to open the door, but again, he didn't. "When he calls you, you call me. Beyond that, it's over for you."

"Beyond that, he murdered my father."

"Goddamn it. You are the most stubborn mule I've met in millennium. I'm letting you off the hook here. No investigation into that subway bullshit, which was all kinds of reckless endangerment and fucking with public transportation. Now go back to your life before I change my mind."

"He's not going to stop until—"

"Until I nail his ass to the wall," he said, and he opened the door. "It gets too goddamn dangerous from here, McCall. Understand? Too dangerous for you."

"Until *we* nail his ass to the wall," I said.

He rolled his eyes in pain like Jimmy used to do when he wanted to toss me into the East River. "You're back on my shit list," he said, stepping into the interrogation room.

"That didn't last long," I said.

"Never does," he said, and he shut the door and arrested Lisa Lowe.

65

ANY PREPOSTEROUS THEATRICAL THING

Posey had said my plan would play like a "Cecil B. DeMille," meaning with a cast and crew the size of an army, and holy shit, she was right. There is a tall tale in the theater community of a young *Village Voice* reporter assigned the task of tallying the total number of off-Broadway theater companies in the five boroughs of New York. The story ends with the reporter dying of old age before he can finish counting.

The point of that old chestnut is that Dennis and Posey were beloved way-off-Broadway icons in the sense that they were the eccentric aunt and uncle of an outside-the-box community of actors and theater people, several thousand at least, who would do any preposterous theatrical thing Uncle Dennis and Aunt Posey asked them to do.

And tonight, Tuesday night, the first night of the World Series, the all-hands-on-deck performance for which Dennis and Posey had sounded the bell was at Blue Bar, where they needed their extensive, extended theatrical family to pack the place to the rafters and act like rabid sports fans—drinking beer, eating sliced steak sandwiches on homemade sourdough, and bantering about batting averages.

The Blue Bar casting call was at four thirty. I arrived at six forty-five. Game One, Dodgers versus Red Sox at Fenway, was at eight o'clock. Pregame analysis was on every flat-screen TV in the joint. The bar was packed with hundreds of people, and I recognized a ton of them as actors, singers, dancers, directors, choreographers, and musicians from musicals past and present. Not one of them let on they knew me. They were in collective character, as directed by Dennis and produced by Posey, who'd been busy planning the performance all afternoon.

I wore a Boston baseball cap pulled down low, a Red Sox hoodie, blue jeans, and a backpack. I was here to root for the Sox. I put on a Boston accent and approached the triumvirate of hostesses, two of whom I knew from when I'd been Danielle, the red-haired management consultant.

"Is Blue here?" I said to Hostess Becky, a Bismarck blonde who wanted to be a movie star but would probably wind up doing the weather back in North Dakota.

"On his way," she said.

"Justine?" I said.

"In her office. Would you like to leave a message?"

"No thanks. I'll catch them a little later," I said, and I sat on one of the plush blue velvet sofas beneath the Wall of Champions. There were ten other people in the lobby. Half were actors. Half were friends of actors.

Harold arrived at ten past seven. He glanced at me and everyone else in the lobby, looking for trouble, but didn't recognize any of us and went into the first-floor bar.

I waited three minutes and followed him in. There were two hundred sports fans in the room. Thirty or forty were familiar, including a half dozen or so Schmidt and Parker Players. It was a packed house. No way in hell to get a seat at the bar. And yet to my amazement, though not to my surprise, Harold had procured two adjacent stools. I ordered an Allagash White on tap and stood where I could watch the action.

Stanley Stein, looking none the worse for wear after his midweek home invasion, strolled in at seven twenty, forty minutes before game time. He took one of the empty stools, opened a newspaper, and got busy reading. The bartender put a draft beer in front of him without the bookie having to say a single word. Harold was at the end of the bar. He and Stanley never looked at each other once.

Within two minutes, a middle-aged woman sat on the empty stool beside Stanley, and I knew three things: the bookie was open for business, the brown-haired businesswoman was in a ladies' room somewhere in the building, and it was time for me to head to the third floor and change my clothes...and my hair...and my eyes.

I passed Dennis and Posey on the stairs up to the second floor. They were in costume and character: Dodger fans having a baseball conversation with another couple. Neither one spoke to me, but we made just enough eye contact for me to know they and the cast were ready to rumble.

Roger was stationed on the stairs up to the third floor. He was with a date but couldn't help himself as I went past him. "Looking good, Boston," he said to me, tipping his own Boston baseball cap in my direction.

The stairs were the spine of the building and also of my plan, which is why Dennis and Posey were charged with the first-to-second-floor staircase and Roger had command of the second-to-third-floor staircase. Justine would have to be rerouted when she tried her trip to the third floor to collect the six grand from Blue, but at sort of the same time, Blue would need easy access, so there was a team in the lobby, a team on the first staircase, a team on the second-floor landing, and a team on the second staircase. Success or failure fell on the staircase actors.

The third floor was standing room only. And here's where the magic of Dennis and Posey came clear: everyone on the floor, two hundred people, was an actor. They were throwing darts and shooting pool and drinking beers and eating burgers. They were watching the pregame talking heads on TV. They were playing foosball. Chloe was at the eighteen-foot Grand Champion shuffleboard table with half a dozen Schmidt and Parker Players. It was the biggest performance I'd ever been a part of. A Cecil B. DeMille, no doubt.

I walked into the ladies' room, locked myself in one of the stalls, emptied my backpack, and became Blue Bar's new general manager. I went with the *Coyote Ugly* look—black sweater, tight blue jeans, cowboy boots—I'd seen Justine wear when I'd met her in her office three days ago. I finished my ensemble with a shoulder-length blonde wig and green contact lenses and checked myself in the restroom mirror. I looked almost as much like Justine as Justine looked like Justine.

I exited the bathroom and walked across the crowded room toward the bar. Seeing so many theater people on their marks made the third-floor feel like a stage set, like an honest-to-God show was about to begin, so I got the same butterflies I always got just before the curtain opened.

It wasn't until I passed Chloe at the shuffleboard table and she said something like "Go get him, girl" that I remembered the point of the production—busting Blue in his own bar—and my heart broke for the tenth time since last Wednesday, when I'd caught Eric with half of the embezzled twelve grand and Blue told me in his office I didn't have to point my investigation at him. *This is work, not theater*, I said to myself. *Business, not pleasure.*

The crowd cleared a path, and I made my way to the bar, where an empty stool had been reserved for my character. I sat on the stool and ordered a beer. I didn't recognize the bartender. Was he an actor? How in the world had Posey pulled that off?

My back was to the room. From behind, even Blue would think I was Justine. I checked my watch: seven forty. I'd overheard Justine tell Blue if he hurried from the airport, they would just make it in time to bet six grand on the game. Blue would be here any minute, which meant Justine would be on her way up right about now.

But she would run into a human wave of sports fans traffic-jammed on the stairs. She would get halfway up, and another wave would come behind her, and she would get sandwiched between them, unable to move up or down or side to side. She would be trapped as the wave moved slowly up the stairs and into the bar on the second floor. When Blue arrived, he would be allowed to pass. When Justine finally broke free and made it to the stairs up to the third floor, a new wave would catch her on its way down and another on its way up, and she would be swept back into the second-floor bar. It would take a choreographer and producer of Dennis and Posey's avant-garde skill to orchestrate this chaotic ballet, but I had confidence they could pull it off and had to admit I was sorry I was going to miss it.

I also had to admit this whole thing with Blue had been a setup since Jerusalem Joe's Chinese BBQ welcome party. He'd come to the House of Emotional Tics not to hire me to catch the crook but to cast the case at Griff and Adam (who had figured out Blue was stealing their bonus money), throwing enough suspicion in their direction that they'd leave without any official fuss. The point had always been to put Eric in place so Blue could keep on keeping on with Stanley Stein, who he'd been gambling with for years, since way back in the Justine days, and with whom he was in a horrible hole.

And with me playing his patsy, it had all worked out just fine—Griff was marrying a millionaire forty years his senior, and Adam was on the run somewhere in the Great Northwest. It was true Blue had not counted on me catching Eric in the act, but even that hiccup had proven to be prophetic because (as she herself had said) the stars had aligned to bring back the beautiful Justine in time for the first game of the World Series. The rub was that Blue had not figured on falling for me, or me falling for him, or the two of us falling for each other. Romance had not been part of his plan.

Or part of mine.

But it had happened. We'd made love and shared our life stories, although he'd left out the part concerning his gambling problem and, oh yeah, the part about Justine. But I'd left out plenty of parts too. I mean, it had only been a month. We'd have shared more and more as the months moved on. Now there would be no moving on. Now there would be regret and remorse and sadness.

The crowd would ebb and flow as Blue crossed the room. They would smile at him and say hello and even stop and ask his opinion about the game or for his autograph. He was famous, Blue was, especially in his own bar, and the cast had been coached by Dennis and prepared by Posey. The lights were up, the curtain was open, the play was begun, and I could see it unfolding in my mind's eye. I could feel it in my sad soul.

Blue would see Justine waiting at the bar, her back to him. He would cross the room and touch her shoulder, and she would turn around, and he'd be holding a folder filled with papers and an envelope with six thousand embezzled bucks, just as they'd discussed. Except *she* would be *me*, and he would be guilty, and I would be heartbroken.

And just like that there were tears in my eyes. *Jesus Christ*, I said to myself. *Get your shit together, Kate. You don't want him to find you bawling at the bar, do you? You don't want him to think...*

And then he touched my shoulder. I'd had no idea he was already in the room. The crowd was electric, and my heart was pounding so hard and so loud it was a hurricane in my head, so I couldn't hear a damn thing. It was ten minutes to game time, and I'd been so lost in my own romantic sadness that I'd fallen out of character. But I was a professional, so I made myself recover quickly, wiped away the tears, and turned to confront him.

Except it wasn't him. It wasn't Blue holding the file folder.

It was Mary.

66

THE LORD OF HOSTS WILL DO
BATTLE FOR US

I was shocked. I couldn't blink. I couldn't speak. I could hardly breathe. It was *Mary*? How the hell could it be Mary? There were no arrows pointing at Mary. All the arrows were pointing at Blue. It *had* to be Blue. It *couldn't* be Mary. In retrospect, every minute of my investigation, from Griff to Adam to Eric, had been about *Blue*. Not Mary. Blue.

Mary was the grandmother I never had. She was loving and kind and rushed off to Pennsylvania at the drop of a hat to celebrate family milestones with spark and fire and light that made me want to curl up beside her on the sofa and drink cocoa and talk about dreams and men and life. She'd shown me the pictures and told me the stories. I knew the faces and the names of her children and grandchildren. I'd felt a part of it, like I'd been in Allentown with them, along for the hayride of their Lehigh Valley lives. She'd shared the death of her husband. I'd seen her wipe away tears.

Mary was my *inside man*, helping me with my case, finding the flower receipt from Barbara Bloom when Griff gave roses to Diane Swain, running through the Blue Bar books so I could see how the money moved, checking the deposit slips against the register readouts, overhearing Adam tell a cook that he, Adam, only needed a hundred grand to open his own joint, feeling the same disbelief I felt that it could be Blue, that it *had been* Blue from the beginning, guiding me toward Blue's bag man: Eric the Red.

Mary was one part Doris Roberts, one part Aunt Bee, and one part Blue Bar bookkeeper, office manager, den mother, jailer, judge, and jury. She knew where the bodies were buried, for Pete's sake.

IT WAS *MARY'S* IDEA TO HIRE A PI IN THE FIRST PLACE. BLUE HAD come to her when he couldn't catch the crook himself, and *she'd* convinced him to hire a private investigator.

No way it was Mary. No freaking way.

Yet it was Mary standing next to me, holding the file folder, just like Justine had instructed her to. Not Blue. Mary.

She looked as confused as I felt. I could see her working through it. Was I Justine? I resembled Justine—the blonde hair, the green eyes, the *Coyote Ugly* party vibe. But there was something decidedly *not* Justine about me. Yes, yes, something *absolutely not* Justine in the woman waiting at the bar who resembled Justine. But if I wasn't Justine, then who in the hell was I?

I snapped myself out of my stupor before she could figure it out. "Hello, Mary. I believe that's for me," I said, taking the file folder from her hands.

While I flipped through the folder, Chloe moved the crowd into position, which was bellied up tight to the bar to my left, then arcing out and around, forming a solid semicircle five or six people deep until the crowd wrapped all the way tight to the bar to my right, twenty feet across, maybe ten feet deep at the crest of the arc. We were alone, Mary and me, in the open space, a proscenium, as it were, and we weren't going anywhere, which became clear when the cast locked arms like an arch of Spartans.

It was in that moment Mary confirmed for herself that I wasn't Justine. I could see the confirmation in the anger of her jawline.

I held up the envelope I thought I'd find and in fact found hidden in the middle of the stack of papers. "I wasn't expecting to see you here," I said.

"This isn't what it looks like, Danielle," Mary said.

"We have to establish what it looks like before we can establish that it doesn't look like what it looks like," I said. "Want to tell me what it looks like?"

She glanced at the crowd and said nothing.

"Let me put it a different way," I said. "Want to tell me how in the world you knew to put six grand in an envelope with an index card that says *Dodgers in five*, hide it in a file folder filled with fake work papers, and bring it to the third floor at seven forty-five on Tuesday?"

She shot me a shrewd smile filled with animosity and condescension. I'd never seen anything like that look in her eyes all the times we'd been face-to-face.

"I had no idea that envelope was in there," she said with Mayberry sincerity, her smug level turned to ten. "Blue left that folder on my desk with a note asking me to hand it to Justine tonight at seven forty-five on the third floor."

"You were already here. That's why nobody saw you come in. You got here before I did," I said. "You were waiting for me, for Justine."

"I flew in from Allentown, came right to the bar, checked my office for messages and mail, found the envelope with Blue's note, and came straight upstairs. I don't like to be late." She looked at her watch and smiled at the crowd, fully recovered and back in Aunt Bee office manager mode. "I've always been a punctual person."

Something about Mary smiling at the crowd, the way she did it, made me pause, but I didn't know what it was, so I let it go.

"You're saying you're the messenger, totally innocent, no idea what this is all about?" I said.

"Of course that's what I'm saying, Danielle. It's the truth," Mary said, moving around the proscenium, addressing me and the crowd, comfortable in her skin.

"Do you mind if I call bullshit?" I said, leaning against the bar, watching her move stage right.

"You do whatever you like, dear. I'm going downstairs," she said.

But there was no way for her to break through the arch of Spartans. Dennis and Posey had been firm with the cast about that. The most muscle-bound actors were in the front row.

"I think we should wait for Justine?" I said. "I'm sure she'll be right along."

"Ladies and gentlemen," Roger said on cue from the back of the pack. "Justine enters with a flourish."

Roger deposited Justine in the proscenium and took his place at the top of the arch of Spartans, exactly center stage, so to speak, which was typical Roger. Dennis and Posey were in the second row, on either side of Roger. Chloe took a front row position closer to the bar. All arms linked up again.

"Hello, Justine," I said. "Thank you for playing."

Justine stared at me, stunned. I was her, and she knew it. "Who are you?"

"Kate McCall. I'm the private investigator."

"Kate McCall. Your real name," Mary said. "I'll be sure to mention it to the police when you're done with this ridiculous performance."

There it was again. A reason for pause. The way she said the word *performance*. Whatever it was, I had to move on because Justine was most unhappy.

"Do you have any idea how much trouble you're in?" Justine said to me.

"No, but I have a good idea how much trouble *you're* in," I said, holding up the envelope with the six grand and the *Dodgers in five* index card.

Watching reality hit Justine in the face was a pleasure, I must say, but I knew I had no time to enjoy it because the show was picking up speed.

"You should know, Justine, that Mary threw you under the bus in front of all these people," I said. I was on the move, walking the swing of the arch, gesturing at the crowd and at Mary and Justine. "She said Blue left the file folder on her desk with a note saying she should deliver it to you on the third floor at seven forty-five. She put the whole embezzlement thing on you and Blue. According to Mary, she had nothing to do with it. That's her story. There's no mention of the phone call that outlined how you two were going to play this thing."

Justine glared at Mary. "You're kidding me, right?"

"I was protecting you, Justine," Mary said. "We both know you called me and planned it out step-by-step."

"She's lying," Justine said to me and to the crowd. "She called me. It was her idea. Her money. I didn't know she'd stolen it from the bar."

"How could I steal the money?" Mary said, taking center stage and confronting Justine head-on as I stepped back to the bar. "I have no access to the cash at any point in time. You're the one with your hand in the registers. You and Blue."

"You're lying," Justine said to Mary, and then she looked at me. "She's lying."

"I think it's clear to everyone that you're the one who's lying, Justine," Mary said to the crowd like a prosecutor closing a case. "And in any event, it's your word against mine."

"That would be true," I said, "except Justine has a witness."

The crowd said, "Oooooooh."

"And who would that be?" Mary said.

"Me," I said. "I overheard the phone call. I know it was you, Mary. Because you said you'd be back just in time to make the bet on Tuesday."

"That was Blue on the phone," Mary said. "It wasn't me."

"Blue's not coming back until tomorrow," Justine said. "I spoke to him about it. He told me he spoke to you too."

"That's not true, Justine," Mary said. "And even if it were, she can't possibly prove she overheard that phone call, can you, Kate?" Mary said.

My mouth fell open, but no words came out. I couldn't prove it.

"That's what I thought," Mary said. "So Justine says I'm lying, and I say she's lying, and we both say you're lying, and now we're all going to have to wait until tomorrow when Blue gets back to work it out. So if everyone will get out of my way, I'm walking downstairs to my office to get my jacket, and then I'm going home."

I saw the cast's collective knees buckle, and I felt it all slipping away. If Mary left the proscenium now, no one would ever see her again. She would vanish into the shadows and that would be that. Justine would be off the hook too because she would say she had no idea why Mary was giving her the file folder and would have absolutely no idea why there was an envelope with six grand cash money hidden in the papers. And I would lose the case and lose Blue in the same breath.

Mary walked to Roger, at the top of the proscenium, dead center of the front row of the arch of Spartans, and said in her best Charlton Heston stage voice, "The Lord of Hosts will do battle for us. Behold his mighty hand." And she spread her arms like Moses in *The Ten Commandments* (an actual Cecil B. DeMille movie!), imagining she might part the people like Charlton parted the Red Sea.

And that's when it hit me, why I'd had cause to pause. She

was an *actor*. Mary was an actor. Community theater, I felt sure, but an actor nonetheless.

"Nobody moves a muscle," I said, and I pushed off the bar and marched to the front of the proscenium. The arch of Spartans held their ground.

"Was any of it true?" I said to Mary, and I held her eyes, and she knew what I was asking, and she walked away from me. I followed her.

"Marcus's eighteenth birthday party?" I said. "Alyssa's oldest, Gregory, proposing to Alexandra in the high school gym, the marching band, every peony in Pennsylvania, every balloon in Lehigh Valley?"

She was flustered and kept moving. I stayed on her. Justine stepped out of the way, as mesmerized by the change of momentum as everyone else.

"Growing up on the same street, dating since middle school, both becoming pharmacists, planning it all out in high school and calling it *romantic destiny*, remember that, Mary? Remember romantic destiny? What about that? What about romantic fucking destiny? Was it all an act? Were you acting the whole time?"

All eyes were on her, and she folded in the spotlight, meaning she froze, *went up*, forgot her dialogue, lost her character.

"Yes, you were acting the whole time," I said to the crowd. "You know how I know? Because you're an actor, Mary, and actors act. You found a hint of reality in some bullshit somewhere and wrote your brazen Blue Bar story around that single sliver of truth. You cast yourself as the honest Allentown, grandma bookkeeper, Blue's one true confidante. You said, 'Oh, Blue. You can count on me. I'll stay close to the case and help the investigator any way I can. We'll solve this together, Blue. You and me.' You didn't actually say it out loud, though. You said it to yourself. That's called *internal dialogue*, Mary. In case you didn't know."

"I know what it's called," Mary said in an offended huff.

"The only reason you stayed close was to point me in the wrong direction, hoping I'd give up and go away before I caught you. You know what? I fell for it, and so did everybody else. But in the end, and this *is* the end, you ran out of talent. You weren't as good as you thought you were. You're an amateur, Mary. Community theater gave you away."

"I studied with Stella Adler," she said. "I'm more of a professional than you'll ever be, so if you're done harassing me in front of all these people, I'll go home and wait to hear from Blue."

"You don't have to wait," Blue said, entering the proscenium from stage left.

Mary and Justine were both taken aback. So was I, for that matter. The crowd gasped as one. It was a gasp mixed with *oohs* and *aahs*, as were all gasps regarding Blue. Meaning, if you were a sports fan, you knew he'd never given up a run in the playoffs; if you watched the news, you knew you'd seen him on TV; and if you were a woman, he was so freaking handsome you just gasped with an *ooh* and *aah* any time you saw him.

"You're back," I said because Justine and Mary were speechless.

"It was always Tuesday or Wednesday, and then it turned into Wednesday, and then it ended up being Tuesday," Blue said. "Sometimes you just get lucky."

"Better to be lucky than good," I said to him.

"I can explain this," Mary said.

"So can I," Justine said.

"No need," Blue said to them. "I heard everything, and then I called the police."

Mary went white. Justine rolled her eyes and shook her

head. The stars, it turned out, weren't as aligned as she thought they were. Not all the lights were green.

"I didn't leave that folder on your desk, Mary, so what's going to happen now is we're all going downstairs to wait for the detectives," Blue said.

And then Large Sarge appeared out of nowhere, an amazing feat for someone that size. Large Sarge drilled Mary and Justine with his eyes and said, "You both coming with me," and they exited the proscenium, and the curtain closed on our little drama.

Blue and I followed Large Sarge, Mary, and Justine through the crowd and across the room, and the arch of Spartans began to cheer, celebrating our bravura performance. When I reached the door to the third-floor landing, I turned and did a curtain call curtsey, thanking them from the bottom of my heart for a job well done. "The play is only as good as the cast," I said. They went wild.

"I still don't know how she did it," I said to Blue as we went down the stairs.

"The police will do that part," he said.

"And the other part?" I said.

"What other part?" he said.

"Us, Blue," I said. "You and me. *That* other part."

"You play today's game today," he said, "and tomorrow's game tomorrow."

"Fair enough," I said. "What time tomorrow?"

67

THE THING ABOUT THE WORLD IS IT COULD TURN AGAIN

What a welcome change of pace to get grilled by a detective not named Logan. Maybe it's that the white-collar crime beat is not as grisly or gruesome as the homicide beat, not as bloody or brutal, but NYPD embezzlement specialist Detective John Fonvielle was cool and calm and even polite. He was in the neighborhood of forty years old and was focused to the max, attached at the hip to his iPad, which was super-charged and connected to every law enforcement app in the country. (I know that because I asked him, and he told me.) He was soft-spoken and thorough, thorough, thorough. I told him everything I knew about the case—except the bit about Adam murdering Ricky Cordoba's Chihuahua with a baseball bat because, I reasoned, being exiled to the Washington wilderness for the rest of his days seemed like punishment enough for a douchebag like Adam Stoker. The point is that Detective John Fonvielle was the diametric opposite of Detective Lew Logan...in all regards but one.

Fonvielle interrogated me first, in Blue's office, while his partner babysat Mary in Mary's office and Large Sarge kept

Justine on ice in Justine's office. Blue attended my interrogation, which took an hour and fifteen minutes. When Fonvielle was done with me, he said I was dismissed and that he'd call me again if he needed more information but that he didn't think he would.

I said I wanted to sit in on Mary's interrogation, seeing as how it was my case and I had delivered her with bells on, and Fonvielle looked at me sideways and said gently, "This is an NYPD investigation now, McCall. If you want to pretend you're a PI and play with the police, that's fine. But you have to be grown up enough to take a hint." Which was his kind and considerate way of telling me he didn't care much for private investigators, so I should screw off and get lost. And, oh yeah, grow up while I'm at it. This was the thing Fonvielle and Logan had in common with each other and probably every other cop in New York: they could just barely, though not really, tolerate private investigators.

Blue escorted me out and told me he'd fill me in when he saw me at ten tomorrow morning. He would come to the brownstone, he said, and he would bring coffee.

Wednesday morning, I sat on the front steps of the House of Emotional Tics at ten minutes to ten. The end of October can be cold and gray and wet and miserable, but this was the kind of glorious autumn day that made everyone in the city want to play hooky and ride a bike or throw a ball or just sit on a bench in Central Park and drink in the color of the trees, breathe in the chilled air, and turn their face to the sun. There were no clouds over New York, and there was no breeze, so it was a joy to be outside.

I'd made myself look pretty in my casual way: comfortable jeans, Frye boots, big, soft sweater. I'd put on just enough makeup so it wouldn't look like I was wearing makeup, and while I was doing that, looking at myself in the mirror, I'd realized I was nervous. *I'm forty-five years old*, I'd said to myself. *I shouldn't be nervous about talking to a man I've already been intimate with*. When you're fourteen years old and nervous about talking to the boy two lockers down, that means you like that boy and you want it to work out with him. Guess what? When you're forty-five, it means the same thing.

Right at ten, I saw Blue coming down East 83rd Street from First Avenue. He was carrying two cups of coffee. He was the most gorgeous coffee delivery guy since guys started delivering coffee.

He came up the walk, handed me my cup, and sat on the steps beside me. He smiled but did not kiss me. He seemed happy about things, settled in a way I hadn't seen him, and I thought that might be a counterbalancing omen to the fact that he didn't kiss me. I couldn't help overthinking my romantic life even though I knew that was probably the problem with it. One of the problems.

"Where do you want to start?" he said.

"Mary," I said. "Business first." As the words came out of my mouth, *business first*, I realized that was another reason romantic relationships were weird for me.

Her name was not Mary Capp. It was Brenda Robertson. She was not from Allentown, Pennsylvania. She was from Garden City, Michigan. She had falsified identification papers, including a driver's license, Social Security card, and various credit cards and department store debit cards. She had created the widow Mary Capp persona and was living that life because she was wanted in three states for embezzlement and was a fugitive from the law. And she owed several bookies big bucks too, so she was on the run from them as well. She had a gambling jones she couldn't escape, and it did her in.

She'd tried to weasel her way out of it, Blue said, putting all her community theater skills in play, but Fonvielle found her real identity on his iPad, and it was all over but the shouting. She'd lasted several years at Blue Bar before temptation gave way to planning, and planning gave way to getting her hands on the cash and betting it with Stanley Stein.

"If you've got a gambling problem *and* an embezzlement problem *and* you're on the lam from the law and the mob, then being the bookkeeper at a sports bar is probably the wrong job at the wrong time," I said.

"Especially if they're going up against you," Blue said.

"I got lucky," I said.

"Better to be lucky than good," he said, and we smiled at each other and clinked coffee cups.

She had drilled a dresser-drawer-size door through the back of her locked filing cabinet, through the wall into Blue's office, and through the back of Blue's massive, heavy-duty, block-of-steel gun safe that said Winchester on it.

"Either me or Griff would do a final count," Blue said, "fill out a bank deposit slip, attach it to that stack of cash, lock it in the safe, and give a duplicate deposit slip and the register read-outs to Mary, or Brenda, or whoever the hell she was, or is, and then go to the bank within a day or two or sometimes more."

"She waited for *sometimes more*," I said.

"Yes," he said. "If there was fifty, sixty, eighty thousand in the safe, she would get to the office early in the morning, hours before anyone else showed up, open her back door, steal five or six grand, rewrite the deposit slip, rework the register readouts, and there was no trail at all. No way to catch her."

"You and Griff never noticed, I mean, I know you never noticed, but you never saw the back of the safe was compromised?"

"It wasn't an open hole. It was still a solid block of black steel, except with a piece carefully cut and concealed that could be pulled out and put back from her office. If you're not looking for a carefully cut and concealed piece you can pull out and put back, then you're not going to see it because in your wildest dreams you never think somebody would do that. Who would do that?"

I nodded. The obvious answer was always the hardest to see.

"I guess the least of her problems is that you fired her," I said after a while.

"No doubt," he said.

"And Justine?" I said. "You fired her too?"

"She says she didn't know Mary stole the money from me," he said. "No, I didn't fire her."

It took me a few seconds to process that. "We're talking about the other part now, aren't we?" I said.

"Yes," he said.

"I saw the photograph on the wall in her office," I said.

"We were engaged once," he said. "But we were young, and we flamed out before we got married."

"Flamed out?"

"They say opposites attract, and that's true, but we were exactly alike, two cuts of the same cloth, and we fell in mad love and got too hot, too close, too fast, and we were too young to handle it, and we flamed out. Then the years passed, and the world turned, and she came back, and we were still in love. It just worked out that way."

"The thing about the world is it could turn again."

"She needs me."

"And I don't."

"You didn't even phrase that as a question."

He was right. "You can't change people, Blue. If you were exactly alike then and you flamed out, why do you think the final score will be different this time?"

"I'm not keeping score, Kate. I don't see it like that."

"I know you don't," I said. "I don't either."

And then we were quiet for a while. Just sipping coffee,

watching the cars go by on East 83rd, both of us looking for what to say next.

"You thought it was me," he said, finally. "Stealing my own money and betting it with Stanley."

"Toward the end," I said, sadly. "I did."

"I'm sorry I made you think that," he said.

"It's just what happened," I said.

"He's known me a long time, Stanley Stein. I don't know what he told you about me, if he told you anything, but it was probably all true," he said. "I've been in Gamblers Anonymous for three years. He doesn't know that. Nobody does. I told Justine yesterday, and she said she'd do it with me."

"That's good," I said. "Really, that's good."

He handed me a check. "Balance due for PI services rendered," he said.

I looked at it. "I can't take this."

"You have to."

"You owe me two weeks. Three grand. This is fifteen thousand."

"You saved me ten times that."

We looked at each other, and a wave of emotion went through us.

"Are you buying me off?" I said.

"I'm saying thank you," he said.

We held each other's eyes. There were a dozen things I wanted to say—*don't go, give me another chance, you're the best thing that's happened to me in years.*

But instead I said, "You're welcome."

And then he stood up, and I stood up, and we embraced, and he walked down the steps and down the path to the sidewalk, where he stopped and turned back to me. "Your money's no good at my place. You're on my tab for as long as I own the bar."

"I'm Jimmy McCall's daughter," I said. "You sure you want to do that?"

"Positive," he said.

"You're a terrible businessman," I said.

He smiled and laughed. "Always have been."

And then he walked away. I took a deep breath, went up the steps into the brownstone, and pressed on.

68

HANG ON TO YOUR HALLOWEEN HAT, HONEY

FOR MANY ACTORS, THE LAST WEEKEND OF A SHOW CAN'T COME too soon. By the end of the run, they're sick to death of the thing, tired of the cast, and worn out playing the same character, singing the same songs, and dancing the same dances. They want to go home, get back in their lives, and have normal human weekends like their next-door neighbors.

The exact opposite was true for me. It was always at the *beginning* of an original D-Cup production where I would say to myself, *Dear Lord of the Footlights, do I really want to do it again with this screwball group of actors, in this madcap, maniac musical, in this wacky, way-off-Broadway theater? Don't I have something, anything, even one thing better to do with my time?*

Of course, the answer was always no. For me, by the final weekend, the last two performances, I loved the show, cast, songs, music, dancing, costumes, makeup, ritual, magic, and majesty so much I didn't want it to end.

And so it went with *Blood Song and Dance*.

Friday night's *Blood* was a beautiful thing. But Saturday night's *Blood* was the best night of the show ever. Posey and the band were on point, Chloe stayed in character (meaning the right character in the right play at the right time), Roger kept his leading man melodrama to a minimum, the supporting Schmidt and Parker Players were perfect, fake blood spurted only when and where it was supposed to, and I had my finest performance in the entire eight-week run of the show.

Maybe it was my way of saying so long to Farina LeBleu, the Cajun vampire who worked her Grand Central Station day job (*day job!*) selling one-way midnight train tickets out of New York while harboring her secret dream of being a night-club singer. I'd had so much fun playing her, singing her songs while wearing fangs, dancing up a storm in skintight black leather and skyscraper stilettos, pouring my heart into a vampire who had no heart but dreamed of singing her way to one.

Or maybe I just needed to bite some people in the freaking neck.

Or perhaps I was pumped because the final curtain coincided with the start of the annual, D-Cup Halloween Bash, the off-off-off-off-Broadway party of the year, in which season subscribers wore costumes to the performance and schmoozed with the Schmidt and Parker Players after the show, both sides celebrating the symbiotic nature of live theater by getting rip-roaring drunk and dancing in the aisles until the wee hours.

Dennis and Posey pulled no punches with their D-Cup Halloween gala. There were caterers wearing skeleton costumes, serving hors d'oeuvres that looked like spiders and scorpions and snakes and other creepy crawlers. There was a twelve-piece big band on the stage, every musician wearing an elaborate Frankenstein costume, calling themselves the Darmstadt Dozen—Darmstadt being the German town that was home to the castle that inspired Mary Shelley's 1818 Gothic novel that changed the world of monsters for hundreds of years to come. And there was a scary fortune-teller dressed as the Wicked Witch of the West, who set up shop near the bar, including an actual raven in a cage and a crystal ball with smoky fog that swirled and whirled and changed colors.

Matthew had traditionally attended two performances of my shows, one the first week and the other the last show of the run. He had *always* been in the audience for my closing curtain since he was a boy. But I hadn't seen him in days and days, the longest we'd ever gone without speaking, and I knew he was a heady brew of angry, upset, disappointed, frustrated, irritated, exasperated, and bewildered with me, and I wasn't sure he would show for the show.

But he was there. He came without Caustic Nina, who had seen *Blood* with Matthew in the beginning of the run and remarked afterward that being there once was still being there too much.

I was so happy to see him, and I think he was happy to see me too, despite my PI pranks and misbehaviors, legal and illegal. He looked handsome and confident, every bit an assistant district attorney on the rise. He knew it was a special night for me, so he made every effort to keep his aggravation out of sight.

We embraced after the show, and I bought him a margarita, and we sat on the edge of the stage and watched the Halloween party heat up. He said he was dressed as a DA, and I came as Farina, except I didn't wear the fangs—because I had tequila to drink—and I added the top hat I'd worn at the end of the second act, when I drank the blood of the last remaining humans in the play.

I asked Matthew about his job, and he told me he'd been working bone-crushing hours, but his cases were interesting and his career was fulfilling and, anyway, he liked working because Jimmy had taught him work built character—and I had shown him it was true by living my life that way. I looked at him to see if he'd meant the part about me, and he smiled softly and said he did, even though he was still mad. I nearly cried. I told him how proud I was of him and how much I'd missed him lately, and he said he'd missed me too, which nearly made me cry again because I knew he meant that as well.

He asked me about the next musical, *Psychedelic Sunday*, and I told him word had leaked that there were two orgies in the play and the entire run had already sold out.

"Who knew sex onstage would be such a big seller?" I said.

"Everybody?" Matthew said.

And we both rolled our eyes and laughed and laughed.

I asked about (Disagreeable) Nina, and he told me that all was well on his home front, that (Displeasing) Nina was fine and also working hard, and that I shouldn't be surprised if he proposed to her soon. I kissed his cheek and told him that would be wonderful news, and that I was thrilled for him and (Distasteful) Nina, and he believed me, and I congratulated myself on being a fabulous actor.

He asked me about my embezzlement case, and I told him how it had shaken out. He said he wasn't surprised I'd solved it and that he was kind of, almost, sort of, maybe getting used to the idea I might be a PI after all. But only for cases like that. White-collar crime. Adultery. Postal fraud. Not murder. Which led him, of course, to Logan.

"Logan told me what happened with Lisa Lowe," he said. "After he told you to stay away and I told you to stay away, you still saved her life and punched the killer in the jaw."

"I didn't win," I said. "But I didn't lose either. Call it a draw."

"There are no draws with this guy, Mom. Logan's right about that. He'll come after you with a vengeance."

"He won't come after me, per se. If he did, he'd be admitting I got the best of him, and there's no way he's doing that. But he *will* invite me to play again."

"And you'll decline the invitation?"

"I can't."

"Why not?"

"Because he killed Jimmy."

Then we listened to the Darmstadt Dozen and ate mozzarella sticks with marinara—that looked like worms dipped in blood—and marveled at the costumes and drank another margarita.

"You still have the Colt?" he said after a while in his I'm-getting-the-last-word-on-this-because-I'm-a-responsible-grown-up-not-to-mention-your-only-child voice.

"I do," I said.

"So you'll defend yourself if he comes after you, but you won't go looking for him just because he asks you to. I have to go. Nina is waiting up for me, so just say it so I can sleep at night."

"I'll defend myself if he comes after me, but I won't go looking for him just because he asks me to. Not without Fu."

"You're impossible."

"I'm Jimmy's daughter. You're his grandson. We're built that way, Matthew."

After that, he went home to my near-future daughter-in-law, and I drank margaritas until the Darmstadt Dozen began to play Halloween songs or songs related to Halloween or to monsters or scary things in general. They started with "Thriller," rolled into "(Don't Fear) The Reaper," and then big-band-jammed to "Sympathy for the Devil." With each song, a new group of Schmidt and Parker Players took the stage and improvised choreographed dances that blew the D-Cup away.

"Feed My Frankenstein," "Ghostbusters," and "Somebody's Watching Me" all brought the house down. Everyone knew every song, and the actors and the season subscribers sang them arm in arm, cheek to cheek, margarita to margarita.

Dennis, Posey, Roger, Chloe, and I took the stage for the great Warren Zevon's "Werewolves of London," and I put in my fangs, and we had a drunken blast. And then the Schmidt and Parker Players and the season subscribers came together for

Bobby Pickett's classic "Monster Mash," and we nearly blew the roof off the old brassiere factory.

After that, I danced my way to the bar, ordered another drink, and by chance turned my head to the wicked witch fortune-teller while I waited for the bartender to make magic in a glass. The witch wiggled a bony index finger in my direction, gesturing for me to join her for a quick jaunt into my future.

I don't like having my fortune told because I think the whole thing is a scam because it's always the same future in my future: you'll meet a tall, dark, handsome stranger; you'll come into a small fortune; there will be a death or a birth or a marriage or a divorce or a new job or a lost job or a wave of success or a bout of failure in your family. The fortune-teller is irrelevant. It's the same forecast every time. But I'd had more margaritas than I could remember and thought I might forget whatever she said anyway, so I slid down the bar and sat across the table from the witch and her raven and her smoky crystal ball.

She drilled me with her eyes, and then she gazed into the swirling smoke, and her jaw dropped open. "Hang on to your Halloween hat, honey," she said, "because come Monday morning, your universe turns upside down and inside out."

My jaw dropped open too. "What the hell kind of fortune is that?" I said.

"I didn't make it up, Vampira. It appeared in my smoke."

"My universe appeared in your smoke? My work universe? My theater universe? My romantic universe?"

"All of the above," she said. "Look, whatever you're drinking tonight, keep drinking it because Monday morning everything in your script gets rewritten."

The way she phrased that thought threw me for a loop because (a) I was already loopy from the tequila and (b) Monday morning was the first day of principal photography for *Kung Fu Fu*.

"What time Monday morning?" I said.

"Do I look like a clock to you?" she said.

"Check the smoke," I said. "Maybe it's in there."

She looked deeper into her crystal ball and said, "It's not an exact science, but I'm thinking nine forty-five."

"You made that up," I said.

"Here's my number," she said, handing me her business card. "Call me at ten and tell me I'm wrong."

69

WELCOME TO THE JUNGLE

I SLEPT UNTIL NOON ON SUNDAY, WHICH SOUNDS GOOD ON PAPER but was rough in real life because I'd gone to bed drunk at six in the morning. When Dennis and Posey throw a Halloween party that celebrates the closing of one show and the opening of another, that's what time you get home. Drunk is just part of the equation.

But I dragged myself out the door and took a taxi to Raul's because I'd scheduled two hours of private coaching at twelve thirty and there's no canceling on Raul once he puts you in his book. If you cancel once on Raul, he tortures you worse than he would have in the first place for the next two weeks so you never cancel again. If you cancel twice, you're done boxing at Raul's. Nobody cancels twice. Or maybe they do and I just never see them again.

I showered and crawled back into bed after boxing, slept more, did laundry, read a month of magazines, slept again, cleaned my house, made a pot of chili to last all week, took a nap, balanced my checkbook, caught up on my House of Emotional Tics paperwork, and just generally did things I hadn't had time to do since Blue hired me at Fu's Jerusalem Joe BBQ way back when at the beginning of October.

Throughout the day, I couldn't help counting down the hours. The Wicked Witch of the West had looked into her smoke and said my universal shit would hit the fan at nine forty-five Monday morning. *Nineteen hours to go*, I told myself at two forty-five Sunday afternoon *Fourteen hours to go. Ten hours.* What the hell could she have meant by my script gets rewritten? What kind of thing is that to say to someone who's had too much to drink?

I put on my PJs at midnight, read through LaTanya's *Kung Fu Fu* outline (it can't be an actual script if it has no actual dialogue), and reviewed Monday's call sheet. Most of the time, filmmakers don't shoot scenes in chronological order. They shoot the middle at the beginning, the end in the middle, and the beginning at the end—or some esoteric combination of those three. LaTanya was shooting the end at the beginning.

As written in the outline, the scene before the final scene had me and Fu and LaTanya arresting Charlie and Al, despite the drug dealers being jacked up on Warren's crazy chemical cocktail that imbued them both with super karate powers. Detective Steinberg (Fu) was simply more super at karate than they were (imagine that!), and his partner, Detective Cassie Barnett (me), had a haymaker that could knock a bad guy into next week, and Captain Rashida Jewel (LaTanya's character) could kick like a kangaroo, so in the end the renegade cops and their renegade captain hauled the renegade drug dealers to the pokey. The final scene in the film was getting the bomb off the bus before it blew up. But LaTanya wasn't making any commitments as to whether we would make it in time to rescue the passengers.

"I get some money, McCall," she'd told me, "we blowing up a damn bus."

"What about the passengers?" I'd said.

"You think Scorsese tying his shit up in a damn bow?" she'd said.

We were shooting in the House of Emotional Tics lobby, LaTanya's logic being if we started in the lobby of the building we all lived in, then no one would flake the first day. I turned out the lights and set my alarm. It was twelve forty-five. *Nine hours to go.*

Everyone made the call (eight a.m.), including Warren, even though he wasn't acting in today's scene because his mad scientist character got arrested in the scene before the one we were shooting today. Warren was here because he was the crew, which meant that today he was the cameraman because LaTanya couldn't shoot because she was acting. We would all take turns being the cameraman throughout the shoot. What could go wrong?

Anyway, we blocked and lit the scene and then LaTanya said she'd made a character adjustment we needed to discuss before she said *action.*

"It being Halloween," LaTanya said to the cast and crew, "I woke up this morning and had a mondo moment of character magic going to make this movie mystical, mythical, and mind-blowing all in the same miraculous minute. I say *miraculous* because this be nothing short of a motion picture miracle."

I'd forgotten it was Halloween. I looked at my watch. Eight forty-five. *One hour to go.*

"Whose character is being rewritten?" Warren said, opening his script (outline) to take notes. In addition to being the Halloween cameraman, he was also the script supervisor, gaffer, grip, first assistant director, second assistant director, craft service crew, and transportation captain.

"Al, until this morning, your character was a day-in, day-out drug dealer," LaTanya said, "typical Hollywood criminal. Seen him once, seen him a thousand times. So we going to turn him up to ten and turn him loose on film fans around the world. He not just another drug dealer; he a *zombie* drug dealer."

"You got to be fucking kidding me," Al said. I think he rolled his eyes, but they were beyond bloodshot and set so far back in his head it was hard to tell. The point is Al was hypersensitive about zombie conversations because he knew that even without a lick of makeup, people on the street, just ordinary folks on First Avenue, thought he already was one.

"Zombies are big box office. Brad Pitt playing zombies. You want to sell tickets in Indonesia, you got to have at least one damn zombie in the movie," LaTanya said.

"What's the backstory?" Charlie said. He'd arrived on set and announced he'd already smoked a ginormous joint to get into his character, a pot-smoking drug dealer. "Can't have a zombie without a backstory. The audience is smarter than you think they are. Especially in Indonesia."

"Got blown up in your meth lab," LaTanya said. "Except he didn't die. He just kept on dealing drugs after he was dead."

"Like it," Charlie said. "Wait, I got a meth lab?"

"In your backstory, Charlie. In a movie," I said. "Not in real life."

Al hated the whole zombie idea. He wanted nothing to do with the new take on his character, so he and LaTanya argued about it for a while, and then Al stormed up the stairs to his room. We all went after him, and he and LaTanya yelled at each other through Al's door for thirty more minutes. Al finally agreed to be a zombie if he got associate producer credit, and LaTanya said that was fine (because she knew associate producers never get meaningful back-end participation and have no power on the set). So Al opened his door, and we went downstairs and took our spots in the lobby, and Warren held the camera, and LaTanya called *action*.

But in that same second, before we could start acting, Edie

and Ray, carrying grocery bags, came into the lobby with another person right behind them.

"Here we are," Edie said, "and we're bringing this nice man with us."

"Says he's been on TV, but who the hell knows where he's been?" Ray said. "I never met the man. Anyhow, trick or treat."

For their Halloween-morning trip to the market, Edie and Ray had worn their costumes, although with Ray every day was Halloween, so it was hard to tell where his clothes stopped and his costumes started. Today, he wore Loudmouth golf pants that sported crazy-colored jack of diamonds from top to bottom and a New Orleans Saints football jersey with shoulder pads. Actual shoulder pads. He wore dress shoes—one laced, one loafer. Edie wore a pink poodle skirt with a poodle on it, pink saddle shoes, and a white button-up blouse monogrammed with her name in pink letters. And pink bobby socks. Frilly. Her hair was up on her head in a bleached-blonde poodle cut.

"He's looking for you, Kate," Edie said, starting for the stairs, Ray right behind her. "His name is Richard Gottfried."

"Says Shavelson sent him," Ray said. "But who the hell knows? I never met the man."

Gottfried was my age, maybe a little older. He had eyes the color of copper and curly brown hair dusted with gray that came down over his ears and below his neck. He was thin and only an inch taller than me. But the thing about Gottfried was that he looked familiar. I recognized him, but I couldn't put my finger on where, and it bothered me that I couldn't figure it out. I knew I had to deal with him, especially since he'd told Ray that Shavelson had sent him. But I couldn't get past Ray's outfit.

"Ray, shoulder pads?" I said, wondering what crazy concoction of prescription medication would make an elderly man wear pads in public.

"I was wondering the same thing," Gottfried said, and everyone nodded.

"I got no shoulders anymore," Ray said to Gottfried, to me, and to the group. "The pads make me irresistible to women. Ask Edith. She's about to pull up that poodle skirt and let a linebacker do the dirty work."

"Don't worry about me, Kate," Edie said. "I'm keeping a full-back in to pick up the blitz."

Ray said something about busting into her backfield, but they turned the corner at the top of the stairs, and we were all spared the rest. I turned to Gottfried and was again struck by how familiar he seemed. I opened my mouth to ask him why that was, but he spoke before I did.

"What are you guys shooting?" Gottfried said, gesturing at Warren holding LaTanya's camera.

"Martial arts masterpiece," LaTanya said. "Got everything but a budget."

"Join the club," Gottfried said, and he smiled when he said it, and I knew that smile, and in that instant, I figured out just who Richard Gottfried really was.

"You're Rick Gotti," I said.

"All my life," Rick said.

Everyone's memory kicked in at the same time.

"Smart-ass, wild-child sitcom star and standup comedian," LaTanya said.

"Welcome to the jungle," Rick said, quoting his signature line from the show that had made him both famous and infamous when he was fifteen years old.

"Drugged out, dropped out, burned out, and bottomed out," Charlie said.

"The good old days," Rick said.

"Hollywood's baddest bad boy when you were still a boy," Warren said.

"It was all downhill from there," Rick said.

"I heard you're making a comeback," Al said.

"Just when I thought I was out, they pull me back in," Rick said, doing his best Pacino from *The Godfather: Part III*.

"I heard you're out on bail for murder," I said. "I heard you killed comedian Kenny Cochran in cold blood in the backstage dressing room of Vincent Valentine's Joke Joint in the East Village."

It had been in the gossip and entertainment pages of all the papers. Cochran was doing a routine that sounded a lot like Rick's, same gags down to the delivery. Rick accused him of stealing his stuff on Facebook and Twitter, and Cochran blew him off and called him out for being an addict and a user and a loser and worse. The comedians had an ugly, public, digital shouting contest that was nasty enough for national attention, and then Cochran was dead on the floor at the Joke Joint. Rick's mug shot was front-page news for a day—until someone else was dead on another floor in some other place. The story was that Joke Joint security took Rick down within minutes of the murder. The child star was booked and bailed, and the pretrial hearing was the week before Christmas.

"That's why I'm here," Rick said. "The guy who killed Cochran is going to kill me next. He thinks I'll name names at the hearing, namely his name. Believe me, I'd like to, but I didn't get a good look at him. Except he thinks I did, so he needs me at the bottom of the Hudson River, so I need a bodyguard to get me to the pretrial alive because I can't prove I'm innocent if I'm dead. Shavelson said you're the best."

I checked my watch. Nine forty-five. *Freaking fortune-teller*, I said to myself.

I looked at Rick, now in his late forties, saw the fifteen-year-old wisecracking kid from TV, and quickly weighed the pros and cons of the case.

The cons were legion. Rick Gotti was trouble with a capital *T*. He was a spiritual, emotional, and intellectual hazardous highway. He'd dragged dozens of decent people into the muck of his own messed-up life and then kept on keeping on with his bad habits, bad behaviors, and bad intentions. To be his bodyguard was to invite all kinds of unscrupulous Karma into my life. Not to mention if someone was trying to kill him, that person might try to kill me too if I was in the way, which is where I'd be if I were Rick's bodyguard.

There was only one pro: money. And that wasn't so much a pro as it was a fact of life. I'd spent all of Blue's bonus paying off a maxed-out credit card and had only two maxed-out cards to go. I knew it was one crappy pro against dozens of reasonable cons, but after years of living on credit, it felt good to pay down debt. Sometimes money talks louder than reason. More than sometimes if you're an off-off-off-off-Broadway actor.

"Three fifty a day," I said.

"Shavelson said three hundred," Rick said.

"You want me to find your dog, that's three hundred," I said. "You want me to save your life, that's three fifty."

"I want you to save my life," Rick said.

"Did anyone follow you here?" I said.

"No," Rick said. "I took four cabs and crisscrossed the city."

"Wait in my house," I said, gesturing at my door. "I've got cable and there's food in the fridge. You'll be safe here. We'll work out the rest when I'm done shooting."

"You're in this martial arts masterpiece?" he said.

"I'm the star," I said.

"Co-star," Fu said. "Fu star."

"Fu you, Fu," I said.

"Fu you too," Fu said.

"I thought you were a private investigator," Rick said as I unlocked my door and let him into my apartment.

"I am," I said.

But I was also an actor.

THANK YOU

I hope you had as much fun reading *Emboozlement* as I had writing it because I had a blast. If you did, it would be most excellent if you could help other mystery lovers find the book by leaving a review and sharing the laughs.

Honest reviews of my books help introduce them to new readers. I would be deeply grateful if you could find a few minutes to post a positive review about *Emboozlement* or any of the Kate McCall Crime Capers. It only takes a minute to leave an upbeat word or two. Thanks again.

FASTEN YOUR SEAT BELT!

Get Gottiguard, the Fourth and Final Kate McCall Crime Caper, and fasten your seat belt!

Kate McCall is determined to make sure it's finally curtains for her father's killer. But her first priority is playing body-guard to the bad-boy standup comic who hired her to protect him while he tries to prove he's innocent of murder. That is until the real culprit takes a shot at her client just as her dad's assassin sends her a clue to his next victim. Will Kate have the last laugh and nail two murderers, or is she about to suffer a fatal punchline?

FIND OUT HOW IT ALL GOT STARTED!

Get Workman's Complication, the first Kate McCall Crime Caper, and find out how it all got started!

Kate McCall dreams of basking in the bright lights of Broadway. But after her PI dad is found dead in a NYC elevator, she has no choice but to split time between show business and the family business. When her vampire musical fails to pay the bills, she accepts a workman's compensation case that's sure to put her acting chops to the test. On her way down the trail of clues, she can't help but get sidetracked by her father's unsolved murder. Will Kate crack her cases before playing detective becomes a role to die for?

KEEP THE LAUGHS COMING!

Get Swollen Identity, the Second Kate McCall Crime Caper, and keep the laughs coming!

Kate McCall hopes she can balance her passions and her PI practice. Struggling to keep both on stage, the way-off Broadway performer finds herself in the deep end of a billionaire's allegedly stolen identity. But her role as a super-sleuth takes center stage when a corporate crime scene replicates her father's unsolved murder. Can Kate shine a spotlight on the killer before she loses her part for good?

ALSO BY RICH LEDER

<u>ROMANTIC SHADES OF FUNNY</u>

Juggler, Porn Star, Monkey Wrench

<u>DARKER SHADES OF FUNNY</u>

Let There Be Linda

Cooking for Cannibals

Extraterrestrial Noir

<u>KATE MCCALL CRIME CAPERS</u>

Workman's Complication

Swollen Identity

Emboozlement

Gottiguard

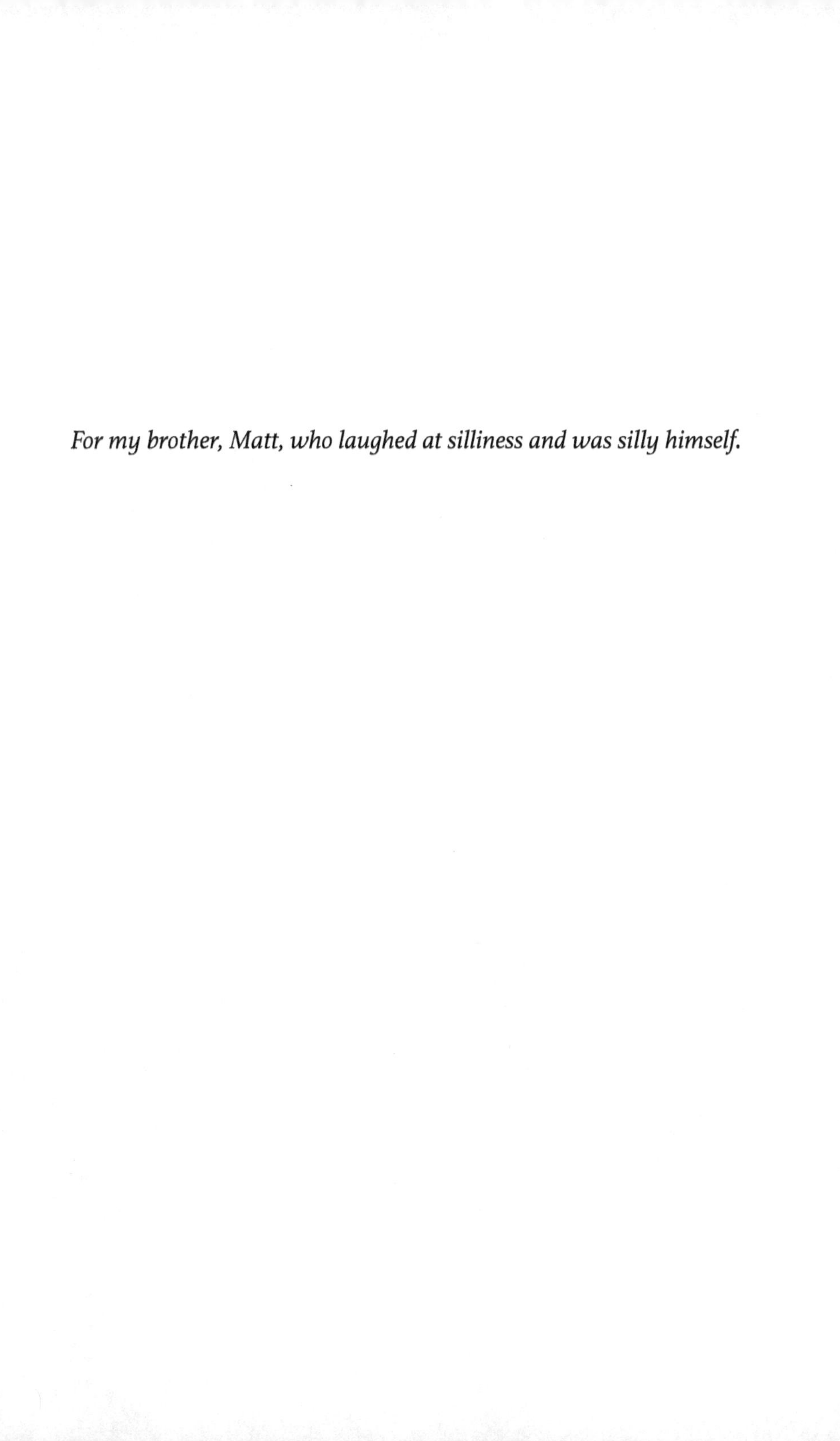

For my brother, Matt, who laughed at silliness and was silly himself.

ABOUT THE AUTHOR

Rich Leder's screen credits include 19 television films for CBS, Lifetime, and Hallmark and feature films for Lionsgate Entertainment, Paramount Pictures, Tri-Star Pictures, and Left Bank Films. He has published eight novels through Laugh Riot Press.

He has been the lead singer in a Detroit rock band, a restaurateur, a Little League coach, an indie film director, a literacy tutor, a magazine editor, a screenwriting coach, a commercial real estate agent, a wedding guru, and a visiting artist for the University of North Carolina Film Studies Department, among other things, all of which, it turns out, was grist for the mill.

Contact Rich through his website: www.richleder.com